PRAISE FOR KRISTY CAMBRON

"As intricate as a French tapestry, as lush as the Loire Valley, and as rich as heroine Ellie's favorite pain au chocolat, *The Lost Castle* satisfies on every level. The three time lines weave and build upon each other as the three heroines navigate dangerous times and unravel ancient secrets. Kristy Cambron's writing evokes each era in loving detail, and the romances are touching and poignant. *C'est bon!*"

> —SARAH SUNDIN, AWARD-WINNING AUTHOR OF *THE SEA BEFORE US* AND THE WAVES OF FREEDOM SERIES

"It's been a long time since I've been so thoroughly engrossed in a novel. Kristy Cambron grabs you from the start and weaves a fabulously intricate and intoxicating tale of love and loss. Her settings are breathtaking, her historical detail impeccable, and her characters now dear friends. *The Lost Castle* kept me spellbound!"

> —TAMERA ALEXANDER, *USA TODAY* BESTSELLING AUTHOR OF *TO WHISPER HER NAME* AND *CHRISTMAS AT CARNTON*

"An absolutely lovely read! Cambron weaves an enchanting story of love, loss, war, and hope in *The Lost Castle*. Spanning the French Revolution, World War II, and today, she masterfully carries us into each period with all the romance and danger of the best fairy tale."

> —KATHERINE REAY, AWARD-WINNING AUTHOR OF *DEAR MR. KNIGHTLEY* AND *A PORTRAIT OF EMILY PRICE*

"Readers will be caught up in themes of family, loyalty, and courage—as well as a mystery and even a bit of a fairy-tale romance—in Kristy Cambron's *The Lost Castle*. Cambron weaves together the lives of three very different women with vivid emotion against the lush backdrop of France."

> —BETH K. VOGT, CHRISTY AWARD-WINNING AUTHOR

"Cambron's lithe prose pulls together past and present and her attention to historical detail grounds the narrative to the last breathtaking moments."

—*PUBLISHERS WEEKLY*, STARRED REVIEW, FOR *THE ILLUSIONIST'S APPRENTICE*

"Cambron has written a gripping tale of suspense that will please her growing fan base."

—*LIBRARY JOURNAL*, FOR *THE ILLUSIONIST'S APPRENTICE*

"At once a love story and a mystery, *The Illusionist's Apprentice* will appeal to anyone who likes novels about strong, enigmatic women."

—HISTORICAL NOVEL SOCIETY

"Cambron takes readers on an amazing journey into the world of vaudeville illusionists during the Roaring Twenties. This novel includes an intriguing mystery that adds adventure and suspense to the intricately detailed historical drama."

—*RT BOOK REVIEWS*, 4½ STARS, TOP PICK!
FOR *THE ILLUSIONIST'S APPRENTICE*

"Prepare to be amazed by *The Illusionist's Apprentice*. This novel will have your pulse pounding and your mind racing to keep up with reversals, betrayals, and surprises from the first page to the last. Like her characters, Cambron works magic so compelling and persuasive, she deserves a standing ovation."

—GREER MACALLISTER, BESTSELLING AUTHOR OF *THE MAGICIAN'S LIE* AND *GIRL IN DISGUISE*

"With rich descriptions, attention to detail, mesmerizing characters, and an understated current of faith, this work evokes writers such as Kim Vogel Sawyer, Francine Rivers, and Sara Gruen."

—*LIBRARY JOURNAL*, STARRED REVIEW,
FOR *THE RINGMASTER'S WIFE*

"Historical fiction lovers will adore this novel! *The Ringmaster's Wife* features two rich love stories and a glimpse into our nation's live entertainment history. Highly recommended!"

—*USA TODAY, HAPPY EVER AFTER*

"Cambron takes a real person, Mable Ringling, and breathes fictional life into her while staying true to what is known about this compelling woman. The novel is an intriguing look into circus life in the 1920s . . . but the author's gift for writing beautifully crafted sentences will draw readers into the story and the fascinating world of the circus."

—*RT BOOK REVIEWS, 4 STARS, FOR THE RINGMASTER'S WIFE*

"Cambron vividly depicts circus life during the 1920s. With a strong supporting cast of friends and family—including a nemesis or two— the women experience heartbreak, loss, hope, and triumph, all set against the colorful backdrop of the 'Greatest Show on Earth.'"

—*PUBLISHERS WEEKLY, FOR THE RINGMASTER'S WIFE*

"A novel that is at once captivating, deeply poignant, and swirling with exquisite historical details of a bygone world, *The Ringmaster's Wife* will escort readers into the center ring, with its bright lights, exotic animals, and a dazzling performance that can only be described as the Greatest Show on Earth!"

—*FAMILY FICTION*

"In true Kristy Cambron fashion, *The Ringmaster's Wife* is packed with emotional depth and characters who charm their way into your heart within the first pages. Engaging and poignant, this is a must-read!"

—*MELISSA TAGG, AUTHOR OF FROM THE START AND LIKE NEVER BEFORE*

"A soaring love story! Vibrant with the glamour and awe that flourished under the Big Top in the 1920s, *The Ringmaster's Wife* invites the reader to meet the very people whose unique lives brought the Greatest Show on Earth down those rattling tracks."

—JOANNE BISCHOF, AWARD-WINNING AUTHOR
OF *THE LADY AND THE LIONHEART*

"The second installment of Cambron's Hidden Masterpiece series is as stunning as the first. Though heartbreaking in many places, this novel never fails to show hope despite dire circumstances. God's love shines even in the dark."

—*RT BOOK REVIEWS*, 4½ STARS, TOP PICK!
FOR *A SPARROW IN TEREZIN*

"In her second book, the author again interweaves a story from the present with a tale from the past. Both Sera and Kája must find courage to battle for a future against impossible circumstances."

—*CBA RETAILERS + RESOURCES*, FOR *A SPARROW IN TEREZIN*

"Fans of the author's first book will gravitate to this tale of the power of faith and love to cope with impossible situations."

—*LIBRARY JOURNAL*, STARRED REVIEW,
FOR *A SPARROW IN TEREZIN*

"Well-researched yet heartbreaking scenes shed light on the horrors of concentration camps, as well as the contrasting beauty behind the prisoners' artwork."

—*RT BOOK REVIEWS*, 4½ STARS, TOP PICK!
FOR *THE BUTTERFLY AND THE VIOLIN*

"Cambron expertly weaves together multiple plotlines, time lines, and perspectives to produce a poignant tale of the power of love and faith in difficult circumstances. Those interested in stories of survival and the Holocaust, such as Elie Wiesel's 'Night,' will want to read."

—*LIBRARY JOURNAL*, FOR *THE BUTTERFLY AND THE VIOLIN*

The
LOST
CASTLE

BOOKS BY KRISTY CAMBRON

The Ringmaster's Wife
The Illusionist's Apprentice

THE HIDDEN MASTERPIECE NOVELS
The Butterfly and the Violin
A Sparrow in Terezin

The
LOST
CASTLE

a novel

KRISTY CAMBRON

THOMAS NELSON
Since 1798

The Lost Castle

Published in Nashville, Tennessee, by Thomas Nelson. Thomas Nelson is a registered trademark of HarperCollins Christian Publishing, Inc.

Published in association with Books & Such Literary Management, 52 Mission Circle, Suite 122, PMB 170, Santa Rosa, California 95409–5370, www.booksandsuch.com.

Interior design: Mallory Collins

Thomas Nelson titles may be purchased in bulk for educational, business, fundraising, or sales promotional use. For information, please e-mail SpecialMarkets@ThomasNelson.com.

Scripture quotations marked NIV are taken from the Holy Bible, New International Version‎, NIV‎. Copyright © 1973, 1978, 1984, 2011 by Biblica, Inc.‎ Used by permission of Zondervan. All rights reserved worldwide. www.zondervan.com. The "NIV" and "New International Version" are trademarks registered in the United States Patent and Trademark Office by Biblica, Inc.‎

One line quoted from the song "Blackbird"; lyrics written by John Lennon and Paul McCartney, released in 1968 on *The Beatles* album. Copyright owned by Sony/ATV Music Publishing.

Brief quotation from Paul Verlaine's poem "Chanson d'automne" ("Autumn Song") in chapter 21, published in his first collection *Poèmes saturniens* in 1866.

Publisher's Note: This novel is a work of fiction. Names, characters, places, and incidents are either products of the author's imagination or used fictitiously. All characters are fictional, and any similarity to people living or dead is purely coincidental.

Library of Congress Cataloging-in-Publication Data

Names: Cambron, Kristy, author.
Title: The lost castle / Kristy Cambron.
Description: Nashville: Thomas Nelson, 2018. | Series: A split-time romance
Identifiers: LCCN 2017038971 | ISBN 9780718095468 (softcover)
Subjects: | GSAFD: Christian fiction. | Love stories.
Classification: LCC PS3603.A4468 L67 2018 | DDC 813/.6--dc23 LC record available at https://lccn.loc.gov/2017038971

Printed in the United States of America
18 19 20 21 22 LSC 5 4 3 2 1

For Margaret and Juanita Maxine,
with fairy-tale love, for unlocking the legacy
of childhood stories in my life.

If I'm honest, I have to tell you I still read fairy tales,
and I like them best of all.

—Audrey Hepburn

PROLOGUE

Your people will rebuild the ancient ruins
and will raise up the age-old foundations;
you will be called Repairer of Broken Walls.
—Isaiah 58:12

Present Day
Les Trois-Moutiers
Loire Valley, France

Crumbling walls were rare, beautiful things.

They could display vulnerabilities without shame, for they'd already proven their worth in surviving generations-deep fractures and a multitude of fallen stones.

Ellie held her breath as Quinn rowed their dory along the back of the moat surrounding the castle ruins. Her first full view in a clearing of weathered stone, night sky, and moon glow unimpeded by the thicket of trees. Save for a bird's distant cry and the delicate ripple of the oars cutting through still water, the forest, too, appeared hushed. Maybe even in league with their plan.

To be struck down so—she hadn't expected it, even when she'd found herself face-to-face with the object of her quest. She edged up in her seat, kneeling in the bow. The dory wavered with the instinctive move. The only way to catch herself was to grip the side, digging her nails into weathered wood and peeling paint as she stared headlong into the storybook scene.

Moonlight illuminated castle walls.

Ghostly ruins took shape before her eyes, forms cutting through the mist and rising against the backdrop of trees. A shiver commanded attention as the chill of a night breeze swept along Ellie's skin, dancing wavy locks of ebony against her cheek. She brushed them back without care.

Quinn held the oars out in the water, using the drag to slow them, the dory bobbing like a cork on the surface. They drifted there for a moment, quiet in the shadow of what the locals called *The Sleeping Beauty.* Château des Doux-Rêves—the castle of sweet dreams.

"There she is," he whispered, his Dubliner upbringing still managing to shadow even the few words spoken between them.

"No wonder they call her *The Sleeping Beauty.* Now that I see her . . . She's every bit of both, don't you think?"

A whisper of stories, hushed for generations, drew Ellie like a string had been tethered to her heart. Enough that she could focus on the silence of the place, as if the hallowed walls and tumbled stones had a secret language all their own. What remained was long buried—ivy-covered stone, hemmed in by scrub trees and underbrush that had faded from green in the last of summer's days and now burned with the height of autumn's gold. Roofless bones spread from foundation to sky in crumbling turrets and an impressive tower that slept six stories high. Arched doorways and intricately carved filigree window frames were frosted under shades of white-blue light, working together to cut a form like lace had been punched into the ink sky.

She'd convince Quinn somehow. Trek back through the woods

on foot if she had to. Anything to find the story buried in that place.

Ellie shifted her gaze. The view, previously concealed from behind the castle, opened up to a clearing—a valley hidden by the grove of trees. She stared at a sight she'd seen before.

The rock wall . . . rounded arch and the opening for a gate that was now missing . . . arbor rows spread out behind in a vineyard rich with the harvest to come. Though time-weathered and now buried under thicket and thorn, this place was familiar; an ethereal memory she hadn't lived herself, but one that remained etched in her mind nonetheless.

A forgotten photo had been taken there in the summer of 1944. The very place her grandmother had once stood.

The scene where her own story had begun.

ONE

The letter recounted devastating news: Baron le Roux had been shot dead.

He'd been discovered facedown in the cobblestone street outside Saint-Lazare, his grown son, too, laid out beside him as wheat barns burned in the background.

Aveline Sainte-Moreau abandoned her mother's instruction on the strict propriety of a lady's posture for the first time in her life, sagging her ball gown in a mass of satin and panniers crumpled against the stair rail. She fused her gloved palm in a white-knuckled grip around a scrolled iron spindle, holding fast, tears rolling free from her lashes, her breaths hollow and shaky as the full weight of her sister's letter washed over her.

Reports out of Paris were far worse than anyone had imagined. Closer too, when names put to the dead were among those of their family's most intimate acquaintance since childhood. How could it be that a noble rank of chevalier, the legacy of a baron, and his only son—Gérard, Aveline's own brother-in-law—was thriving one day and simply wiped from existence in the next?

"What of Faubourg Saint-Honoré?"

She scanned Félicité's letter, searching for mention of the section of Paris in which her own family held residence. Her heart thumped, turning flip-flops beneath the bodice of her gown.

No matter the contents or consequences, even if her world would come crashing down in the span of a single missive, Aveline could not deny herself the penned words. Were her father and sister out of danger? And what of their home? And the friends whose lives were in possible jeopardy but streets away from the Le Roux estate?

> Baron Le Roux's manor has been felled by fire, the family routed with nothing but the clothes on their backs. An assemblage of armed men gathered at the gate bordering the clergy land at Saint-Lazare. Rumor had circulated that they hoarded wheat, salt, and other food supplies, and the people set out to plunder. I know you do not wish to hear of these grievous circumstances, given your sympathies for the rabble—but you must. Father was most aghast when he learned what you'd done. The story of the mysterious lady with the violets is all over court, and he had much to cover on your behalf. Though your name was saved from discovery, thus is the evidence that your sympathies were most ill placed.
>
> We hear tell the baroness and her daughters have been detained in the city. Where and for what purpose we do not yet know. I write these words now only because I stayed with Father and we saw the flames illuminate the night sky. The rabble took torches to the baron's house and wheat barns, burning them to the foundation. All that remains now are blankets of ash and earth mounded over for fresh graves.
>
> I'd hoped to rendezvous with my dear Gérard for your impending nuptials, but now, all is lost. He left to defend his

father's home and did not return. Rest assured, dear sister—
Father and I have not been assailed.

We are safe . . . but hopelessly broken.

Aveline stopped, running her gloved fingertip over a misshapen circle that blotted the last letters inked on the line. One of her sister's tears?

She squeezed her eyes shut on a sharp intake of breath, daring to imagine the horror and almost immediately wishing that she hadn't when the image of lifeless bodies and burning estates flashed through her mind. "God save their souls."

Desperate for a reprieve from the brutality on the page—and her sister's none-too-gentle reproach of the ill-placement of her sympathies—Aveline turned her gaze to the view looking out from one of the second-story windows of the Château des Doux-Rêves.

The last of evening's light toyed with the twilight sky, sifting shadows through the great canopy of trees that hemmed them in on all sides. A swan danced through the circular moat below, disturbing the water in a rippled kiss along the castle's outer walls. Horses nickered from the nearby carriage house, jovial and quite unaware that anything was amiss in their part of the world. Their innocent melody of clip-clops and neighs drifted through the air as carriages descended upon the road to the front gate.

The castle-turned-château was to be her new home in a fortnight, once she married Philippe, the Duc et Vivay's son. But all thoughts of an elegant white muslin gown, calligraphy-tipped invitations, and a country chapel teeming with high-ranking guests had darkened under a cloud. Was Aveline to suppose they'd move forward without a pause, now that Paris was in upheaval and her own brother-in-law had been killed? Given the rising state of bloodshed in France, everything in their world was poised to change.

Marriages. Alliances. Even love . . . How could such luxuries of the heart survive when death remained such a cruel provocateur?

Candelabras stood guard at marked positions down a hall of leaded glass. The windows lay bare to the night sky, all having been left unlatched along the terrace. A breath of wind caught an edge of curtains, dusting the thick brocade with movement. The solidarity drew Aveline, inviting her to a safe haven while she fought to restore her shredded composure. She'd need all once she descended the stairs. And it wouldn't be long now. A chorus of chattering party guests and tinkling crystal had begun to drift up the stairs, signaling that the engagement fête had already begun.

Aveline leaned against the wall of glass, one slippered foot in the hall and the other mingling with the world just outside on the stone terrace.

Guests of the beau monde emerged from the carriage doors: high-coiffed ladies bedecked in ivory and gold, their male escorts brandishing powdered wigs and equally elegant simpers. They shared oblivious gaiety, from their smiles down to the tips of their buckled shoes. How was it possible that the atrocity of bloodshed could coexist with the luxury of peace, just half a country away? Charred estates had already begun to dot the skyline in Paris. And now that the populace had a taste of vengeance, she couldn't help but fear which estate—and who—might be next to satiate their hunger.

"*Excusez-moi*, mademoiselle."

Aveline jumped at the intrusion, jerking her hand upon the stair rail.

Félicité's letter drifted from her fingertips. Aveline watched, helpless, as the folds of paper fluttered down to disappear in the shadows of the grand first-floor entry. She hastily wiped her gloved palm under her eyes, drying any evidence of tears lest someone question their existence on such a night.

She turned to find Fanetta, the maid who'd been assigned to her upon arrival at the castle, a composed statue waiting just behind.

"Je suis désolée." The young woman began her apology, her auburn-tipped crown in a modest bow, even as her gaze drifted over the stair rail. "I am sorry to disturb you, milady."

Aveline stole a glance to where the letter had fallen. She'd have to wait and retrieve it when she ventured downstairs. Until then? Smoothing her composure was all she could do. She straightened her carriage with a notch of the chin, the strict demands of her station so second nature, they owned her even without the benefit of her mother's presence. "Yes. What is it?"

"Pardon, but Lady Sainte-Moreau had wished to attend your toilette this eve. She bid me to fetch you and ask after the time to arrive." Fanetta shifted her attention to Aveline's ball gown. Ivory and blush satin fanned out in lithe folds at the sides and back— graceful and lavish, but clearly not the cut of an afternoon tea gown. "But it appears your ladyship has already dressed for the evening . . ."

She was weary of the fashion in Paris for women of her station to engage in a grand ceremony of the toilette time. Who needed a gaggle of attendants to flit over a lady's every whim? For the future Duchess of the House of Vivay, it would be a near ironclad expectation. But they weren't in Paris. Aveline was to be ushered into the highest ranks of the French peerage while hidden away at a château in the Loire Valley, and she hadn't the stomach to continue the fluff of court a single day longer.

Not even on the night of her own engagement ball.

"I hadn't the inclination to delay in preparation for the ball merely so as to garner an audience before it. The toilette was simply impossible this eve."

"Of course, mademoiselle."

Awkwardness befell the air between them, Fanetta's station

understood but clearly in conflict with a decree from Aveline's mother. The maid waited for Aveline to voice her bidding, keeping her eyes downturned until she received it.

"What I mean is, I'm afraid I haven't anyone to observe the delicacies of your coiffeur this eve, Fanetta. My mother is the only lady in residence who would care to keep up the practice of Paris. But just between our ears, might we help my mother to quietly forget the impropriety as long as she is here visiting with us—and then we may abolish the practice thereafter?"

A spark of amusement flashed in Fanetta's eyes. She inclined her head, working diligently at cloaking a smile. "Very well, mademoiselle. I daresay her ladyship may have already gone downstairs. She left in haste, as she did not wish to risk also missing your debut."

"And she will not. I've been assured the announcement will not come until midevening." Aveline tugged at the tiny creases of her gloves, a task employed to hide the slight tremble of her hands. "She will have ample time to find her honored place in the dining hall when the duke calls the party to attention."

"Of course, mademoiselle. Then I shall give you this." Fanetta outstretched her hands on a curtsy and presented a gold filigree trinket box glittering from the center of a silver letter tray. "I was told to take it to your chamber for presentation during your toilette, but you had already gone."

"What is it?"

"A gift—for mademoiselle."

"For me? But who . . . ?"

"The Duc et Vivay's son. Just as your family has commissioned an engagement portrait of your ladyship to gift your betrothed, you are offered a gift in return. I'm told to relay that when you accept this token you are now a part of the House of Vivay, and wear it this eve so the Duke et Vivay's son knows the bride-to-be the moment she enters the ballroom."

A gift so her betrothed would know her on sight? It read as thoughtful, but perhaps still the hallmark of a matrimonial arrangement brokered between two fathers.

Young women of her station were seldom given the compliment of knowledge beyond the art of fan waving or how to breathe in a corset, let alone the freedom to decide whether a man's temperament made him a worthy candidate for marriage. After not even seeing her betrothed's face, Aveline would enter the ballroom with every disadvantage imaginable—especially after her sister's missive had so weighted her heart. Philippe, on the other hand, could enjoy anonymity for as long as he wished.

All she could do now was breathe deep and pray the gesture was a forecast of some tenderness to come.

Aveline took the trinket box in hand, adding a polite, *"Merci,"* before gently lifting the delicate clasp. The hinge gave without a sound, revealing the treasure inside: a gold fox brooch edged in diamonds, citrine, and tiny pearls. The precious stones winked back at her, the soft lines of the fox tail glittering in the candlelight.

"A fox." Fanetta nodded approval. "That is a gift befitting a queen of this house, as the symbol of the Vivay family."

"It is a curious creature for a family crest."

"Fox roam free in the vineyards in all directions, mademoiselle. Feeding on the grapes, hunting for bird nests in the arbors . . . generally causing disruption for the workers here. But they've long been associated with the House of Vivay. Why, the deep wood beyond this hall of windows is so named *Bosquet du Renard* because of them."

Fox Grove. Aveline hooked her gloved fingertip around the edge of the drape, looking to the twilight world beyond the glass.

An obsidian sky dotted the mass of shadows with stars, pinpricks of light piercing the bower of trees.

A place for hiding, it seemed.

"I knew the family managed more than one estate. It is quite favorable to hear that the winemaking enterprises are thriving, if not inhabited by a mischief maker or two."

"Thriving they are!" Fanetta bit her bottom lip to temper her enthusiasm, then tossed a look over her shoulder, as if attentive ears should not be privy to a tidbit of gossip she simply couldn't contain. "The House of Vivay is thus known to boast a very renowned label of wine, named after the fox. It's said the king himself even keeps the *Renard Reserve* stocked in his royal wine cellar. And the wine is produced right here, in the heart of the valley. The Duc et Vivay and your husband-to-be own it all."

"I knew the duke was engaged in provincial enterprises, but I'd not been made privy to them—at least not until now. I look forward to learning more as long as I'm here."

A wall clock betrayed the brief respite with deep-chested chimes echoing down the hall. Fanetta took heed of the warning that time had bled thin, and turned to look back toward the wing of ladies' rooms.

"Do you desire powder for your hair? Violet, I think, would best bring out the tones in your ladyship's eyes and the gold of your hair, of course. We still have time if you'd like to go back."

"No, *s'il vous plaît.*" Aveline closed her eyes and pinched the bridge of her nose, sorting her thoughts for the remaining desperate moments before she'd be presented.

She'd swept powder over her face and dotted the tiniest bit of rouge to her cheeks, knowing her mother would comment had she worn none at all. But just thinking on it caused the whalebone corset to strangle the breath from her lungs—even more than usual. It was ambitious to breathe in one on a good day, let alone on thus. She could stand no more plucking or primping for court . . . not when her world had been cast into such dizzying array.

"No more powder. I think I'd prefer to just be me tonight."

"Certainly. If you'd wish not." Fanetta paused, still gripping the tray out in front of her. "And what of the brooch? Would you like to wear it?"

"My betrothed has asked me to." Aveline had held tight to the brooch, having enclosed it in her fist like a lifeline. She exhaled, letting go, and extended her hand, palm to the ceiling. "So we should comply with the request."

Fanetta set the tray on a sideboard, waiting as Aveline joined her at the oversized gilt mirror dominating the wall. She took the brooch and went to work, affixing the trinket to the elegant embroidery of the square-bodice ball gown.

Instead of reveling in her reflection, Aveline saw a powdered and primped lady who would descend the stairs with all eyes watching, one who wore a rehearsed smile and a golden brooch, but who was fairly trembling beneath yards of satin. She was poised to step into the coveted role of mistress of a grand château and multiple estates, and become a social princess in the top ranks of the beau monde: France's most elite nobility.

The nobility from which she'd secretly wished to escape.

The same nobility that was hated—and, with proof now, *hunted*—with hastening fervency.

"There." Fanetta retreated a step to admire her handiwork. "You are perfect. Surely an engagement ball is just the beginning to your happiness."

"*Oui*, I'm sure it is."

Aveline looked at the brooch dominating her reflection, the fox standing out against the blush satin. It glittered at the row of embroidery edging the top of her bodice, the citrine turning a deep, blazing amber in the candlelight.

Fanetta met her gaze. The partygoers' revelry teemed in the background, reminding them both that the party wouldn't wait for its guest of honor.

"Will there be anything else, mademoiselle?"

"No. Merci, Fanetta."

"Then I will take the trinket box back to your chamber and leave you with this—a note from the Duc et Vivay's son." The maid pulled an ivory note card from the pocket of her apron with *Aveline* written on the front in a lovely, looping script. "And bid you have the evening of your dreams." She offered a faint smile and with hastened steps disappeared into the shadows of the glass-walled corridor.

Aveline stood, feet frozen. Heart battling against the expectations of her position and the ever-present weight to perform them. She'd been jarred by penned words again, but this time, it appeared they were from Philippe—*her fiancé.*

A fresh longing stirred that her betrothed's words would match the thoughtfulness of the gift. Aveline ran her fingertip under the crease to break the circular red seal: a red fox fashioned there too, the image of the Renard crest pressed deep into melted wax.

Drawing in a steadying breath, she read, a gloved fingertip resting on the brooch as her one connection to him. But within seconds . . . the last thread of hope to which she'd clung unraveled by the impact of mere words:

> Find me in a blue coat with the Renard crest on the lapel.
> If you and your mother wish to remain unharmed, please—
> do exactly as I say.

TWO

PRESENT DAY

MARQUETTE, MICHIGAN

Ellison Carver responded to the urgent voice mail the only way she knew how—by speeding her Jeep across town so fast she nearly blew the leaves clean off the trees.

It should have been her favorite time of year, when the rhythm of October frosted the air and painted the shores of Lake Superior in deep oranges and burnished golds. But Ellie barely had time to notice. Not when she'd received a summons for the second time that week, with news that her grandmother was ailing.

The stop sign at the end of the street intervened with a fleeting suggestion to pause, which she'd almost missed for driving on autopilot. She slammed on the brake. The tires cried out, jerking the vehicle to a halt against the rain-dampened road.

Ellie sat. Jeep idling. Leaves drifting in front of the windshield. She cooled her breathing as rain gathered in trails upon the glass, snaking down it before the wipers could sweep them away.

"Don't borrow trouble," Grandma Vi had always said. *"Don't borrow—but be sure you don't set out to buy it either."*

If it was life-threatening, Laine wouldn't have left a message. No, her best friend since grammar school would have called an ambulance first and met Ellie at the hospital second.

Ellie nodded, believing her own story, and eased her grip on the steering wheel.

This wasn't it. It wasn't the day she would lose her.

Surely we have more time.

Logic won out as she turned onto Lake Shore Boulevard. Even then, the sight managed to inspire a hard-fought smile. The Marquette Harbor Lighthouse greeted her from the rise over Lake Superior with cheery red walls, sparkling white-trimmed windows, and lake views that worked overtime to mimic the expanse of the sea. This marked the point in the drive when Ellie would consent to let fear in, but only for the few seconds it demanded. After the lighthouse faded into the rearview, she'd exhale and slay the beast of worry—if just for a little while. Only then could she tackle whatever each day might bring.

So it was sweep in Ellie-style: She found the closest parking spot when she reached the Maple Ridge Care Center, slammed her Jeep in park, and hustled through the last drizzles of rain to the front doors. Once she'd punched the visitor's code on the inner door, she managed her pace in high-heeled boots so she wouldn't look like an overcaffeinated sprinter charging down the hall—just a granddaughter with well-placed concern.

It was easy to spot Laine at the check-in station for the Alzheimer's unit: tall frame, sleek suit, and tidy chestnut chignon were dead giveaways from behind. While she may have been the care facility's activities director, that title meant little in the moment. She turned around, spotted Ellie, and dropped whatever she'd been doing to meet her in the hall.

Relief flooded in for those reasons alone.

"She's alright, Ellie. I was sorry to call you away from work but—"

"No. It's okay. I asked you to keep me informed."

Ellie slipped out of her peacock-blue coat and ivory tucker, then tossed them over an upholstered chair near the common room hearth. Without missing a step, she eased over to the doorway of her grandmother's room and paused to peek inside.

A figure stood by the room's lone window, and now that the rain had eased, afternoon sun cast a soft halo around her.

Whispering felt right, so Ellie leaned in closer to Laine. "How is she?"

"It's like I said on the phone." Laine eased an arm around Ellie's elbow, joining her in inspecting the petite form in the back of the room. "She's not causing a fuss. In fact, she hardly makes a peep until you get here. That's just about the only time she lights up. But she's been unsettled—most of the week really. I know you're aware that she's gradually sleeping more hours of the day. That's of note on its own. Couple that with the agitation since this morning, and it's enough that we thought we should call you."

"Agitation? About what?"

"That's just it. We don't know."

Viola Carver—Lady Vi, as she'd always been known—was the town pillar, retired college professor, and independent grandmother who'd raised Ellie since she was eleven years old. She still owned her signature pixie cut, though the deep ebony color grandmother and granddaughter had once shared was now frosted white.

A favorite cardigan was draped over her shoulders, the one in the soft hue that matched the rare shade of her violet-gray eyes—like Elizabeth Taylor's, she'd always teased. She'd been quick to admit that though her father had selected the name *Viola* for her eyes, the Hollywood starlet had actually worn them better. Then a wistful smile . . . the dimple in her left cheek—they'd always made an appearance when she told that story. Mere shades of them remained now, existing only in Ellie's memory and in the framed wartime photos on the wall.

Grandma Vi parted the drapes with careful fingertips, caught up by some sight through the glass. Peace lasted only a few breaths before she dropped the gauze curtain back into place and took to wrestling her hands, softly, slowly, turning one aged palm inside the other.

True. That wasn't like her at all.

If there was one manner of decorum Vi had always taught her granddaughter, it was that a lady never fidgeted. Fidgeting meant a lack of solidarity. An unwillingness to trust. A woman mustn't ever sacrifice those things. They were important to her once, but the bleak world of Alzheimer's toyed with that reality enough that those virtues had wasted away along with the rest.

"She's been like this most of the day."

"What? Just standing by the window?"

Laine nodded. "Yes. Standing. Pacing. And wringing her hands—" Vi turned her hands inside-outside again. "See? Just like that. And then she rests her palm over her lapel and closes her eyes."

Ellie's heart slammed in her chest. "She's not in pain, is she?"

"No." Laine reached out and patted her hands. Ellie hadn't even realized she'd extended them until the warmth of two palms encased her own and squeezed, offering reassurance. "It's nothing like that."

"You're sure?"

"I don't think it's that kind of pain, Ellie."

Laine's usual smile had faded behind a creased brow: one of those half smiles that meant she put on a brave face, but was showing real concern at the same time.

"What did Kathy say?" She was the charge nurse on staff and

ran a tight ship. If anything was amiss, Kathy would have been the first one to notice it.

"She checked her vitals first thing this morning. And we called the doctor in before I telephoned you. Grandma Vi is not in any physical danger at the moment. It's just . . . she's very anxious. I hated to call you from work, especially when I knew you'd drop by this evening for your usual visit, but I thought you might be able to settle her."

"What about music?"

No—not this time, by the downturn of Laine's eyes.

"Billie's been singing all morning without making a dent. Reading aloud didn't work either. She couldn't seem to sit still for it. Nor to eat. The doctor said we could give her something to calm her down, but it's your decision."

"No. Let's not go the medication route just yet. If she's awake and alert, she'd want to remain that way—that much I'm certain of." Ellie sighed, letting go of a breath she hadn't even realized she'd held captive in her chest since the drive over. "Maybe we'll get lucky and she'll recognize me today. At the very least I could open the family albums and get her talking about the old days. She'll like that."

Laine nodded. Her brand of empathy was simple but steadfast: encouragement that could only come from a friend who'd become family herself.

"You're brave, Ellie. You just have to keep on being brave. For her. For yourself too."

Brave.

It was the last thing Ellie felt.

Terrified maybe. Unsure. Staring down loss every day. Those were adversaries that felt far more real than any companion of bravery. She hovered in the doorway, feeling a sting in her chest as Grandma Vi hovered in front of the drapes.

"Everything . . ." Ellie stopped, the words lost. Why was it emotion could strangle her voice at the very moment she needed it most? She cleared her throat. "Everything I have left in the world is in that room, wearing a lavender cardigan."

"I know. And that's why I'll be here. And I'll be honest, no matter what."

Honest. A strange thing to reply. Ellie turned back, still lingering in the doorway. "Honest about what? Has something happened?"

"Grandma Vi was asking for her brooch today."

"The brooch." Ellie hung her head.

Of course. Now it made sense. If Grandma Vi wanted her heirloom brooch, no doubt her thoughts had stalled around the memory of Ellie's grandfather.

Married for more than sixty years meant that past memories were now stronger than her present. The cherished memento from their first year of marriage was probably a sign she was waiting on her sweetheart to come walking through the door, when he never would again.

Laine hesitated, sympathy edging down over her features. "She insisted on wearing it this morning when Kathy came in to check on her. And now she's been looking for it everywhere since. I didn't learn of it until I came in this afternoon. It may mean nothing, but we still thought you should know."

Thank you, she mouthed, wishing some of that bravery Laine thought she had could see fit to show up. "I'll see what I can do." Ellie drew in a deep breath and stepped inside.

Billie Holiday's sultry voice was on constant loop, lilting from a stereo on the bureau. Grandma Vi stood by, tapping an index finger against the windowsill in offbeat time with the music.

Framed black-and-white photos—the ones artfully displayed on her grandparents' cottage mantel for decades—were still present, though some silver had tarnished and the mass of them were now pressed in a smaller space on a sideboard against the wall. Picture postcards documented her grandparents' life on a pin-board over a twin bed. Hawaii. The Grand Canyon in 1953. Niagara Falls. Even Hackensack, New Jersey, once. a flat-tire diversion on one of their many cross-country road trips through the early years of marriage.

And though her grandmother didn't read any longer, books packed every inch of built-in bookshelf space spanning the wall beneath the window: lovely worn spines lined up in perfect rows, story after nostalgic story, still so much a part of who this woman was that Ellie couldn't have pictured Lady Vi without them.

"Grandma?" Ellie tilted her head to the side, looking to the far-off point her grandmother had settled on outside the window. The view showed trees, leaves flirting with autumn, and a parking lot full of cars that glistened in the sun.

She eased in. One soft step forward. Then two. "Grandma Vi?"

"Yes?" Vi turned, only then having realized a guest was behind her. She stared through Ellie with unfocused eyes, like she was nothing more than a vapor in the room.

"It's me. It's Ellie," she whispered, holding her fingertips in a self-point at her chest. "Your granddaughter."

See me, her heart willed. *Look at me and really see me . . .*

"Yes, dear. Come in."

Her grandmother was far too gracious to admit she didn't know Ellie. That was usually the way of it. Vi would pretend, out of ingrained politeness, and Ellie would be yet another strange guest who'd come to haunt her.

This was likely one of those days.

"I'm Ellie." She paused, praying anything she said could trigger something concrete in her memory. "Do you . . . do you know who I am?"

"Of course I know who you are." Vi's eyes behind her glasses focused on Ellie, her brow wrinkling as if she was troubled by something. "You needn't keep telling me."

A laugh bounded from Ellie's lips before she could stop it.

Yes, this was Lady Vi Carver. The petite Englishwoman was back, if only for a moment—her wit and spark still a drumbeat beneath the surface.

"Right, then. It appears we won't need to say that again." Ellie took her by the elbow and kissed her cheek gently, hoping to lead her to the wingback chair waiting behind them. "How are you, Grandma? Would you like to sit?"

"No. I'll stay at the window." She patted Ellie's hand but eased her elbow free nonetheless. "The rain has stopped."

"But the chair is just there. You can still see out the window, and at least you won't tire out. I can sit with you if you'd like."

Vi kept her hand over the lapel of her sweater, fingertips running along the seam and winding around the edge of a button, as if grazing an imaginary something in its place. "My brooch? I can't seem to find . . ." She turned, scanning the shadows in the room. She drifted knotted hands over the table surfaces nearby, breaking Ellie's heart. "I've misplaced it."

"The brooch is at home, Grandma. Remember? You asked me to keep it at the cottage."

"The cottage . . ."

"Yes. The home Grandpa built for you? Your brooch is there. But I can bring it for you anytime if you'd like to wear it. How about tomorrow?"

Vi turned away again. Had she followed any of the last bit of conversation? Ellie exhaled and surveyed the room. They needed a distraction to draw her grandmother away from the imagined world that held her captive at the window.

Ellie retrieved the leather-bound album from the bedside table. "Would you care to look at photos while we wait?"

Those violet-gray eyes sparked to life when Ellie approached and opened to the photo mounted on the first black page. Vi settled onto the chair, though noticeably perched on the edge of the cushion, in the event she needed to spring up.

It was so like her to agree, but to do so on her own terms.

Vi ran her finger over the edge of a photograph of a young man in an officer's uniform. His hair light, his smile a soft crease without teeth showing. "He's handsome."

Ellie leaned in closer, resting over the arm of the upholstered chair. This was the difficult part—navigating conversations when Grandma Vi remembered only pockets of the past. She'd tread carefully. Not stir up anything too bittersweet if she could help it. "Yes. Quite handsome. Very distinguished, I'd say."

"I know him . . ."

"Yes. He was Dr. Frederick Carver—your husband."

Vi stared, head tipping in a soft nod.

"Grandpa. You married him after the end of the war." Ellie turned another page, filling in the blanks she knew were there. A toddler in a cowboy hat stared out from the vintage photo, smiling with a six-shooter stuck in the waistband of his denim. "And you had a son, Eric. This is him on his third birthday. It's always been one of your favorite photos."

Vi nodded, but whether she remembered who they were was a gamble. She turned from the photos, gaze drifting to a far-off world outside the window. "Is he coming to see us?"

"Um . . . no, Grandma. Not today." Ellie swallowed the lump in her throat. "Both he and Grandpa have been gone for many years now."

"He understood, you know. The day at the chapel changed

everything, but he still married me. He was a good man." Vi turned the page back and ran a fingertip over the edge of her husband's photo. She brushed Ellie's hand with her index finger, then tapped the photo again. "A very good man."

"Yes, Grandpa was a very good man. You've always told me that." Ellie tilted her head, trying to follow despite her grandmother's frequent mental rabbit trails. "But you said he understood something. What changed?"

"I did." Vi shook her head and drew a hand up to her lips, carefully pressing them against her fingertips as if kissing something good-bye.

Ellie eased back and closed the album cover. "Maybe that's enough for today. Hmm? Why don't we go to the dining hall? Or order some tea and sit on the veranda? It's not too chilly for it if we find you a quilt."

"*No.*" A firm refusal was new. Vi again tapped the spot where the brooch would hang. As the song on the radio drifted into Benny Goodman's "Always and Always," she smiled—a faint, far-off look that washed over her countenance. "I need to wait."

"Grandma, wait . . . for what?" Gently, slowly, Ellie whispered the words. "Who do you expect is coming?"

Vi issued a glance so sharp it struck like an arrow.

A huff was all she offered before turning to the bookcase in a nimble move that had Ellie jumping to her feet with her. Vi squinted and ran her index finger over the spines, searching through the rows of books.

Ellie stood behind, her hands aching to brace her grandmother against the potential of a fall. In her zeal to find whatever she sought, Vi could have an accident in a blink. Ellie peeked out the door to find Laine watching from the hall. All she could do was shrug, standing by clueless as her grandmother continued her search.

"Grandma, can I help you? What is it you're looking for?"

Vi pulled a volume down from the low shelf; one tucked away and forgotten, perhaps for its condition. Any title printed along the spine had faded, and the leather cover was cracked and worn thin at the edges.

"It's this one." Vi settled back on the edge of her chair to keep her attention fixed on the window.

Ellie stood behind as her grandmother gave a loving pat to the title, embossed on a rust-toned cover with elegant gold leaf design: *Histoires ou Contes du Temps Passé.*

"But it's . . . French?"

"Oui." Vi nodded, as if it should need no further explanation. "*La Belle au bois dormant*—The Sleeping Beauty." She offered the book to Ellie, seemingly rushing her about the business of finding the fairy tale in the book's pages.

Ellie obeyed, thumbing to the Contents section, trying to decipher the French she'd heard and find anything close in print. "La Belle . . . " she started, searching, flipping pages, skimming through hand-tipped illustrations that might match the story of a sleeping princess.

She hadn't a clue what she'd do when she got there, given she couldn't translate more than a few phrases in French. But perhaps Grandma Vi would simply enjoy holding it. Seeing the illustrations. Maybe falling back into whatever memory she'd associated with the text.

Something slipped from the binding and fluttered to the floor.

"I'm sorry. I . . ." A card, faded and forgotten, stuck halfway under the edge of the chair. She stooped and picked it up, then turned it over in her hand.

Vi looked back at her, her eyes focused.

Too focused.

"See?"

That was just it; Ellie could see. And she couldn't for the life of her understand what she was holding. The card wasn't a forgotten bookmark, but a photo—one she'd never set eyes on before. It lay in her hand, weathered and colorless except for the vintage tint of sepia.

The image showed a young woman sporting victory rolls, the coiffed barrel curls framing her face in ebony, with a telltale dimple in her left cheek and a 1940s-style notched-collar dress highlighting her figure. She sat atop an old stone wall. Barefoot with legs demurely crossed at the ankle, she was luminous, beaming up at a man in the photo. He stared straight on to the camera, an arm casually draped around her waist—a young, sun-kissed soldier type with wind-tousled waves covering his forehead, and a grin that went on for days.

He was dashing, to be sure. And the romance of a couple in the midst of a sun-drenched vineyard in goodness knew where might have been one of the most enchanting things Ellie had ever seen. It could certainly set a romantic's heart to beating. And Ellie had always thought she owned such a heart, but in this instance, she was forced to retreat from the notion.

Because while the woman was her grandmother, the man was most certainly *not* her grandfather.

Ellie flipped the photo to the back, finding no comment to place or name them. Just a penciled date: *June 5, 1944.*

"Grandma?" She held the photo out, tapping her index nail just under the young man's face. "Who is this?"

"I had to keep him there—with *The Sleeping Beauty.*"

Ellie looked to the book again, flipping through the pages to see if any other secrets were tucked away in its binding. But there was little else than a penciled word—an uneven *Criquet* scrawled in the front cover. A child's hand practicing letters? That told no tales on its own.

"You mean you wanted to keep the photo in the book? By the fairy tale?"

"No. The castle."

And that, she hadn't expected. "A castle . . ."

Ellie had been sorry for some time that she'd never pressed Grandma Vi for more stories about her life during the war. She'd shared some, of course—the courtship with Ellie's grandfather, how she'd gone back to London for a time after the war, and was one of the first women to graduate from Cambridge in 1948. But Grandma Vi had always glossed over the war itself, summing up the years with a sentence or two about what their generation had fought for.

"There's a castle. A real castle . . . in France somewhere?" A nagging sentiment pricked her insides, that there were stories— secrets no one knew. Maybe not even her grandfather. Or her parents. Were they hidden, like an old photo? Forgotten so long, their story had faded with the black-and-white image?

"Why have you never mentioned any of this before?"

Vi tendered a graceful tip of the lips—a knowing smile? "Because I was not ready to share him."

That declaration was soft but witty. And the hint of a smile too? Classic Lady Vi, but the timing was breaking her heart all over again.

"This man. Is he family?"

"Not any family you would know."

So much for that angle. "A friend, then? Maybe an acquaintance of Great-Uncle Andrew? Or someone you met during the war?"

"He said I could find him in the chapel, the one at *The Sleeping*

Beauty. If I wore the brooch, he'd know my answer the moment I stepped through the door."

"The brooch? I thought Grandpa gave it to you." A wave of doubt washed over Ellie. "You wore it in your wedding photos. So I thought Grandpa . . ."

"He wanted me to have it." She paused, long seconds ticking away from the clock on the wall. Tears? Were those . . . tears forming in her grandmother's eyes? "It was all he had to give."

It had been ages since the last time Grandma Vi had been able to feel anything enough to cry. It must have been important, whatever memory she was lost in, if she was so overcome that its remembrance could stir an emotional response to defy even the firm grip of Alzheimer's.

Ellie slid to the floor by Vi's lap, covering her grandmother's delicate hand atop the book's cover.

The turn in the conversation had made her almost too afraid to ask, but Ellie drew a deep breath and whispered, "Who were you waiting for? Is it . . . ?" She swallowed hard, charging headlong into a question she wasn't sure she wanted the answer to. "Is it this man?"

"He said he'd come back for me." Vi looked out to the grove of trees again, her eyes cloudy and wet behind her glasses. She shook her head, gazing down at her empty palms. "I should have stayed behind, like he'd asked. But I was scared. And so young . . . And then, I couldn't. It was too late."

"I don't understand. What was too late? What couldn't you do?"

Lady Vi Carver came back that day. If only for moments in a small nursing facility room, she sparked back to life. With a twinkle in her Elizabeth Taylor eyes and a familiar dimpled smile. Accompanied by tears. Through loss and the storied pasts of fairy tales, forgotten photos, and heirloom jewelry—

"Become his wife, of course."

Tinges of shock pricked Ellie's skin. "His wife . . ."

"That's right." Vi ran her index finger over the photo's worn edge. "I need you to go to *The Sleeping Beauty*. Find him. Tell him I accept—before it's too late."

THREE

Viola Hart didn't dare think of the last time she'd eaten.

Food. Water. Even survival—such things were an extravagance when dodging the realities of war. Her stomach had given up its harrowing pangs long ago as the drudgery of long days and sleepless nights blurred into one another.

Railroad tracks littered with the remnants of abandoned wagons and trucks—rusting ghosts from the 1939 exodus of Paris—cut paths through the never-ending span of countryside on her trek from La Roche-Guyon. Vi had followed the metal graveyard lining the tracks, hiding just far enough into the darkest parts of the woods so as not to be seen. And keen she was to notice every sound, avoiding the rhythmic drumming of marching Nazi patrols and the grinding of tank treads that had gutted parts of the countryside like angry metal tillers.

Hunger festered as she continued moving, staying put only as long as necessary to ensure her safety before moving on, finding little to hope for.

Even less to eat.

She'd uncovered parsnips from an old garden some days back. Wild mushrooms under a felled log in the forest. Guinea eggs nested in the hedgerow of an abandoned farm. Vi had even come upon an overturned truck boasting a treasure: two cans of sardines that had been lost under the wreckage along the rail lines. Tin reflected in the sun, giving away their hiding place. She dug them out by scraping her nails in the dirt and sat in the midst of the metal graveyard to feast like a queen. But that was days ago. Too many to count. And her clothes had been near hanging off her frame before she'd started running.

Other than those scanty gifts of provision, little was left that hadn't been picked clean or bomb-withered long ago. The forest was barren. France was being choked from the inside out, and her hope to flee from it had all but faded. At least until she saw the old chapel—its humble stone spire and cross rising out of the morning mist like a mirage, drawing her to it.

Vi had come upon a storybook castle first, the ruins of stone walls enveloped in a thick layer of ivy. She'd rather have hidden there, to get lost in its crumbling secrets and forget the world for a time. Maybe sleep in one of the lofty rooms and imagine the soirees that had enlivened it centuries before. But it boasted a wide moat of murky water on all sides but one. And despite the enchantment of blossoming trees creating a blush canopy to line it, the road that led to the castle's façade had fresh tire tracks cutting through. If SS guards were in this little vineyard town, it appeared they were patrolling the Loire Valley's vast kingdoms of castle ruins, searching for enemies of the Third Reich.

Enemies, *like her.*

The bumps of tire tracks beneath her soles were enough to make her settle in the tiny chapel peeking out from behind the ruins. The roof looked sturdy enough to keep her dry if the sky decided on a spring rain. And she'd almost missed spying it, so chances were good any patrolling eyes would too. With dawn not far off, it seemed as good a place to rest as any.

Vi huddled on the floor of the abandoned chapel, surrounded by crates of pears and a burlap bag of unshelled walnuts she'd found stowed away in the hollow of a stone altar. By who, it didn't matter. With a world cloaked in obstacles, hunger had been turned away long enough.

It would wait no longer.

Sitting in the shadows, Vi bit into a pear's flesh, letting the juice run down her chin. The taste was sweeter than anything she remembered. The rest, kinder. If there had been any pews, they were long gone. The floor was cold, but still the altar beckoned her to lean back and finally breathe deep, savoring the respite from a constant battle for survival. She surrendered, too weary to think of anything save for being grateful that a pear and an old chapel had become her unwitting saviors.

Raw emotion pricked at her eyes, threatening a flood to come pouring out. Vi shook her head against it, forcing the tears away. "You will not cry." She broke the silence with words that echoed against the ceiling. "You will not . . ."

Not when she'd narrowly escaped.

Not when others had given their lives to get her out of northern France altogether. She owed it to their fight to keep going . . . to keep running . . . to stay alive—no matter what. The SS were still out there, no doubt turning over every stone in France until they found what she'd stolen. And tears wouldn't change that.

The beauty of a stained-glass window behind the altar drew her attention instead, doling comfort in the central image of a mature Christ standing watch over the space. It was hushed but power-ful, the King in pristine ivory robes, with sky blues and rich royal purples stained around in delicate design, an awakening image of peace in their war-torn world.

She bit into the pear again, the sweet combination of honey and tart pulling her back to the present. Moments of longing at stained glass windows were a folly Vi couldn't entertain. Someone had stored those wares in the chapel. Though she desperately needed the rest, the owner could come back at any time, and she could ill afford a break now.

She'd been denying the truth, for a few precious moments anyway. The only option was to line her pockets and venture out into the forest again, running and praying for the best—her stomach she'd have to fill later.

Vi had only begun to stuff pears and handfuls of walnuts in her canvas messenger bag when the sound of a sliding bolt sliced through the empty chapel, echoing off the walls.

She stopped chewing, her palms instantly freezing in midair.

The heavy chapel door spread its weight in a creaky cry of weathered iron hinges. Footsteps echoed through the chapel a scant second later, the soles of shoes—or, *God help her*, military-issue boots—grinding into the soil of dirt and dried leaves that had gathered in piles upon the stone floor.

Each step was slow, steady, penetrating through the frantic beating of her heart.

Fear taunted as Vi swallowed the last bit of fruit in her mouth, its sweetness having turned bitter on her tongue. There was only one entrance she knew of: the door at the east end of the chapel. The door with the lock Vi had managed to pick and the bolt she'd left unlatched until she could slip out again, unheard and certainly unseen.

That intention fizzled now as she scanned the room, inching up on her knees to peek through the shadows.

The door stood ajar.

Someone had indeed entered—and was still inside.

She sank back down, her thoughts racing so fast they could be pinging off the walls. Maybe she could surprise the intruder? Jump up and run without warning? Knock them down and head for the door to escape into the woods?

No. The SS guards had guns ready for us last time and weren't afraid to use them.

It was certain she'd be shot in the back before she could get five paces out the door.

Think, Vi. Think.

Smashing through a stained-glass window could prove deadlier to flesh than a bullet. Throwing pears and walnuts at a soldier with a machine gun was feeble—completely out of the question. The old straight blade she'd found along the railroad lines some towns back was still in the bottom of her bag, but it would cause too much noise to dig it out now. And what good would a chipped, rusty razor do against a soldier's automatic weapon?

All that remained was for her to fight.

Vi ran her nails along the grooves of stones at the altar base.

The foundation was weak, but she hadn't time to dislodge any of the stones. Her last recourse was a weathered wood crate. It would prove a paltry weapon against the Nazis' guns, but what choice did she have?

A board hung loose and Vi gripped it, finding it gave without fight or sound. Two rusty nails protruded from the end. They might at least prove some point, if she could connect them with her attacker's body.

She held fast in a white-knuckled grip, determined to give them the best whipping she could, or go down swinging in the process.

The footsteps grew closer.

Hold . . .

Closer they came, God help her.

Vi slammed her eyes shut for a split second, listening. Trying to calm her breathing at the same time. Wishing she'd never seen the treelined road or the hidden chapel. If only she'd passed by the ruins instead of letting them draw her in.

Hold fast . . .

When she was sure the intruder was but a step away, Vi shot to standing, wielding the board like she'd seen the cricket players do on campus at Cambridge—out, away from the body, ready to crash the target with a confident, steady grip.

She pulled back to swing, the air slamming in and out of her lungs.

"Arrêtez!" a man shouted, immediately lowering a rifle that had been braced against his shoulder.

To yell "stop" . . . was it for her, or himself?

He extended a hand out in front of him and repeated, "Arrêtez," this on the exhale of a pent-up breath, indicating he'd been as startled as she. He pulled his finger back from the trigger, enough to encourage her to resume breathing.

The man lowered the rifle to point at the floor, then scanned the chapel, his feet iced in place. He covered all corners of the space quickly, then turned to her with a tilt of his head to one side.

Even through a mass of shadows, the golden tint of his eyes examined hers. *"Êtes-vous seule?"*

"Yes. I'm alone." Why she'd responded in English without thinking, Vi couldn't guess—unless it was so ingrained as her first language that it tumbled out her mouth due to exhaustion and a half-starved state. But it was a mistake at that, and mistakes meant death here.

She didn't dare make another.

"Bien." He let out a rough sigh. "You're English."

Though displeased with her presence in the chapel, to Vi's relief the man didn't appear truly threatening. Annoyance was a marked improvement over murderous intentions any day.

He eased the butt of the rifle to the floor and leaned against it like a makeshift cane. "Well, you can speak *Français* for a start. And lower that. I'd rather not take a board to the face if I can help it. Terrible way to start the day."

Yes, she supposed she could ease off a bit. Vi allowed her arm muscles to go lax and lowered the board, but she still kept it down at her side—just in case.

He ran a hand through a crop of dark waves that tipped over his brow, then searched the shadows in the small chapel again, perhaps doubting she'd been honest with him that she was indeed alone.

"Why in God's name didn't you speak French?" He lowered his voice to a vehement whisper, adding, "Do you have any idea how dangerous it is to speak English here?"

"I . . ." She shook her head. "I honestly don't know why I spoke English. I haven't spoken to anyone in . . . well, in a while."

"How long is a while?"

"Long enough to know what a mistake that was."

He sighed again. "So, English, do you mind telling me what you're doing here—besides pilfering the food we put back from winter stores?"

Vi kept her lips pursed. Any outright lie at what she was doing would have been ridiculous in the middle of a war zone. Not when France was blasted to bits and she looked like some lost creature from the woods. She drew upon her experience to come up with the best tale. She'd have to make an explanation as close to the truth for it to be believable, but far enough away that he'd not question her further.

"You have no answer?"

She nodded, willing her countenance to read as innocent as a milk maiden's. "I'm bound for my family's dairy farm in Vercors."

He did a double take. "Vercors? Aren't you a bit far north? And west, for that matter? What sees a dairy farmer's daughter lost this far into wine country?"

"Visiting, to care for my uncle. But there have been some . . . complications. So I'll be heading south to rendezvous with my family."

He paused, as if searching the chapel for an uncle they both knew was not there. "And your travel papers?"

Vi could have choked on her breath. "Why do you want to know about my papers?"

There'd been no time to manufacture new papers, and even if she had them, her old forgeries were grossly out of date. Without valid paperwork, it would take a mere shred of suspicion for a local villager to turn her in to the nearest gray uniform. She'd be up before a Nazi firing squad before dawn.

"Your silence is an answer whether you know it or not." He shifted his weight to his other foot as he leaned against the rifle. "So, you're waltzing through Nazi-occupied territory, spouting off weak explanations in English, with zero papers to explain what you're doing here. Oh, and thieving from our limited food stores. Is that about the way of it?"

Vi straightened her posture before him. If he stood to drag her before the firing squad's guns, she'd go with every ounce of brash she had left—including courage that set her spine ramrod straight. "I wasn't thieving."

"*Menteuse*," he said, smiling as he called her a liar, and pulled a kerchief from his pocket. He tapped his chin and tossed the linen square to her. "There's a half-eaten pear on the floor. Between that and your face, I'd say there's a bit left out of your story."

The dirt. The pear juice must have left trails down her chin.

Vi closed her eyes, wishing she hadn't remembered she still owned any vanity at the moment.

She'd found a straight razor some days back and sawed at her hair, chopping it to her chin in case the SS were circulating a photo with an ebony style down past her shoulders. Lucky for her she was made of stout stuff, enough that she could forget how it gutted her to watch her locks burn in a makeshift campfire, or what the jagged and mismatched ends must look like at the moment.

War changed everything. Vanity of every kind was extinct in their savage world, and the imperious stranger should have known better than to chide her for a white lie to survive in the midst of it.

Vi wiped her face, soiling the white kerchief as he studied her with a cool stare.

"Are you well? Do you need medical attention?"

A curious thing to ask, especially if he was debating on turning her in. She'd expected to need an undertaker far sooner than a physician.

She shook her head. "No."

"You may not need one yet, but you will if you don't take better care. Don't you know trespassers will be shot on sight? Signs are posted all along the road. And in town—no one stops at the castle. Period."

"I can read." Vi needn't tell him it was in six languages—French and German included. "I didn't come by the road or through town, so if there were signs, I missed them."

"Then how did you . . . ?"

"By train."

It wasn't an outright lie. Vi had come by train—along the tracks, anyway. Still, the furrow in his brow told that he wasn't drawn in that easily.

"Well, English, your story just keeps fanning my interest." He lifted his rifle and pointed out toward the road leading to the castle. "Train lines have been shut down to passengers for years, especially the foreign, paperless kind. Only Nazi-occupied train cars come in or out now, and they own every road for miles. You'd never have made it through by car or rail. So try again."

Blast. He was more astute than he'd let on.

"I followed the tracks on foot, staying just inside the tree line."

"And why is that, pray?"

"They don't bury mines along the tracks."

That seemed to trigger a deeper level of understanding in him.

There was a longer pause after each explanation she gave, like the cogs and gears had begun turning in his mind, connecting things Vi would have rather kept inactive. But this was different. A tiny twinge to the lips, a crease at the corners of the eyes— amusement of some kind. And he wasn't averse to letting it show.

Vi had gone too far. Made herself too knowledgeable. A bilingual milkmaid was rare enough. But a foreigner who knew of communication wires and land mines? That was a bona fide unicorn in the occupation zone—unless, of course, there was more than she was telling him outright.

She backtracked. "Everyone knows the Nazis wouldn't dare risk their ability to move supplies and troops by severing their own communications lines."

"Everyone, hmm?"

"The risk is high of being seen out in the open, but it's far safer than going through the towns. As I'm a woman traveling alone, I'm sure you'd agree someone like me would have to choose the lesser of two risks." She shrugged, feigning ease as if she were in a shop window picking out a new Sunday hat. "So you can see how I missed the signs."

"Oui. I can. But whether you happened upon them or not, they are still posted. And *Boches* don't hang them for kicks. There's no trespassing. Not here or at the castle ruins. The Nazis will shoot you on sight. That's to say nothing about interrogating you for being caught amongst our food stores. I'd rather not advertise where we're keeping supplies if I can help it. I'm not interested in being hanged anytime soon."

"They'd hang you for that?"

"Or put a bullet in the back of the skull, but some say that'd be for the lucky ones. The rest are sent away to a work camp and never return."

"Forgive me, sir, but in case you haven't noticed—there is a war on. If you wish to keep your food a secret, then I'd consider stowing it in a more clever hiding place," she fired back, keenly remembering to keep her tone soft enough to avoid being heard by anyone who might be lingering outside.

Vi tossed the kerchief back at him and tipped her chin up a notch.

He caught it in one hand against his canvas jacket, with just the hint of a smile. "You don't need to instruct me on war. I know quite enough about it already."

"As do I. And I wasn't—"

A sound cut through the silence between them—the snapping of a tree limb somewhere?

"Shh!" he ordered, dropping the kerchief. It drifted to the floor, almost in slow motion, as their eyes locked and he pressed a finger to his lips.

Slowly, he stepped in front of her with the rifle raised. Vi dug her nails into the board in her hand, standing frozen behind the tall, sun-swept haven of his shoulders. He turned an ear to the door. Listening. Their breathing and the amiable sound of trees swaying in the breeze the only noise to occupy the silence.

Sunrise was already streaking yellow in a line across the stone floor, piercing the chapel with colored light sifted through the stained glass. Strange, but Vi could hear birdsong in the stillness, a melody just as lovely as ever. And a loud cry cut the morning—a hawk maybe, circling somewhere overhead. It was peace. Defiance even, as if nature itself resisted war with beauty in the birth of the day's first moments.

They waited. Joined by the marriage of half sound, half silence.

If Vi could judge, that little something she'd seen flicker in his eyes—golden, soft, and steely at the same time—spoke volumes. His three-quarter profile said he was young. Midtwenties maybe. And even in the shadows of the chapel, Vi could discern a steadiness she desperately needed to believe in, especially when a split wooden board was the only thing that stood between her and meeting her Maker. He was willing to protect her without pretense, and that was rare for a stranger to do in a war-torn world.

After no threat presented itself, the man lowered his weapon and turned back to face her. "Whatever you need, it's yours. Just take it and go." He tilted his head to the open door and stepped back out of her path, keeping the rifle braced on the ever-so-slight hitch of a limp in his right leg.

"Maybe I should ask if you're the one who is well."

He shrugged off the comment, as if used to such things. "There's no time to be anything but well around here, not when we're trying to stay alive."

Vi eyed him as openly as he looked on her. They both knew what this was—survival. She was battling to stay alive too. Sans food. Or travel papers. And with uniformed Boches crawling through the countryside.

Staying alive was relative at the moment.

"Does that mean you won't turn me in?"

"I must be mad, but no. As long as you leave and never mention this conversation to a living soul."

She should have been overjoyed, but as Vi looked out to the freedom beyond the chapel door, a familiar pang struck her midsection. Out there was a war-ravaged countryside; that world held nothing for her. It was the blackness of war. Bombs raining from the sky. SS guards patrolling the rule of Nazi law over the French citizens, their own government held captive by Hitler's iron fist a country away.

Out there? Vi hadn't a prayer. Death and destruction were rampant, and likely there was not another peace-filled chapel left standing in all of France.

The man watched her, even as she worked things out in her own mind. He seemed to be waiting for something, almost as if he could read her thoughts and watched to learn if he'd been correct in his judgment of them.

Noting her pause, he pointed to the pile of deep-rust Anjou pears that had already been skimmed from the top. "Please, don't grow a conscience now. If it helps, I absolve you of any wrong. It's far more dangerous for you to be here than it is for me to have a dent in our food supply." When she opened her mouth to reply, he added, voice still weighted in a whisper, "And before you go too far, I'd rather not know—whatever it is."

"Rather not know what?"

"The reason why you, an obviously learned but naive Englishwoman, could expect to blend in here. You're no dairy farmer's daughter."

"I speak French." She winced at the meager submission.

"So you said. But there's more to being French than speaking the language. We're watched here—far too closely for me to engage in any association with you. So please ensure the safety of everyone on this land by leaving it now. Take the food and go."

Tears? Vi would never show them.

Not now, not ever.

Even when fear threatened to wreak havoc on her insides. This was the time to summon what Viola Hart was truly made of. She abandoned the wooden board to the stone floor and stooped to replace the pears in the crate, one by one. She then scooped walnuts from the depths of her canvas bag, rolling them from her palm into the burlap sack on the floor.

He watched her, leaning on that rifle without another word.

When she'd replaced what she'd taken, Vi stood, her vulnerability exposed before him. She made the decision to do the only thing left that could possibly save her life.

"Please hide me," she mouthed, dropping her voice to a fervent whisper. "Hide me here, or I'm dead."

FOUR

July 14, 1789
Les Trois-Moutiers
Loire Valley, France

Aveline halted at the top of the grand staircase.

A formal announcement would come any moment and she'd be forced to summon an air of serenity, though her insides wrestled in turmoil. She scanned the crowded entry for any sign of formal wear bedecked with the Renard crest.

Had Philippe's note contained a threat against her alone, Aveline wouldn't have ventured down to the ballroom at all. She would have slipped out the service entrance, absconded with one of the horses from the carriage house, and been well on the way back to Paris before anyone was the wiser. But considering her mother's life had been threatened as well, Aveline had little choice in the matter. She'd have to locate her mother in the throngs of guests, show her Philippe's note as proof of the dark omen, and get them both as far away from the castle as possible. Now, she'd been captured by the futile effort of searching a mass of blue jackets moving through the foyer.

Black. Navy. Even shades of robin's egg or gray—all gentlemen's coats could have passed for blue in the desperate search of her mind's eye. It would not improve with her announcement. A sea of faces would beam back—revelers celebrating her debut without an inkling as to the battle of nerves raging within her.

Aveline held fast to the note, burying her gloved hand in the graceful folds of her gown and with a deep breath, backed away down the hall. Instead of falling into a sea of ball gowns and fluttering fans that created a colorful mosaic of congratulations, she found the service stairs Fanetta had used before and swept through the back hall by following music to the ballroom.

It took some doing with her face cast down, but Aveline's gaze finally landed on the marigold brocade of her mother's gown. She'd found a perch, twittering with a cloud of guests who'd gathered opposite a grand marble hearth. He mother appeared gleeful, no doubt exclaiming the many charms her daughter had employed to garner such an advantageous match.

Aveline wasted no time. She moved through the entry as a member of court would, with perfect bowing and spreading smiles to the gentlemen and ladies who stepped in to greet her. That would have to do for now—cordialities that didn't require her to speak.

When at the hearth, she hooked an arm around her mother's elbow, attempting to ease their backs to the wall. "*Mère*—"

"Where have you been? They have not yet announced you." Francesca Sainte-Moreau lowered her voice, pausing to comment on her daughter's tardiness, then turned an about-face to inspect the merits of her appearance.

"I know that. I did not wish them to."

"And why have you no powder? And mere traces of rouge."

Aveline leaned in, though she employed her gaze to still move about the room, searching for any sign of Philippe over her mother's shoulder. "I must speak with you. *Now.*"

"Stand up straight, Aveline. Honestly," Francesca huffed, using the adept maneuver of tugging at the back of her daughter's bodice to straighten her posture, then flipped open her fan for a distraction she could speak freely behind. "Do you have any idea what a poor reflection this is on your father? You are tardy. To your own engagement ball. Fortunately, I was able to use the weariness of travel as a lady's excuse. But I passed your betrothed by the dance floor already, and he was quite worried when you didn't appear as expected."

"He's already here?" A shiver swept prickles the length of her spine.

Aveline returned her gaze to the dance floor. Too many people. Too much twirling satin and coiffed hair to see a fixed position through it all. If they could just stand still for a moment . . .

"Of course he's here, and quite anxious to meet you."

"Which one is he? Was he wearing a blue coat?" Aveline squinted, peering through the rows of dancers to the bystanders gathered on the other side of the room.

"Of course! That is the fashion, is it not?"

Francesca Sainte-Moreau was in fine form. The form Aveline knew well. She wasn't a heartless woman. Just fanciful, with eyes that were easily diverted by all things glitter and gold. And as she had two daughters to marry off, her occupation had been in assuring her daughters' futures. How little she knew—both daughters' perfectly packaged tomorrows appeared in jeopardy now.

"Listen to me, Mère. I haven't time to explain, but we must go this instant."

"Go?" Incredulity emitted in an effortless gasp. "Where have you a mind to go in the middle of your engagement ball?"

Aveline lowered her voice to a whisper. "I cannot explain here, but you have to trust me. We must leave. We'll take a coach from the carriage house—I saw them lined up at the front gate. We can persuade a coachman away. I'll lie if I must. But we will head out on the north road to Paris. It will take some time to get there—"

"We are not going to Paris. Certainly not until you are wed."

"I don't know what we'll do for money . . ." Aveline's thoughts warred within her, fear and practicality battling for dominance. They could barter their jewels. Her hand flew to the brooch on her bodice—how ironic if the gift would provide their means of escape. And there wasn't time to send word to Papa. A missive could take two nights to reach him.

No, they'd simply have to leave, and not stop until they'd reached Paris.

"Enough of this." Francesca pressed her lips into a fine line and sank her gloved fingertips into the back of Aveline's arm, her nails applying pressure. "I will not listen to another word about this engagement. Do you hear me? Your father worked in earnest to forge this alliance and I will not allow childishness to be the fall of it, especially after that nasty business of your consorting with peasants in Paris. Take your place, daughter. And a grand place it is. You will be mistress of this castle, the woman to provide heirs for this land. Does that mean nothing, that you have been chosen to carry on the legacy of this great family?"

"Baron le Roux is dead."

The blunt force of the declaration delivered the blow she'd expected. Francesca's jaw drooped open, her grip falling lax on Aveline's arm.

"Dead . . . the baron? Surely not." She laughed, a wavering cackle released under her breath, and flitted her fan to wave air against her face. "Why would you say such a wicked thing?"

"It's true. I received a missive by courier. Félicité sent it just this eve. It's what kept me. The le Roux family was attacked and their estate burned to the ground."

And now, she had her mother's attention.

"And . . . what of Gérard?"

Sorrow clung through each heartbeat. Aveline just wished they had time enough to remain in its company. "I'm so sorry."

"*Comment est-ce possible?*" Francesca melted against the wall behind them, looking like she gripped the chair rail or else she'd faint dead away.

"I wish it was not so. But it can be. *It is,*" Aveline whispered, answering her mother's question with nothing but regret.

"What of Isabella? The baroness and her daughters?"

"Félicité did not know. Nothing is certain, except that safety in Paris is no longer assured. The men were felled in front of their family, Mère. And the whole of their estate is left in ruins." She paused, hating to have no answer for the pleading in her mother's eyes. "Do you understand what I'm telling you? Papa and Félicité are safe—for now. But the violence is spreading. We cannot outrun this forever."

"I will not believe it. Where is this letter?"

"Lost." Aveline shook her head. No time to explain. "They were soon to announce my name and I had no choice but to join the party without it."

All the while they stood, they were watched. Men gazed their way, bowing, as was cordial if they met Aveline's eyes. Was Philippe out there somewhere among them, watching their discourse even then? Ladies, too, watched, curious about the young woman who'd been elevated from nowhere to attain such a station.

Aveline cast her gaze down, turning away from them.

"We'll retrieve the letter on the way out. I know where it is."

"You cannot think it possible to leave now, when there are revolts in Paris? If this news is true, then we ought to stay here where it is safe. Consult the Duc et Vivay. And Philippe." Francesca straightened up, as if her corset had been drawn tighter with her resolve. "Yes. That is what we shall do. After the ball, you will take this letter to your betrothed and he will instruct us in the matter."

"Mère, I should think this is one decision I may make for our safety without instruction from a higher-ranking male. But besides that, it is not possible now." She spoke quickly, lowering her lips to her mother's ear, entreating with a fervent whisper. "I was bound to tell you the grave news of Gérard, and then . . . I received this." Aveline pressed Philippe's note into her mother's gloved hand, squeezing for good measure. "Read it."

Francesca obeyed, her face transforming from an air of inquest to numb shock in a matter of seconds. She crushed the note in her palm and looked up too, staring through the throngs of guests turning circles on the dance floor. "Who would dare send something like this to the future daughter-in-law of the Duc et Vivay? Your fiancé will have this gentleman's head, whoever he is!"

Francesca obviously wasn't thinking beyond the toxic merge of fear and fury that had swept into her mind. "You don't understand. It is by Philippe's hand."

Aveline stared back, meeting her glare with doe eyes, saying everything without the necessity of words.

"The Duc et Vivay's son?" Francesca raised her chin, letting loose with a chirping laugh. "Impossible! Someone is entertaining themselves with a cruel jest against you, dear. It's a folly—not the bequest a fiancé would dare give his betrothed on the eve of their presentation."

"It is no jest. It was delivered by his staff, a note from the duke's son, accompanied by this." Aveline ran her gloved fingertips over the top of her bodice, grazing the fox brooch. "Who else could afford such luxury as this? It is a gift, he said, so he'd know his bride-to-be the moment she stepped into the ballroom. Surely you must see that whatever the motive, I cannot marry such a man. Not until I have a proper explanation for why a threat would accompany a gift that only he is in a position to bestow. And I'll not stay another moment in the house that would threaten our family—"

A blast shook the walls, deafening Aveline's entreaty.

A hail of tiny crystal knives cut through the gaiety of the ballroom as windows shattered above them. The quartet's strings halted with off-key screeches, sending the revelers into shrieking fits on the dance floor. Sharp whistles penetrated the sky, ending with glass rain that pierced the air a second time.

Aveline tugged at her mother's wrist on instinct, pulling her down to shield her head from falling debris.

The two-story Palladian windows lining the back of the ballroom blew out, one by one, their leaded glass shattered as stones sailed through the sky. Wind breezed through the jagged lines of glass that remained in the frames. The crystal chandelier had gone dark, eerily rocking back and forth from the impact of stone and glass. The flickering flames of candelabras were snuffed of their candlelight too, making the perimeter of the dance floor a hazy memory.

Aveline peered through the darkness, no longer searching for a coat.

It wasn't possible to follow the note's instructions if she couldn't find the man who had given it to them. All she knew was the warning had been real. Somehow, Philippe had known what was to come and he'd tried—and failed—to warn her in time.

"This way!" Aveline tugged her mother through the throngs of the disoriented, retreating to an alcove under the stairs.

Chaos swallowed the room like a raging sea.

She peeked out from their vantage point, watching in horror as a rock shattered the mirror over the marble fireplace at the end of the ballroom, sending the weight of the gilt frame to crash down, glass skidding across like ice had been let upon the dance floor.

Tiny flickers of flames came into view then, bobbing up and down in the distance.

"God help us."

Dories appeared on the water. Men with torches—too many to count—had made their way across the moat and now collected along the château's outer walls. Without warning the dance floor was lit up again, this time by fiery torches that sailed through the air.

Fire tore into the château's insides, eating up curtains and. exploding the accelerant of broken champagne flutes from a refreshment table that had been cut down to the floor. A hail of smoke and hungry flames tore up the walls, devouring age-old family portraits, and licked at the hems of ladies' gowns.

Francesca fell deeper into disrepair with the fiery explosions. She curled into the curtains like a panicked child, burying her face in the velvet with each boom.

"We must get out of here!" Aveline wrapped her palms around her mother's shoulders, trying and failing to pull her away from her iron grip on the hanging velvet. "Do you hear me?"

Loud pops burst through the pandemonium then, smaller explosions as rocks pounded through glass and felled pictures on the walls, one by one.

Ladies fell away in their haste to flee, sliding on glass and debris that shredded their delicate satin slippers. One side of the ballroom had become a makeshift battleground, where men had lined up behind the overturned punch table, loading muskets and firing into the madness beyond the château's walls, while others formed a line hoisting buckets of water to douse the flames.

She searched for the blue coat. Surely Philippe would have

lined up with the rest of the men in defense of his father's estate, like Gérard had done when his father's home fell under siege. But black smoke invaded the scene, creating cinder-laden shadows that darkened the air.

It was impossible to make anything out now.

Aveline coughed into her palm, the smoke searing her lungs with each breath.

Fear of flying debris was one thing, but they couldn't hope to hide from fire. Not if the castle was to be brought down to ash and rubble. They were not going down with it. She squared her shoulders against the mere idea.

In a blink a flash of blue whisked past their hiding place, jarring Aveline from frenzied thoughts of escape. She peered through the smoke, steeling her eyes to stay with the willowy figure. The man had dark hair, long and tied at the nape, and a royal blue coat she'd been searching for. But the Renard crest would have been on the front, and that she couldn't see.

He moved back and forth, whisking ladies from the dance floor and depositing them in the entry behind men splashing buckets of water against the roaring flames.

Aggravated by the evening breeze, the flames licked higher. Closer. Deadlier as they eyed their victims under the stairs. Aveline could see them, roaring like a fire-breathing dragon come to collect its prey. She hadn't time to consider whether it was a smart decision or not; it was either stay in fear and get eaten by the flames, or flee and take their chances with the musket shots.

Aveline ripped her gloves free.

"Here—" She shoved the crumpled swatch of fabric under her mother's nose. "Cover your mouth." She kept it there, pulling Francesca's shaking fingers up to replace her own. "Hold it here, breathe like this. We must run. Do you understand?"

Francesca nodded, though weakly.

Aveline dug her nails into her mother's elbow, yanking her along behind her. "Then go! Now—" she shouted, covering her own mouth with a satin glove as she steered them into the storm.

Francesca proved deadweight—a useless stupor in yards of brocade, allowing herself to be dragged along like an oversized doll. Aveline stretched an arm over the small of her mother's back, bending her over at the waist as they ran. They sped along the wall, avoiding the fire as best they could, tripping and falling with skirt strips tangling round their ankles. They reached the front hall, but it, too, was imperiled.

Flames had consumed parlor chairs and rugs on the second-story landing and were eating up brocade curtains where Aveline had stood only moments before. Their only exit was the front façade, where she'd watched the carriages unload with party guests. It was before them, freedom behind front doors that had been stripped bare, their hinges torn and splintered wood hanging as if made of paper.

The blackness of night beckoned outside, the flicker of torches buzzing like fireflies kissing the water. Aveline paused behind one of the thick doors, making wood her shield.

Shadows passed by: men running. Flashes of satin gowns flew past as women scattered and hid in the shrubbery. To the left, a bright-orange glow burned where the carriage house had once stood—it, too, now consumed. Horses trampled by with empty carriages, doors swinging in the runaway madness.

Aveline pushed her mother forward through the doors. "Run! Down the road! We'll hide in the grove until morning. I will come and find you."

This was their battlefield: fire and ash come to claim them. All that was left was to summon grit and pray slippered feet would carry them. Aveline could do nothing but watch her mother amble through the darkness, until the orange glow reflecting off her skirts had faded into the night.

Félicité's letter . . . the half-imagined portrait she'd sat for . . . the fiancé she had yet to meet—all were poised to vanish that night. And they would not be listed among the dead. She drew in a steadying breath, then raised her torn skirts to follow down the stairs.

Without warning her vision was jarred, blurring her sight as blackness flooded.

A blow to the side of her head sent Aveline careening for the doorjamb. She fell, crumpling against it. Searing pain shocked the breath out of her lungs, forcing unconscious tears to her eyes. They mingled with smoke, somehow, the wetness burning her eyelids.

She scratched her nails down the wall, desperate for sight, for anything of substance to hold her from the tidal wave of dizziness dragging her to the floor. It proved futile. The pile of satin skirts did little to cushion her fall, so she had a sense of bumping into things—people? Furniture? Why hadn't her face slammed against the marble floor yet?

There was no pain. No sense of up or down, right or wrong. Just falling. And then the oddest sensation that she was flying— maybe both. Her world had been overcome by fire and smoke, and somewhere in the midst, Aveline had been whisked away from it.

Night air overtook her, washing her skin with a coolness that replaced the oppressive heat. The limbs of knotted trees stretched out in a canopy above her, air laden with smoke and flashing cinders suddenly left far behind. Aveline flew through it, seeing the blur of stars overhead, the sky wild and dark as chaos faded into the background.

"Stay with me."

The voice startled Aveline to focus.

A hand brushed against the side of her head, then patted her cheek, like her *nounou* used to do when she was to wake each morning.

"Can you hear me, mademoiselle? You must stay awake."

A man. His tone was firm but edged in worry.

"Open your eyes . . ."

Aveline battled, blinking against the canopy of green overhead.

"Bien. Keep them open."

She tried, failing to focus on the man's profile above her.

They were still flying, dizziness toying with her senses. The air smelled fresh and clean somehow. And the glow of orange and yellow flames dissolved into an ink sky, black shadows, and still forest greens. Aveline allowed her head to sag, chin to chest. And then she saw it, flooding the view before her: a blue coat.

A coat with a crest on the lapel.

Gold embroidery. It was a fox, the Renard coat of arms that had plucked her from the dragon's breath. Aveline raised a hand to the embroidery, battling to stay awake as she ran a fingertip over the rows of thread.

"*Philippe* . . . ," she exhaled, finally giving in as her fingertips fell away from the light touch of gold stitching, and blackness triumphed.

They were safe.

FIVE

Ellie stood at the edge of the mist, staring out over a crossroad cutting through sun-swept vineyard hills.

The country road mirrored the landscape she'd passed for much of the drive from Tours: fog-laden hills and hollows, winding roads, the occasional gated entrance or quaint cottage. Vineyards and châteaus, of course. A rich expanse, no doubt, but not clearly mapped for a directionally challenged American who could have used a French lesson or two long before an intrepid spirit led her to hop on a red-eye bound for the Loire Valley.

Fortune had intervened before it was too late, catching her attention in the form of an old wooden sign peeking from the overgrowth on the side of the road. It boasted lovely names—in white-painted letters and accent marks near faded from the sun. They could have been châteaus or estates, just as easily as country town names. And the arrows pointing in all directions offered little help. But little was better than none. So Ellie had parked her Fiat and hopped out, trying to match names to the guidebook map she'd picked up at the airport.

Despite the sign that pointed seven ways to nowhere, the vast landscape was exactly as she'd dreamed. A never-ending span of rolling hills cut a broken line against the horizon, layered with a feast of greens, rich ciders, and autumn golds. The sun peeked over the highest crest, sweeping through the landscape like a silent protector, mingling with grape arbors spread out as far as the eye could see.

"Well, if I have to be lost, this is definitely the place to do it."

Though the sun's searching rays were just starting to wake the land, they offered scant warmth. Ellie was grateful for her Northern Michigan constitution right then. October could still be brutal in early morning, and she'd packed smart out of instinct: fingerless gloves, layering sweaters, and lined hiking boots—just in case. She shivered into her blanket scarf and pressed the folded map under her elbow as she turned in semicircles, arrested by the calendar-worthy landscape.

Grandma Vi had been persistent one day out of hundreds since her diagnosis. That alone would have been enough to spark some investigation on Ellie's part. But then the brooch . . . the photo . . . the discovery of a lost love and the breaking open of a story she'd never known existed. As fairy-tale romances went, Ellie had to admit that finding the man in the photo and giving him her grand-mother's decades-long answer to a secret proposal was up there.

A quick Internet search had produced images of a castle of the same name as Perrault's famous fairy tale. It was nestled in the Loire Valley—the area of France Grandma Vi had mentioned a time or two before. And that was it: Ellie left Grandma Vi under Laine's watchful eye, boarded a plane with little else than a photo and raw nerve, and stepped out in their race against time.

I wish you were here, Grandma Vi. You'd love this.

And then she thought of the old photo and the long-ago

captured views that might have been locked away in her grand-mother's memory.

But I wonder, have you seen this before?

Emotion dared her eyes to remain dry as she snapped photos on her phone, until the rumble of an automobile echoed up the hill and pulled her from her thoughts. She scrambled, waving, intent on flagging the driver down.

A vintage truck in faded evergreen—looked like an old Ford—which struck her as odd to have been in France. Despite impressive rust patches, wooden slats lining the bed, and an engine that sounded like it was sputtering on its last leg, it still rolled up over the rise. The brakes whistled, slamming the truck to a stop directly behind her rental.

Wistful thoughts of the view faded, replaced by the hope that the driver might be able to point Ellie in the right direction. She hadn't seen anything but rock walls and trees, vines and the occasional cottage for ages. Maybe this passerby was better at reading maps than she was. Better yet, maybe he was a local who could solve the mystery of the crossroads and simply tell her which way to go.

Ellie trotted up to the door, but when zeal threatened to get the better of her she eased off, burying her riding boots in the dewy grasses along the field. A tourist traveling alone in a foreign country best be on the cautious side. She slipped the map behind her and smiled, ready to speak from a safe distance.

A man cranked the driver's side window down, calling, "Mornin'," over the sputter of the engine. Ellie could decipher little else over it but took a hopeful step forward when she heard at least one word spoken in English.

That was a good sign.

"I'm sorry. What did you say?"

He cut the engine. "I said, good mornin'. Is there a problem with your rental?"

The man was younger than she'd expected, given the vintage ride. Thirty, maybe. Probably around her age. And not bad to look at. Not at all, with dark hair tucked behind his ears in a longer, laid-back style, and a jawline that looked like he'd purposefully avoided a shave. He proceeded to stare at her through green eyes so sharp, she bet they could knock a person flat had he wanted them to.

"My rental?"

"Rental." He nodded over the top of the steering wheel to her Fiat. "Sticker in the back window. Gives it away every time."

Ellie's heart sank a little. His old rig obviously wasn't a rental, so she'd hoped that meant he was a local. But with that Irish brogue weighing his voice down, there was no way he could be French. Chances were he knew as little about the landscape as she did.

"You're Irish?"

The question tipped his brow a shade. "There's a problem with an Irishman offerin' to aid a stranded motorist?"

"No. I didn't mean it like that. Sorry—it's just that you might not be able to help unless you're from around here. I couldn't understand much of anything they said in that little town back there. They know about as many words in English as I do in French, so we bumped into a bit of a crossroads, so to speak. But by your accent I'd have guessed you might be a tourist and I was hoping that's not the case."

"A tourist like you, ya mean?" He tossed a glance down at the half-hidden map in her hand. "I didn't think they still made maps that folded."

"Yeah. They do, apparently. I found it in a bookstore at the airport. And good thing, because my GPS hasn't once found a signal out here. If I could just read this thing. But I'm hoping you can help point me in the right direction."

"So, nothin' wrong with it then?"

Kind of gallant to ask.

Ellie turned toward the little Fiat. It sat, quiet and still, the jet-black color cutting a sharp outline against the field mist.

"The car? No, it's fine. A little on the small side but—"

He nodded, satisfied enough by midsentence to cut her off. "I meant not broken down then. You do realize you're parked."

"Yes."

"In the middle of the road. With your car door open, so no one else can get by?"

"Is it?" Ellie glanced up at her car. The door was indeed open, efficient in blocking him or anyone else from getting around it on the tight one-lane road. "I'm sorry. I didn't know the roads here were so tight."

"It's alright." He wasn't annoyed, thank goodness. A man of few words, yes. But at the very least, he seemed cordial enough that Ellie felt she could ask for help.

"But if you could help me, I'll be out of your way that much faster."

She flipped the map so it was right side up to him and pointed her cherry-red index nail at the spot she'd circled with her Sharpie.

"I'm looking for the Domaine du Renard. You might have heard of it. It's a vineyard around here. According to the map, it says it should be . . ." She waved her hand out over the span of rolling hills past her car, gesturing out into the heart of it. "Right there. But as you can see, it's not. It looks like I've come to the ends of the earth out here. A beautiful end, but still not what I'm looking for."

"Right there." He tossed a glance to the span of fields and cocked an eyebrow. "You sure about that, yeah?"

What good was it to pretend? Ellie could barely handle the driving, let alone reading signs in a language she hadn't studied since seventh grade. Finding an estate house smack-dab in the middle of the French countryside was beyond her at the moment. Best to be out with it. The sooner she got to the vineyards, the sooner she could start investigating the photo and get back home.

"No, actually. I'm not sure about much of anything anymore."

"The Renard is up the ridge, not down." He extended an index finger over the wheel, pointing to the treed hills out in front of them. "That way. About two kilometers, then turn left at the rock wall. Follow it back to the end."

Ellie held the map up over her brow, blocking the rising sun as she looked up over the rise. So the vineyard was up the hill? Good. She just hadn't gone far enough. And even though there seemed to be some old rock wall every hundred feet or so, a well-known vineyard would have to have better signage than the one she'd initially stopped for.

"What a relief. Then that's where I'm headed."

"There's a tastin' room—open until nine. The wine shop a half hour later, except on Sundays. And the restaurant is seasonal, but it's still open for a few more weeks. That'll save you from gettin' lost on the way back to town, if you're in a pinch and need a bite. Breakfast and noon meal. Night meal's on your own, though."

"So you work at the vineyard?"

"In a manner of speakin'."

Finally, a real stroke of luck. He was headed right to the front door she needed to knock on.

"Great. I can't tell you what a relief this is. Do you mind showing me the way? It's actually freezing out here, and I would love to find my room at the estate inn—preferably one with a fireplace so I can warm up and check my limbs for frostbite."

As if triggered by something she'd said, the man's countenance changed in an instant. Cordiality melted away, his casual air
replaced by a distance in the eyes and a firm cut to the jaw.

He kicked up the engine—a none-too-subtle signal he was
ready to be on his way. "Sorry to disappoint you, miss, but the
estate house is privately owned. It's booked by reservation only.
There aren't any of those this time of year. Ya ought to head back
down the hill—stay at one of the inns in town."

"Oh, but I do have a reservation." Ellie turned to her phone.
But just like the use of the GPS, she had no Wi-Fi access. And no
Wi-Fi meant she couldn't hope to show him her e-mail reserva-
tion. "Well, I do when my e-mail's working. Does the estate have
Wi-Fi?"

"No."

"No Wi-Fi? Really? Surprising."

"No—you're not goin' to the estate."

Ellie rocked back on her heels, sobered by the finality in his
tone. While the reasoning was unclear, the look of determination
in his face was not. She wasn't getting an invitation, regardless of
her purported reservation status—the same status she'd already
paid for.

Ellie folded her arms over her chest and leveled her glare, challenging him with what she hoped was a look as stubborn as his.

"Sir, I've paid an advance deposit for two weeks—more, if necessary. My credit card has already been charged. Now, I may not
need to stay the duration of the booking; it just depends on how
long it takes to find what I'm looking for. But I'd prefer to speak to
the owner before I make a decision."

"What could you be lookin' for out here?"

"Presently? The estate house where you work. I paid extra for a
vineyard staff member to show me the Loire Valley, so I'll leave the

rest to my tour guide. If I could just get access to my e-mail, I could confirm it for you."

"Sorry. Not able to help." He rolled the truck forward, adding inches. "If you please, then."

Maybe he was a looker not two minutes ago. But the Irishman had developed a bit of a surly smirk for no apparent reason. Ellie made the command decision that one moody local wasn't going to put a damper on the trip, just because he'd decided to wake up on the wrong side of the vineyard that morning. It didn't matter if it was two kilometers more or two hundred—she'd come this far, and she was going the rest of the way.

"Fine. Thank you for your time." Ellie dipped her head in a polite nod. "I can always go knocking on doors up the hill. Maybe they can help me find this Titus Vivay."

The truck engine cut off with an abrupt, coughing jolt.

If the poor auto had finally died on that last sputter, the man might be regretting the clipped edge to his conversational skills. Ellie may not know much about the metric system, but a couple kilometers' walk was bound to be far enough to be a nuisance, especially when he wanted to be on his way. But no way was he in line to receive a ride after the cool reception he'd just dished out.

Ellie turned on the sound of the driver's-side door creaking open.

He'd stepped out, then clicked the door closed behind him. Odd, but he wasn't boorish as she might have expected. Instead, he took a few steps toward her but stopped still a healthy distance away, then looked down on her with an amiable attitude once again in place.

Something flashed in his eyes. Narrowed, but with a softer crinkle between the brows. Was it . . . concern? She wasn't sure what to make of that.

"I'm sorry—what name did you say?"

"My reservation was made with the estate owner, a Mr. Titus Vivay. Why?"

"Judas!" He slapped a palm against his leg, then turned to stare out over the fields with his hands braced on his hips. He hung his head, shaking it back and forth. "That's what I thought you said."

"Is . . . that a problem?"

"It is when the man has been fightin' any form of modern technology for the last sixty years and only now decides to use a computer just so he can defy me. And my own grandmother helped him. What makes him think he can just rent out rooms in our house?" He exhaled low, as if frustration had mounted to tipping. "I'll kill him. No—first he's goin' to make this season's wine, then I'll kill him. Or at the very least, break his laptop so he'll stop invitin' strangers to set up housekeeping under our roof."

"Your roof?" The barb struck her then. "Hey, what kind of stranger do you think I am, anyway?"

"You're American."

She shifted onto a cocked hip. "Meaning?"

"That's quite enough chancer for this morning."

Chancer? Ellie made a mental note to research the term as soon as she had Wi-Fi access. It didn't sound favorable in the least, and she wanted to be on his level if she needed to dole out a zinging comeback later.

He turned back around, greeting her with irritation flashing in those eyes of his. "And yes. It's *my* roof. Or ours. The family's home. And he probably used my laptop too. The one he didn't care to turn on to update the books in the last two years, as fate would have it. But that's beside the point. We have a harvest to bring in. You can see the fields, yeah? That's fog. That means it's cold. Another week of this and there'll be frost, and then we can kiss the melon harvest good-bye."

"Melons?"

He sighed. "Not melons. *Melon de Bourgogne*—white grapes. But it would be an entire label lost for the year and I'm not going to let that happen, no matter what harebrained scheme my grandfather finds himself a part of. We don't have guests durin' the harvest. Period."

That didn't make sense. "But I read somewhere that vineyards do take in tourists and pay them to hand-cut the grapes. It stands to reason that you would need help instead of turning it away at harvesttime."

"I'm not interested in what all the other wineries are doin'."

The man's temper hadn't truly flared—just his frustration at the surprise of a reservation at an inopportune time. That was something Ellie could at least try to understand. But flying thousands of miles and trekking through tourist towns with only a rental car, a guidebook, and some inherited grit meant she wasn't backing down either. Not when she had her grandmother's photo in her pocket, an abandoned castle to find, and precious time ticking away with each passing hour.

"He's your grandfather, this Titus?"

The man ran a hand through his hair on a half eye roll to the sky. "Yeah, heaven help me. He is."

"And he lives at the estate house, does he?"

"Until he finds a way to displace the lot of us. But for the moment, yeah. He's there."

"Good." Ellie marched over to her car and tossed the map on the passenger seat. Followed by her phone. She got in and poked her head back out, calling over her shoulder, "Since you speak English, I might need you to translate to work this out. So if you please, kindly show me to the estate. I've had a rough night in town and a long drive already this morning, and that's all before I've had any coffee. What I'd like is just a bit of perspective and a lot of caffeine. And hospitality, if you can manage it. Then I'll retire to my room and be out of both your and your grandfather's way."

"It's Quinn Foley. Not Vivay—grandfather on my mother's side. But you're in luck, miss." He motioned around a bend in the road, the one that trekked up over a rocky ridge. "He hasn't gone into town yet this mornin'. So come on. Let's go get your money back so we can send you packin'."

SIX

APRIL 22, 1944

LES TROIS-MOUTIERS

LOIRE VALLEY, FRANCE

Gunfire rocketed through the trees.

"Stay down."

The man wasted no time in issuing the order, just raised his rifle over a fallen tree and scanned the dense thicket as more shots echoed overhead. He'd only just led them out of the chapel and begun a steady trek through the woods when a rapid succession of gunshots had cut through the trees. Several steps later, despite the slight hitch of his limp, he halted and pulled Vi down to her knees in the underbrush beside him.

His demeanor read as straight confidence, enough that she obeyed. But she wasn't a novice at running from a threat. With what she'd seen, Vi had been war tested long before now. He might have stopped to consider that if she'd been running from guns herself, she knew when to keep her head down and would do it on her own.

"It's alright." He shot a glance back at her, just once, then turned back to the direction of the gunfire.

"Why do you say that?" Vi stared ahead. Watching. Adjusting

her knee away from a stone bent on cutting into her flesh as they held their positions.

"Because you're shaking."

Vi edged back. *Blast!* She'd crept up so close behind that she'd fused her nails into the moss-covered log and had pressed up against his back. She relaxed her fingertips. Her hands were shaking on their own, and being so close, he certainly would have felt it.

There went her plan to declare an assertion of courage.

"Well, I consider it a victory that I am not screaming in terror, to tell you the truth," she whispered back, still scanning the forest for the telltale uniforms of Nazi gray. "I'll take silent trembling and a cool head over that any day."

His profile eased into the hint of a smile. "As would I."

Nature stilled in response to the gunfire. Its usual sounds were replaced by something far more eerie: a melody creeping through the trees.

Music? Surely not.

Vi strained her ears, listening, waiting as notes drifted closer. The *ping-ping* of high-pitched notes lilted through the trees like a lost music box.

"What is that?" she whispered, seeing no movement against the overgrowth of fern, felled trees, and rocks that covered the forest floor around them.

"A gramophone. The Nazis probably found a stash of wine and are taking their jollies out with target practice on the castle ruins."

"And they do that often?"

"Not as a rule, no. But we've seen it before. Sometimes they look to pick a fight in town. Other times they amuse themselves with whatever they have at their disposal. It's something to do while they wait."

That was little explanation. "While they wait for what?"

"The Allies."

"The Allies?" Vi swallowed hard. "You're quite sure of that."

He nodded, his eyes fixed in front of them. "They're coming. We just don't know where or when. But it's a rumor that persists enough to keep the Nazis locked in their posts. So now? We all wait. And pray to God to sustain us."

A rumor.

Vi nodded. How many in France believed the Allies were coming? And what would happen when the truth finally played out? The intelligence she'd been privy to was more than rumor. More than innuendo she'd heard of Hitler's military leaders at Château de La Roche-Guyon.

She clutched the messenger bag at her side, instinct eager to keep her secrets close. His attention wasn't broken by the action though. He appeared not to notice—just pointed a finger over a ridge ahead of them.

"There's enough cover beyond the hill that we should be able to slip out unseen. It's something of a good hike, but we'll be able to get out if we go right now." He looked down at her shoes and shook his head. Dirt-caked shoes with thick heels probably weren't what he'd hoped to see. "I hadn't remembered what you were wearing. With the accent I was half afraid to find a pair of heels on you. But lace-up oxfords are close enough to it. You won't be able to keep up."

"I would have given up these heeled stompers a long time ago, had I been given a choice. The old coat and dress too. But war is not a garden party, monsieur. You take what you can and hold on to what you have. I learned that about the same time I started my career in pear stealing."

That comment garnered a genuine smile from him. "I suppose you do have to make quick getaways in that line of work."

"If you say we'll escape Nazis with itchy trigger fingers, then I'm more than ready to make any getaway you'd like. You just might find that in the end, you're the one who has to keep up with my oxfords."

Mustered courage in her words was something she used to overshadow the opposite tells of her physical presence. He must have known it because Vi could still feel the slight quiver of her hands. She hid them in busyness, adjusting the bag's strap over her shoulder instead.

Hunger. Fear. A combination of both—whatever had caused the trembling, he either hadn't noticed or simply let it go without comment. With one final check over the vantage point to the direction of the castle, he edged forward like he was about to spring.

She stopped short, pulling him back at the elbow. "Wait."

"What?"

"Your name?" she whispered. "I can't keep calling you *monsieur*, and I sure don't want you calling me *English* again. I shouldn't want to keep smacking the sod who's rendering my aid."

"For a Brit you sure don't pull any punches."

"Aren't we in the business of survival? Your words. If we're risking our lives with this run, I'd like to at least be on a first-name basis in case I have to curse you for getting me killed."

"I'm not sure what good it does to exchange names when we'll only have to part ways again. It's safer if we don't know anything about one another."

"Safer how?"

He wasn't ready to elaborate, apparently. Neither was she. So they were at a hefty stalemate in the middle of the woods.

"Julien."

"Is that your name?"

Again, he didn't linger in the details.

"You're English, so . . . Lady. That's your name while you're here. Anyone asks, that's what you reply."

"That's fine for the French, but you do realize what *Dame* is in English? You don't have to be terribly clever to connect the dots on what that implies."

She could think of a list of less flattering things to be called, starting with mud-caked pear-stealer. But he'd moved on, pulling his rifle down, preparing to run. Lady it would have to be for now, and she'd pick a fight over propriety later.

"We'll head northwest. You'll see a small riverbed after a kilometer or so. There's only one way over—a stone bridge they like to keep up with random patrolling. We'll have to cut over in the other direction, along the forest, where it's shallow enough to wade through. Then across the vineyards to the opposite tree line."

Vi sighed low. "Is that all?"

"For the moment, it's enough." A pair of errant pistol shots pierced the woods. Julien shifted his glance in the direction of the sound. It was followed by the faint echo of laughter somewhere far off, though it only lasted for a few seconds. "Ready, Lady?"

She nodded.

It was then or never—and she'd come too far to accept never.

"Allons-y!" He sent her off with the whispered shout of "Let's go," then jumped out on her heels and lapped her to lead the way.

The trek through the woods was faster than she'd imagined, especially since she was in foreign surroundings and Julien didn't appear exactly surefooted. Still, they angled over rocks and around overgrown thickets, moving at a quick pace.

Twigs poked at her legs. Branches—the scraggly, sharp kind— punished with unyielding snaps as they swept by. Vi ducked and moved each time she felt them reach for her. Best to be nimble or she'd take a limb to the face. She could navigate the rough terrain, though bone weary and hungry as an ox. Running through the woods was her specialty now, as was hiding from hunger. Even death. As long as Julien could keep pace against those things, so could she.

The landscape muddled in a blur of greens and ruddy browns, trees and earth. The ground was soft from spring rains—disastrous if the sole of her oxford caught in the forest floor. She could turn an ankle or worse. Vi picked up her feet as best she could, keeping her gaze locked on Julien's back, minding her footing even without a sense of direction as to where he was taking them.

The same landscape bled by like a moving picture show until she'd lost sense of anything but trees. Underbrush. The sound of water as they crossed rocks lining the streambed. More earth and sky and running.

Then—*gold*.

That's what swept in around them. The overgrowth of the thicket broke open and the vineyards spread out before them, rolling in hills of lush vines, greens and warm golds awash in sunlight piercing rays through the clouds.

"This way." Julien led them into the vineyard rows, his gait in a steady half run.

Vi had seen the Loire Valley's grape arbors before, though most she'd passed by had been burned, picked clean, or withered as casualties of war. They bordered roads, uneven. Bombed out and littered with the carcasses of horses and abandoned wagons and— Lord help her—the occasional crumpled body . . . The remnants of death were left to rot for days, weeks, even months now. It was stark, to have passed by darkness as if unaffected.

But then, in a snap: life again. Vines covered with scores of tiny grape buds, vibrant and green, and young leaves shining under a glaze of morning dew. The view became otherworldly—a mirage of normalcy in their war-ravaged world, with row after cultured row of life flourishing under the warmth of the sun.

Julien didn't stop, so she didn't either, not even when her side issued a sharp hitch from the pace. Vi ran with her shoulders drooped but her head up, keeping in step with him as they passed through arbor rows.

The forest landscape was finally revived, creating a thick tree line at the opposite extension of the vineyard. He led them over a rise, taking her hand to help her climb the rocky incline. He released her when the ridge leveled out. An expanse of a stone wall took shape, running behind a humble cottage tucked in the crest of the incline. It was hidden, with lofty trees overhead and a vantage point of the break in the canopy, a perfect view of the long road to the castle below.

Vi stood, taking in a fairy-tale view of castle spires climbing through the trees, grazing the clouds. "What is this place?"

"Old winemaker's cottage on the estate." He'd slowed to a walk but kept moving, intent upon getting them under cover. "This way." Julien pulled a key from his pocket—one of the old, iron kind that rusted in the folds of intricate carvings along the shaft. He turned it in the tiny lock hole in a weathered wood door, then led her inside.

Two steps in, Vi bent over at the knees, still trying to catch her breath. Julien recovered more quickly, gripped his rifle tight in one hand, and clicked the door closed with the other.

Dark fabric blacked out the windows, but a thin veil of sunlight peeked under the door, just enough that Vi could begin to make sense of the cottage layout. It was a single ground-floor room. Stairs snaked up the far wall, looking dangerously aged. There were no other doors that she could plainly see and few furnishings, save for an oversized bookshelf, near empty, that dominated a corner tucked behind the stone fireplace.

Julien stepped into view, arms braced across his chest and a severe clench to his jaw. "That was incredibly foolish."

They were the absolute last words she'd expected to hear. Vi shot up to standing, her breaths still rocking in and out. "Pardon?"

"You trusted me."

"Of course I trusted you—it was either that or risk getting a bullet in the back. I hadn't any other choice."

"Didn't they train you at all?"

"Who?" She swallowed hard, feigning her best show of innocence. "Train me for what?"

"What are you, a secretary masquerading as a spy?" Julien shook his head, making no effort to hide what he felt about such a ludicrous idea.

Vi's heart rate kicked up a notch, the drumbeat echoing in her ears.

What? How much does he know?

The Nazis may not have been the only ones to circulate her photo. The thought rocked her, that Julien may know more about her than he was letting on. But that was pure speculation, and it would require her to reveal too much even to inquire.

Julien flitted his glare to the rifle he'd leaned up against the table, then rested his eyes back on her. "How did you know I wouldn't put a bullet in your head right here? Or turn you in to the nearest uniform for a pittance of food? You must be smarter than this if you mean to stay alive here longer than five minutes. They shoot milkmaids too, you know. And secretaries. The multilingual kind go first."

As much as Vi hated to admit it, he was right.

Men at war wouldn't hesitate to work out their trigger fingers. And truth was, besides the name Julien had given and where he stashed food rations, she knew next to nothing about him. He could have been in league with the Nazi presence in nearby Loudun, and that would have been it; a firing squad in the town square with her as an example to the rest.

"You're right. I wasn't thinking . . ."

Julien didn't take it further, much to her relief.

He crossed the room and tinkered with the surface of a sideboard against the wall. The small flicker ignited the end of a matchstick with a *pop*. He cupped his hand around the flame and lit a kerosene lamp, then turned around to face her.

"Only use the lantern if absolutely necessary. I lit it now so you can get your bearings. Bumping into things could signal your presence inside. The matches are in the sideboard, top drawer. But take care with them. They're a luxury now—all we've got left."

He walked the length of the room, casting a glow on the back corner beneath the stairs. The light revealed a cot and a folded woolen blanket, a wooden stand with a metal pitcher and chipped porcelain basin, and a floor-to-ceiling shelf with empty mason jars and stacks of books.

"Pitcher and basin in the far corner with water left over from yesterday. Soap next to the basin and a towel on a bar under the window. There's an old hand mirror in the drawer but it's cracked, so mind you don't cut yourself."

"A broken mirror. Isn't that bad luck?"

"Let's hope not, for both our sakes. We need all of it and more at present."

Vi paused at the bottom of the stairs, looking up. They were steep and wooden planked, with a flimsy rail overlooking the room where they stood. "And up there?"

"A loft. Sleep there if you'd like, but it's near empty. We used the last of the furniture to feed the woodstove last winter."

She ran a finger along the edge of the bookshelf. "But not these."

"They're bolted to the fireplace. Would've taken too much effort to dislodge them when there's firewood growing all around the cottage. But don't worry. They'll have their day. Another winter like the last one and this cottage may be reduced to kindling and a pile of stones." He looked around and sighed. "I wish it were more, but this is all we have to offer you."

We.

It was the first time she'd considered that this man may have a family. She had to know. If it was the case, a wife—children even—she'd put them all at risk just by being here.

"You have a family then?"

He nodded. "Every person on the vineyard grounds is part of our family. Unless they're the enemy. The enemy we tolerate. Watch. And keep our rifle sights trained on in the event we're forced to defend against their threat. Boches are our enemy around here, and any indifference on their part eventually becomes our ally."

The fact that he'd make such a distinction didn't sit well.

"Which do you think I am? Family, or enemy?"

"Neither. You're invisible right now. That is, until I decide what to do with you."

"You said you'd hide me here . . ."

"Yes. And I'm sorry if this is not what you were expecting, but it's the way it must be. With no disappearing back to the castle ruins or the chapel. If they think anyone has helped you, we're all at risk. I won't take that chance. Do you understand? If I let you stay here, you *stay*."

Julien was right. Besides the sparse furnishings and a central stone hearth, there wasn't much to the space. No running water. No bathroom facilities. Certainly no phone line. It was like some woodcutter's cottage she'd read about in a fairy story—tucked away, forgotten by time, just like the castle. She couldn't think of a single friend back home who would give up her rationed nylons or her lipstick, let alone rough it out in some rustic hovel in the woods. But if he thought the surroundings were a detriment to her, they were just the opposite.

Even for its lack of comforts, the cottage was what Vi needed most.

It was her third savior of the day.

"Can you abide by my terms?" He'd already placed the lantern on the table and stood off behind her, quiet. Waiting. Watching her as she took in what the cottage offered.

"Thank you, Julien. I'll stay." To look around and feel a measure of safety was so foreign, she'd almost forgotten what it felt like to have her heart beat at a normal decibel. "And I'm grateful. Truly."

"Thank me by doing as I ask."

Vi wrapped her hand around the cross-shoulder strap of her bag. "And how long am I to be here?"

"We'll see tomorrow. For now, rest. Will you need anything else tonight?"

"Wait—you're leaving?"

He cupped his hand around the lantern's glass hurricane, preparing to extinguish the flame. "Yes. Before anyone realizes I'm gone, and certainly before I have to explain why. I'd rather not lie my way through breakfast if I can help it. Stories always manage to come to light, no matter how we try to protect them. If no one asks a question, then I don't have to provide an answer. If there's no answer, then there's no you."

"And that's what you're doing then, protecting me?"

"I'm protecting everyone." He surprised her by retrieving a pear from one pocket and setting it on the table. "For lunch." And then another, setting the fruit side by side. He lowered his head to her, offering a polite nod. "And dinner, though I wish it was more."

"It's enough." She tipped her shoulders in a light shrug, patting the canvas bag against her side. "I didn't mention it, but I kept back some of the walnuts too, just in case. Couldn't risk going hungry if you'd said no."

Julien nodded again and let a soft smile spread his lips in a speechless *touché*. He picked up the rifle and carried it over, extending it to her. "Do you know how to fire one of these?"

Viola took the rifle, wasted no time inspecting the chamber to see if it had a live round. It did. She then checked that the sight was level, eyeing a stone she picked in the far wall, then lowered it in a firm, double-fisted grip in front of her.

"I think I can manage."

"Right. Well, then I'll leave you to it. And I'll bring you water in the morning, before sunup if I can. Until then, stay out of sight. And get small in that loft if you hear the slightest noise outside."

She nodded. "I will."

"Bonsoir, Lady." He left without another word, the sound of the door bolt jarring and final.

Vi went to the window and slipped her finger against the black woolen fabric, enough so she could see him disappear into the woods.

The same view rose behind him: castle spires peeking up over the tops of the trees. The sun pierced the sky above it now, in the spot where clouds had once met the ground in layers of morning mist. Other than a slight touch of wind that kissed the treetops, no movement stirred along the road. No sound. The gunfire had stopped and music no longer carried through the trees, though she doubted she could have heard it from that far away.

There was only . . . stillness. Her body protested with the realization of it.

Safety brought the nagging ills of her weary physique back to the forefront, her stomach lurching and muscles crying out for attention. She turned to the pitcher and basin first, pouring water over her cupped hand.

Washing was the first, weary step.

Vi took time with it, though the water stung like daggers against her skin. But she couldn't care. It was a luxury to wash—to feel like a woman, even human again. She reached for the molded lump of soap, a sickly beige color smelling of turpentine. Washing pain away with the dirt and grime tingeing the water.

The cracked mirror she left in the drawer. Maybe another day she'd take it out. But not today. Exhaustion befriended her the moment she'd replaced the towel on its rack.

Vi picked up the rifle, carrying it to the back corner of the cottage. The pears and walnuts would also have to wait their turn. And the rest of the forest would have to pass the time without knowing where she was. Because in that moment, Viola Hart felt her physical hunger abate. The hunger for a safe haven was now satiated, and for however long it lasted, it was enough.

She leaned her back against the wall and slid down to the floor.

The rifle she laid by her right hand, for quick access should she need it, and pulled her knees up to her chest. Vi would do as Julien asked. She'd stay put. Remain invisible to the world, and try to sleep in the meantime. Above all, she would protect her secrets—starting with the fact that he'd been an answer to her most desperate prayers.

He was her fourth savior in one day.

SEVEN

"Mademoiselle . . ."

Aveline had been lost in the void between sleep and waking for some time, until the anchor of one word pulled her from it.

But spoken in a man's voice? Surely not. Her mind was playing tricks on her senses. If she'd fallen asleep, it would have been in her private chamber, a space no man other than a lady's husband or father, or perhaps a physician on the most serious of occasions, should ever be allowed entry.

She fluttered her eyelids, battling to open them and confirm what was real.

Fitful sleep had enveloped her. For how long, she couldn't know. Aveline had fought through a similar madness before, when she'd been infected with the putrid throat as a child. She'd survived under a cloud of furious fever then, with days that were lost to her memory.

This sleep had felt like that, the alternating between oppressive heat and biting cold, pain enveloping and then easing in fractures of memories . . . A cool cloth bathed her brow. Words, spoken by whom, she didn't know, encouraging her to fight. To wake, to battle, and then to rest as waves of fits continued to ebb and flow.

It was then Aveline remembered the last moments in the castle, with glass rain and a wall of flames, the grip of fear that should only exist in nightmares—never so in real life. The halls of leaded glass, marble floors, and royal furnishings of gold and crystal. That was the view she'd expected to find. The only one her mind had known. But she opened her eyes, surveying a room in stark contrast now.

Crown molding had become a thatched roof, plain and pitched in a severe vault overhead. The elegance of carved furnishings—an oversized armoire and gilded bed with brocade curtains, a writing desk and tea table made to host trays of fine china and sweets— they'd all vanished, exchanged for a simple four-poster bed and stiff, line-dried linens that scratched at her skin. A bureau, chipped pitcher, and washbasin lined the wall closest to the bed. A single window had been opened. It spread threadbare curtains to dance out in the breeze, washing plain stone walls in veils of white.

The only object that did not belong in the humility of the space was her silver-and-ivory-handled brush laid out atop the bureau, though the paired hand mirror was missing. The curious addition of a vanity stool was pushed up against the wall, elegant with rolling carvings in the legs, a tiny drawer with a gold claw pull, and a tufted velvet cushion in a deep amethyst shade—the only splash of color in a very earthy, bland room.

"Mademoiselle?"

The floor creaked with someone's shift of weight.

Aveline turned, the absolute certainty of a man's voice this time prompting her to seek its owner. She settled her gaze on a form, just edged in shadow, standing across the room.

He leaned back against a stone chimney that cut a line through a railing to a ground floor beyond. He stood silent, one trouser leg crossed over the other, arms folded tight across his chest, wrists peeking out from the rolled cuffs of a white linen shirt. Dark hair had been neatly groomed, combed, and tied at the nape. Light eyes greeted her, soft tawny and nonthreatening, just beneath a brow that seemed to relax in relief.

The sight of him eased her trepidation. Not much, of course, but the tiniest sense of danger had been erased when he stood his ground, making no move to approach the bed.

Or *her*.

"*Bonjour*." He offered the greeting on a respectful half bow.

Awareness that she was indisposed fell swiftly, prompting Aveline to pull the blankets up to her chin. Her body reacted to the move, tiny twinges of pain searing the hands she'd moved.

The man righted his posture in reaction to her grimace, then turned away.

"You may come up. She's awake." He called down a set of stairs in the corner of the room, then stalked back, took the pitcher, and handed it off to someone in the shadows of the stairs. "Bring fresh water. She'll have need of it."

Aveline released the death grip of her right hand clutching the bed linens but still kept covered, as any proper lady would. They were not alone. She hadn't any other answers, save for that. But it was enough to start breathing evenly again.

He held a hand out and took a half step forward when she shifted in the bed, perhaps anticipating that the next thing she'd do was try to stand. "Please, don't get up."

"Why?" Her voice sounded foreign, graveled, as if someone else had muttered the single word instead of her.

"It's ill-advised. You've had quite a shock."

Aveline sat up, eager, but her head still swimming. She leaned back against a wooden headboard, battling the dizziness with the only anchor she had at the moment. "So it did happen?"

"Yes. It did." His nod and pursed lips confirmed the somber truth.

He didn't need to explain further. The castle had been eaten up by flames. Party guests scattered, mauled by flying stones, satin shredded by glass. Their entire world had been turned on end in the blink of an eye. Odd that all could be confirmed in such a tiny, unfeeling word as *it*.

"You needn't worry," he said, taking a cautious step forward. "You're safe here with us."

Aveline nodded, her next question coming without pause. "Where am I?"

"We'll explain all." He turned toward the pitcher on the bureau, poured water into a glass tumbler, and brought it to her. "Here. First—drink. Before you try to speak."

Aveline reached for it, her arms feeling as if an extension of someone else's body, until even the slow movement tore pain down her left arm. It stole her breath this time. She slammed her eyes shut, blocking out the man for long seconds as she drank in deep, steadying breaths.

"Slowly," the man whispered, matter-of-fact. She opened her eyes to find him standing over her, water glass in hand, waiting.

She took it—every movement slow, painful, exhausting—and drank, the coolness of water a balm to the gravel in her throat.

"You've taken a blow to the head. And you'll need to move with care until your burns are fully healed. The length of your arm up to your shoulder and neck, and down the leg to the ankle."

Under normal circumstances, Aveline would have blushed for a gentleman to talk of such things as a lady's leg and ankle. But she looked to her arm as she handed the water glass back, finding it wrapped in taut linen strips that extended from shoulder to wrist. The only skin she could see was pink and inflamed—angry hues that blistered a red line against the porcelain skin of her wrist.

"We've had a woman to tend you. Her mother was a healer, so she's quite versed in how to care for your injuries. Everything was done with proper care—for a lady of your station."

Aveline's body eased back to life then. It seemed every pulse of damaged cells strained to declare their injury at once. The left side of her face, her neck, her arm and leg too, down to the foot—it all burned, the skin searing hot and dry at the same time, as if embers had been raked under the surface.

Every movement brought tiny waves of torture. She raised tentative fingertips, brushing them against something rough—the apple of her cheek no longer covered with the softness of youthful skin. The place her lady's maid would have dotted with powder and rouge the night before felt foreign, almost chapped now. The skin cracked along her brow, even as she closed and reopened her eye.

"My face too." She wanted the pain to stop, but only slightly less than she wanted the truth. "Is that what I feel?"

"Just try to be still . . . You're alive. And you are safe. That's what matters."

He reiterated the statement, that Aveline was safe. But he seemed less sure of something this time, as if he could see fear overtaking her. Her left side may have burned with pain, but the rest of her felt brought back to life, with sparks of energy that made her want to jump from the bed and run down the stairs if she didn't get straight answers.

"You've been injured, mademoiselle. Quite seriously. It's for your own good that you remain here," he said, tenderness meeting her from his eyes even as he set the water glass upon a table by the bed, then retreated to give her space, all in the span of a few breaths.

"You must stay. For now. I cannot allow you to get out of this bed. Do you understand?"

She eased away, sliding her shoulder back against the safety of the headboard. For the first time she felt the unease of a prisoner, though she wasn't certain why.

"My mother—" Aveline's thoughts turned back to the last sure events she could remember. "I wish to see her, monsieur."

"She is not here. But we did get her out in time."

"Out of harm's way at the castle, you mean?" Aveline cleared her throat, calming her voice, and pushed back tears, trying to sound strong, though inside she was melting.

He shook his head. "The north road. It took some doing, but we've received word that she is safe. And as soon as possible, I promise you will be reunited."

"That is not possible. My mother would not leave the Loire Valley voluntarily. Not now."

"I don't believe any of this was voluntary."

"Both my father and sister are in Paris at present. They were to rendezvous with us for the wedding. But . . . things have changed. Is that where my mother has gone, until we reschedule the nuptials?"

"Mademoiselle, I'm sorry, but your marriage ceremony will not take place as planned—at least not now."

"Because of the attack on the castle, you mean. Did the chapel burn too?"

"No. It did not. But the wedding has been postponed"—he stopped, giving a noticeable clearing of his throat—"indefinitely."

The recollection struck her then, searing more fiercely than burned skin ever could.

Memories of the felled castle faded into something else . . . a blue coat. A golden crest in elegant embroidery. And a face she couldn't make out fully, looking down, and a voice telling her she mustn't go to sleep. But she had. And the memories of the night before—the fire, a coat and crest—were all that remained that was sure.

A distressing thought cut into her heart—her fiancé was dead. That was what this man was trying to tell her.

"You are not Philippe."

Aveline already knew it somehow, but he confirmed the truth with a soft shake of the head. "No. I am Robert. Monsieur le *vigneron*—master winemaker for the Duc et Vivay."

She straightened up, squaring her shoulders against the worst. "Is my fiancé dead?"

"No, mademoiselle." He shook his head again, though his eyes were stormy with something else she couldn't place. She remembered then, the hazy sight of a man in the ballroom, a blue coat flashing by, whisking party guests away from glass rain and smoke . . .

"But you were there. I saw you, helping the duke and his son, calling up fighting men to resist the attack from the boats. Was it not you I saw in the ballroom, seeing people to safety?"

"I wouldn't say we could put up much of a fight. We did the most we were able at the time. You were struck down, caught under falling timber before we could reach you. We hadn't a choice but to bring you here, to the winemaker's cottage. You're still on the outskirts of the duke's estate, but you've been asleep for three days now."

"The castle burned . . . three days ago?" Aveline slammed her eyes shut against it.

Against *him*.

She shook her head in defiance. Disbelief too, plaguing her. Nothing made sense. Not the scattering of her family. An attack that left the castle in smoldering ruin. The faceless image of her betrothed, still a mystery to her. And now, the loss of three days' time when her mother, father, and sister were possibly in some measure of jeopardy.

"I don't wish to distress you, but you need to know the truth. The seriousness of this situation here, and in Paris."

"What of Paris?" Her gaze flitted up, meeting his.

"News has trickled out; the Bastille has fallen."

Félicité... Papa...

"Fallen. The prison in Paris? You mean it was attacked?"

"I mean felled completely. Stormed by the populace the same night of the attack here. There were few prisoners to free, but they were after the stockpile of weapons. With the people starving . . . it was only a matter of time. Now, it is feared the king's rule is in disarray. The people have begun to rise up, just as they did in the Americas. We'll continue to see the ripple effects in the Loire Valley, even as Paris clings to life. They say it is inevitable now."

"What is?"

"Revolution."

Swimming head, burning skin, aching heart—they all warred against her.

Aveline raised her right hand, the only part of her that didn't seem to hurt, and steadied it against her brow. "You said my mother is gone from here. North, yes?"

"She is."

"Very well. We shall have to send word to her as soon as possible. She will be in a state, wondering if I've suffered the same fate as Gérard."

"Who, mademoiselle?"

He didn't know to whom she referred, but Aveline hadn't time to explain.

Too many thoughts demanded her attention, just as too many

fears outranked her ability to fully grasp what the fall of the Bastille prison could mean. Her mind was fixed on the temporal—what must be done and what she could effect from her bed.

"Monsieur, I'm sorry, but it is too much to explain now. I'd ask that a courier go to my father this very day, if it's not been thought of before now. He will be in Paris, surely awaiting such a missive. I can give you the exact location of the estate."

"Forgive me, but I've already seen to it. By now your father will be aware of what has occurred, and that you are safe. We await his reply concerning you. In the meantime, we'll hide you here."

Hide me . . .

"Why is it necessary to hide me?"

"Forgive me, but there is much to say. Too much at the moment. But whatever is left, I've taken the liberty to have it brought here."

Aveline looked to the near-barren bureau top. Meager though it had been, her trousseau was most assuredly gone. The books she'd brought. Philippe's brooch and even Félicité's letter . . . all burnt to ash or lost in the chaos, it seemed. She was to be a guest among strangers—without the comfort of any familiarity.

It was too much. To think. Feel. Make sense of anything in the moments after waking from such a terrible dream.

"You say I may not leave this bed, and I give you my word that I will not. But I should need some assurance as to the safety of the estate, and this cottage, both for my mother's care when she returns, and for my own now. I know you are not in the habit of taking orders from a woman, but I assume the sacking of a duke's castle should give some allowance for impropriety. And as I am the only ranking member of my family left to render such decisions, I would ask for your help to fulfill them."

"At your service. Tell me what you have need of and I'll see to it."

That was curious, if he meant it.

"I wish to see my fiancé so I might discuss these matters with him. We haven't met, formally . . . but that will have to be overlooked for now." Aveline shifted in the bed, uncomfortable both in body and at the prospect of meeting her fiancé in such a state. But matters of vanity would have to subside.

"Mademoiselle—" Robert stared back, this time without the former softness in his eyes. Something in him had gone cold. Aveline wasn't sure she wanted to know why.

"But surely Philippe is aware of all this."

Robert shook his head, saying nothing. Just issued a glance.

Something was terribly wrong.

"Pray go on. Whatever tidings you have cannot be worse than what has already transpired here."

"I'm sorry, but your fiancé is presently unaccounted for."

She swallowed hard. "But you said he was alive."

"He is."

It was some small measure of relief, but not enough.

"Captured then?"

"No." The line of his jaw flexed. "Fled."

The single word sliced through Aveline's heart like a serrated knife, cutting her with pain all over again.

Philippe fled? He left his family . . . guests . . . me . . . even as his castle burned?

Aveline refused to accept that her fiancé could have tucked tail and run, leaving the castle and his party guests to fend for themselves.

"You're quite sure he's alive?"

Robert nodded. "Yes. It is by God's grace that there was no loss of life. We had minimal notice of the attack—not enough to send guests out into the grove without defense. The duke and your fiancé were aware of what was happening, and they were seen fleeing on horseback, riding away in the first waves of the attack."

"That is impossible." Unable to accept the possibility of such cowardice, she demanded, "Who saw them to claim such an injustice?"

"I did."

Aveline's thoughts drifted to the brooch.

The gift that she'd foolishly thought would give some understanding of a man's character. How naive she'd been, to think a simple golden trinket could define a man's innermost virtues.

"You are mistaken. That cannot be the character of the man my father has assured is a gentleman of the highest rank. Philippe is a man of honor, from a family with a most prestigious name."

"I agree. If it is proven to be the man's character, it is not befitting his family name at all."

"There you are. As master vigneron, surely you are aware of the fortitude required to manage the duke's estate, to look after the farmers who tend the land and the people who live and work under such an immense yoke that the wine production demands. Philippe would not dare abandon them."

"I am well aware of the people's plight here."

"Then surely there is an explanation."

"If there is, I'd like to hear it."

"Perhaps a misfortune has befallen Philippe, or else he would be here in your stead. With all that has happened, perhaps the rabble seized him and the duke as they were going for help? Maybe took them back to Paris?"

He closed his eyes for a breath, as if her question had pained him in some way. "Please. Don't use that word."

"What word?"

"*Rabble.* Please do not call them that." He paused, shook his head. "They're people, like you and me, and not what you label them."

"I know of the *Third Estate*, monsieur. And the problem of taxation against the masses. I am well aware of what occurred at the Estates-General on 5 May of this year. You do not need to instruct me on labels and the reason for applying them."

Robert started, his mouth slightly aghast and his brow curiously tipped at her mention of the commoners' estate—the lowest rank in the *ancien régime* of their society—the working and starving and dying people who survived on the rungs below both the clergy and the nobility.

If he was astonished, he hid it, though not completely.

"Housing costs have risen by 80 percent in some areas," she went on, hard-pressed to stop once they'd broached the subject of taxation upon the masses. "While wages for the working haven't seen a rise more than a quarter of that in the last decades. The people see only the taxes of a palace in Paris, with both king and clergy who understand nothing of the extremity of their circumstances. The prolonged deficit of hunger has driven them mad. It is understandable to a point. But I will call the people rabble if they behave in such a manner. And here, with torches that felled an innocent man's castle, I call it deserved. They deserve the fiercest punishment leveled by God himself."

Women were not expected to possess a mind for politics. Or economics. Those topics were of little use outside a ladies' salon. So whether she'd shocked him mattered little. Aveline had seen it before: a gentle tip of the head. Bewilderment in the eyes. Adopted consternation on the face of a gentleman each time she made a statement that defied the constraints of her station—and those strict appropriations of her gender.

Robert stared back, studying her. Perhaps searching for a retort in light of the fact she possessed a brain of some function, and a head for figures that expanded beyond counting how many pairs of evening gloves she owned.

"You are very direct, mademoiselle."

"I must be. These are uncertain times. To be direct is the only foothold we possess."

"Then I will do you the courtesy of being equally forthright. As the whereabouts of both your fiancé and the duke are unknown, it is incumbent upon us to look after you. That we will do as long as you are left to our charge. But I assure you this: If your fiancé does come back and dare show his face to the people he abandoned, I'll level a fist so far into his jaw that he shall not remember his own name."

Any reply she might have owned died in her throat.

Robert had adopted an emotion far beyond anything Aveline had thought. Steady on the surface, his was a fury that boiled beneath the surface—and seemed only just held at bay. How much longer might it be restricted, if at all?

"Pardon, Master Robert?" A lady's intrusion behind them had been soft, her words respectful and meek from across the room. "I've brought water for mademoiselle."

Aveline entertained little hope to reconcile much of the news she'd just received. Her recourse was to turn away, or else weep in front of him without filter. She looked to the window, sunlight the only thing she recognized as constant, and bit down on her bottom lip to suppress the wave of emotion.

"I will leave you then. Au revoir."

Robert's response was clipped: a bow and boot falls echoing with each step he took away from them. Tired stairs groaned as he stepped upon them, then his footsteps faded with a slam of a door. He'd gone from the cottage completely.

Aveline found herself truly washed over in that moment, first from the shock of pain and injury, perhaps more for the stark revelations of cowardice Robert had leveled against the estate masters. She wasn't sure any measure of courage was left in her. Thankfully, Robert had taken his leave. Perhaps with a woman, she could think clearly. Breathe again. Maybe even crumble, if she needed to, and receive grace in doing so.

She turned, lifting her gaze to meet the other occupant of the cottage. Her lady's maid stepped into the light. "Fanetta?"

"Mademoiselle." She dipped her head in a bow.

Fanetta bore a weakness of spirit, with eyes red-tinged as her auburn hair, and a brow tipped in sorrow. She wasn't dressed in formal service attire as she'd been at the castle. Rather, she wore a simple dress of linen, the bodice and skirts in faded indigo, and gripped tight to the porcelain pitcher in her hands.

"I don't understand . . . What are you doing here?"

"We rescued you, mademoiselle. Or rather, Master Robert did. He brought you here and we've tended you in secret." Fanetta set the pitcher on the bureau, then turned back, her eyes lined in worry. "The vanity stool too. He brought that, with whatever else he could from your chamber. But no one must know where you are."

"Why tend me in secret? He said something about hiding me. What do I need safety from now that the castle is burned to the ground and my fiancé is missing?" Aveline did cry then, tears rolling from her eyes, begging their due. "And you're a part of this! You brought me the brooch . . . the note . . . You knew this was going to happen, didn't you? So why? What in heaven's name is left to steal or kill?"

"You are, mademoiselle. *La Belle au bois dormant*, they're calling you—the beauty sleeping in the wood, like in Perrault's fairy story. You've become a fable in the last few days, even before the smoke ceased rising from the ruins. The duke and his son fled under their noses. But you are the princess that simply disappeared into the night. They vow to do anything to find you, to make you an example of their anger at the duke—and the king."

Aveline flitted her glance to the stairs, the loft's only exit.

Fleeing France after her mother or attempting to make her way to Paris, alone . . . There was little she could do with a broken body. Even less without the aid of a carriage or horse. Should she try to usurp her captors, Aveline wouldn't make it far before collapse or capture.

There was no choice. She must place her trust in the hands of strangers who were of the very populace who wished her dead.

"An example. I see." She exhaled, praying now only for survival. "And what do you say?"

Fanetta leaned over the side of the bed, taking the palm of Aveline's uninjured hand in her own. "The same thing that Master Robert does—that we would die before we hand you over to them."

There it is again—Master Robert . . .

"Why do you call him Master?"

Fanetta shook her head, as if the answer should have been plainly known. "Why, he's the master vigneron on the estate."

"Yes, that he said. But is it the reason for his title?"

"He is a man of the people, yes. A matchless worker and well respected among all here. Master Robert has always served as a bridge between the nobility and the people working beneath them. He took you as our responsibility out of character, seeing as your fiancé is the one who fled. No doubt that is why he made no mention of his title. A winemaker has none by rule, unless of course he's a master vigneron, and here, demands respect as the duke's younger son—and your fiancé's brother."

EIGHT

Present Day
Les Trois-Moutiers
Loire Valley, France

"Titus!" Quinn called out his grandfather's name the instant he stopped in front of the estate house, cutting the truck engine with a jolt.

Ellie shifted her Fiat to park at the end of the circular drive. She peered through the windshield, taking in the scene before her. When the online description of the vineyard inn had noted an estate house, it wasn't kidding. If this Quinn Foley thought she'd be in the way of the harvest in this three-story pile of weathered stone and glass, he was a shade out of touch with reality.

It was more romantic than a cottage, a little larger than a house. Actually, a lot larger. Enough to swallow up Marquette's town hall without extraordinary effort. Still, size didn't detract from its endearing qualities. Dormers boasted old-fashioned charm. Heavy wood doors couldn't hide under a round stone archway: a give-away of the structure's rustic attachment to the land. Oversized lantern sconces hung on either side of the entry, their gas flames still flickering through the last shadows of morning.

Quinn obviously didn't see the surroundings the same way

Ellie did. The amour of a French provincial scene may have cap-tured her, but it failed to cool his heels. He stormed across the wide drive, quickstepping it to get to the front entrance.

The spell broken, Ellie scrambled to gather up her purse and phone. No way was she losing this argument because she wasn't present in the middle of it. If there was any defending of her corner to be done, it would be from inside the estate too. She sucked in a deep breath and hurried off in pursuit.

Ivy stretched up the estate house walls, mingling fresh and green against stories of stone and leaded glass. Ground-floor win-dows stood open behind a row of weathered wood shutters, inviting crisp morning air to drift in freely. And as if in partnership with one another, the aroma of cooking food floated back out, offering an intoxicating *bonjour* to road-weary travelers.

The unmistakable aroma of freshly baked bread . . . sizzling bacon too? Even the luxurious hint of wine managed to perfume the hilltop air. And French press coffee . . . Ellie closed her eyes, drinking in the richness. She pulled herself out of the stupor when she blinked. Seconds later, Quinn pushed the front doors at the center and disappeared inside. She followed, awkwardly so, turning the corner into his world.

Sunlight streamed in, high timbered ceilings awash in gold.

Quinn ignored a parlor—the epitome of quiet country charm—stalking through without hesitation. But Ellie did pause, slowing up to prevent her ballet flats from clip-clopping against the slate entry and around an iron-spindled staircase that wound up the opposite wall and stretched out in a lavish bell curve before her. A span of windows lined the back wall, sun and earth and sky unobstructed by drapes. A stone veranda stretched over arbor rows trekking down the hill, painting a maze of greens and autumn golds.

Cream walls . . . wainscoting . . . antique furniture trimmed in grommets and deep espresso woods . . . Ellie could have imagined it all long before setting foot inside. But it was the unexpected that arrested her—an oversized hearth, distressed through white paint and generations of unobstructed sunlight, and the rather remarkable painting of a woman in eighteenth-century dress commanding notice over the mantel.

Ellie stood, exhaling low. "So this is what HGTV looks like in France."

She'd have lingered, but Quinn swept through a brick archway down the hall.

Music—a light instrumental melody—drifted from somewhere in its depths. And suddenly, laughter.

Ellie kept walking, slowly for a few steps, listening to the mix of melody and the idyllic notes of the French language being tossed back and forth. A woman's laughter became joy drifting out from the back of the hall.

One second it hadn't been there and in the next, it simply became . . . a *home*.

It reminded Ellie that while generous in size, the estate house was not an unfeeling manor. Storied maybe, and oh-so-French, but not at all haughty. And somehow, it didn't seek to greet her as a stranger. Just the sounds of easy conversation, laughter that made it feel like she'd walked through those halls before, and incredible views of the vineyards with a quiet presence the modern world couldn't seem to touch.

It felt an intrusion to step uninvited into a family's private moments, so Ellie hung back, hovering in the shadows of the kitchen's arched stone doorway.

The lightness in the room fizzled as Quinn marched in, directing his attention to an aged man with thinned gray hair, olive skin, and a rather remarkable presence, perched at the head of a farmhouse table. His shoulders were haloed in sunlight and strings of herbs and lavender sprigs that had been tied up on a wooden rack behind, their colors drying in the sun.

"Titus?" Quinn didn't bother to soften his direct tone. *"Qu'as-tu fait?"*

I wish I could remember what that means.

Sitting in a waxed canvas jacket and work pants, a simple white oxford unbuttoned at the collar, and uneven rolls at the cuffs, he sipped on a half glass of wine and took his time fiddling with the folds of a newspaper. Permanent laugh lines edged his eyes, painting him as one who favored amusement instead of irritation.

Two women stood off behind, looking alike—startled but familiar. They both wore silver-gray chignons at their napes, one in a dress in varying shades of blues, rust, and cream, the other in crisp ironed chambray. Homemade aprons draped down to protect their fronts from flour. They halted in kneading dough on the butcher block of a long center island, their smiles lost and eyes turned wide when Quinn barged into the room.

How Ellie wished she had her seventh-grade French textbook now.

The French began flying so fast that she was able to pick up only one or two words out of every twenty. There was *difficulté*— she recognized that in Quinn's explanation of the situation, or *her.* And he'd taken particular effort to emphasize the word. Maybe she was causing that for him. She also heard *d'argent*—"money." And *Américaine.* That one she was sure of, just as she was about the way Quinn said it, like it wasn't meant to be anything near a compliment.

Based on the conversation they'd had on the road, Ellie could guess what Quinn was saying. How this tourist insisted she had a reservation and how she'd already paid out the duration of a two-, maybe three-week stay—much to his very apparent chagrin. No doubt he was petitioning the old man to get out his checkbook and fix the error so they could get her out from underfoot as quickly as possible.

Titus responded, calm and controlled, shrugging off his grandson with an assured wave of his hand. *"Tu t'inquiètes trop."*

"I *do not* worry too much. This is serious. If you'd only listen to reason . . ." He seemed frustrated, rambling in English when Titus didn't appear to follow. So perhaps the old man spoke only the colloquial French of the Loire Valley? "I can't help ya if you refuse to let me. It's not why I came all this way, to be countermanded at every pass." Quinn added a soft rebuttal in French after that— whatever it was, whispered under his breath—and suddenly, the air in the room turned cold.

Gazes shifted to her.

The women stilled, their chattering long having died away, leaving the music drifting alone in the background. The old man noticed her for the first time too. He squinted at the doorway, looking with great care. And to add insult to the injury of not being wanted at the place she'd expected to be welcomed as a guest, the old man's countenance visibly hardened when he settled his gaze on her.

Quinn turned to look at her too, and though he seemed a bit sorry about it all, he still peered back with determination set in his unshaved jawline.

Ellie had never wished she could melt into the floor so badly in her life.

Forget the photo. Cast out the idea of finding the castle. Certainly abandon the feeling of empowerment that came with traveling across an ocean to find an untold story. She actually toyed with the idea of ending it all right there, but let it go just as quickly because of one thing: the image of her grandmother standing at a window. Alone. Waiting. Waiting for who, Ellie needed to know. And something told her this valley might hold the answer. Maybe even the gentleman before her could know something about the answers she sought.

If she must sacrifice a little pride to uncover truth, then so be it. "Hello . . ."

You're in France, Ellie.

She shook her head. "Uh, bonjour . . ." Half waving from the doorway, she stepped into the light. "I'm Ellison Carver—Ellie, from the United States. Michigan actually. I don't know if you're following a word I'm saying, but I have a reservation . . . to stay. Here at this estate."

One of the women—the seeming older of the two—flitted a glance over to Titus. He didn't return it, just kept his countenance solid and his gaze unwavering, offering no indication of where his thoughts might be.

It seemed like a good idea to hold up her phone, thinking of the e-mail she couldn't load. Ellie did but lowered it just as quickly, lest they think she was some sort of foreign phone salesman. Without Wi-Fi she couldn't access her e-mail anyway, so it would probably only work to confuse matters further.

"I made a reservation last week, to stay here for a few weeks. Your grandson found me a bit turned around out on the road and was kind enough to help me find the estate house." She tilted her head back toward the hall and the French country house view of the path they'd walked from the entryway. "It's beautiful, by the way. Um . . . *C'est belle*, I think. *Une belle maison.*"

Maybe that was enough of an explanation so he'd honor her booking. After all, it was a business transaction. He couldn't just cancel at the last minute, could he? Tell her to leave and go back to the little town when she'd already paid in full? Ellie would have to give him a piece of her mind if he did, and that wasn't how she preferred to kick off her research.

Titus said nothing. Maybe he didn't need to. Just exhaled low and with effort pushed his chair back from the table. He stood and reached a hand for a carved wooden cane braced against the table-top. He leaned on it with one hand and picked up his goblet in the other, swallowing the last long bit of wine in the glass. Then he crossed the room, taking slow, measured steps, stopping only when he stood toe to toe with his grandson.

Quinn responded, holding his arm out to his grandfather. Titus felt for it, settling knotted fingertips on his forearm, and gripped tight.

"Oh . . ." Ellie exhaled, realization swift to flood over.

The old man was blind, or close to it. He'd looked in the direction of where she stood, not because he could see her, but because of what Quinn had said. And perhaps for the sound of her voice.

It opened a vault of questions.

He raised his chin, whispering swift, almost inaudible words up to his grandson. They were final, apparently, because he stared squarely into Quinn's face when he said them, a lack of sight unable to diminish his authority. He punctuated his words with a stern finger point to the floor.

To Ellie's surprise, Quinn sighed and added, *"D'accord"*—a one-word concession.

Whatever disagreement had existed ended with the patriarch's victory.

Titus turned toward the hall. He paused to offer a gentle nod to Ellie, then made his way out of the room. She watched his finger-tips tracing the wainscoting down the length of the hall, until his shadow disappeared.

The great Titus Vivay may have faded somewhere into the span of the estate house, but he'd left quite an impression in his wake. Ellie wasn't sure what to make of it. He didn't appear unkind, just resolute—despite advanced age and weathered body. If he was the head of the family, business or otherwise, he'd certainly mastered the role well, down to the way he silenced opposition with a few whispered words.

"I'm sorry about that," Quinn offered on a sigh. He rubbed a hand to the back of his neck. "My grandfather can be . . . rigid at times."

Ellie peered into the depths of the hall. "What did he say?"

"In so many words, that we're to honor your reservation."

"You are?" A smile swept over Ellie's lips she couldn't contain. There were but a few words spoken, but Titus had sided with her. That was a victory even if she hadn't earned it herself.

"Thank you. I mean, I hope it's not an imposition if I stay, but I am grateful. And I would have liked to thank your grandfather for that. Will he be back soon?"

Quinn shook his head and braced his hands at his sides. "Not for a while. I'll be drivin' him to town. Always goes first thing. We'll be back when the men disperse, so he can spend the rest of the morning with his vines."

His vines.

It was an odd perspective—like the rows of grapes were more than just plants. Like they had a soul somehow, and the family patriarch was the only one who understood them at that level.

Quinn shot a glance over his shoulder, apparently only just realizing they still had an audience.

He slipped behind the kitchen island and whispered something to the women, then dusted a peck to each of their cheeks. They drank in the attention, flitting like mother hens over a chick—a very tall, handsome one.

Titus may not have been under Quinn's spell, but the women sure appeared to be.

Quinn walked back to Ellie's side, offering a polite smile. "They said since you're stayin' on, I should take your bags up to your room. It's the door at the top of the stairs. Suite at the end of the hall. Do you have your keys?"

Ellie dug the rental car keys out of the bottom of her purse, then dropped them in his outstretched palm. "Here."

"Good. Then just . . . make yourself at home."

"Wait, you're leaving me here?" Ellie stared back, dumbfounded. Did he actually expect her to converse with two women who didn't speak a syllable of English? "But I don't speak French. How am I supposed to talk to them?"

"Don't worry about that. These two speak the language of food. I just hope you're hungry." He leaned in, adding with a whisper, "They'll have you fluent before you know what happened to ya."

It was then that the room broke free from tension.

Joy eased back into the space of brick and rustic wood, of baking bread and crisp morning air as Quinn introduced his grandmother, Helene, and Auntie Claire—his grandfather's sister. They were the vineyards' accomplished cooks and, no matter the barrier of grumpy menfolk or languages spoken, appeared to be gracious hostesses.

They flitted and fussed over Ellie, whisking her into the depths of the kitchen, drawing her from the doorway with a tug of the hand. She picked up on the words for *beautiful* when Helene patted flour from her hands and took Ellie's face in her palms, kissing her on either cheek.

Auntie Claire wasted no time in pulling out a chair at the breakfast table and ushered her down in it, telling her she needed

to *Mangez! Mangez!* and then mounding a plate with croissants
and *pain au chocolat*, yoghurt, and fresh fruit.

Ellie was lavished with attention. Truly, the women were light
in an already-golden place. Why, every storied estate should lay
claim to wise cooks, with freshly baked bread and flour-dotted
aprons in its innermost soul. Two weeks or twenty—she could get
used to the flavor of life in this place, so much so that Ellie had
almost forgotten why she'd swept into the house in the first place.

"Mr. Foley?"

Quinn stopped short of scooting out the door and turned back
to her. "Yes, Miss Carver?"

"What was it that he said? Your grandfather, before he left
the room?"

"Without gettin' into too much detail, that you paid for a tour
guide and you're going to get one."

"Who?"

He sighed, tossing the car keys in his palm. "Me."

NINE

Plane engines cut the night sky, the roaring dying off in the direction of Whitehall Road.

Vi slowed her trek down the hallway, pausing in a quiet commons alcove just outside the dining hall doors. She hugged the stack of books in her arms, drawing them tighter to her chest, as her gaze drifted up to the tiles above her head. The ceiling lamp stirred on its chain, just a shiver, as if an invisible breeze had been let in the office and chose that instant to sweep overhead.

Another bomb blast.

That one had been *close*. Too close for anything near to comfort in the days and long, bomb-riddled nights they'd endured since September.

Vi slammed her eyes shut.

Thinking. Waiting. Nibbling on her bottom lip. The muscles in her shoulders tensed and fell lax again, pulsing in time with her heartbeat. She tried praying, words falling from her lips in a feeble attempt to advocate for the poor souls who might be in harm's way.

But even they felt jumbled—stirred by the blast their building had felt down to its bones.

She found the wall, leaned her shoulders against it. She'd stay here for a moment or two only. Surely that would be long enough for the planes to pass by and leave them be. But the Luftwaffe was aiming to cut the beating heart out of their fair city. If aircraft were headed for Whitehall, that meant bombs could rain down over Trafalgar Square, the houses of Parliament, and Scotland Yard . . . all within a short trolley ride of the hall in which she stood.

As if on cue, lamps wavered in a haunting line down the hall. The bottoms of hefty porcelain domes jostled like tea bells strung out on a clothesline. Vi gripped the wooden chair rail at her back, felt the wall vibrate against her palm. Was it the building's trembling she felt or her own?

"Viola Hart. There you are! I've been searching high and low."

Vi turned, half expecting to find an air-raid warden barreling down the hall instead of Carole, one of the other secretaries in the library wing. She had a similar scolding in her tone though and wind in the rolled curls of her chestnut hair as she hotfooted round the corner.

She halted near where Vi stood in her tucked-away alcove. "Did you feel that?" Carole's gaze, too, drifted up. Specks of dust—from where, who knew?—floated from the ceiling in tiny clouds. "Another close one."

"Too close, I'd say."

"Books rattled from the shelves. Nearly scared the wits out of us back in the library. So you'd better get your stompers a moving, doll. I came to fetch you. If this keeps up, we'll have to be more than a charitable library organization for the empire; we may well turn into newsmakers ourselves. We're headed for Charing Cross Station to wait it out."

"The Underground?" Vi shot her glare over to the window facing the street, forgetting for a moment that it had been covered over outside with a layer of sandbags, and blackout shades had been installed indoors some time ago. "Is it safe to be out on the streets right now?"

"That answer is above my pay grade. But safe as it is anywhere in London these days. And quite better than spending the night in our musty old basement here, drinking tepid tea and noshing that leftover stew from the dining hall. I'd rather take our chances with the rations at the Tube station canteen." Carole flashed a charm bracelet with gold and red cherries dangling round her wrist. "And the company just might have its perks too."

"That's new."

"Sure is. Met a chap in the RAF last time the sirens carried us underground." She winked. "Promised I'd keep an eye peeled for his uniform next time."

The building rattled, a nearby picture frame jangling against the wall with a fresh blast. Air-raid sirens hastened in, their maddening cry causing Vi to jump nearly out of her skin.

They exchanged glances, knowing hearts connecting through locked eyes.

In London in 1941, sirens deafened wartime promises with aching regularity. Each time their call began, they swept in with a sense of urgency, though Londoners had been greeted by them dozens of times before. But this night, something was different. The air stopped feeling . . . normal. The drumming of typewriter keys and the telephone rings that often echoed through the offices . . . clinks of dishes in waiters' hands and the chatter coming from the dining hall—the usual background sounds, even for the late hour that it was, fell into an eerie silence.

Carole reached out, easing the books from Vi's hands. She

stacked them on a telephone table nearby, then hooked Vi's handbag over her wrist to the elbow. She offered a crimson-lipped smile, something so in-character for the office girl with the Able Grable high spirits and dishy smile.

"You shine up real nice, you know," she whispered, prompting Vi to release her grip on the wall. Carole's attempt at normal so welcome in the midst of madness that it drew a smile to her lips as well. "Brilliant duds."

Vi tipped her shoulders in a light shrug. "It's from last year, but I thought for tonight . . . why not?"

She straightened the jacket of the pretty spring suit—the one her mother had made—a deep lavender, the color to match her eyes. She'd worn it with pearls and her last pair of nylons that didn't have holes in any place that would show. And beetroot juice lip stain wouldn't do for that evening. Vi had held back a tube of Tangee lipstick saved through rationing, a vibrant splash of color dubbed *Red Majesty*, and had tucked it in her handbag for later.

And it was later.

Despite bomb blasts and the sirens' cry, Vi would endure it wearing a bright smile.

"A lot of good shining up does for us now. But at least we'll be the best-dressed ladies in the Tube." Vi opened the tortoise-resin handles on her purse and dug inside until she found the lipstick. She held it up, victorious. "So, Charing Cross Station?"

"That's a gas that we're going there, I know. We were supposed to be hoofing it at the Blue Lagoon Club, and we end up sleeping in the Tube station anyway. If I snag my last pair of nylons trying to get down those steps, I'll go absolutely mad."

"At least it's not far." She linked her arm with Carole's and forced a brave smile. "Let's go. We'll swipe this color on our lips and descend into the abyss of tracks and RAF uniforms together."

Vi drew in a deep breath, her last before the roar of planes infected the sky and the screech of air-raid sirens was overtaken by an eerie whistle that slashed the night.

A savage burst enveloped them, blasting the world to bits.

Dust and plaster. Brick and books. Walls, those shivering ceiling lamps, glass from the windows, and grit from exploding sandbag barriers outside—all crumbled down in a massive would-be grave.

The oddly sweet smell of propellant—cordite?—filled Vi's nostrils first. She coughed under its weight. And then blinking and inhaling and choking through dust this time . . . The few breaths she'd managed to capture were taken over by smoke rising from the dining hall—the blackness burning straight down to her lungs with each new breath.

A fireball had burst through, intense heat and smoke invading the length of the dining hall and their little alcove just outside it. The telephone table had vanished in a blink, along with the stack of books, their paper and wood bones strewn through the hallway. Loose paper, smoldering and singed in the corners, drifted down in a haunting ticker-tape parade.

Vi brushed at the floating debris, feeling strangely numb and calm somehow, as one would sweep cobwebs from an attic's corners. With ears ringing and lungs punished, the relentless toil for each breath a fresh battle, she climbed through the rubble, scraping the flesh on her hands and knees, shredding the nylons that had seemed so important but moments before. And as if the sirens' call and the whistle of bombs had not been hellish enough, the worst came in the bomb blast's aftermath.

All manner of sounds haunted the air in chilling cries from both man and machine: the grinding of engines and raining of bombs from planes overhead . . . The otherworldly crackle of fire . . . Low moans and terrified shrieks—shouts of first responders with fire wagons wailing on the streets. Or were they coworkers around her? Maybe Carole, for Vi had already lost her in the pile of debris. Vi heard her own cries then too, tears falling, mixing with smoke and ash and a new, terrifying silence as she clawed at the rubble with her bare hands.

"Carole?" She could scarcely whisper—her voice sounded foreign to ears still ringing from the blast. She drank deep of dust-filled oxygen, summoned her lost voice, then bellowed a series of guttural "Help!" shouts down the hall.

The world of the Royal Empire Society had become oddly loud and silent at the same time, encompassed in both light and darkness, giving Hitler's barrage an authentic face for the first time.

War was not a game of rationed lipstick and spring suits worn in the Underground. It was raw and real and happening with savage consequences all around.

Their world had been ripped clean in two and Vi, the unprepared secretary still in the midst of her Cambridge education, didn't know the first thing about being a hero. Her world had been stories: English and literacy and languages. All words. And social impact at a charity that invited women as members and sought to spread knowledge throughout the king's empire. Heroism had never entered her mind, unless it was found in the character of a book. And now, fighting, clawing through rubble, she felt beaten by the dragon of death in its first real blow against her.

Cries echoed louder. Fire popped and sizzled. More whistles, from somewhere, and then a fresh shaking in what remained of the building around them.

Another blast—this one not direct, but close.

Where are the fire wagons?

"Carole?" Vi heard her own cries, over and over, shouts mingling with the rest of her coworkers, pleading for help. She kept digging for life, though terrified that she'd find nothing but death. Her friend was no longer standing at her side, with painted lips and a sassy toss of curls over her shoulder when she talked.

Carole . . . Carole.

The last horror her eyes remembered clearly as the debris field flooded with help from the street: men moving in slow motion though they hurried in Vi's direction. Digging, clearing debris, unearthing a lifeless palm and wrist that extended from the rubble, with golden cherries covered in a layer of dust . . . and blood.

APRIL 23, 1944

LES TROIS-MOUTIERS

LOIRE VALLEY, FRANCE

The roar of plane engines wrangled Vi from a deep sleep.

She jerked awake, greeted by the cottage's weathered wood rafters overhead, trying to judge if the sounds were real or merely ghosts of her imagination. For nearly every time she fell into sleep, vivid dreams took her back to the Royal Empire Society's Northumberland Avenue headquarters, and the night in 1941 when her life had taken its first detour.

Sweat tickled her brow.

Vi swiped at it, trying to focus, to remind herself where she was. If she waited, the memory of that night would fade and within seconds the bomb-blasted room would turn into the place she'd last closed her eyes in sleep—this time, a hidden winemaker's cottage in a Loire Valley vineyard.

The castle ruins . . . the treelined road to the castle and Julien's

face, staring at her from behind a rifle . . . The events of the day
before brought her back to the present. With trembling hands she
felt around the cot. The rifle barrel was as she'd left it, lying cold
and still beside her. She wrapped her palms around it, clinging to
it like a lifeline.

There was no drone of planes overhead, no coworkers crying
out for help . . . no Carole lost in the debris again, to her absolute
relief.

You are safe, Vi told herself. Over and over, even if it was a lie,
she said it.

Breathe . . . Breathe . . .

You are safe.

Planes or not, something was cutting through the night, stirring now that her senses were fully awake to notice. A distant hum
pulled Vi up to sitting. Curiosity drew her to the window, the
rifle fused to her grip. She parted the blackout fabric so she could
look out.

The forest was shrouded, layered in shadows, night having moved in after she'd slept through the whole of the day. She
squinted, peering through the trees.

Yes, there was movement. Something mechanical. Vehicles?
The shadows advanced through the night like an army of legion-
naire ants, marching the long road to the castle. She counted no
fewer than four great, lumbering beasts—oversized box trucks—
their headlamps extinguished. Men, maybe women too, wearing
mismatched clothes, moved about in one accord, as if they needed
no instruction to accomplish a task through the darkness.

Vi watched long enough to see the trucks ease to a stop and
men jump from the back, moving about, tossing wooden crates
from truck beds to waiting arms. With nimble authority, men disappeared through the trees like ghosts gone to haunt the castle

ruins. The process of unloading, carrying, and disappearing went on only for mere moments—not long enough for her to decipher any purpose other than to arrive and then disappear again. The who, the why, even the what—they remained a mystery.

And then, silence.

Just as suddenly as they'd appeared, the trucks retreated, the hum of their engines vanishing back into the night. The men, too, were absorbed into blossoming trees and the forest reverted to its natural existence. Shadows remained, only trees disturbed by a gentle breeze that toyed with their limbs and young leaves.

She watched for long moments afterward, waiting. Wondering if men would filter through the trees, climb the ridge, and—heaven help her—find the winemaker's cottage with the stowaway hiding inside.

But the forest slept.

No more trucks. No men. Certainly no plane engines or terror raining from the sky like she'd experienced during the Blitz. This was not London but Nazi-occupied France, a place with no laws or rules, save for the ones dictated by the savage creature that was war.

Vi finally let the blackout curtain drift back into place and allowed the lure of sleep to call her back. The RES bombing had been the first time anyone had died before her eyes—but she feared it wouldn't be the last. That she was certain of. Exhaustion swept over her and she melted onto the cot, collapsing as her world became painted in the blackness of sleep once again.

If only dreams would consent to leave her in peace . . . for one precious night.

TEN

Aveline parted the velvet coach curtain.

The driver had stopped their coach and four on the street in front of the long, paved courtyard at the Chapelle de la Sorbonne. She peeked out at the domed chapel and church complex that back-dropped a street bustling with commerce—an outdoor market teemed with patrons, goods, and merchants, all bustling and buying, in spite of the dreary weather.

Spring was toying with them, keeping Paris under skies of a colorless gray, plaguing the streets with a chilling drizzle that refused to release its steadfast grip on winter. It was curious, then, that even on such a day the church steps were covered over with the masses. Dressed in scraps and huddled against the elements, a succession of somber faces created a striking contrast against the lavishness of Corinthian columns and fountains spread through-out the courtyard.

They'd lined up along one of the expansive wings of the complex, preparing for what appeared to be a processional behind

114

an old wooden barouche, its wagon wheels stilled and workhorses' hooves clip-clopping even while at temporary rest.

Raindrops had weighted the peacock feather on Aveline's spring hat. She waved it back out of her face and rubbed her gloved palm in a circle on the glass, doing her best to see through the marred view the window provided. "Why have we stopped, Papa?"

"Ah . . . the mundane beast of business."

Baron Évrard Sainte-Moreau flipped open the golden cover of his pocket watch. Cathedral bells chimed outside the carriage, and he grunted approval as he replaced the timekeeper in his vest pocket. "Nine o'clock. Bien—right on time."

"Business this early?" When Aveline realized he intended to explain no further, she pushed, asking, "And at the church?"

Évrard issued a customary furrow of the brow and an *I'll-put-up-with-you* smile—the look he always gave Aveline when she questioned the merits of something she was to know or care not a thing about. He should have had a son in her, he maintained, for Aveline was far too *curieuse* for her own good.

The man of *la noblesse* would concede that his younger daughter had been gifted with both his noble lineage and her mother's beauty—attractive qualities when the time came for her to marry. But he'd noted that the addition of an inquiring mind to her person both amused and perplexed him. He enjoyed Aveline's attention to wit and inquiry, though she doubted he'd ever encourage her outright use of either.

He much preferred she keep the peculiarity of such character flaws secret from the knowing world.

"Yes. At the church, *petite fille*." He reached over, dismissing her with a tap of his index finger to the book in her lap. "See to your reading, if it amuses you. But stay here. Keep the curtain drawn. And mind you don't go looking for *les problems*, hmm? You needn't burden yourself with the woes of the world—unless they are matters a lady can discuss in the privacy of a salon."

Her spine stiffened, almost on its own.

"And if woes greater than dress fittings and needlepoint should interest me?"

He pitched an eyebrow. "Then I may have to pay heed to the titles you select from my library. What is it you're reading today?"

"Nothing of consequence." Aveline ignored the barb and slid the book under her cloak, shielding the title from his view.

She slid her gaze back to the people beyond the coach curtain. Their line had begun moving along, haltingly, a bleak procession lumbering through the rain. "This is a holy place, one for restoration and reflection. Woes should be banished, should they not? Whatever kind of trouble might we find here, Papa?"

"Indeed." He tapped his walking stick on the floor of the coach. The door opened, mist sweeping in as the coachman stood by, his wig and uniform peppered with the blast of raindrops. "I shan't be long."

The coach released her father's weight and the door clicked closed behind him, leaving Aveline alone—and effectively blocked out. She turned back to the gathering stretching down the paved walkway.

The mass had begun to move and the barouche wheels made their slow, ambling turns as the workhorses labored, cutting ruts through the muddy street. Something was piled in the wagon bed— bags of wheat? Perhaps a load of turnips or goods going to the market? But the wagon appeared as if it might proceed on to the busiest part of the market. Why, then, was a processional trailing after it?

Aveline craned her neck, trying to see, finding that the velvet and fogged glass worked together in obstructing her efforts.

The parade of souls warranted explanation, at the very least,

to the bend of Aveline's curious nature. There was no cause for a
trek in such weather. Why, there were even children—some quite
young and struggling to keep up on tiny legs—teetering along with
mothers and fathers or weaving in and out among the adults. These
were the discontented, the lowly *paysans*, Aveline's mother would
have called them. The peasants who crowded the alleys of the city's
underbelly, and the lion's share of the crude assemblage she'd been
taught to overlook.

They turned away from the formal cemetery gates and stopped
short of the market, instead filtering along a sodden alley between
the church building and the next block. Their path disappeared
round a cover of trees, the crowd bleeding away through the adjoining park and chapel cemetery.

Aveline pulled the hood of her cape over her hat, her decision
made, and rapped her palm to the glass on the door. The coachman
hesitated only a second, then opened the door with a nod.

"Mademoiselle?"

"Oui, Durand. I'm coming out."

He fumbled for a breath but opened the door the rest of the way
when she moved without giving a chance for him to deny her.

Aveline reached for his hand and climbed down without explanation. She glanced down the road in front of them. The line of
people moved past the small cemetery, their shadows fading behind
rows of monuments. Even with their slow, steady gait, she'd have to
quickstep it to keep the people in sight.

"Stay here, s'il vous plaît. I shall return momentarily."

"But, mademoiselle—whatever shall I tell the baron?"

"You shall tell my father nothing, Durand, do you understand?
He will not even know I've gone." She pulled the hood closer around
the sides of her face. "I shall return long before he does."

"But to go out unchaperoned . . ."

Aveline notched her chin, rain peppering her nose and cheeks with tiny pinpricks of cold. She offered a sweet smile, hoping it would melt the coachman's defenses enough that she could slip away in the pursuit.

"Honestly, Durand. I am quite capable of taking a stroll through a church courtyard." She crooked her gloved finger at the rows of vaults and monuments, their uneven height creating a ghostly backdrop against the mist. "And I'll be right over there. You may keep me in sight if it eases your trepidation in the least. That's a chaperone in a way."

The assemblage had all but faded, their palette of ruddy browns and weathered grays blended in against the moss-covered gravestones and monuments that dominated the front portion of the courtyard. Budded trees hung low overhead, and green tulip shoots peeked up through the earth in beds bordering the stoned path— the garden's job to remind mourners that spring was poised to bloom again, even in such a place.

The signs of life might have brought comfort, but the people passed them by without notice and kept walking, heads down to the waterlogged earth beneath their feet. Aveline swept along the path, careful to keep the heels of her shoes from slipping against uneven cobblestones. She moved along, noting she'd turned a corner out of Durand's line of sight, and tried to ignore the nagging in her midsection for the angst she was likely causing the old man.

Like the much larger Paris market at Les Halles, a market bustled outside the courtyard, with street vendors already serving coffee and sweets from *les patisseries* nearby. Early morning deliveries of fish and meat had come and gone, evidenced by the pungent odor that filled Aveline's nostrils in a near-overpowering wave. She raised a gloved hand to protect her nose, or else blanch and go no farther.

Farmers shouted prices for greens, root vegetables, and barley, and sold wedges of cheese wheels covered in wax. Water bearers stood by with barrels aplenty, selling their fountain-drawn water to eager Parisians. A butcher chopped a meaty carcass upon a block not far off. The sight of slopping bits and stray cats dancing circles around the man's feet flip-flopped her stomach. She turned away from blood pooling in the street, grateful for the distraction of a flower cart nearby.

Aveline eased closer to the soft scents of flora. She perched just under a wooden overhang, observing the gathering of people as they slowed by a hole and a mound of sodden earth. The horses were brought to a halt and men released the back of the barouche. Another jumped upon the wagon bed, and to her horror, what might have been bags of wheat or market goods was revealed to be something altogether worse.

Limp bodies piled high.

Countless, wrapped in fabric—certainly not fine Indian muslin. Perhaps linen or . . . burlap? It took two men to unload each. Reaching, straining to lift, then quite unceremoniously dropping corpses in a line, filling the depths of a crevice that had been dug in the earth.

Her breath was stolen.

How could one possibly maintain an even cadence of breathing, in-out, in-out, with what she was witnessing? There was no dignity in this, no reverence for loss. Mourning had devolved into the most commonplace of occasions, one that might accompany any day of the week. A market day, even, judging by the unaffected exchange of goods and coin that occurred right over her shoulder.

Aveline watched, her heart feeling twinges beneath the satin of her bodice.

A woman clutched no fewer than four little ones to her skirts.

Another, despite bystanders who attempted to uphold her at the elbows, was felled at the knees, the front of her splashing down in the mud. Rain, sorrow, muck and mire—they were the silent witnesses to a blemished countenance of church life. It was unlike any service Aveline had ever attended. Her limited experience had been one of formality, where mourning ladies dotted tears behind veils and gentlemen masked emotion with a near-foppish eloquence.

But this was life in Paris—and death in France.

Death as routine. The raw and real minutiae of life as she'd never witnessed it before, where the immense weight of grief mingled with the humdrum of daily whatnots and responsibilities.

Surely God could see them. And would intervene?

Whether tears or rain, Aveline didn't know—a trickle of water trailed down her cheek. She swiped at it, a heartbroken anger surfacing at what she'd witnessed. This wasn't a stage play—children had lost parents, and wives were without husbands. She turned away, finding the reality too great, and instead looked at her hands.

They were covered in satin gloves of a soft dove gray. Beneath them, a floral gown in a cheerful cherub pink. They rendered her so out of place in the confines of the world in which she stood. The realization washed an unexpected wave of contrition over her.

"*Pardon moi*, mademoiselle."

A voice plodded, interrupting the shower of guilt.

Aveline turned to find a woman perched at her elbow—quite haggard. Dirt-smudged and rough. Though she was also young. Maybe even near to Aveline's nineteen years. She bowed, keeping her head ceremoniously tipped low, and extended a bouquet of violets. Their petals were brilliant; tiny masterpieces of lavish purple that stood out against the earthen conditions around them.

"*Aimeriez-vous acheter une fleur?*"

Would I like to buy a flower? Aveline shook her head.

"*Une violette* . . ." She pulled a single bloom from the bouquet and pushed it into Aveline's hand. "Just one, mademoiselle."

"I'm sorry, but I haven't any money." Aveline looked down, sickened the moment she'd claimed it, even if it was truth.

The woman grumbled and turned away, no doubt dejected by what she believed was the flimsy excuse of a noblewoman. She busied herself with the careful arrangement of flowers on her cart, giving Aveline no notice thereafter.

It stunned her that she hadn't thought of it before then: She hadn't any need for money. At least not like this woman did. Not even for a single long-stemmed violet.

The Sainte-Moreau estate boasted a manicured garden and kept an award-winning gardener on retainer. Aveline's mother held accounts at the most exclusive clothiers and arranged private fittings for their special occasion wear. Everything was bought with nothing more than a selection and a smile. It meant that beyond the affectations to feed their social standing, money was subordinate in Aveline's existence. Everything on the estate—in her life, really—was commissioned and managed by the hand of her father. And one day, when she married, that responsibility would fall to her husband.

If Aveline desired a flower, she'd not have to stand in the rain to purchase one. She was of age and, if her parents had their way of it, would be fixed in an advantageous marriage with all due haste. It was probable that one day soon she could but step outside and pluck petals from a bower in her private garden. Hers was a life bursting with every color of the rainbow. Not like the woman she turned back to then, who was so worn and weathered to have been so young. How much would it cost to buy a single hue for a near-colorless existence?

"Excuse me, but can you tell me what is happening there?"

The woman didn't look up. She must not have needed to. "A paupers' burial, that is."

Aveline bit her bottom lip with her teeth. So it was exactly what she'd never seen before, but feared nonetheless.

"Why here . . . why line up at the Chapelle de la Sorbonne? I thought all burials were banned within the city center."

The woman scoffed this time and tethered her hand to her hip. "You mean what are they doing at a church for your people?"

"No, I didn't mean to imply—"

"Death duties. They're paying their tax and tithe to the church." She leaned in, close enough that Aveline could see the shade of brown on her teeth. "Reparations, because they had the nerve to live and die in the la noblesse world. Catacombs not ready to take the number of dead. Where else would they go?"

La noblesse—nobility. The woman's temper seeped out, and she'd spat the word like a plague.

"How much?" Aveline stared back, pondering her reply as raindrops gathered and dripped off the lowest point on the front of her hat.

"Excusez-moi?"

"Je voudrais acheter une violette." Aveline sorted through the bouquet, finding one that shined brighter and bolder than the rest, and pulled it free from the company of its sisters. "This one. I would like this one."

The woman started, bewilderment tempering her former hostility. "But you have no money. You said as much."

"That is correct. I haven't any." She laid the violet on the cart before her. Aveline unhooked pearl buttons at the wrists and tugged her gloves free, then slapped them on the weathered wood beside the bloom. "I assume you barter. Will these do?"

"Mademoiselle . . ." The woman snapped a glance over her

shoulder, as if she expected the king's guards to show up, shackle her, and cart her away to prison for daring to consider something that was so far above her station. "Is this a jest?"

Aveline turned back to the funeral. The assemblage was still there, though some of the crowd had begun to disperse as men heaped shovelsful of earth on top of the mass grave.

"*Non.* These gloves for one violet. They're new, I assure you. And of the finest quality. But I haven't time to dither." She turned back, leveling a steely glare at the woman. "So, do we have a deal or not?"

The woman's hesitation vanished. She swiped the gloves with a hand more deft than Aveline would have given her credit for and pocketed them, mumbling a quick, "*C'est fini*—done. But mind, I won't be giving them back."

Aveline drew in a deep breath and nodded, sated. "Fine. Because I wouldn't take them. Not if you were to offer the whole of the contents on this cart. I have what I want."

Whether the encounter left the woman in a stupor, Aveline wouldn't know. She hurried off without looking back. Time was wearing thin. She had an answer now—a terrible, mind-numbing reality for why the people gathered. But no doubt her father would return soon with blood boiling should he learn what she'd been about.

The cobblestone path was deserted near the street. But soon the lonely souls from the paupers' burial would fill its way again, walking back to rejoin the world beyond the garden.

Aveline swept out in the rain, hurrying lest her father see the evidence of the elements upon her shoulders. She stopped, seconds only, to lay the violet upon the edge of the path. She kissed bare fingertips to her lips, then brushed them against the rain-dampened cobblestone and turned away.

The trek back was made in more haste—speeding through the market, avoiding anything that might mar or soil her garments—until she found the nearly tormented Durand and the carriage waiting exactly where they had been.

She hurried over, brushing rain from her shoulders with bare palms.

"Mademoiselle." Durand's shoulders sagged. He appeared quite breathless, which pricked her heart even more. "I was quite overwrought when you turned the corner."

"Well, you needn't have been." Aveline took his hand to step up into the carriage and settled on the bench seat. She arranged her skirt in a flow around her, smoothing and flopping the fabric, hiding the edges that had seen the most rain. The skies were still covered in a gloom that darkened the inside of the coach, enough that it would save her from notice.

"See, I am quite well."

"Of course, mademoiselle." He nodded, decorum firmly in its place.

Aveline dared to look in his eyes though, finding some softness there. Some care for the way she'd troubled him. And though her mother would have fainted dead away at the thought of a member of their house seeking atonement from a servant, Aveline offered her most genuine smile in reparation.

"*Je suis désolée*, Durand, for the trouble I've obviously caused. This kind of nonsensical business shall not be repeated in the future."

"You needn't apologize to me." He leaned into the coach then, lowering his chin ever so slightly, and slid her copy of *The Wealth of Nations* onto the bench. Aveline took it under the fold of her gown and looked back, knowing her gaze held questions.

"A worthy choice. One to be read with much sense and

intention. But without the necessity of gloves, I'd say?" He bowed, tipping his head in a slight show of solidarity.

Just as Aveline knew he'd hidden the book lest her father come back and find it, Durand had followed her, far enough that he'd have left the coach in order to see to her safety. He'd seen all and, without explanation, told her he'd keep her secret in full.

The coach door closed and Aveline was left alone again.

Hands laid bare in her lap, fingertips still shaking—these were not the effects of weather, no chill of rain. It was the gradual opening of her heart, to see with new eyes the world around her. Velvet curtains could no longer shield Aveline from a truth she longed to see. And now, perhaps, she could find a way to add color to.

Aveline watched through fogged glass as the watercolor shapes of mourners drifted past the coach. They disappeared into the corridors of the market, scattering back to their lives, leaving the brilliant hue of a violet left to honor the dead completely unnoticed.

Theirs was a world washed over in the colors of earth and rain. But hers? Lavish violets that would not stretch beyond the confines of a private estate garden. Aveline knew now she wanted to color the cobblestones—one by one if she must.

If this was life and death in France, she could ignore it no longer.

JULY 27, 1789
LES TROIS-MOUTIERS
LOIRE VALLEY, FRANCE

Robert spotted Aveline the moment she left the doorway of the winemaker's cottage. He eased the steady cadence of ax chopping through wood, bringing the blade to rest on the ground at his feet. "Did I wake you?"

"No. I've been up for some time. Fanetta brought tea and said it would be permissible if I stepped outside today. Just for a few moments, to take a turn around the cottage, mind."

"If you're steady on your feet, then yes. It's fine."

"And the sun this morning . . ." A smile began to build on its own. "I'm grateful to actually feel the warmth, rather than just see it through the loft window."

He nodded, and they stood for a breath, their lack of familiarity apparent. She not knowing what to say to a stranger, and he offering the only aspect she'd seen of his nature thus far—which was a well-mannered reticence. She was grateful but had no idea how to manage even the smallest conversation with virtual strangers all around.

Aveline had heard vague mention of a younger son on the estate, even before her maid had confirmed it. Now, it was the first time she'd really looked at him. He owned a strong profile. A firm jaw. A reserved manner and kind eyes. Seeing him in the midst of laboring as if he hadn't a thimbleful of noble blood running through his veins, she was reminded how little she knew of the family that held her in their care. Just as the faceless Philippe, he was the Duc et Vivay's son. Yet as the younger of the two, Robert would not inherit an inch of the ground upon which they stood.

Were his likeness and his nature shared with his older brother at all?

"What day is it?"

"Monday."

"Then I've slept through church service by a full day. That is something my mother never would have allowed."

"The rest is good. You look well." He fumbled, then backtracking, added, "I meant, you are well. Oui?"

"I am, monsieur. Thank you." She held her left arm out waist high, showing the absence of the wrappings covering her burns. "We still have a way to go, but Fanetta says I am much improved—as well as that I am to call her Fan, just like you and everyone else. And the pain is easing some, so there are some comforts to speak of."

"That's a relief to you, I'm sure."

"Yes. Fan is kind, and self-assured with her knowledge of healing, but a mite strict. I'm afraid I could bear it no longer, staring at the ceiling. No matter the pain that accompanies moving about." Aveline looked over her shoulder before continuing in a whisper. "I'm afraid I had to gently insist she let me leave that loft room, or I would flee from it the first moment she turned around."

He suppressed a smile. "That I can believe."

The loft room had been her lonely view for too many days to count. There was no mirror, however, and Fan was unable to produce one, so Aveline hadn't a clue as to whether she truly looked well at all. Save for what she could determine from the shoulders down, Aveline hoped she was semi-presentable, even with the remnants of burns that had begun their slow heal.

Fan had wound Aveline's hair under a Spanish net, twisting it in a low chignon at her nape, and had found her a round gown of linen. Though it lacked the courtly ruffles or russets Aveline had become used to in her gowns, the deep rust color, square neckline, and slightly higher empire waist proved lovely. Pleasant even— made more so by the fact that a corset and panniers had been left out entirely. The absence of restriction was an added measure of repose in her surroundings.

"Fan has taken great care with me. And I'm grateful. Truly."

"She's a kind girl. And a steadfast worker. Sister to the man who runs the winepress. Both of them are respected on the estate."

"Your father's estate?"

"Yes. I suppose you'd have learned that at some point. My father's estate." He nodded, though he didn't give the appearance of haughtiness in confirming he was the duke's son. Nor did he elaborate.

"Why didn't you say who you were?"

Robert turned back to the bulk of wood, pulled a log from the pile, and resumed chopping. "Would it have made a difference?"

"Of course. You are the Duc et Vivay's son—that makes a difference to me. Is that why you helped me the night the castle was overrun, because we are to be family?"

"It is, yes."

"But you would not have rendered aid otherwise?"

He stopped midswing, a tightness taking over his countenance. Surprise, maybe, that she'd judged him so.

"I would hope a gentleman would render aid to a lady wherever it should be needed, mademoiselle, regardless of her station. But yes, on that night, Fan was your savior far more than I. She and her brother, Gabin, overheard the plan making threats against the estate. The rhetoric of those who would rise up against their masters. When Gabin's efforts at stifling the uprising failed, they turned to me. By the time I'd received notice of an impending attack, we hadn't the ability to let the castle of its party guests. We believed it a greater risk to leave them roaming the woods. But though she delivered my note, I would have you hold Fan and her brother blameless in what's happened. This is not their doing."

"Somehow I knew that already, but I am grateful for the truth. And I do hold them blameless. As I do you. It is my opinion that you did all you could to prevent this atrocity. And thank Providence there was no loss of life. Castles can be rebuilt far more easily than broken lives."

"Very true."

"But now that it's over, I don't know . . . what you mean to do with me. Unless Philippe returns or until I am transferred back into my father's care, I haven't anyone else to turn to." She drew in a deep breath and raised her chin a notch. "So I should like to hear your intentions."

He hesitated in the rhythm of chopping, meeting her gaze. "My intentions are to keep you safe, and keep you well. The rest I leave to your father and fiancé. I sent a missive to Paris straight-away, the night of the fire. They would be aware of what's occurred by now."

"I see. And a reply?"

"None yet. Regardless, I made the decision to shelter you here until you are well enough for a coach journey. But even then, I hesitate to put a time to your departure. There is risk with travel by road even on a good day. But now that Paris is in upheaval, I couldn't allow you to go back until we know it is safe to do so."

"And your vineyard is not in upheaval?"

Robert turned his attention to studying the mingling of trees around them. Rays of sunlight cut down through the trees, dancing through the bower overhead and waving about on the ground at their feet.

"The sun should do you some good."

Not seeing the connection in the abrupt change of subject, Aveline sent a sidelong glance to the thicket of trees past the ridge. "Yes . . . it is why I came outside this morning. In part, anyway."

"What I mean is that you should spend more time outside. As much as possible. I don't mean to cause injury, mademoiselle, but your skin is—"

"An abhorrence." Aveline swallowed hard. "I can imagine."

Though she had yet to see her own reflection, it was not difficult to guess how he might behold her. It did no good to hold illusions; burns scarred. Left traces. And judging by the pain that lingered as her skin fought to heal, Aveline couldn't suppress the monstrous images her mind invented.

His gaze met hers, unwavering.

"You misunderstand. It is a detriment." Robert spoke gently and took a half step forward. "But only to your safety. Your skin is porcelain. Ladies of la noblesse alone can claim such. Here, the women labor under the sun and their skin shows the hours spent in the vineyard. And your hands—I'd wager they've not seen work. Forgive me, but those who toil in the arbors will take notice of that immediately. If you're discovered it will put you at risk. And though we will try as long as we may, we cannot keep you hidden away in this cottage forever. If we want to see you reunited with your family, we must allow you to hide while blending in until such time as we can arrange it."

"You mean to make me work the land?"

"No. Certainly not. I would not ask that you truly labor like the rest—only give the impression of it if your presence at the cottage is found out."

Aveline scanned the small clearing around the cottage.

He'd split reams of wood—half a wall high already—and had stacked them against the stone wall with great care. Linens had been strung up on a cord of twine tied between the trees. Women's work, no doubt. Most likely by Fanetta's toil. But he tended the land same as a servant and showed no conceit in it.

That merited notice.

"And if I should want to work?"

He shook his head, not giving her an inch. "It's not safe."

"Why is that?"

"Mademoiselle, I hesitate to add to the misery of your circumstances by being forthright—"

"No. It's alright. I prefer it, as a matter of fact." Aveline drew into herself, wrapping her arms around her middle—with care, of course, for the pain in hasty movements.

Robert watched her, twisting his hand around the ax handle, like he battled with how to soften whatever blow he had to deliver.

"Please, monsieur. I am not as fragile as my injuries would lead you to believe."

"Alright." A pause, deep inhale, and leveled gaze later, he added, "They are still looking for you."

"They . . . you mean the men who waged war on your family's home?"

"Yes. They came to the vineyard first. Demanded entry here that very night. Fan hid you in the woods until it was safe. And we circulated the talk that you'd fled with your mother. Taken the north road back to Paris. They watch it now, searching every peddler's wagon that happens through. But as we still don't know exactly who was in the revolt, I cannot allow you to be put at risk in working alongside them long enough to find out."

Aveline paused, nodding, seeing the value in his argument.

Much like her father's intense opinions, she guessed. But then, this man was not familiar with her tenacious nature. Paris would not assure her safety; that Aveline accepted now. Yet she couldn't see how this threat was any worse. Stone walls could be stormed and estates felled in the city just as easily as they could in the countryside. The Bastille had proved that.

Fear would only end if she was willing to stand up to it.

"And . . . if I should still wish to work with them?"

"Why would you desire to work?"

"You labor here, do you not? Your family rank is above mine. If I'm to be elevated to the wife of the future Duc et Vivay, shouldn't I work as my future brother-in-law does? This will, after all, become my land too. Would it not do that alliance good to work in the sun, arm in arm, with the people who support us, and understand why their plight drove them to see no recourse but to fell the castle of the very family who sustains them?"

His posture stiffened, and his brow tipped up in a swift wave of shock. "You would hold the men behind flaming torches blameless too?"

"Not blameless, no. But I would pay them the compliment of seeking to understand the impasse of life here at this country estate. Are they well cared for?"

"They are."

"And what of taxation?"

Robert shifted his stance, the pause evident. "We tax them no more than the law requires."

"I see. And perhaps therein lies our problem. Is it not customary to tax the people's use of another man's land? The right to live and even die in their own country? Perhaps Fanetta's brother is taxed for the use of your winepress, to produce the very wine that is received in the king's salon at Versailles. You may wish to see if the people you trust are truly your allies. Or allow me to work alongside them and learn it for you."

Aveline paused, trying not to consider how her appearance might have been altered. Maybe by a wide margin. All vanity aside, she would use whatever bargaining ground they had.

"I wasn't presented at the ball. Not formally. The only ones to have seen my face and know who I am were a select few in service, and like Fan, I'd wager they are loyal to your family. So where is the risk if no one will recognize me?"

Something twinkled in his eyes. Amusement, perhaps? "Forgive me, mademoiselle, but your opinions are near to revolutionary."

"So I have been told on occasion." She walked over to the line, running her hand along the seam of a sheet. Dry. They could come down and her bed changed with them. "May I see to these?"

"You may. As long as you are well enough to do so."

A sense of purpose washed over her. A small one, but purpose nonetheless. One that had nothing to do with former affectations of a Paris peeress, and everything to do with answering the call of the secret questions in her heart.

She tugged at the sheet, easing it free while careful through twinges of pain, and gathered the fabric in her arms before it touched the ground.

"I am well, sir. Thank you. So well, in fact, that you may expect me to finish this work before you complete yours." Aveline turned, found the slow build of a smile evident upon his face, and returned the civility with a faint one of her own. "And I will be out here at sunup tomorrow, whether the Duc et Vivay's son is awake yet or not."

ELEVEN

The view owned a *c'est bon*-worthy description, just like in every Provençal movie Ellie had ever seen.

French doors and a private balcony presided over a span of vineyards and an abundant landscape of trees beyond. The doors had been left open, a breeze toying with white gauze curtains. Powder-blue walls and windows stretched from floor to high ceiling. A fireplace with elegant carved moldings and an oversized hearth lent the room its classic, French château feel.

Ellie sat on the edge of the bed, absently combing her fingers through her hair.

It was a perfect room. *Too perfect.* In an estate house basking in the heart of wine country. Nestled in hills, all laden with a coming harvest. And her grandmother's castle—it was out there, quiet in its slumber, waiting to be discovered.

For the first time, in spite of the beauty around her, the solace pricked Ellie with the full impact of what she'd done. It had been far too easy to whisk away—run from her impending troubles. She'd given herself two weeks. Maybe three. But Laine's e-mails and the time ticking away on the clock would determine how long she had to delve into Grandma Vi's story.

Only two weeks. And did she expect her life to change in that time?

"Well, I'm here, Grandma. Secrets or not, I made it. So what in the world do I do now?" she whispered aloud, even exhaled, feeling the weight of nearly everything in her life coming down on her in the moment.

The sound of a boot rapping on the door startled her. Ellie shot up and turned, flattening waves behind her ear with a quick hand.

Quinn stood in the doorway, a suitcase in each hand. "Where would you like these?"

"Um . . . on the floor by the armoire is fine, thanks."

"Right." He stepped in and set the luggage down as she'd asked. "Towels are in the cupboard. En suite is through that door. The meal for guests is at half day—but in the dinin' hall, the one facin' the front drive."

"Oh yes. Thank you." She'd seen it. And received his veiled meaning also that the kitchen and breakfast room she'd wandered into earlier were reserved for family only.

"Your room key." He handed it to her, tending his head in a respectful nod, and moved as if to leave without another word.

"Thank you."

Say something . . . anything.

If Ellie didn't at least ask him about seeing the castle, develop some rapport right then, it may prove difficult to crack the veneer of hospitality later on. That was, if he possessed it at all.

She edged a step forward. "I'm sorry about that down there . . . your grandfather? I didn't know. He's . . ."

Quinn stopped in the doorway, turned, shoving his hands in the front pockets of his jeans. "Blind. Or near enough to it anyway."

"What I mean to say is I didn't know. And I didn't set out to cause any trouble. I'm sorry if I did."

She meant it. To see the old man was struggling—it cast new light on her stay. Finding answers to the questions surrounding the castle ruins had been paramount on her mind. But seeing anyone in a similar situation as she was with Grandma Vi sparked a sudden sense of empathy she couldn't ignore.

Thinking of how he'd taken time to fold a newspaper in his hands, she asked, "You read the paper to him?"

He nodded. "Every mornin'. He can still see some, light and shadow. Shapes. Enough to know where to walk without bumpin' into things. But no longer type set on a newspaper. And certainly not a laptop screen. Those two ladies in the kitchen take pity on him and do his biddin' to rent out rooms in our estate house. It won't get better, unfortunately." Quinn tipped his shoulders in a light shrug. "Fightin' the world—it's his way. He lives by the old rule of life here in the Loire—somethin' his Irish grandson would know nothin' about. So when I said rigid, what I really meant to say was stubborn as a hundred-year-old goat, and that's being kind. He's near enough in age and constitution to make it an accurate description. It's not an argument with you."

She smiled. *Good. Apology accepted.* "I'll keep that in mind next time I interrupt a family breakfast."

"I see you managed to sneak away from my grandmother and great-aunt before they heaped a third plate in front of ya."

"And here I thought the French didn't have more than a café au lait and croissant for breakfast. It's been an education. Bread. Pastries and fruit. No cheese though. Something called *brioche Suisse*. And even bacon?"

"Ah yes. The rashers. My grandmother orders those special now that there's an Irishman in the house."

"That, and for the American tourist it seems. I'll never need to eat again."

"Oh, you think you won't but ya will. And in just a couple of hours, if they have anythin' to say about it." Quinn checked his wristwatch and edged back toward the hall, as if time called him to walk away. "My advice—find a clever hidin' place to stay out of sight during midday. But that tip's free. Best o' luck then."

"Well, I was actually wondering . . ." Ellie stopped him again, feeling unsure this time.

Maybe it was the room.

Maybe the color of his eyes. Or his openness about what had occurred in the kitchen. Whatever it was, something hooked in her midsection and added the slight flutter of butterfly wings to the mix.

". . . if you could take me on a tour of the grounds this morning? I'd like to get started on my research right away."

"Research." Quinn leveled his eyes in a slight squint, as if the word meant she owed him more. "You here for work then?"

She nodded. "Of a sort. That's why I paid for a tour guide. I need someone to show me the grounds. The vineyards . . . the roads in and out of town . . . especially any castle ruins or rock walls in the vicinity. I'm looking for something specific, and for lack of better words, I'll know it when I see it. So that means I'll need to see everything."

"You don't say."

If Ellie showed him enthusiasm, a hardworking spirit, maybe he'd see value in the fact that she wasn't just there to pass the time tasting wine and visiting tourist shops. She was there to work. For answers. Surely he'd soften up a bit when she told him what she really sought. Locals always wanted to talk about the history of their land. He'd be no different.

"Yes. So if you can just show me around, I'm sure . . ."

"It's not a good time. I have business to attend to."

"You mean business out there?" She tilted her head toward the window. "In the vineyard?"

"It is the reignin' enterprise around here. And I'm still learnin' the ropes."

Ellie sat in an upholstered chair by the hearth and swiped the boots she'd discarded nearby. "Good. Then I'll go with you"—she pulled a boot up one leg—"and we can stop off on the way back." She slipped into the other boot and stood, ready to go.

He shook his head. Apparently, she'd lost him.

"Stop off where?"

Ellie pointed to the view through the open doors: a thicket of woods, with the tips of white stone turrets jutting out against the highest leaves. "There."

Quinn shot his glance to the same view from the balcony but didn't make a move to really look at what she was referring to. Maybe that meant he didn't need to. He knew exactly what she wanted to see. It seemed a story he'd heard before. Had heard and, for whatever reason, didn't appear to warm to at all.

"Don't be tellin' me that's why you're here."

"In part. Yes. I came to see the castle," she stated flatly, and folded her arms across her chest. "Is that a problem?"

"Well, I hate to disappoint, but that's not goin' to be possible."

"Why on earth not?"

"It's closed to the public. I may be new around here myself, but even I know it's been that way for decades. And forgive me, but one American's stubbornness isn't likely to change that. Ya probably should have Googled a bit more about it before you set out."

"If you think calling me stubborn will dissuade me, you're on the wrong side of that argument. I take it as a compliment. And this is France's valley of the kings, isn't it? Tourists come here for that purpose—to see castles and châteaus, to taste some of the best wines in the world. Even a castle in ruins would garner some interest in a setting like this, right? Surely there's an owner I can speak to? At least try to persuade them to just let me look for five minutes. Or at the very least, I could speak to your grandfather about it, with you to translate. You can't tell me I came all this way and now it's just . . . not possible."

Quinn waited.

He was patient but also . . . annoyed? One could have heard a pin drop for how quiet he'd remained through her explanation. And though he was a good eight or so inches taller than her petite frame and probably thought he was a load tougher, Ellie stood her ground before him.

"You say you want to talk to the owner?"

Ellie nodded, adding a touch of surly to her tone. "Just give me the chance."

"Fine. Grab your shades. Sun's warmin' things up outside."

Turned out Ellie needed the sunglasses.

Sunlight drenched the vineyard rows in which they walked, she keeping a few steps behind Quinn.

He walked slowly, with a laid-back air that would never fly in the faster-paced America, even in her small town. He could have been strolling through a park for how little he cared for the time. If they were headed to see the castle's owner, she expected he had little interest in reaching the destination before dark.

"So what is it?"

Ellie paused, more than a little surprised to hear him engage in conversation at all. He seemed the keep-to-himself type. "What?"

He looked back, didn't miss a beat even while taking a few blind steps. "The story that brought you here."

"How do you know I have a story?"

"Everyone does." He smiled. Skeptical. "Said yourself you're researchin'. What's it for then? Let me guess—ya one of those idealistic writer types?"

How funny that he'd nail that down. Grandma Vi had always pushed her to consider writing. But she'd let it go . . . a dream that was too far off to grasp.

"No, actually. I have a normal job as an analyst at a pharmaceutical company. I have a desk. A home. Friends who have all grown up in the same small town. No idealistic anything here."

"But you still have a story, don't ya?"

Ellie did of course own a story, but she hadn't a clue how to tell it.

Hers was a photo. A brooch. A woman in lavender whose secret past had been cracked wide open by the fresh jabs of Alzheimer's. And . . . loss. The story stirring in her heart at the moment—Ellie couldn't speak of it, even if it was the truth.

She couldn't say how a funeral had shattered an eleven-year-old girl's rose-colored glasses years ago, dispelling any illusion of childhood fairy tales. On a rainy day in November, her grandmother had become both father and mother, teacher and helper, confidante and friend for the years that would follow. She'd stepped in to create a sense of normal—making blueberry scones at midnight, staying with Ellie in the kitchen long after the funeral mourners had left the house that night. But now, recalling memories like that . . . Ellie didn't have the faintest idea how to reconcile the fact that her grandmother had kept something from her, something buried so deep inside, and had only just shared the image of a woman whom Ellie now feared she might never truly know.

How could she possibly say all that to a stranger? Death and loss and blueberry scones . . . they were heavy when they came as a package. She couldn't even begin to work it out in her own mind, let alone try to explain it to an irked Irishman.

"Some stories can only be told when they're ready. I'm not even to the first chapter yet."

"So you're lookin' for the ideal France. The vineyard or castle photo from the desk calendar. Is that about the way of it?"

"I think I had one of those calendars once. Is that so terrible?"

"It is when tourists spend their time fantasizin' about somethin', and they're let down when it's never as good in real life."

"I don't think there's anything wrong with a little dreaming. You know, France practically wrote the book on romance. Ever heard of a city called Paris?"

Quinn stopped on a dime.

He turned, staring back with a curious look in his eyes.

The sun burned down on his shoulders, illuminating a faded maroon tee with an Irish pub logo splashed across his chest. Typical, Ellie thought. And she bit her tongue against saying out loud that he had a pretty cynical outlook too. The glare confirmed it two times over.

"You're lookin' for romance, are ya?" His eyebrows edged in, creasing in humor. He looked to be teetering on the edge of bursting out in laughter.

"Maybe I am. But certainly not the kind you're referring to." It would have felt a little too good to slug him in the shoulder of that faded pub tee. Ellie turned her attention to the sky. The landscape beyond the vineyard row. Anything so she wouldn't have to see him laugh at her. "All the romance I need is in the castle."

He shrugged, walking on ahead of her again.

"You and all the rest. They all think they'll find it here. Runnin' away from a breakup. Midlife crisis. Lost a job or relationship faded out . . ." Ellie perked up at that, felt the jabs that edged so close to her own life, tried to ignore them and keep walking. "You name it. And then there's you. People like you show up, always alone, demandin' to see a castle they know nothin' about. And they're shocked when someone dares to tell 'em no."

"Well, what would your grandfather say about it, if he knew what I'm looking for?"

"He only talks of the grapes—and that's in French. Good luck with anythin' else gettin' through."

Ellie sighed. Much like the sign at the round outside the vine-yard, they weren't getting anywhere.

She guessed Quinn Foley was one of those guys—the slightly prideful in thinking he could figure her out at first glance. A psy-chologist in training, no doubt. With few if any entanglements to tie him down. Maybe he lumbered along through the vineyard rows with no clock to manage or schedule to keep. There were few responsibilities she could see, other than to drive his grandfather to town and watch as their employees brought in the grape harvest.

Still, he'd turned his attention to the vines, inspecting the full-sized grapes as they walked on, bright green on the vine, and seizing an opportune time to show he was an expert craftsman nurturing the vines' progress to greatness. Doing it all for her benefit? She wouldn't have put it past him.

"Why this castle, when there's hundreds of others? Have you come here because of the name: *The Sleeping Beauty*?"

"It sounds enchanting, but no. Not all of it, anyway."

"No knight in shinin' armor?"

She bristled at the intrusion into her private life. "No princesses or towers either. Just a regular person. Sorry to disappoint you, but

I have a fairly normal life. I'm not looking for anything but a few answers to something you wouldn't understand."

"And how's it workin' out for ya then?"

"Not exactly as I imagined. But I'll keep going. Roots don't move unless you dig them up, right?"

"You won't be moving these." Quinn pointed, then stood back. "There's your castle—or at least, the road down to it. Shut up tight, just like I told ya."

They'd come to the end of the long arbor rows, in a clearing that met an old country road, grassed over, parting gangly trees in a line far down into the darkness of the forest. And what almost stopped her heart—a hopeless barrier in the form of a high stone wall. Iron gates brandished intricate scrollwork, with rust and scrub bushes growing up into the heart of where the two sides met, a heavy chain and lock . . . and a sign that screamed *Passage Interdit* and *Propriété Privée* in garish red letters.

"It can't be." Ellie stepped up to the gate, wrapping her hands around the scrolls. "You can't even see the ruins from here. How far back does the road go?"

"Far enough to keep pryin' eyes and curious minds out. Look." He pointed at a near-invisible metal wire that cut from the sides of the gate and all the way down the tree line on both sides, as far as the eye could see. "Electric fence. And up there. See the top of the fox crest engraved in the stone wall?"

A small camera had been wired there and stood watch, a light blinking plain as day, mocking any would-be tourist's plight.

"There's another one every ten meters or so. Add that to random patrols around the castle itself, and you're lookin' for trouble if you try to go in there. Your passport won't do ya much good if the authorities confiscate it."

"But why show me this if we can't get in? I thought you were taking me to speak to the owner. Where is he?"

"Unavailable. Titus says he lives away—is owner in name only. But to every question you pose, this is what he'd say."

"How do you know what he'll say unless you let me talk to him?"

"Because countless have asked before you, and this is what we tell them—there's no trespassing here. It's private property. The owner does not want the grounds disturbed, and no manner of pushin' will change his mind. That's how it is."

Ellie stepped back, abhorred that he hadn't mentioned it sooner. "You're on the payroll to keep tourists away?"

"No. I'm not. But to my grandfather, we're a neighbor and so we honor the owner's wishes."

"You're his watchdog then." Ellie shook her head, disappointment leveling a clean blow. "You might have said."

He sighed, kicked his heel into the earth, and looked up, though the sun was cutting high and threatened to blind him for it. "Look. I didn't want to make ya angry. Just discourage you from tryin' to go any further with this. You're booked to stay here and that's the way of it. St. Peter himself couldn't change my grandfather's mind once it's set on somethin'. So you might as well accept the terms. Go tour the other castles. Drink wine. Snap photos for the desk frame and have a grand time. Then go back home to your life, and leave this place be."

He forced a smile, one of those gentle tips at the corners of the mouth that meant someone wanted to feel sorry but didn't. Not enough for her to believe it, anyway.

"The castle's earned its peace, Miss Carver." Quinn tipped his head in a nod, then left her alone there. "Let the past stay buried."

Strolling away to some other part of the vineyard, she guessed.

Maybe so she could have some time to think about doing what he'd said. Snap some photos. Maybe post a selfie at the castle gate so she could at least tell her girlfriends she'd been there. And perhaps drown her sorrows in his family's wine after. But that wasn't her.

"Whether you've earned it or not, you don't want peace. Do you?" Ellie whispered out into the road's long void beyond the gate. She wrapped her hand tighter around the iron scrollwork, feeling the roughness of rust and the coolness of metal against her palm. "You don't want it or I wouldn't be standing here right now. You have a story to tell."

Quinn's warning had been valiant. And the No Trespassing sign did have a quaintness about it, printed in French she couldn't read. But while Quinn's revelation of his role as caretaker of the castle perimeter had come with a jolt, it only served to remind Ellie who she was in turn.

She was Lady Vi's granddaughter—and that meant she wouldn't take no for an answer.

TWELVE

APRIL 25, 1944
LES TROIS-MOUTIERS
LOIRE VALLEY, FRANCE

Vi shot up in bed, waking with a start.

The fitful routine of sleeping like a stone and waking again had dogged her for more than two days. Beams of sunshine fought to break into every crack in the cottage's walled façade. She scanned the room. All was quiet and still—as it should be in her hideaway.

Hunger slammed her, the aching in her stomach finally demanding its fair attention now that her weary body had restored its sleep reserves.

Julien had dropped provisions by sometime as she'd slept, leaving a crate of pears on the table. Vi swung her legs over the cot in a fluid motion and drifted to it, leaning the rifle against the tabletop. She took one, biting in, this pear too tasting heavenly as the fruit had in the chapel days before. But there was no savoring it. She ravaged through bite after bite, chewing and swallowing as if she no longer owned a sense of taste.

"Alouette, gentille alouette . . ."

The singsong melody of the French schoolyard song—and

a little girl's voice behind it—drifted, soft and seemingly uncon-
cerned, from just outside the cottage door.

"Alouette, je te plumerai . . ."

Julien had left water and food, but she hadn't spoken to him
in days. He'd warned her to stay silent no matter what she might
hear outside, but he hadn't said a word about unexpected guests—
certainly not a sprite singing her awake from the cottage doorstep.

The sound of a key invading the lock on the door nearly stopped
her heart. Jiggling first, then clanking in the heavy iron keyhole,
the key fought to turn.

Vi reached for the rifle. In her haste, it slid along the tabletop and slammed down in a great *clap* against the hardwood floor.
An abrupt halt to the singing followed, and the key fell silent in
the lock. And then the little singsong voice was replaced by foot
stomps, quickly retreating. There could be minutes only before the
little girl brought an adult to investigate the odd sounds in what
was supposed to be an abandoned cottage.

Panic flooded her mind.

Clean up. Hide. Make it out as if you were never here.

The habit of removing any trace of her presence was something
Vi had picked up early on. She'd already folded the towel and emp-
tied the washbasin into the rubbish bin the night before. Now she
swept up pears from the table, dropping what remained of the core
in her jacket pocket. Turning to the cot next, she rolled the blanket
and stowed it under. The last and critical thing for her, Vi slid the
strap of her canvas bag over her shoulder, making sure it fit snug
behind her back.

It wasn't a few moments that the door jiggled again, with no
singing to accompany the noise. The key turned in the lock with
a precise *click*. The hands that turned it did not belong to a child
this time.

Vi raised the rifle, praying beyond hope that it was Julien.

She swept up to the second-story shadows, keeping her shoulder pinned behind the stone fireplace with only a tiny fraction of her body and profile exposed.

The door creaked on weary hinges. Daylight flooded in a stream across the floor, illuminating the table and chair in the center of the room. The end of a rifle extended past the open door first, then light was cast on the arms that held it: surprisingly enough, a woman—her body lithe under a beige dress and mustard cardigan, unbuttoned over a belly round with child.

She was fearless, at least from every indication of her solid stance. An expert too, it seemed, as she scanned the space with her gaze leveled through the rifle's sight.

"*Sortez!*" she shouted, her voice even and strong as it echoed against the rafters.

The woman paused, floorboards creaking ever so slightly as she shifted her weight to look over every corner of the ground floor.

"I said come out—*now*! Or I swear I will set this cottage ablaze with you locked inside."

"That shall be very hard to do if you are dead."

The woman froze. She kept the rifle fully raised but did not turn. Didn't look up. Just kept breathing, her shoulders rising and falling with even strides.

"Drop it!" Vi's voice matched the woman's own brand of steady. "Slowly. No noise or I pull this trigger."

The woman obeyed, lowering the rifle. With effort that strained the small of her back, she set the weapon on the floorboards at her feet. She righted herself again, slowly, hands raised to the waist.

"Now step back. Four paces. Keep those hands in the air." Vi descended the stairs behind her, one by one, the aged wood creaking with each step. She kept the rifle raised, stepping down and around, stopping to face the woman.

Vi stared back into wide fawn eyes, a pert nose, and a youth-fulness that managed to soften even her most ardent stone-face. The woman was young—probably a couple of years under her own twenty-two. Lovely olive skin was haloed by the sunlight behind her, making the fabric of the skirt around her legs almost translu-cent. Her hair was fashioned in an intricate braid, rich and dark, tumbling over the front of her shoulder.

They eyed each other, Vi's rifle her sole companion for sur-vival, and the woman in front of her staring back with an equally stern set to her jaw.

"Step back. Toward the door."

The woman kept her hands raised waist-high, taking slow, measured steps in the direction from which she'd come. Vi took one forward to each she took back, knowing the woman was in no condition to spring for it, and stopped when the other rifle grazed the tips of her oxfords. She bent and scooped it up, keeping her rifle trained as she swept the other's strap over her shoulder.

"Where is Julien?"

The woman's face changed, a twinge cut into her brow, then smoothed away again almost immediately.

"You heard me," Vi demanded, rifle raised and arm muscles tensed. She shifted her glance from the woman to the door. "And you obviously know who I'm talking about. So where is he?"

"Marie!" A tiny girl, the pigtailed owner of the schoolyard song, swept into the cottage on tiny feet and wrapped her arm halfway round the woman's middle. "Please don't hurt her, lady. Can't you see? She's going to have a baby." She clung to the woman, palms spread wide in a tiny protection of the woman's belly. "This is my cousin."

"Go, Criquet." The woman pushed the child behind her back, nudging in the direction of the open door. She pointed to the sun and the freedom beyond. "Fetch your brother."

"Marie, stop!" A tall form moved in through the door, blocking the sun.

"It's alright. This woman is with us. She won't hurt anyone." Julien stepped in, taking command of the woman and child, his hand raised in calm. He turned to Vi. "Lady, stand down. Please."

Vi nodded and immediately lowered the rifle to her side.

"She won't harm us, Marie." He stepped over to Vi, holding his hand out palm to ceiling.

He looked dead in her eyes. No words needed; she knew what he was asking.

Hesitation still owned the better part of Vi's judgment. She shifted her glance from the face she trusted, to the woman she didn't, to the wide-eyed little girl, who couldn't have been more than eight or nine years old. All three souls looked to her, waiting while she calculated the risk.

"You may keep the one I gave you last night, oui? Just give me that one."

Vi slipped the strap of the woman's weapon down from her shoulder and, without a word, placed it in his outstretched hand.

"Who is this, Julien?" Anger flashed in her eyes.

"I was going to tell you. But if you'd honored my request not to venture into the woods on your own, none of this would have happened. How many times must I ask this of you?" He turned his attention from the woman's obvious acrimony back to Vi.

He ran a hand through his hair, frustration seeping out on a sigh. "This is Mariette—Marie for short. My brother's wife. And this little troublemaker who found you this morning"—he sent a stern look over to the little girl, who lowered her head to stare down at her buckle shoes—"even though she knows she's not to go into the woods alone—is Criquet. My sister." He made a low whistle sound against his teeth, drawing her attention back to his face. "We'll talk about this later."

"My book, *s'il te plaît?*" Criquet turned, pointing to the bookshelf by the corner with the cot. A mishmash of goods occupied the shelf: a basket, soiled gardening gloves, a weathered hand spade, and a stack of books. "Last time we were here. I left it. I can't sleep without it."

"*Ne t'inquiètes pas*, Criquet. I will fetch your book for you."

Vi stood, silently watching.

The explanations for who they were turned out to be quite suitable, though the thought of Criquet searching for a beloved book, only to be frightened by a stranger hiding in their cottage—it must have been terrifying. She felt sorry for the little girl, for an innocent devotion to reading had stirred such angst.

Marie, on the other hand, her venom was clear. Devotion or not, she couldn't see past the intruder in their midst. Vi actually thought if she'd had the rifle in hand, the mother-to-be wouldn't shy away from using it, despite anything Julien had to say. She stared up at him, an icy indifference evident in the lines of her face. Quite different from the hero-worthy gaze Criquet had lavished upon him.

"Your brother would never agree to this. He left you in charge, to look after his family. Is this how you would repay him?"

"You're my family too."

"And yet you hide stowaways in the cottage?" Marie's words were spat, toxic and accusing, at the man who had defused the confrontation that could have ended so terribly. "I will not have"— she slid her steely glare over to Vi, inspecting her from lashes to toes—"*this*, under my husband's roof."

"You don't know what you're talking about." Julien leaned on
the rifle on a deep sigh, the same way he'd done the day before. "Do
not question me for doing what is right, Marie."

"Right?" she scoffed. "This is not right."

"I had little choice in a matter you know nothing of. I understand this was abrupt, and in light of the shock you've just endured,
I will overlook your hostility. I'd have explained when the time was
right. But you must know I always have this family's best interest at
heart. I would not allow a threat under my brother's roof. Not with
you both here. Not for one single moment. Do you understand?"

The flex in her jawline eased, evidence that she'd backed down
a shade by the softness in his tone and the authenticity in the
words he'd chosen. Marie took Criquet's hand in hers though, drawing the child closer, just in case the stranger was still a viper in
disguise.

"I will not question you now. But you will make her leave from
this house. This instant."

"Take Criquet back to the estate house," Julien countered, his
voice steady. When she didn't move, he just stared back with softened eyes. "Marie. Please? Do as I ask. We'll discuss this later."

Marie issued a seething glare in Vi's direction before she turned
in a huff and tugged Criquet out into the sunshine with her.

Vi watched them go, silently, until their shadows disappeared
over the ridge.

Julien turned back to her.

He'd resolved the decision he'd made for her to stay, but something else looked to have lately knocked the stuffing out of him. Dark
circles rimmed the underside of his eyes. His brow was furrowed
and dark, partially covered under tousled waves that hung down,
shielding his eyes from looking at her. He had a strong face—one
that Vi might have thought handsome if he'd walked into the Blue

Lagoon Club once upon a time in London. But here, in the mix of shadow and light streaming in through the cottage door, the young man in Julien looked more mature than his obvious years.

Embattled. Troubled and hopelessly worn out.

"I'm sorry for that. There was a problem in the vineyard this morning. Something I couldn't avoid, and . . ." He cut his explanation short on an overt sigh. "I meant to come earlier. Now I know I should have."

"Well, I suppose I know why she was so angry. I would be too if I found a drifter on my property, especially with the state of things, a child to look after, and since she's . . ." Vi cleared her throat. Who talked of such things as babies with a man she'd spoken to in total for less than half a day? The proper Brit in her recoiled that she'd been clumsy enough to lead into it, with no way out.

"Nearing her time, of course." He smiled then, a curious curve that spread wide on his lips, as if he enjoyed her lopsided attempt at discretion a little too much.

Grins like that didn't exist in the heart of war-torn France; they belonged on the cover of *LIFE* magazine. Why, the office gals who filled the dance floor at 50 Carnaby Street wouldn't have known what to do but buckle at the knees over a smile like that. And there it was, shining down on her.

"But you misunderstand. Marie thinks I'm, uh—" He cleared his throat. Straightened up and tried to add a more serious bent to his features. "Keeping you."

"Keeping me?"

"Yes. That you're kept. Here."

His gaze flitted to the cot, and a rush of understanding fluttered the length of Vi's insides. The nostalgia she'd felt in his smile melted faster than an icicle in summer. She turned away in shock, a blush burning her cheeks. "Oh . . ."

"Which I'm not, of course," he rushed out, tripping over his words. "No expectation."

Vi gripped the rifle a little tighter, issuing clear intention. "You're right there's no expectation!"

"Exactly what I said, no expectation whatsoever. The cottage has been used by soldiers in the past . . ." Julien shook his head. His turn to squirm through an explanation now. "That's beside the point. You are here as our guest. I'll make sure Marie understands that in full, and that there is no reason to mistrust you."

Vi might have held on to her embarrassment if she hadn't felt as weary as he looked. Even then, adrenaline was still fighting her on her way to calm, and her stomach had begun a fresh battle by once again clawing with hunger at her midsection. She needed food. Rest. A safe haven from dreams and imaginary planes blasting horror from the sky.

"Well, might I ask you then what your intentions are? Knowing, of course, that I am quite capable of using this rifle against you if you should dare to try anything at all."

Julien's smile had faded some, backtracking to what she read as kindness in the eyes again. He tilted his head toward the entrance. "The door's open."

"Are you asking me to go?"

"No." Julien shook his head slightly.

The narrowing of his eyes, an arm braced in a loose fist at his side, the sturdiness in his stance—even with the weight he'd eased off the injured leg—showed he earnestly meant what he was about to say.

"I'm saying we'll offer you shelter at the estate house. No more hiding in the woods. If you really are running from something or someone, it's best to hide you in plain sight. We have laborers here. Dozens of them. Women and children mostly, and some of the aged men who were deemed unfit to fight. They're not conscripted into labor for the Nazis because they work for me, and we supply a large portion of wine to Hitler's fighting forces. They leave us be, as long as they believe we're obeying their law, bringing in the harvest, and living under their yoke of fear."

"And why would you do that for me, a complete stranger?"

"Because it's the right thing to do."

Vi started, doubting anything in the grip of war could be that simple. "What about the little girl?"

"Criquet."

"Where are her parents—your parents?"

"Dead." He straightened, easing weight off his leg. He seemed to notice how her glance had drifted down and cleared his throat. "Our mother when Criquet was born. Father drank himself into the grave not long after."

"I'm sorry."

"Me too." And he looked it. "My brother and I . . . and Marie. We're her parents now."

"Look, all jests of your sister-in-law's wrath aside, why would you permit me to stay with your family? With your parents gone and your brother off fighting? You don't know who I am."

"Is there a reason I shouldn't trust you?"

"Of course not."

"Then leave Marie to me. From my view of it, I'll have someone else close by who knows how to handle herself with a firearm. And let's just say we'll all have an extra pair of eyes to keep Criquet and her curiosity from pitching over the second-story balcony of the estate house. Everyone wins."

It was against her better judgment, but Vi couldn't pinpoint a rebuttal he'd accept. So she nodded, figuring she could put up with Marie's brusque attitude for a day or so anyway. All Vi needed was a safe stop for a few days. Then she'd move on, and the estate house would fade into another stop in a long line of war's grim memories.

"Very well. I'll stay."

"One more thing." He eyed her without filter. "How many trucks did you see the other night?"

Vi swallowed hard, trying to decide what kind of game he was playing.

Not one of those men had come within a hundred paces of the cabin. It was too dark and far too secluded for the truck drivers to have seen anything that far up on the ridge. No one could have known she was there . . . unless they already did.

"Is that why you look so tired?" Vi stared back at him, no longer caught off guard by Julien speaking as if she were his equal in matters of espionage. What mattered more was that he'd trusted her. "That was you out there with those men. How long has it been since you've slept?"

He brushed it off. Just stood, waiting for her answer. "Just answer the question. How many trucks, Lady?"

Without hesitation, she clipped, "Four."

"And men?"

Vi drew in a deep breath, enough to cover a full explanation.

"No less than twenty. All able-bodied. Certainly enough that they could be conscripted to work for the Nazis, I'd say. But curiously enough, they're scurrying about like worker bees in your woods. I'd say you spend more time in this cottage than you'd care to admit. Perhaps as a lookout? It's a perfect vantage point to clock Nazi patrols on the road to the castle. And I'll save you from inquiring further—there were over forty crates. Give or take a few. Some that required two grown men to carry. Stands to reason the wares in those trucks were more than crates of pears or bags of walnuts. Or cork for bottling wine. I'd say, more like antiaircraft weaponry.

Or rifles, perhaps? Maybe ammunition. In any case, I'd say that should answer your next few questions. So, is that enough? Are we finished? Because even if you're not hungry, I am."

Julien nodded. The general retreated again. "Bien."

"What's good?"

"That my instincts about you were dead on." Julien extended his hand, offering a shake on it. "We received word through the wire that His Majesty's Special Operations Executive organization had a young linguist go missing in Paris a few months back. You wouldn't know anything about that, would you?"

They have a wire?

Vi hesitated only a moment as the thought sank in, then, with her decision made, placed her hand in his. One firm shake and she let go, turning toward the cot and bookshelf in the back. "It's SOE for short, you know."

"I'm aware of that, Lady. But I said it for your benefit."

"Then we know where we stand, don't we?"

She knelt and, thumbing through the small stack of books, found the only title befitting a little singing fairy. She tucked the book under her arm and walked back, offering the copy of *Histoires ou Contes du Temps Passé*.

"Here. I'd wager Criquet will want her *Mother Goose Tales* for bedtime."

Julien nodded. But instead of taking the book as she'd expected, he tipped his head to the door so she could take it herself. "Welcome to the resistance, Lady."

THIRTEEN

It was said that a deep wood like *Bosquet du Renard* should be enchanted.

In folklore, the very nature of "Fox Grove" fit the definition. It could be home to dragons and fairies, gnomes or elves, if one believed in such things. All manner of mythical creatures could inhabit its secret corners, though Aveline believed in only one of them: the elusive fox, which after several days of working in and around the cottage, she still had yet to see.

She could hear their whimsy—a shuffle and a bushy tail whisking away behind her while she pulled down linens from the line, or evidence of mischief around the rubbish bin, meaning the fox had looked in on the scraps left over from the last night's meal.

After days of waiting for a missive from her father, mother, or the yet-absent Philippe, the monotony of cottage life was beginning to weigh heavily upon her. Robert had seen to sending her books, but having surely missed her brother-in-law's burial and waiting for further account of affairs in Paris, she found they failed to hold her attention. Even Robert and Fan had been in and out, leaving her unattended for longer spans of time as they saw to their responsibilities in the vineyard.

Aveline was seeing to refilling the water buckets at the creek—a task Robert could have done for her, but she'd preferred to venture the short way on her own and prove to herself, if no one else, that she wasn't completely dependent. The buckets were only half-full, and she kept to ginger movements with her burns still healing, but she raised the wooden yoke over her shoulders, balancing for the trek up the ridge.

And there he stood.

A fox.

Just as curious and clever as she'd have guessed he would appear. Bobbing his head slightly, shimmering, brilliant orange-rust fur down to the ivory tip of his tail, two black boots making a stark contrast as front paws padded back and forth.

Notorious for their reticent nature around humans, foxes usually kept a fair distance and only emerged from their hollows when shadows lingered at dawn and dusk. But this one was inquisitive and had abandoned his clandestine nature by boldly stepping out at midday. He kept his eyes keen to Aveline, watching intently, though she moved only as much as it took to breathe and maintain the balance of the load across her shoulders. And then, as quickly as he'd appeared, the animal turned and darted off with nimble speed, fleeing down the long road that cut through the heart of the wood.

Aveline lifted the load from her shoulders and eased the yoke to the ground, then secured it on a sturdy bank at the water's edge. And though she hadn't a reason other than capriciousness, she swept off in pursuit of the wary bandit's tipped tail.

The fox had been far too agile for her to rival in a long skirt and Fan's shoes that were a size too large. So she gave in, easing to an idle walk as it swept under a log and disappeared into the inner depths of the wood. She walked—no longer in pursuit of a fox but instead wandering down the castle's road.

It might have been different, had the castle not fallen. Had Philippe stayed and their marriage taken place as scheduled. As it was, Aveline had spent the better part of the fortnight during which she was to be readied for their marriage celebration battling back from injury with no clear direction as to her next steps. Save for the castle, which she hadn't seen since the night of the uprising.

The road would take her there, if she wished to know what had become of it.

The grove drew her closer. Like the fox, it too owned a kind of enchantment. Step after step she walked, with the distant call of birds overhead, the whisper of a breeze through the trees, and the occasional crack of tree limbs falling somewhere in the depths of the thicket.

And suddenly, there she was—in a clearing surrounded by moat waters on all sides. Transfixed by the sight before her, walking the road that led to its façade, moving through the shadow of the once-beautiful Château des Doux-Rêves as it emerged from the trees.

The impact of seeing black bones contrasting a blue sky sent her hand flying to her chest. Aveline stopped, the horror icing her feet in place, and rested trembling fingertips on the bodice where the brooch had once been pinned.

The stone walls still reached to their former height, but the roof no longer existed. It had lost its high pitch, the corner turret reduced to jagged edges instead of a smooth cone on top. Strips of blackened fabric blew in the breeze on the ground floor. Birds flew through invisible glass barriers, windowpanes and ceiling no longer impediments, to perch on the crystal chandelier left teetering in the foyer.

Aveline proceeded down the path, stones crunching beneath her feet, until she reached the front steps. One of the heavy wooden doors hung low on its hinges; the other was gone completely. She pushed it back with a *creak* and dipped her head under the surviving lintel to step inside.

Too many days had passed—the ruins no longer released smoke curls into the sky. But the impact of the fire still laid her heart bare. It had once been a majestic pillar in the valley. Now it was a ghost. Where the Duc et Vivay's former glory had been on display, birds roosted and rainwater left sodden. Where guests had descended from carriages and swept into a grand foyer, only a shadow of the castle's former might, with a missing ceiling and charred timber, remained.

Footprints marred the layer of soot and debris in a trail through the foyer: indication that someone had recently passed through. Looters, perhaps. Or maybe Robert had seen to a salvage operation and gathered men to reclaim any family heirlooms that might be left to them. Whatever the case, little remained but scorched remnants.

Light reflected off a surface, glinting enough to catch Aveline's eye. Drawn to it, she passed by the remains of the grand staircase. She stooped in the alcove beyond it, the light concentrated there, and dusted soot from an object left under a pile of debris.

Her heart caught at the smooth surface that reflected back.

The remains of a looking glass lay with a charred gilt frame, one of the mirrors that had lined the second story of the entry hall. They, too, had succumbed to the fire, resting in a pile beneath timber and the blackened remains of a legless settee.

Aveline wasn't prepared. Not for the sight the mirror reflected.

Evidence of the fire damage lingered in the walls around her, but also upon her. She'd expected some damage, but never of the severity she saw in the mirror.

Hers was the face of a stranger staring back.

Golden hair and eyes Aveline recognized as her own, but the skin trailing down the left side of her face was tainted—almost beyond belief. She swallowed hard, forcing herself to bear turning her cheekbone to the light. Porcelain skin was marred by waves of pink and red, in angry blotches of uneven pigmentation. She tried grazing her fingertips over the skin on the apple of her cheek, but pain seared her. She eased her touch over her jaw . . . followed the sting of burns along her neck . . . stopping at her collarbone and the exposed burns along the collar of her dress.

Her hand shook, wobbling the glass fragment with unconscious force as the weight of her altered reflection sank in. Hers was not the face of a lost princess. The people may search, but they'd never find that girl again. The future Duchess et Vivay, the one who might have been, vanished in that moment. Instead, a new and blemished reality emerged to take the former princess's place.

"My apologies, mademoiselle."

The softness of the address jolted her, and Aveline dropped the shard of glass. It shattered, splintering into tiny pieces against the marble floor.

Aveline hadn't made it past disbelief to shed any tears, thank heaven, so there would be nothing to hide before she faced him. She turned, finding Robert in the doorway. His gaze flitted down to the remnants of the mirror at her feet, then back up to her face.

"We were worried." He drew his eyebrows together as he tilted his head back toward the road behind them. "Fan found the discarded water buckets."

"I . . ." She swallowed, her tongue still numb enough that it interfered with speech. "I'm sorry. I didn't mean to cause you concern."

"Don't trouble yourself. I wondered when you'd come back here. I've been expecting it, actually. It's how I knew to check the ruins." His jawline softened and he held out a book. "I brought *Utopia*, as you requested."

"Merci." Aveline ran her hands over her skirt, battling for composure by smoothing out wrinkles from her dress. "I suppose anyone should be curious, after all this. And it looks like someone has beaten me to the task."

She hurried, even for taking prudent steps around timber and debris, until she joined him at the door. She hesitated at the threshold between the castle's scarred remains and the world outside, hovering in the doorway as she eased the book from his grip.

"Oui. The footprints. That would be us. Once we saw the people to safety, we've been watching for ongoing smoldering of the ruins and slowly assessing the damage. The castle may have sustained the most of it, but we couldn't have the fire spread to the grove, nor the vineyard beyond. The loss was great, but it could have been far worse. No loss of life, thank heaven, and the vineyard survived. So now we see what can be saved."

Aveline straightened her posture, battling not to show him the full weight of her scars—the very ones he'd seen for days on end, without giving her the slightest inkling as to their severity. Or, she knew now, what would likely be their permanence as well. "Yes. That is some consolation."

"Mademoiselle, what you saw—" Robert confronted her then, gently, halting her from fleeing the castle steps with a tentative hand to her marred wrist. He studied her, his gaze lingering upon her burns. "I should have told you. Should have given some warning before you . . ."

"It makes sense now. A brush without the hand mirror. A stool with no vanity. I understand why you and Fan sought to protect me from the truth. I accept it as a great kindness."

"A kindness." He looked at the soot-covered floor beneath his boot and kicked at a piece of scorched wood in his path. "Is that what it was?"

"Oui." Aveline nodded with a fervency that surprised even her. "It is benevolence to show me the truth. That nothing has changed. The castle is scarred, yes—but it is not dead. Not yet. This place can come to life again. I think that's why I'm here. Or why I was brought here. Maybe God's will is tethered to both. And after this, I shall be renewed in my purpose. Or perhaps I see it fully for the first time. Your family *will* come back to this land. The Duc et Vivay, your father, and Philippe, my future husband, will return to find their world much altered. And when they do, they must see that we have not surrendered to this loss. They will find that we are strong, and we have already begun to rebuild."

Aveline turned her attention to the foyer, taking a last look at the charred stairs, birds floating in and out, the gentle cascade of the breeze lifting the remains of curtains.

"I will not"—her voice wavered, cracking with emotion, her hands shaking so that she fumbled and dropped the book on the marble at their feet—"wallow in despair." She tried to stoop to pick it up but paused, somehow unable to.

For days, through pain and uncertainty, Aveline had banished tears as weakness. But standing in the broken shell of what should have been her fairy-tale world, their oppression came to call with a ferocity that this time she couldn't hope to control. Without the luxury of pride she crumpled, burying her face in scarred fists.

"I will not abandon what hope remains in this place. We will rebuild."

Though she'd expected he would discount her wave of emotion—simply retrieve the book and dismiss himself from her presence—the opposite occurred. In the next breath, strong arms enclosed her and she was gifted the gentle freedom to weep.

Aveline released her fists, and forgetting that he was not her betrothed, she melted into the front of Robert's shirt, falling into the security of being hemmed in. He remained silent, his heart beating beneath her palms, steadfast while she continued breaking apart. Shattering like the fractured mirror she'd dropped against the marble floor.

They stayed there long moments. The length of time she needed to feel safe again.

"You'll see," she breathed out, whispering against his chest. "She will rise again—we'll bring her back from the ashes."

Robert's chin came down to rest on the top of her head, bobbing slightly as he agreed. "I have no doubt, Miss Aveline, that you will."

FOURTEEN

"A *chancer* is 'a dodgy opportunist who manipulates a given situation to his or her own maximum benefit.'"

Quinn didn't stop playing his guitar, just kept up the finger-picking of a soft melody and smiled at the outcome of Ellie's colloquial research.

"I see you found the Wi-Fi password."

She held up her phone. "Do you want to verify my reservation? I can show it off now."

"We'll trust ya for it." Quinn tilted his head toward the iron-lattice patio chair across from him. "Have a seat."

Ellie wrapped her sweater around her middle and slid onto the cushion, tucking her legs under her.

Night sounds mingled: a crackling fire in a stone pit nearby. The clink of wineglasses and chattering of guests on the tasting-room terrace up above. The drum of insects singing, the melody of doves cooing the grape vines to sleep. The soft strum of the guitar, merging sweetly with the vineyard's song. The reign of peace was

166

so lulling, Ellie leaned her head back against the cushion, almost forgetting for a moment that she wasn't alone.

Quinn broke into her thoughts, bringing her back. "Go on. What else does it say then?"

"Well, the dictionary used an example of how a fortune hunter might swoop in on an unsuspecting old widow and relieve her of the burden of her family jewels. Or in the present case, convince an old winemaker to share the mystery surrounding his neighbor's fairy-tale castle. You may apply whichever example best fits the present description."

He replied with a light laugh only, surprising her again with how at ease he could seem in a stranger's presence.

Quinn had claimed little interest in the castle's history. And none at all in disturbing its ruins. But somewhere along that road, Ellie found it was his lack of interest that most piqued hers. Maybe she'd have a better chance to learn something if she gave him no choice but to open up.

"You think I'm a chancer? That I'm here to manipulate Titus— or you, in some way, as long as I get what I want in the end?"

"No. Wouldn't say that exactly," he said, attention lost in the vineyard hills.

"Then what would you say?"

Quinn stilled the guitar strings with the palm of his hand and snapped his gaze to her, the firelight contrasting light and shadow across his face. "You still have that phone?"

Ellie held it up and leaned in, ready to do business. "Right here. Just give me the castle owner's number and we'll call him right now. And you can even blame me for the lateness of the hour."

"Why don't ya look up *olagonin'* while you're pickin' through that dictionary of yours?"

"Is this a trick question?"

"Go on. Look it up. O-l-a-g-o-n-i-n," he said, and started fingerpicking the strings again. A new tune she couldn't make out, but somehow instantly liked.

Ellie typed it in, hit Search, and laughed. "You were about your moaning and complaining, hmm?"

"Somethin' like that, at least where my grandfather is concerned."

"Forgive me if I'm prying, but why are you down here when your family is up at the estate house? Is it because the two of you don't see eye to eye?"

The familiarity of his smile faded away again, leaving the aloof Irishman who'd first greeted her along the road.

"We aren't on holiday, Miss Carver. There's a strict way of doin' life here, and I'm only just figurin' that out. If someone doesn't manage things, then the wine bottles are goin' to stay empty. If the bottles are empty, we have nothin' to sell."

"Ellison is fine. Or Ellie, if you prefer. Either way, you're stuck with me for the next couple of weeks. It might go easier for us both if you can call me by my name."

"Alright. Quinn, then." He nodded.

"Fine. Quinn it is. And I wasn't questioning why you worked late. Quite the contrary. I was asking why you missed a French country *dîner* with your family. Your grandmother prepared a plate for you—coq au vin. She said it was your favorite as a boy. I admit I had no idea what to expect until I tried it."

"And?"

A soft breeze brushed by, carrying the chill of evening with it. Ellie leaned forward on instinct, scooting the chair a bit closer to the fire.

"Well, I think simply calling it chicken stew would be one of the world's great travesties. But if I'm honest, I wondered why a stranger who can barely speak to them was seated at their table instead of their own grandson. I watched your grandmother and Auntie Claire in the kitchen. They didn't use a cookbook or a recipe card. They just did what they do best. You could almost taste the years of practice love even, that went into the dish. You could see it, in how your grandmother served Titus at the table. And hear it, in how they tried to teach me even a few words in French. It was dismal on my part, but . . . still there. Even if you don't speak the same language, don't even live on the same continent—somehow, everyone understands love."

"And you think I missed it."

Ellie shook her head.

Her thoughts turned to Grandma Vi just then. What she wouldn't give for a dinner. For a dish without a recipe. For laughter and smiles. And for the making of memories instead of regular e-mails from Laine, reminding her of Alzheimer's progress in stealing their world.

All of it was wrapped up in the one thing they no longer had, and that was time.

"You haven't missed it. Not yet," she whispered, stealing a breath to turn away and blot at a rogue tear weighing her lower lashes. "But you might if you're not careful."

"France wasn't on my list, if that's what you're wonderin'. In truth, I haven't stayed put in any one place near a decade. I come back through to look in from time to time, usually on my way to the next stop. Titus never needed anyone before—the vines have always been his. But I'm here now."

"And you're staying?"

He shrugged the question off. "We're tryin' to figure things out. That's the way it's goin' to have to be for right now—complicated."

"You mean . . . you came here because of his health." She looked up the ridge, the far-off glow of the estate house windows welcoming even then. "You're worried about him."

"That's one way of puttin' it. He'd say he's old as the dirt on those hills out there. But you pick up and move when the story changes, yeah? Not altogether different from you, I'd say, flyin' off on a whim to chase after an old castle. It seems we've just found some common ground. How unlikely is that?"

Ellie shifted in her chair, just listening as he played, the level of familiarity of talking family dynamics with him shifting the air a bit more. Finally, she found it; the notes connected to a memory. She recognized the melody and eased into a soft smile, tipping her chin toward the guitar.

"I've been sitting here wondering why that song is so familiar. And then it hit me: 'Blackbird.'"

Quinn started this time, his gaze popping up to meet hers without hesitation. "You know your rock 'n' roll."

A laugh came easy. It felt good to smile at a memory of her father, instead of the usual feeling of bittersweet that accompanied the remembrance of long-ago days from her youth.

"More I know my Beatles. Not the lyrics—just the melody, thanks to my dad."

"Your dad plays?"

"He did. Always played for me."

"But not now?"

Ellie shook her head and glanced away, the look in his eyes a little too open for comfort. The fire seemed a safer place to land, so she stared back at the flames, getting lost in the crackling dance.

"No. My parents died in a small plane crash when I was eleven."

He edged up in his seat, strings silenced beneath his palm. "I'm sorry."

She shrugged, finding protection in avoiding closeness. "It was a long time ago."

"But a long time ago doesn't make it easier, does it?"

Their eyes met, somehow sharing in a bittersweet understanding exchanged over the fire. Life was real. And messy. And never as clear-cut as in the pages of fairy stories. Castle or not, there were broken people who had to live in that kind of world.

"Look, about this morning. The castle? And the owner . . ." She held up her hand, softening her defense when he reached over to return the guitar to its case. "I'm not digging. I'm trying to apologize. And I wouldn't have pushed at all if I didn't have a very, very good reason."

"Which is?"

Something kept Ellie from voicing it—at least not all.

"I need something real."

"An iron gate and fence aren't real enough, yeah?"

"I mean, I want to sit down with the owner, look him in the eyes, and ask all the questions that the ruins pose out there. There must be some way to appeal to him. I know chancers may have asked before me. To be honest, I probably came here as one of them. But there's something about this place that seems . . . almost untouched. Like you wouldn't even need fences and cameras to keep the rest of the world out. The castle may be asleep, but that doesn't mean it's dead. It still has life in it. Don't you want to find it? Let it breathe again?"

Before it's too late, she wanted to add.

"What if it's not up to me?"

"Is it?" She stared back. What if Quinn was the owner? He hadn't outright denied anything. "Up to you, I mean?"

He sighed, his gaze cutting over to get lost in the fire dance.

"Look, you say you want to see somethin' real. It's that important to ya?"

"Yeah. It is."

"Fine. You want a story, we'll give you one." He flipped the clasps on the guitar case and stood with it in hand. "Let's go."

"Where are we going now?"

"To town. The story you're huntin' is there."

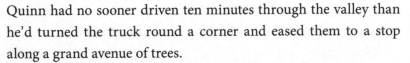

Quinn had no sooner driven ten minutes through the valley than he'd turned the truck round a corner and eased them to a stop along a grand avenue of trees.

The center of a little town greeted them with a grandiose nighttime *bonsoir.*

A gangly canopy of trees and tent tops held in the glow of stringed lights, spreading a web of glitter against the night sky. Bordering streets were blocked off and boasted long rows of wooden stalls and tents owning royal-blue, red, and candy-striped awnings. The sound of the French life was all around: folk music from a wine tent not far off, the chatter of tourists and locals alike, bartering goods and engaging in a little provincial gossip. Carnival games elicited the enchanting high-pitched laughter of girls and boys.

They stepped from the truck and a breeze swept by, carrying with it the perfumed scent of flowers and sweets to envelop the air. Ellie stood still, hanging on the truck door. What could possibly have been more enchanting than the view from where they stood?

It was impossible to keep the awe out of her voice. She didn't even try. "Where are we?"

Quinn chuckled low, as if he'd expected such a reaction.

"Loudun. And this, Miss Ellie, is your first official tour." He paused only to step around her, easing the door from her grip to close it behind her. "Welcome to the *le marché nocturne*—the night market."

"Marché nocturne . . ." She turned semicircles in place, overwhelmed with the whimsy of it all. It was at once nostalgic and new, inviting and yet foreign—this eclectic mix of sights and smells and sounds that she never could have read about in a travel book.

"Come on with ya then." He nudged her in the elbow and tipped his head to the street. "Let's go feed that hunger for explorin'."

Ellie had no idea what a night market could have to do with the story of her castle, but it didn't matter. She fell into a wonderland of French life. Stalls of sweets offered heaven—pain au chocolat, crepes filled with hazelnut and chocolate spread, and artful stacks of *macarons* in crayon box hues.

Savories were not far off, which they sampled but didn't buy, especially not after the filling estate house meal Ellie had just put back. The rich artisan flavors of local cuisine were in abundance: buckwheat galettes, *fruits de mer*—a hearty seafood stew—the intoxicating aroma of fresh bread and roasted chicken, oysters and escargot—which Quinn couldn't convince her to try—*pommes frites*—the sister to American french fries—and of course, a treasure trove of local wines.

They came to a stall with a reclaimed wood counter stretched over dark toasted barrels. Ellie recognized the red logo and unmistakable vineyard label splashed over a cream banner: *Domaine du Renard*.

"So this is you!" Ellie exclaimed, delighted to see patrons lined up, making their expert choice from among Titus's bottles of family wines.

"It is. Night markets are usually only durin' the summer holidays, but they pick up again the weeks before Christmas. The

Renard has always had a place here because this is the heart of the
Loire Valley. If you were wantin' a real story of the land, here it is.
The food. The wine. The history and the people. Everythin's right
in front of ya. The market's your best place to research—not a pile
of crumblin' rocks in the forest."

"If that's true . . ." She exhaled, her mind toying with the
prospect. "Then you're going to have to do some fine work to
convince me."

Quinn leaned into the stall, accepting a handshake from the
young man behind the counter. They exchanged a greeting in
French so fast, Ellie was proud she actually caught a few words.

"You always greet the merchant first," he whispered, offering
instruction. "In a shop or marketplace, it's done out of politeness.
But Marcel is the vintner—wine merchant for our vineyard, so
we're on a first-name basis. That makes it a mite informal, mind.
In the States you're used to a bit more levity than they'll give you
here. And I don't care how bad your accent might be, you always
say *bonjour* and never *hello*. It'd make ya the definition of a rude
American to do the other way."

"Got it." Ellie smiled, greeted the seller with an expert "Bonjour"
that even Quinn couldn't find fault with, then ran her fingertips
over the rows of shiny glass bottles. "So, if this is yours, your family's story for generations, I should probably hear about it too. Teach
me. What does Titus have?"

"What doesn't he have is the question." Quinn pointed to a crate
of bottles in a vast selection. "We've got the *vins rouges*—the reds.
Cabernet franc is a classic choice. But people come to this part of
the Loire for the steady supply of *vins blancs*—you'll recognize that
as the whites. There's a sparkling *Chenin blanc*—Saumur—made
from the best grapes. And this is a *Vouvray*. We sell out of that
label nearly every year." He cocked an eyebrow like he was sharing

a secret. "It's a little fruit and a whole lotta sweet. Big with the tourists, mind. So you might like it."

"Ah, but I'm not a tourist today, am I? I'm a local now. So keep up. What's next?"

"Then you'll be wantin' to know about the *Muscadet*—the locals' favorite. Always served ice cold."

"And the Muscadet is a white too?"

He grinned. "Muscadet is the best of everythin' here. It's my grandfather's signature. He's known all over for it."

Ellie ran a fingertip over the crisp white label. "*L'Aveline?*"

"Family name somewhere back there. That's all I know. There's somethin' of a legend here in the town—story of a lady who came to marry a prince of the Loire Valley, but she disappeared into the woods before the marriage could take place. Never heard from again."

"And that folklore is supposed to dissuade me from going into the woods, hmm? Subtle."

"Take what you like from it. But you'll see the name and hear the story all over the markets. It goes back somewhere around the time of Napoleon himself. So Titus won't hear of changin' it. Not for anythin'. Says lightnin' would strike him down if he dared try."

"Good." She laughed, somehow picturing Titus saying exactly that in French words she wouldn't need to translate. The idea fit in any language. "Not good about the lightning strike, of course, but for the name it is. Because it's perfect. I don't know how, but . . . *L'Aveline*. It just fits this place. If it's part of the history of the land— your family's land—you shouldn't consider ever changing it."

The glow of the twinkling lights and market goods lured them back to the wanderlust of the rows and they walked on, Quinn hushed unless she asked a question, and Ellie battling not to chatter on with them. They passed jewelry booths. Leather goods.

More sweets. Freshly baked breads. No produce or butchered goods though, as Quinn said those were reserved for the morning markets. The ones for the weekly shop. But there were Christmas ornaments and whatnots for the tourists, and the splash of colorful cut flowers for the locals. Carved wind chimes hung in a booth, magically stealing the breeze and turning into a woodwind melody.

It felt like hours they walked, Ellie awestruck and Quinn, hands in his jeans pockets, putting up with her every exclamation. It wasn't until the sellers began packing up their wares that he checked his watch.

"It's late."

Ellie looked around, noticing, too, that the lights were growing dim and the size of the crowds had dwindled to a crawl. "Yes. When did that happen?"

He looked down on her, offering the rarity of a genuine smile. "Somewhere between one patisserie stall and the twentieth?"

"Now pain au chocolat might be the one French phrase that I actually do know by heart. And I'm convinced it's a glorious one. If we got lost in the pastry section of this place"—she popped the last bit of a chocolate croissant in her mouth and crumpled the brown paper—"then that's a memory I will forever cherish. And I thank you for treating."

"Call it payback for scarin' you off the castle grounds today."

"Ah, but that was just today," she quipped, keen to remind him that she couldn't be bribed into forgetting. Ellie tossed the paper into a nearby wastebasket, American basketball style. "We'll see who wins tomorrow."

"Win or lose, you do realize you're walkin' away from a night market with nothin' but a bit of buttered dough in your stomach."

"Am I? I don't guess I did. Must mean I'm content with my lot in life."

Ellie had to admit, it seemed a crime to travel all the way to the Loire and walk away without a single memento of her first tour through the markets. Laine probably would have seen fit to kick some shopping sense into her. And Grandma Vi surely would have disapproved. What lady traveled to France and didn't buy anything?

"We can't have it."

"Can't have what?"

Before she could stop him, Quinn trotted over to the nearest booth. He leaned in, respectful in greeting the seller, just as he'd said one should do. He chatted with a kerchief-clad woman, her eyes bright and aged hands helpful as she showed off the goods she still had spread out upon the table.

He said something that made the woman peek over his shoulder, settling her gaze on Ellie. The woman winked back at him and with careful fingertips sailed her hands over the table until she settled on a selection. After wrapping the item in a brown paper parcel, she went to add twine and he stilled her hand. Then to Ellie's great surprise, he leaned in, whispered something, and kissed her cheek.

The entire exchange left Ellie breathless.

Curious at what he'd said, the obvious charm he could turn on to win over an old shopkeeper in ten seconds flat, and whatever it was that had sent the woman's gaze drifting in her direction . . . Ellie felt the telltale burn of a blush tinge her cheeks. It was unexpected and entirely out of character. Enough that she turned away from the glow of lights and settled her uneasy footsteps on the slow advance to the truck, the darkness hanging over the row of trees along the avenue.

Quinn trotted back to catch up with her seconds into her flight. He held out the parcel and a respectful nod as part of the package. "Here. For you."

Ellie halted her steps, stopping to look back at the woman in the stall. She'd watched them walk away and now, seeing the exchange, offered a nod back to Quinn.

"Did you know her?"

"Seems I do now." Quinn brushed it off with a shrug and a tempered smile. "Go ahead. Open it up."

Ellie obeyed, taking a deep breath and opening the parcel, brown paper crackling against the fresh folds. She swallowed hard, praying that surprise wouldn't dare show on her face. Buried in the center of the folds was a pool of fabric: ivory pin dots set against a deep wine-red.

"They call it the *L'Aveline* print—dyed right here in the Loire." Quinn unfurled the satin scarf and, without warning, slipped it around her neck. He didn't give her a chance to breathe, let alone conjure a response. He just backed off, nearly in the same heartbeat, turning away as if the exchange was commonplace for him.

"Every tourist has to go home with somethin'. So now you can't say we're all mean watchdogs, yeah?"

Ellie fumbled through a quick nod and "thank you" as he smiled, holding her door.

She climbed into the truck and waited, still not knowing what to say, the sentiment having humbled her to silence. What was worse, she very much doubted a wine-colored swath of French satin had affected him in any manner close to how it had her.

To him, Ellie was a chancer—a tourist looking after her own agenda. But there was so much more she couldn't say. Even then, as Quinn fired up the engine and lumbered the old truck away from the market lights, she couldn't bear to tell the truth. Not about Grandma Vi. Definitely not about herself.

How would she have admitted it was the first time a man other than her father had bought her a gift as if they knew the real Ellie?

Something so blasé for him had forced its way into becoming a moment of sudden tenderness—a reminder that she could take the scarf home, but she would soon have little home to return to.

The castle was forgotten again. Instead, Ellie couldn't help but wonder how hours of wandering through a street market had flown by like they were mere moments in time, and yet the silence of a short drive could ache like an eternity.

FIFTEEN

"They told me I could find you here."

Vi stepped over a pile of broken bricks, leveling her footing on a length of busted sidewalk.

She'd sought Andrew out, knowing her brother would be at the Alexandra Hotel as soon as the bombing reports came in. He stood on the sidewalk, hands buried deep in his trouser pockets, numb from staring at the bombed-out shell of his hotel.

The pungent odor of broken sewer lines and coal gas hung on the air. As did smoke. The heavy, bomb-blasted smell she could now recognize as cordite. The hotel walls jutted out in the hub of it, an eerie brick skeleton where the foyer had once greeted guests with convenience and grandeur. It was flattened, along with the spiral staircase and the central lift area, the floor having collapsed down on the basement some time ago. Rescue workers were busy cutting through the upper floors to free as many trapped as they could.

"Look at it." Andrew shook his head, glancing around as bricks were picked through. Piled. Walls teetering against gravity. Smoke rising. As men toiled and— Vi shuddered, seeing a blanket-covered stretcher being loaded in a hospital wagon. "I never thought I'd live to see the day."

"Oh, Andrew. How can this have happened?"

"They told me to wait here. To keep people calm as they come out. But I look around, ready to beg for something to do. Anything, so I don't have to stand here like a clod while our guests are carried out under sheets."

Appearing so much her older brother, Andrew turned to her, showing how life had taken the four years he had on her and run them over in lines upon his brow. The Cambridge chap she'd always known to sport a smile was washed over in seriousness then, his pinstripe oxford, white suspenders, and suit trousers blackened with soot, his face marred with that plus exhaustion. The casual laugh lines she'd always loved about him were gone—faded into worry around his eyes.

He'd gone to war. Already seen soldiers die before him. A bullet had taken its time, searing the mechanics of his arm with irreparable nerve damage, the slight shaking and loss of feeling that meant he could never again be a man in uniform. So he'd come back to London. Back to more death at home.

"You really shouldn't be here, Vi. It's not safe."

"I had to see if you were alright."

He tipped his shoulders in a defeated shrug. "I'm the hotel manager who lived. How can I be anything else but alright?"

Vi hated to see the weight of guilt come down so heavily. She went to him, braced her hands on his shoulders in a supportive half hug from behind. "It's not your fault. None of this. How could anyone know where the bombs would land? Dreadful reports are coming in from all over the city. Even Westminster Abbey has been hit. I heard that on the bus to come here. The Abbey walls still stand, but plaster and debris crashed through the roof. Imagine—in a house of God."

Vi shook her head. After nearly nine months of raids, you'd think they'd be used to it. Horribly used to the sight before them. "How is Mae?"

He nodded weakly. "She's fine. The kids, fine. We lost all the windows at the back of the house and the garden's unrecognizable now, but we're the fortunate ones. More than the poor souls here and over on Carlisle Street . . ." His voice trailed off. His gaze remained fixed on the piles of tumbled brick before them. "You?"

"Fine. No worse for wear. I spent last night in the Anderson shelter behind our building. My flat was untouched, but others sustained some damage. A couple in the neighboring building are gone completely. No serious injuries though. There's solace in that."

She straightened her shoulders on principle; the Luftwaffe wouldn't receive even the compliment of her sorrow.

"And that?" He pointed to the long scratch that stretched from the outside of her left hand and wrapped around the inside of her wrist, the one that had been stitched up after the Royal Empire Society bombing blast weeks before.

"Oh. It's nothing. All healed up now." Vi twisted her hand in the air. "See? Brilliant."

Andrew nodded like he accepted her answer, even though she knew he didn't. Not really. He'd met her at the hospital the night of the RES bombing and since had remained a typical and most protective older brother.

He stared up, the smoldering hotel ruins coughing up gray smoke as the fire wagons' water hoses doused and sizzled the fire that remained. Vi joined him, using her palm to block out the sun, staring up at the span of smoke-stained sky where the upper floors

of the hotel had been just a night before. The fire brigade continued bustling around them, with soot-darkened clothes and weary
bodies, only stopping to chug tea and ration-approved sugarless
cakes from a makeshift food table that had been set up on the street
corner.

"I know this is the worst possible outcome, Andrew. But I'm
here because of this." She tilted her head to the carnage.

He looked back at her, questions in his eyes. "I don't understand."

"I've had enough. Enough of watching our countrymen die in
front of our eyes. Enough of Hitler thinking he's beaten us."

"He will never beat us."

"That I believe is true. In fact, it's why I've come to find you this
morning. If there's anything I can do to add to the fight, I'm ready
to do it." She leaned in, dropped her voice low, and stared him flat
in the eyes. "I want the address."

"It is not the time to discuss this." He shook his head. "Go
home, Vi."

"It's never the time, is it? But I see what is happening plain as
you do. And I'm here. Now. Ready to do something about it. You
cannot deny me this."

"You're the one who's always spouted ideals of pacifism, like
Mum and Dad. You cannot speak peace and war in the same
breath. And Mae would never forgive me if I let her best friend
from university come closer to death than you already have. My
own sister. And what would I tell William and Pippa?"

"You won't tell them anything, except that their auntie Vi loves
them very much."

Andrew stooped for a crumpled bit of paper on the sidewalk—
an early summer issue of *Vogue*, the bathing beauty's legs and image
of a red beach ball singed to black in the cover's corner. He took it
in hand and stood. Rolled it.

He tapped it against his leg, ignoring her.

"I won't be shut out of this war, Andrew. Either you give me the address to the Special Operations Executive, or I'll find it on my own. But my way will simply take longer."

"You're not even supposed to know what the SOE is, let alone where it is." He rolled his eyes in her direction.

"I can guess what you're thinking. But I'm not being naive about this. Andrew, I'm experienced with languages. Proficient, some professors say. Gifted with words, another one said. I'd never thought of it like that until now. Surely that can be of some skill somewhere. A desk in the war office. Translating German transmissions that come in from behind enemy lines. Writing letters. Filing memos. I don't care what it is—I just want to do something."

"And you have no idea how dangerous that something might end up to be. My advice is to take solace in what you're doing for the people here in London, by rebuilding the library at the RES. No one would dare ask for more than that, not after what you've already been through. Your building took a direct hit, Vi. *You* took it—from a two-ton explosive bomb that landed clean on the lot of you. Haven't you been through enough?"

"What I've been through? It is nothing," she said, gritting her teeth and meaning it.

Vi clamped hold of his forearm, begging him to meet her gaze, to look back in her eyes and feel her pain.

"Do you hear me? *Nothing.* Carole will never walk again because of what happened at the RES that night. And the young man? The waiter who was burned alive in that dining hall? I shall never forget his cries. Not as long as I live. They . . . *haunt* . . . me. So please do not tell me that a cut on the hand and a nice, safe job reshelving books means I've done my duty for king and country. Don't you dare overlook what is burning right before our eyes because you're scared. This is my life, and I must be able to choose how the story is going to play out."

He wavered, his eyes searching her face. She prayed they met stone.

Vi needed him to see her resolve. And more than anything, she needed his will to ease, just enough to give her the name of the man who'd approached her at Cambridge that one sunny afternoon more than a year before.

The man in the trench coat and Bogart hat had approached her on a street corner, given her his card, and told Vi that he was an acquaintance of Andrew's. He'd asked her to telephone him, that he'd seen her work and might have a job for her in wartime service. But she'd thrown it away. The whole idea of a prolonged war had sounded quite far away and too fanciful at the time. Who'd want to talk to a woman studying at Cambridge, especially for what was in her mind? It was laughable.

Vi had brushed it off at the time, thinking only that it was a unique approach for a gent to ask a lady for a date. But now that one encounter burned in her memory.

These were not the sidewalks and classrooms of Cambridge any longer. She'd grown up in a year's time. They all had. They stood in a new place—still the streets and sidewalks of old London, but a world that was burning all around them. Andrew needed to see that she was serious. And if he looked back in her rare violet-gray eyes, she prayed he'd see a determination just as notable.

"Give me the address."

"Vi . . . If you do this, there is no turning back."

She swallowed hard, the bitter root of fear being shoved back down to her midsection. "I know that. And I pray that God will never allow me to go back to who I was before—even to those few weeks ago. I must move forward. I don't care if there's no risk, all risk, or something in between. I still desire peace and an end to this war. But sometimes, peace must be earned with the sacrifices of those willing to run into the fight, not away from it."

He sighed, stared down at the tips of his shoes.

"Please. Something in me says I have to do this."

Always, he'd give in.

Whether she'd begged him to read to her as a child . . . to go out on just one date with a gal named Mae, her friend who had a crush on him . . . or now, as the little sister who was stubborn enough to stand on a cracked sidewalk and demand he acquiesce just once more—for the most important time in their lives.

Andrew took a pencil from his pocket, scrawled something on the corner of the magazine cover. "You know Mum and Dad will have my hide if anything happens to you."

She held her breath. "I'm well aware of that."

He halved the bathing beauty with a rip and held the torn cover just out of her grasp. "And that my wife will likely have me sleep in the Anderson shelter for weeks, regardless of whether these ghastly bombings continue or not."

Vi stuffed a laugh. "I'll apologize in my first letter to Mae, I swear it. Just as soon as I'm settled."

"Sixty-Four Baker Street. Ask for a man named Garrick Moran—tell him you're one of the 'Baker Street Irregulars,' and you'll get a meeting. No promises, mind. That's the best I can do." Andrew handed her the scrap, then crushed her in a hug before she could read it. He leaned down, whispering in her ear, "Just come back to us, Vi. Do you hear me? Or I will never forgive either one of us for this."

"I will."

Tears, the real kind—the ones that meant everything was about to change and she must weather it all with newfound courage—

refused to leave them be. She clamped her eyes shut, blocking out
the view of the smoldering Alexandra, and a brother not too proud
to cry over it all.

"I promise. I'll come home."

⁂

APRIL 25, 1944
LES TROIS-MOUTIERS
LOIRE VALLEY, FRANCE

As far as underground armies were concerned, Julien's idea of resistance seemed raggle-taggle at best. He didn't appear dissuaded by
humble means though and ran Vi through a dossier of their condition in each area of the estate house, from upper-floor chambers to
the ground-floor halls.

They passed a library at the bottom of the stairs, the door
cracked enough for Vi to peek in. It was curiously void of furniture
or nearly any books on its shelves—unlike any library she'd ever
seen. It boasted the curious addition of a rather remarkable painting, a woman in full eighteenth-century dress, watching over the
room from a tucked-away alcove.

A dining room stretched out at the end of the hall, and Julien
led her in, stopping just inside. An iron chandelier towered overhead; a grand hearth and fireplace, adorned with a filigree fox crest
carved into the marble above the mantel, took up one wall; and
farmhouse tables with long benches stretched two to a side.

Vi sighed, looking around the hall, knowing it would fill to
brimming with bone-weary vineyard workers and children altered
by war, like Criquet, surviving on meager fare, when it should have

been a grand hall for celebratory feasting. It matched the rest of the rooms she'd seen in the estate house—the stark contrast of one-time elegance and humbling barrenness existing in the same space.

"As you can see, we've evolved into a makeshift *l'auberge*."

Devoid of many furnishings, the open spaces and high ceiling carried Julien's voice against the walls with a noticeable echo.

"We'd call those inns back home. Or public houses. But I believe they were commonly inhabited by highwaymen at one time, and not usually women and children."

"Back home in Vercors?" He smiled, testing the effect of an affable nature and the hint of a smile against somber surroundings.

Vi ignored his cheek. "It's a relief to be past that cover story. But for now, that's all I'll give you."

"Well, I wouldn't discount the people here. Marie keeps things orderly in the kitchen. And we manage to keep everyone fed, which is a minor miracle these days."

"If that is true, then I applaud you. But, Julien, I look in rooms like this and I have to wonder what you expect of me. You've shown me some of what you have here. A roof over your heads and rela-tive safety, as long as you keep employing the people who supply wine to your enemies. And while I haven't seen the food larders, I'd assume you boast some semblance of provision because you have a dining space laid out, which is remarkable considering the state of much in France. That's what I do see, that everything has a pur-pose here. But what I don't see is mine."

"We'll get to that. I've something in mind for you while you're with us." He tilted his head and kept on down the hall, the sound of his shoe sliding every other step. "This way."

Julien owned an assured nature, so much that Vi had almost forgotten about the limp until that very moment. She could guess it provided the reason for his absence from the frontlines but was curious that he didn't speak of it. And he didn't seem impeded from running the entire enterprise. On the contrary, he was both worker and master, capable more than any two men might have been together.

It set her to wonder for the first time, though, where the rest of the men were.

Julien stopped, pointing toward a brick arch and open room splayed with sunlight at the end.

"The kitchen is in the back, down that hall. We'll go through in a moment. But first—the mudroom and a connected water closet." He eased into the bath and flipped a switch on the wall to illuminate the space. "Don't get too excited. It's communal. But we're grateful for running water as long as we have it, even if it is ice cold."

He pointed to the corner of the room. The light shone upon a window, blackout shade pulled and barred from the inside, and a row of three heavy dead bolts spaced down the length of the portal.

"And in the mudroom—a back door to the outside and a hall leading to the cellar. Both watched around the clock."

"By whom?"

"We all take a shift."

"Does that include the rest of the men?"

He sighed, a measure of cynicism weighting the exhale on a slight laugh. "You're looking at most of that list, I'm afraid, if you're counting men in the house who are over fifteen and under sixty."

Julien flipped the light off again and began walking on toward the kitchen. "If we had any others left, they'd last about five minutes here. As it is, even I'm accosted when a new unit comes through Loudun. The Boches see me in the vineyards and think I should be conscripted into one of their factories or sentenced to a starvation death in a Nazi POW camp for being French, able-bodied, and male. I have to show my work papers and explain each time. It's tiring." He patted his leg. "Good thing this talks for me. Never thought the leg would be a savior until now."

"Because it keeps you from fighting?" Vi nearly cringed from behind him—sorry for how the words sounded the moment they'd left her lips. She'd been curious only.

Julien slowed to a stop, turning to her beneath a stone archway that opened to the kitchen. If she could judge a face at all, it appeared to pain him that he couldn't be a part of the fight. And she'd asked a question, unthinking, that chided him for it.

"I'm so sorry. I didn't mean to—"

"No. It's alright. You're allowed to ask. I simply meant the leg is a savior in that it's kept at least one of us here to watch over our family. I take it to heart that God has given me a responsibility here."

"You speak of Marie's husband, your brother, not being here to watch over your family?"

Julien nodded, his brow fixed in a deep crease, and gave a sideways glance into the kitchen. He dropped his voice to a whisper. "My older brother is gone from here, yes. Six months now. There's fear he's dead or withstanding the horrors in a Nazi POW camp. To be honest, I don't know which fate would be worse. But we owe it to him to see that his child is given a chance in this life, and to protect the people on this land. We're determined to cling to hope."

Vi, too, looked toward the kitchen, though she couldn't see in fully past the archway.

The sounds of muffled activity and the conversation of women at work melded with shadows cutting across the sun-drenched floor. Marie must have been in there, and out of respect Julien dropped his voice to save her from hearing the worst presumptions about her husband's fate.

"Then that's why . . ." No wonder Marie had been indignant at their first meeting. Vi's heart sank. "I'm sorry. I didn't know."

"How could you? If anyone could change it, we would. This place is a haven, Lady, for the widows of every man, even before they're lost. This is our resistance—a workhouse of redemption. And the castle ruins out there? It's our memorial to them. A reminder that to work, to defend the land and cling to hope, is to fight back. Even if it's through forced labor. If it's wine we make that is stolen in the end, it is still our job to endure. And we lie in wait until the moment we can rise up. It's the hope that day is coming that keeps us going."

His tribute was moving. Real and steadfast—not like anything she'd expected from a leader as young as he.

"So wine is both a luxury and a necessity."

"Yes. It is everything." Julien opened a heavy slatted-oak door to an oversized butler's pantry and spread his arm wide, inviting her in. "And it's where your job comes in."

Vi issued a sidelong glance, doubting.

"After you," he offered. "But only if you trust me, of course."

She did, somehow, feel a connection to the land and the people already—even to him. There was some kind of unflinching quality to him that stirred her to trust. And so she obeyed. He followed, clicking the door closed behind them, then crossed the room to the back and flipped a wall switch.

The hum of electric lights illuminated a passageway down a set of cellar stairs. He descended into a common larder with a single lightbulb hanging from the timber ceiling and wooden shelves lining the walls. Save for a few rows of canned goods, unmarked barrels, stacked wine bottles, and crates of root vegetables, the larder stood at near empty, painfully devoid of excess.

"Let me guess, you're putting the resident pear-stealer to work down here, to fill the shelves?"

Julien did smile then, his grin sharp. "Actually, that's one of my jobs. But while I wouldn't turn you away if you had designs on replenishing our stock, I thought we'd give you an assignment that might better fit your skills."

"And you have an understanding of my skills?"

He stepped over to a shelf in the corner and, with great effort, tugged it away from the wall.

Vi yelped at the sound, so unexpected and jarring it was to hear wood scraping against the stone floor by a shelving unit that should have stayed against the wall. But just like that, the false front swung open, revealing another round-top, sturdy oak door. He turned a key in the lock and swung it open, then stepped back, allowing her to peer into the void behind.

A dark hollow with stone floors and timber ceiling extended far back, with little to make out save for a dim light that glowed from under a door near to the complete blackness at the end. "What is this?"

He crossed his arms over his chest and tipped an eyebrow, satisfied that in whatever he had to show her, she'd most certainly have interest.

"Why don't you come back and find out? The team's been waiting for you."

SIXTEEN

APRIL 20, 1789

FAUBOURG SAINT-HONORÉ

PARIS, FRANCE

Aveline jammed her fingers against the piano keys, frustration sending her part of the duet to a screeching halt.

She could bear it no longer. Resentment for their purposeless recline in the salon was bound to occur at some point. Days of mindless tune playing and dress fittings for her sister's impending nuptials had left Aveline's spirits raw and fingers unable to find even half the notes to keep up with the music's cadence.

Another matter plagued her; the gardens were coming back to life after winter, and soon would be in full bloom. She could see them, splashes of color beginning to peek from their buds in arbors outside the salon windows. They turned to violets burning in her memory, with the image of a pauper's funeral she'd witnessed the spring prior. Soon, reams of violets would burst to life outside the windows and would torture her with remembrance once again.

"Why do we not pay taxes?" she asked, her voice echoing about the high ceilings.

Félicité had continued a lilting melody on her harp but looked up, fingers fumbling on the strings, the astonishment outlined on her face marking the question an intrusion of their music tutorial. Her fingers drew silent against the strings.

"Aveline, now is not the time," she whispered, shaking her head ever so softly. "Let us return to the gaiety of our practice."

"If not now, then when is the proper time?" Aveline shot back.

"What's this, petite fille?" Évrard drew his attention away from his book, seemingly alerted by his daughters' indiscriminate whispering.

Aveline sat up straight on the piano seat, eyeing him with a softness she hoped would read as virtuousness. Though she still sat in the most demanding pose she owned, summoning the courage to ask about what truly plagued her. "I inquire after our taxes, Papa."

"Taxes? What have you to care of such menial things?" He snorted, then slammed his book closed on a laugh.

"It is curious that we engage in profitable enterprises of goods, yet we do not pay the local *douane* tariffs on such specialty items that we produce and sell. We own property, which should also be taxed. And as wheat is produced on some of those estate lands and we sell at the Les Halles market, I am curious to know whether we are subject to the *octroi* tax levied on products entering the city for sale at the fairs and markets. It is all quite complicated, and I thought perhaps you could instruct me on our enterprises."

He leaned forward on the parlor settee, the wood creaking with his girth. "This is your Gérard's influence, Félicité?"

"Certainly not, Papa. My fiancé would never dishonor you, or bore me, by plaguing our conversation with matters of taxation or politics. I should think that the responsibility of the king and the gentlemen of the assembly, is it not?"

"Quite right." He nodded, then turned his attention back to

Aveline. "Then what is this, Aveline? Someone has stirred your concern where it should not exist?"

"No. Not exactly." She swallowed hard. "What if I died? Would you be required to pay a tax for my death, either to the church or to the benefit of the king?"

"What if you died? Here, here now . . . These are ill tidings indeed." He waved her off with a swat and a chuckle rumbling from deep within his satin vest. "You've been listening to the gentlemen at dinner. Or lingering at the door to my study again. Someone has been jesting with you, complicating matters with ruinous facts and figures to weigh on your feminine sympathies. I shall inform Gérard and the rest of the gentlemen who visit this house to temper their tongues around you from now on. I fear you, petite fille, are too examining of matters beyond your depth."

Aveline ignored the barb that she shouldn't bring her brain to dinner, nor use it afterward, save for card playing or book reading with her mother and the other ladies in the literary salon. If the truth were known, she'd been reading every newspaper proclamation she could get her hands on in recent weeks, and she wanted nothing more than a real inquisition on what it all meant.

"I've been listening to no one but the voice of my own conscience, and it begs for an answer. I would like to understand why we are not required to pay taxes. Neither does the clergy, nor any other member of the peerage living in a grand estate along the Champs-Élysées. The formal groves of the *cabinets de verdure* must require ample money to maintain, and those gardens border the privacy of our own. And what of the king's court and grand palace? Who supplies the luxury afforded him there?"

Papa started, flabbergasted out of his former amusement. "You question our king?"

"*Non.* I am merely inquiring as to who pays for the upkeep

of such finery, and therefore supplies the view we enjoy outside the windows of this very room. Does it fall upon the backs of the bourgeoisie?"

"Aveline," Félicité gasped.

Aveline ignored her sister's vexation. "Has not the king summoned a convocation of the clergy and nobility in the First and Second Estates, to meet on 5 May of this year and discuss matters of the Third Estate's taxation? And as a member of la noblesse, I assume you will be called upon to attend with the other nobility of the Second Estate. Mère said you are bound for Versailles in a matter of days. I wondered if you had an opinion on the matter, that's all."

His face hardened, turning steely in a heartbeat. "Where have you heard such a thing? Surely not in *Le Journal des Dames*?"

"I do not read fashion magazines, Papa. And the *Journal de Paris* is censured by the royal court." Aveline pulled a copy of the *Moniteur Universel* newspaper from behind her sheet music and crossed the room, presenting the printed headline to him. "There are new journals established nearly every day, it seems, to print the truth in Paris and beyond. So the people can stay apprised of events as they occur."

His eyes were sharp, looking from the printed words up to her face. "And who gave you permission to read all the newspapers of Paris and beyond?"

"No one. I didn't think it a matter of wrongdoing." It hadn't crossed her mind that any permission should be required. "Félicité and I have been tutored from a tender age, brought up to read and reason and apply logic when it is needed. You can't think that to become educated on the world we live in a misapplication of that knowledge."

"Knowledge." Évrard crumpled the paper in his fist, rose, and stalked to the fireplace. Gripping the mantel with his free hand, he sagged his head rather than look at her and stared for long moments at the wooden inlay in the floor.

Aveline looked to Félicité for support but found none. Her sister appeared thoroughly discomposed, her complexion having turned white as a sheet behind the safety of golden harp strings.

"You will not speak of this again." His words were cold. Direct and biting, as if she were some stranger in his midst instead of his very own flesh and blood. "Do you understand me? Not in public. And not even in the privacy of this salon. I will keep this blemish upon your character from your mother, as it will only serve to injure her further should these misdeeds become known. I daresay your sister will also keep your shame a secret."

"Shame? But I am political, Papa."

"You are a disgrace!" He slammed the accusation with such a shout, he fairly shook the crystal drops hanging from the chandelier.

Félicité yelped and plucked a rogue harp string in her fright. And Aveline, though so afraid she was near to shaking in her satin slippers, stood resolute in the center of the room. Waiting. Expecting she didn't know what, as she'd never in all her life heard her father raise his voice louder than a song.

"This is"—he turned and tossed the newspaper in the fire—"a barbarism. And it ends here."

"Papa, I—"

"You have a new life coming to you, Aveline." He cut her off and turned, composing himself with a ramrod-straight stance and hands that adjusted his waistcoat back into proper place. "One which you will embrace with the same fervency you attempt to sully this family's reputation."

It was one statement Aveline had been dreading.

Somehow, it struck more fear in her insides than the threat

of his physical presence ever could. For as a baron, her father had the power to make good on any threat he made—especially one in which he'd bind decisions of her very livelihood. And that discussion had been going on for some time.

Aveline was to wed. And if she understood him rightly, that arrangement must have been brokered.

"We were planning to celebrate at the evening meal, but I see that you should like to receive the joyous news now."

"What news is this?" Félicité's singsong voice wavered from across the room, her flighty nature evidenced by the ever-present activity of sweetly prying into Aveline's every affair—at least the ones that didn't drift near politics.

Évrard stared into Aveline's eyes as he said, "Why, your sister is to be married. It is assured. I've come to an arrangement with the Duc et Vivay. He wishes to add to his family's property holdings, and her dowry will see to that. So, Aveline, you will marry his eldest son this summer and be elevated in rank to near a princess of his castle in the Loire Valley. You will provide heirs for one of the most important dynasties in this country."

A girlish shriek floated from across the room, causing Aveline's heart to sink.

"A duke?" Félicité's slippers tapped across the room, and she swung her arm around Aveline's waist, dancing a circle around her at the prospect of such a glorious match. "And I thought becoming a viscountess one day was nothing short of a dream. This is magic!"

"It is, Félicité. Your sister will also need a bridal gown. And a portrait commissioned in all due haste. She will need your advice, as the elder sister and soon to be wed yourself. I daresay your mother was so enlivened with this news, she has already taken the coach to the clothier with my missive, to ensure ample funds are available for the most fashionable trousseau in all of the king's court."

Aveline swallowed hard. What had been a vague inclination was assured now. There was to be no argument. No future life in Paris, and certainly no further interest in the nation's political affairs. She imagined her parents were sending her as far away as they could manage to improve her station—removed from the city streets and the world of the people in it.

"You have been graced with the life of your dreams, Daughter. And I mean to do everything in my power to ensure you accept it." Évrard leaned in and pressed a prolonged kiss to Aveline's forehead.

She slammed her eyes shut, unwilling even to look at him.

She was to be his petite fille no more.

AUGUST 7, 1789
LES TROIS-MOUTIERS
LOIRE VALLEY, FRANCE

"What's all this?"

Fanetta had arrived at the cottage that evening with an armful of deep-jade linen. It turned out to be a round dress piped in delicate rows of ivory at the bodice and an azure scarf she'd brought to weave through Aveline's chignon.

"Trust me." She winked and set about primping for what, Aveline hadn't a clue. "It will be dark by the time we reach the vineyards. There is to be a great celebration tonight. All of the men will have their wives in attendance, and the eligible ones who are unattached shall be free to dance all night."

"But I am not unattached."

"You are if you're my cousin from Bordeaux, come to stay for a few weeks' time."

Aveline bit her bottom lip, holding in a laugh. "Your cousin, hmm?"

"Yes, cousin."

"I don't know, Fan. Robert was against this very thing. Men are still checking the road to Paris. And you said yourself that while tempers have cooled, the townspeople are still carrying the rumor that the Duc et Vivay's princess is hiding in the Loire Valley. What if someone should recognize me?"

"Who would recognize you? I was the only lady's maid in your attendance at the castle, and I won't say a word. By the time you'd made your way into the ballroom, the party guests were dancing so no one could see a thing but the backs of wigs and feathered heads. All the footmen recall is the sight of boats and torches on the water. Without powder and rouge and wearing a common dress, you look quite different. Very much yourself."

Aveline nodded. The memory was vivid for her too.

"No one will inquire. But if they should, I will tell them there was an accident at my uncle's farm and you've come here to convalesce."

"And they will believe that?"

"They will. If I say it is so, and if Master Robert agrees, no one will question it. Because no one would dare question him." Fan reached for Aveline's hands, clutching them in hers. She squeezed, gently, until Aveline lifted her eyes to her. "Shed memories of that night, if you can. Instead, determine to make new ones. I want you to dine and dance all night long. Without fear that anyone should recognize a woman of the people. My cousin shall be merry, for she deserves it. And one day, when Philippe returns, you will remember this celebration. That this became the night in which you truly belonged on this land. With these people. They will accept you as their lady even before they know you as her."

Gratitude warmed her heart.

Aveline hadn't any other friend like Fan, not even her sister, if truth be known. But there they stood, in a quaint cottage room, happy as queens for the bond of friendship.

"But what if someone should think that I—?"

"No one will think anything but that you are the most graceful and beautiful woman in attendance."

Aveline summoned a nod, forcing herself to believe she could go without notice, both for who she was and for what she looked like. Either way, the risk was palpable that she'd be in danger of being hurt.

"In attendance of what?"

Fan winked. "You'll see."

They quit the cottage, taking the long way through the grove, past flowering trees and vast arbor rows and the ridge overlooking the abundant valley below. The sun had tipped beyond the horizon, just as Fan had said it would, streaking the sky in lavish ribbons of indigo and gold.

Aveline basked in it, grateful for the wide-open skies when all she'd been used to was the covering of trees in the thicket and, before that, the soot-laden air in the streets of Paris. Here, the air was clean. The sky vast. The world . . . new. Just as her father had once said. Only this view she now welcomed instead of feared.

Torches had been struck into the ground around the perimeter of a great feast, glowing on the ridge above the vineyard.

Tables, rustic but clothed in fine ivory linen, and benches on all sides were in a semicircle around a great feast of breads and fruit, bowls of lentils, and roasted chicken with parsnips and turnips.

And, of course, pitchers and goblets for wine. A breeze blew, tickling the edges of the table linens and drifting with the aroma of abundance.

It was nothing like the grand engagement ball Aveline was to have attended.

There were no crystal flutes or grand carriages pulling up to a front gate this time. Instead, people walked up the hill. Musicians played mandolins and pocket pochettes, lilting their stringed melody in light tunes as dancing set in. Children teetered, weaving in and out of the frolic, laughing and chasing one another around the tables.

"What is this grand fête?"

Fan smiled and took a single bloom from the small bouquet of wildflowers she'd collected on the walk from the grove. She tucked it in the waves above Aveline's ear and pecked a kiss to her cheek.

"This, my dear cousin, is the *délicieux* party that should have been yours." She slipped her arm around Aveline's elbow, drawing her toward the center of the activity. "Shall we see what kind of amusement we can procure?"

It turned out to be a grand celebration—food and fellowship in abundance, the simple nature of sitting at a table under the stars, alongside the hardworking people on the Duc et Vivay's estate. And though her mother surely would have swooned at the thought of Aveline dirtying her slippers in a field of vines, clapping and smiling as the people danced off full stomachs, it mattered little.

Fan was right; this was the fête she'd have chosen over the grand affair of an engagement ball. The star-splashed sky and unencumbered joy all around became a setting far more lavish than one under the gilded ceilings of a castle.

"Bonsoir. I hear you are Fan's cousin, come to visit our humble vineyard?"

Aveline turned, finding Robert had eased in beside her. He

tipped his head in a congenial nod, hands braced at his back. He, too, was watching the combination of melody and smiles playing out before them.

"You don't mind that I defied you by leaving the cottage to attend tonight?"

"No doubt it was Fan's idea."

Aveline captured the edge of her bottom lip with her teeth and shook her head, unwilling to allow Fan to absorb the blame in full. "But I made the long walk with her."

He nodded again and tendered a semi-restrained smile in return. "Past the road to the castle, I see."

Aveline instinctively raised her hand to the sprig of petals adorning her temple. "Yes. Some of the wild plum trees are still flowering—quite late this year, she said." Aveline pulled the blossom free and twirled it in her fingertips. "But wildflowers blanketed the road along the arbor rows. I thought nothing could rival the sight of the gardens in Paris or the grounds of Versailles . . . and then she brought me here. To see all of this. Though, I must admit, I'm still not entirely certain what we're celebrating. I don't remember seeing a couple exchange vows tonight."

"Wedding celebrations are tame affairs compared to this." He smiled, watching the people dancing in the firelight. "As it is, their frolic tonight is to mark a death."

"You jest."

"Not at all. You said you're familiar with the Third Estate."

She nodded. "I am. What has that to do with this celebration?"

"We received a missive by courier just this eve. The National Constituent Assembly convened the night of 4 August in response to the growing number of revolts in Paris and around the country." Robert held up a piece of folded parchment, to which Aveline held her breath.

"And?"

"The *ancien régime* is dead. No more land tax. And goods' taxes like the *gabelle*—salt, or wine—the people won't have to take a loss to cultivate and sell them. Seigneurial rights of the nobility have been abolished, and the *dîme* tithe to the clergy is wiped out. This means that nobleman, peasant, and clergy—all inhabitants of the provinces are in equal standing before God and king. All is eliminated as of this declaration."

Aveline exhaled and wrapped an arm around her middle, shock reverberating through her. She absorbed the news, then realized what it would mean to the nobles—to him, the son of a duke, standing beside her.

"The feudal system is dead. And yet here you are, celebrating your own noble demise along with the people who used to be subservient on your land?"

"The old order is dead and the bourgeoisie will have a new future. Why wouldn't I celebrate that?"

A rush of happiness flooded her cheeks. She pressed her palms to the sides of her face, the blossom still grasped in her fingertips. "I'm sorry. I just feel what this means. The people in the cities . . . in the countryside . . . they will have the ability to sell all they want. To work for themselves. To live and die in peace, and not to be taxed into their graves. I can't help but feel hope that this decision will lead to a reversal of the course of their lives. I pray it is a lasting, peaceful change for the people of France. And one day, Philippe will return and restore this land. The people here could be treated as equals, and if we rebuild, the castle could serve as a symbol of that. Restored from ashes. Walls rebuilt from what's been broken. There is even a stone wall at the back of the castle—you know of the one that keeps the garden in separation from the outside?"

He nodded. "Yes. I know it well. It was my mother's garden."

"Maybe it could be opened up. Fashion an arch and gate right through its center? Let the children come in to explore the space as they will. Let them take flowers like this from the castle grounds. Aren't we in a position to do that, to give them something that will color their world? To make it a better place? No doubt your mother would be honored in something like that."

Robert remained silent.

She looked to him, expecting perhaps she'd lost his attention in the fervor of her explanation. He hadn't drifted to watch the dancers move through the firelight as she had. Instead, his gaze had drawn in and settled, readily taking in the contours of her profile.

Suddenly exposed, scars and all, she turned away on a weak laugh. "I suppose it's an abhorrence to find a woman's interest in politics. Perhaps I should keep to discussing gardens instead."

Robert shook his head and, through a sideways glance, kept his gaze fixed upon her. "On the contrary, mademoiselle. I told you before—nothing about you is an abhorrence. Leastways not to me." He cleared his throat, the tenderness of his reply stepping over a faint line of propriety. "As it is, I'd come to speak on another matter."

"Very well." Aveline nodded, blocking the endearing sentiment from embedding in her heart. "What is it?"

Robert's profile was solid, and his manner composed at all times. It was odd, then, to see the tiniest flicker of indecision on his brow. He looked as though he wanted to tell her something but was left considering whether to broach it or not.

"Yes?" She leaned in, meeting his gaze. "You wish to tell me something, Master Robert, in the center of all this grand merriment?"

He laughed, lightening at the tease in her voice. "Only that you may drop the pretense and call me simply Robert from now on. Please. I wish it. If you are fetching water and hanging linens at the winemaker's cottage, I cannot have you address me in any other way."

"Cultivating gardens and also restoring your castle, don't forget. I plan to begin work on those as soon as possible. But very well, Robert. I believe I can honor that request."

She curtsied, a low, courtly bow she'd practiced umpteen times for her mother's edification. Somehow, it felt far statelier under the cover of night stars than it could have in the rooms of a grand palace.

"You may call me Aveline. We hold no titles here."

"Aveline." He rewarded her with a smile—the first genuine show of emotion he'd allowed himself. And it suited him enough that she didn't feel scarred. Or royal. Or anything just then but herself. "Done."

"And that was all you wished to ask?"

"The rest will keep for tonight." Robert tucked the parchment in the pocket of his jacket, pulled his arms from the sleeves, and laid it on a nearby bench. He pushed up his shirtsleeve and held out his hand, palm to the night sky. "May I have this dance?"

Aveline dropped the blossom on the ground as they walked to the grass-covered dance floor—more color in her world.

SEVENTEEN

The hum of machinery lulled Ellie from sleep long before the sun had awoken.

She slipped out of bed, padding across the hardwood in bare feet, and parted the drapes to see the activity beneath the balcony.

Even in the smoky dawn, she could see the unmistakable outline of Titus standing before a group of workers, cane in hand and a basket and leather strap cutting across his shoulders. They'd lined up along the arbors, at the ready to fill baskets with the lifeblood of the land. Trucks had been spaced out, their headlights illuminating the haze of fog mingling down the vineyard rows.

Quinn was nowhere in sight, but it didn't take a winemaker to tell Ellie what was happening. Or to irritate her enough to want to confront a certain Irishman about it. It was harvest day—the biggest day in the wine-making life cycle—and it appeared as though she'd been the one person on the estate left out of it.

"If he thinks he's excluding me from this . . ." Ellie sprinted across the room, yanked a pair of jeans from the bureau, and hustled to dress. "Quinn Foley has another thing coming."

Within minutes she'd pinned her hair back into a braided knot at her nape and tugged riding boots over her jeans. After a quick check on her daily update e-mails from Laine—seeing that while Grandma Vi hadn't improved, at least nothing was worse—Ellie darted down the stairs and out the front doors, then slipped in among the group.

If Quinn was reluctant to allow her to nose into the inner workings of the vineyard, she would have to convince him to change his mind. He'd kept her at a distance in the few days since the outing at the night market, passing her only at breakfast, a chance meeting on the road to Loudun, and once in the kitchen for an evening meal. Claiming business, he hadn't offered another tour of anything, leaving Ellie to her own devices of research. She'd explored the nearby town of Loudun, and struggle though she might with the language, Ellie kept digging for any information she could find on the castle—or Lady Vi.

Which amounted to little more than nothing at each turn.

Ellie had stumbled upon a tucked-away café in the heart of town, with an attached patisserie and outdoor tables boasting a view of the town square. And to her delight, in a prominent location overlooking a fountain and small garden, she'd found a plaque written in French—and to cater to the many tourists who flowed through, the glorious addition of the English translation beneath it.

It referenced the castle, commemorating the stand of the people when it had been sacked in July 1789. She'd pressed her palm to the weathered bronze, feeling the raised letters beneath her skin. It answered little, save for stirring her heart to wander back to the vineyard, to somehow make it past the gate and the blocked road leading to the castle.

Maybe this was to be the first step.

Ellie squared her shoulders and slipped in line next to Titus, determined.

"Bonjour, Titus," she whispered, to let him know she was there.

"Ellie." She caught the warmth of a smile soften Titus's profile, and he nodded approval. Quietly. His stance laden with patience and pride as truck engines stirred and workers gathered in the arbor rows around them. It didn't take a broken conversation for him to know why she was there. He simply slipped the basket from his shoulders and, feeling on air, met her palms with the coolness of the leather strap.

"*Le panier.*" He lifted her hand and placed it over the basket's weaving.

"Le panier," she repeated with a nod.

Though he wouldn't see it, Ellie wanted him to know she was ready.

She slipped on the strap, adjusting it crosswise over her shoulders like it had been on him, and added, "Bien," so he would know she was good and ready to get to work.

After reaching inside the basket, he placed gloves in one of her hands, adding, "*Les gants,*" and shears, "*Les cisailles,*" in the other. She whispered a soft "oui" in understanding each time, wrapping the tools in her grip.

There would have been more to ask—which grapes to select, how to cut and handle them, and what to do with the harvest once her basket was full—but she hadn't the words to say. Not in French, anyway. Ellie figured she'd just watch. Mimic. And learn.

Titus moved off, a sated smile still evident upon his lips. His cane hovered over the field grass, searching for obstacles as he walked toward the sound of trucks and people, and supplies to replenish the ones he'd given to her.

His was the role that, despite blindness, had him once again standing before his army—the people who would take passion for the vines and turn it into something real. He appeared thoroughly enlivened by it, and to be honest, Ellie couldn't blame him. She, too, was taken by the bustling sounds, the crisp edge to the morning air, and the swell of anticipation sweeping in with the impending harvest.

It was exhilarating to feel included, to know they'd be outside when the sun began to spread its first golden-orange fingers over the horizon. To hear the rumble of ice machines and trucks, ready to receive the mass of grapes and keep them cool in their beds.

"What's all this?"

Ellie turned. Quinn had picked her out of the line and taken up the space Titus had vacated. She shrugged, keeping her attention focused on the prep of workers around them, as if the activity was normal and she quite prepared to move along with it.

"I'm here to help."

"To help, are ya?" He tipped an eyebrow and crossed his arms over his chest. "Have you any idea how hard this work is?"

"Trying to scare me off?"

"No. Not a wit. Just bein' truthful. You'll stoop for long minutes at a time. Bendin' and reachin'. Carry loads of grapes for hours without rest. And you're late, so you missed out on breakfast completely. You mean to work with the rest, all without a stitch of food in your stomach?"

Ellie wrung out her arms, willing her muscles to awaken. If her pride was to be saved, they'd have to sustain her through the day, and be quick about it.

"I stopped by the kitchen. Already had a pain au chocolat while walking down here. And I thank you for your concern, Quinn, but I'll be fine. In fact, I've already paid you, and this is the tour I want today. A tour of your vineyard. As my guide, do you honestly mean to deny a willing—and paying—volunteer? If you can give me one good reason, I'll go straight back upstairs."

Quinn accepted the challenge with a curt nod. "Spiders."

Ellie had to cover a sharp intake of breath. Even felt the vapor of a chill spread down her arms at the mere mention of the word, which she had to shrug off.

"Doesn't bother me."

"What about if they become your new best friends? Crawl up your arms when you swipe their webs, and drop down on your head when you sit on the ground to cut the low fruit. You can't be tellin' me that doesn't concern you even a little bit. *Vendangeurs* are more than pickers hired to cut grapes for wine-makin'. They contend with spiders and mosquitos, snails, lizards, and even birds tearing up the arbor rows. The scrapin' out of rotted grape heads, staining your hands and arms, ruinin' your clothes even before fruit can go in the bin. You'll freeze all mornin' and be blazin' hot by the time we call it quits at midday. And don't think that's gettin' away with anythin'. You'll still be knackered for the rest of the week after one day of the harvest."

"Whatever that means . . ." Ellie drew in a deep breath, willing courage to ignore what he was telling her and pretend spiders making liberal contact with her skin didn't pose a host of gruesome concerns in the pit of her stomach. "Tell you what. I'll trade you for it—an honest day's work in the vineyards for one glance at the castle. More than six hours of spider-infused hard labor for thirty seconds of face time with a pile of old stones. And you'll never find a better offer in your life."

She thrust her hand out, ready to shake on it. Quinn ignored it, leaving her palm hanging on air.

"You know it's not my decision to make, Ellie."

"How do I? I'm still not certain who the owner is. Could be you.

Or Titus over there? Why don't I just get out my translator app and ask him? Either way, at least I'll be making some progress, which is more than I can say for the last few days."

There. She'd said it. It's what she'd been thinking all along. He'd been ardent in avoiding her, and she hadn't a clue as to why.

"I can't go tourin' until the work's done, Ellie."

"Good. Me neither."

It had been a whim to tuck the scarf Quinn had gifted her into her pocket, and glad she was of it now. It gave her just the right amount of moxie to stand defiant before him. She dropped her tools back in the basket, then pulled out the scarf and covered her hair with a wide band across the top, tying it over the knot of hair at her nape.

"If you and your grandfather can do it, then so can I." Ellie slipped her hands in each glove and fused them to her hips, every inch of her petite frame standing up to his much taller inquisition. "Just point me in the right direction and I'll get to work."

Quinn said nothing else right away, instead just looked at her like he was mulling something over.

Good. He sees I'm serious.

It didn't surprise her. It had been much the same since she'd arrived: Quinn gave an ultimatum, she defied it, he gave in. Ellie was just as certain she'd won when he started to walk away. But he stopped at his truck bed, pulled something from the back, and waltzed back in her direction, a slow smile building on his face.

"If that's what ya want, Miss Ellie, then we'll work you right into the ground." Quinn placed a folded brown-paper parcel in one of her hands and offered a thermos to the other. "Here ya go. Another one of your pain au chocolat and some extra coffee. After six hours of what this vineyard has in store for ya, you're goin' to need it. And by then you'll be whistlin' a different tune."

By the end of the harvest day, Ellie wasn't whistling anything.

Aching shoulders, a screaming back, and a touch of sunburned skin, however, made enough noise to draw more attention than she wanted. Ellie stood at the end of the arbor rows, taking mental snapshots of the scene as she pulled the work gloves from her hands.

It was exhilarating in a way, to feel exhausted but happy and satisfied in the work they'd accomplished. It was a surprise to learn that just like dining around a feast table, she didn't need to speak the language to be a part of what was happening there. The people, Titus and Quinn included, took pride in laboring together. Cutting and carrying to one end. Carefully loading and letting the full-to-brimming trucks lumber off to the winery, to start the hopeful process of producing the year's wines.

She'd even caught Quinn's glance a time or two, glad to show him that she'd filled her basket and gone for another. He'd tipped his head in a congenial nod, smiling in agreement that she'd won another battle in his eyes.

Funny how Ellie could spend years moving from college straight into lackluster office jobs and never feel the same as she did after a single day spent in the sun. It made her long for something real, to feel new roots grow—maybe in a reimagined place. A place that had passion in the soil. Like the vineyard. Or the castle. It made her more determined than ever to carve out a life for herself, and for what past story might enliven the time Grandma Vi had left.

The sound of shoes crunching the dried field grass caused her to turn. And surprisingly, she found the man of the hour himself.

His unquenchable thirst for the land she, too, was beginning to understand.

"Bonjour, Titus."

He'd run his hand along the row of vines, using his palm to see the path to her. She reached out, offering her arm when he came to the end.

"So you have spent an entire day with my vines." He stepped out with her, taking a chance with careful steps. "What did they tell you?"

The jolt of words—*his* words, spoken in perfect English— stunned Ellie to gaping.

"Don't be so surprised." He patted her arm, her silence alerting him to it. "I never said I could not speak English. I merely prefer *Français.*"

"Does Quinn know?"

"Of course. But he knows I prefer it too. And between us, he could use some work on his accent. But do not tell him I told you that, or he'll take away my newspapers."

She bit her bottom lip on a laugh. "It'll be our secret."

They stood, their backs basking in the sunlight, but their faces turned to the cool afternoon shadows of the grove.

"So, what did the land say to you today?"

It was a lovely thought; spoken like a true wine master. Ellie drew in a deep breath, absorbing the majesty of the view around them. "That it's rich. Full of life. And boasts a harvest that just seems otherworldly somehow." Ellie noticed the electric fencing cutting a clear path along its border and sighed. "And then, despite how beautiful everything is, I remember that I'm no closer to finding what I've been looking for than the day I stepped off a plane."

"And what is it you came to find?"

She swallowed hard.

Was this the moment? Perhaps Titus was the owner. Or it seemed he may be counted on as an ally. He'd asked and now waited patiently as she chased her thoughts in circles, looking for an answer that would suit them both.

"Truth."

"Hmm." He paused, with the clear evidence of compassion etched on his face. "But if the truth you find isn't the one you were seeking? What then?"

Ellie had to admit—she hadn't considered that.

Whatever secrets her grandmother had been keeping about the castle, they might change everything. They could alter the way she viewed the woman who had raised her, and that, when her foundation was already wobbly, left her near terrified.

"I suppose I'll have to accept it, whatever it is. But that comes back to the castle. There's a story there. Waiting for me. I can feel it. I can't explain why; it's just there in the silence. And I guess the question now is, what am I willing to risk in order to find out?"

Ellie shook her head, feeling his grandfatherly wisdom enough to graze the side of her cheek against his shoulder. "Does that make any sense at all?"

"More than you know, petite fille. Many have come before you, asking to find the same thing."

"I know they have. I think that's what's scared me more than anything. Did others just give up? Or each time, did they find some truth they didn't expect, then run when it was staring them back in the face? It's like the fox in the grove. They're swift animals who run away from risk just as fast as they can. I keep wondering—is there some terrible secret the castle doesn't want known? And if I find it, will I be sorry? Maybe I'll want to run too."

His laugh was storied—deep and robust, like an aged wine. The reaction as if her question was familiar and the answer given too many times before. "No, dear Ellie. It is nothing like that. Maybe they didn't need the story like you do."

"Then why? Why is it hiding from the world?"

Titus lifted his face, his gaze moving around as if he still had sight, reliving the generations of memories that existed only in his mind. He raised a hand and pointed out in front of them.

"The woods always have the same feel. The same smells and sounds. They never go away once they're burned in our memory. I may not set eyes on the grove any longer, but it is still with me. I see the road to the castle in my dreams . . . blossoms, rain showers in the spring . . . the vines alive in summer . . . fallen leaves and harvest in autumn . . . snow piled from heavenly storehouses every winter. It is the constancy of God, in His time and in the very heartbeat of the land, by which our stories will live on. That is where roots grow deepest. Do you understand?"

"I think so. I'm beginning to, anyway. But I still wonder what Fox Grove looks like from the inside. But you know. You've walked that road."

"Yes." He paused, as if something had moved him to remembrance. "Many times."

She held her breath. "And the castle?"

"Of course. Since I was a boy, and all of my life until I lost the use of my eyes. I still see the stones. The castle sleeps in my memory too."

Ellie turned to him, knowing he couldn't possibly see the longing she knew covered her face. But she was prepared to try, easing her heart out into the open, praying he'd hear it in her voice. Enough that it would touch a place in his heart.

"Titus—tell me, please. The truth. Are you the castle's owner?"

He sighed, an audible show of regret. "I am sorry to disappoint you, but *non.*"

"But you know who the owner is?"

"I do."

"Then can you tell me? Or at least appeal to him on my behalf? I haven't told Quinn the reason why, but I think my grandmother may have visited here once, enough that it changed her entire life. It would have been in 1944, and though I can't show you what I'm talking about, I have a photograph of her. And I need to know if it was taken here. She's not well, and . . . can't tell me any longer. The only way I'll unlock that part of her story—of *our* story together—is to see it from the inside. And I know the answers I'm looking for are at the castle ruins."

Lines deepened around his eyes, weighted by his smile. "I thought it may be something like that."

Ellie squeezed her hand upon his arm. "So you'll help me? You'll appeal to the owner on my behalf?"

He shook his head, sinking her heart. "I cannot do that. But I will still help you."

"How?"

He winked, his eyes focused as if scanning the depths of the woods in front of them. "I know how to get you inside."

EIGHTEEN

Like "resistance," "team" must have been a loose-fitting term for Julien.

By the time he'd closed the false front of the shelving unit and locked the door behind them, he proceeded down the hall at a more agile pace than she'd seen him lead before. Vi followed, needing quick steps to keep up. The sound of voices—conversation, maybe even a radio?—carried through a door toward the end. And curiously enough, she thought she heard the cooing of birds echoing somewhere in the depths of the dark hall, though that would have been more than odd. Improbable really, for the confines of an underground tunnel.

There was no knock or pronouncement; Julien just stormed through the door as brazen as could be.

A man sat before a tabletop of machinery, his back to them, nose down, nursing a cigarette and intently focusing on something he heard over a wire. Julien clapped him on the shoulder and pulled the headset back at the same time, causing the man to jump nearly out of his skin. He hopped up, dancing on his feet, trying to avoid a singe from the cigarette dropped in his lap.

Watching a man of at least fifty hopping about and cursing in French, all the while brushing ash from his trousers, made Julien come alive with laughter. So much that Vi bit her lip through the same.

"That was the last of the Dunhills." The man twisted his heel over the butt, grinding smoking tobacco against the stone floor. Ever the professional it seemed, he stooped and picked it up, scooting the remnants into an ashtray on the desk. "I'll have to go back to rolling my own. And it will be your responsibility to scrub the ash from the floor again."

Julien ignored his cheek, announcing, "*Professeur.* Do look smart. We have a visitor." He motioned for her to come in.

Vi stepped into the center of the makeshift bunker. Where above floors was provincial, the real cover was for the vineyard's rogue communications operation happening belowground.

Radio equipment . . . ticker-tape printing and maps pinned to the walls . . . shelves teeming with books and paper files . . . and rolled maps that appeared weathered and worn at the edges. They made up a treasure trove of information, all packed into the space. And to her great surprise, Vi recognized what looked identical to a German Enigma-1 coding machine sitting on a writing desk in the back of the room. And she had heard a radio. It hummed from the headset the man had discarded on the desk—a transmission continuing on without him.

The man owned a bushy gray mustache and steely hair tucked under a black Basque beret, and though his suit coat and trousers were of worn herringbone, he'd paired them with the amiable polish of a pinstripe shirt and navy bow tie.

"This is Lady, our Brit. The new team member I was telling

you about. Lady, this is Pascal—our communications specialist. He only has two rules in the bunker: a gentleman should always wear a tie, and he insists we uncivilized scamps in the Maquis resistance address him as le Professeur."

Pascal ignored the barb of Julien engaging in a mock bow, instead greeting her by tipping his hat and offering a congenial nod. "Mademoiselle."

Vi had to suppress a smile. It was fair to say she liked the professor from the start.

"He was a theology professor at the University of Paris at Sorbonne until '39. But we got lucky when Hitler moved in and he escaped west, stopping here with us. He runs operations in the bunker, seeing to our transmissions, getting information in and out."

"And you may note, mademoiselle, that this one does not wear a tie. But I hold that against him alone. You, however, may call me Pascal."

Julien rolled his eyes heavenward at the confirmation of being called a scamp, as if he'd been privy to the song and dance on more than one occasion. He let it go, back to the business of scanning the room, as if only then noticing that Pascal was manning the command station alone.

"Where is everyone?"

"Brig is tinkering with the *explosif plastique* again. I told her to take it away from the estate house. I don't trust her not to blow us all sky high until she knows what she's doing."

Julien sighed. "I'll talk to her again. And Camille?"

"Feeding her pigeons. We'll need them soon." Pascal flitted his gaze over to Vi.

"It's alright." Julien confirmed it with a steady nod. "Lady can be trusted."

"Very well." Pascal issued a nod in her direction, which she took to mean as *No hard feelings*, but he had to ask. "Elder took a team out to set up for a retrieval run."

Julien's eyes brightened, and he leaned over the desk, scanning what Pascal had scrawled on his notepad. "We've had another transmission then?"

"Just picked up on it. They said, *The Sleeping Beauty is awake*." Pascal turned to Vi. "That's the SOE code for our team—because of the castle. We listen for it, knowing that the missive is for us when the name comes through."

"Oh, right. Brilliant." Vi nodded, nonplussed but acting as if all of it came as not the slightest surprise.

She was familiar with codes from the Special Operations Executive office and transmission from the BBC broadcast *Radio Londres*. What came as a revelation was that Julien's team had tapped into the anti-German broadcasts rivaling *Radio Paris* and the Vichy government *Radiodiffusion Nationale*—both propaganda-laden broadcasts that were under strict government control. How they'd managed it in a cellar buried in the heart of wine country was no small feat. Not only had they connected to transmissions from Charles de Gaulle's France Libre government while it was still exiled in London, they were actively using the transmissions.

"Another supply drop this week." A satisfied smile built across Julien's face. "That makes two this month. We've never had them that close. Have you heard any chatter?"

"Much more than usual. Transmissions coming in a near-steady stream. That's why I didn't leave when you tripped the door. Something is definitely in the works. And the Boches have stepped up attacks on border towns suspected of harboring resistance fighters."

Vi's heart squeezed. That was exactly the kind of thing they didn't need.

"Then that's why the drops are increasing. The Brits think we may have a fight coming and want to arm as many of us as they can." He scanned the notes on the desktop. "How many drops, did they say?"

"I counted seven fox in the grove, so I called on Elder right away."

"Magnifique, Professeur. We'll need the larger team." Julien looked to her. "Elder is our general, of sorts. He stirs the men in the forest anytime we have a wire. If there's a supply drop or an offensive, he's the man in charge of the operation."

Vi issued a look of what she hoped he'd read as exasperation, for the half-truth he'd given her upstairs. "The men who you mentioned are off fighting, hmm?"

"Don't look at me like that. I didn't lie. I just neglected to say everything where any ears might overhear. In addition to Elder and le Professeur here, we have Camille, who sends missives out by carrier pigeon, if necessary, to communicate with the teams at Loudun and the surrounding countryside. And Brigette—or 'Brig'—is our ever-daring explosives specialist. She's a fourth-generation powder monkey, and though we need her, she does have the ability to stir one's insides with her cavalier ways. You'll meet them all soon. But in the meantime, while you're here . . . we thought a linguist may be of some assistance with the wires."

Vi furrowed her brow, trying to remember if she'd let that bit of knowledge slip. "Did I say I was a linguist?"

"Of course. You must have for me to know it, right?"

Julien shifted his glance from Vi back to Pascal, who paused, excitement blooming in a smile spreading wide across his face. He eased down into the wooden swivel chair at the desk, it creaking as he leaned back and folded his hands across his vest.

"What? What is it?" Julien eyed him, waiting.

"In addition to a linguist, we'll be up one more guest. I have reason to believe Victoria will be arriving with the next drop."

"Finally. Bien." Julien exhaled, his relief apparent, and nodded Vi to the door. "We'd better be off then. And, Professeur, mind you keep a keen eye on the light, would you? Next time someone trips the cellar door, it may not be a friend."

Pascal looked high to the corner of the room and a line of wires that led to a bulb. It blinked for a series of seconds, then shone bright, more than the desk lamp that illuminated a halo around his work space.

"Oui. But as I said, a transmission was coming through and I couldn't stop. Not when we've been waiting for Victoria for weeks. What would you have me do?"

Julien rolled his eyes. "And if I'd been an SS guard? I'd have stopped you from listening fast enough."

"Well, you weren't. So do be off." Pascal shoved by him, absorbed in getting back to his transmissions. He turned to Vi briefly and slipped the headset back over his head with a respectful nod. "*Bienvenue, Dame,*" was the short team welcome she received before Pascal fell back into his world of transmittals and hand-rolled cigarettes.

Julien tipped his shoulders in a shrug. "He's dedicated. I'll give him that."

"I'd say he is. But . . ." She scanned the room again, their headquarters of no mean size, but notable impact nonetheless. "I didn't expect anything like this."

"Good. We're holding our cover well, then. You weren't supposed to. No one knows, unless they're a part of the team."

"Marie?"

He nodded. No explanation required there. "She knows."

There was a little evidence that made sense, given the ongoing hostility that Marie seemed intent to share only with her. She was a part of the team, and a steadfast fighter at that.

Vi turned her gaze down to his shin. "And your leg?"

"I wish I could say that was all an act. Though I am a bit more nimble on my feet than one with a leg damaged by childhood polio should be. Looks worse than it is functional. And that makes it a savior. If they think I can't run, then I'll be able to when it's necessary."

"I see." And she did. It made sense now, the savior aspect of it all. "So what now? Because while I admit I'm impressed with the operation you have going on here, I'm still not clear on everything. Who's Victoria?"

"Come on." He tipped his head to the door. "Let's walk to the end of the tunnel so you see where the rabbit hole leads. Then it will make sense."

"And at some point, I'll understand all of this."

"You will when you meet Gertie." He winked, holding the door for her. "She's Victoria's sister—and together, they'll be the most important members of our team."

⁓

Julien pushed the dory far enough into the water for it to bob on a half float but still be stabilized on the edge of the bank. "After you." He held out a hand for her.

Vi took it and climbed in, ignoring the slight shiver that his touch sent the length of her arm. Julien let go almost as quickly, and she brushed the thought away as she settled on the plank seat, chalking it up to the sense of unease she'd feel in anyone's presence after running so long on her own.

He eased in behind her, pushing them from the bank.

"So, this Gertie. She's out here?"

He nodded, cutting the oars into the water with a steady stroke. "She's at the ruins, yes. It's her home, for now at least. And when Victoria joins us, they'll be out here together. Helping us fend off the Boches in the woods."

Vi turned to stare him down, a thought pricking at her senses. "Tell me the truth. The music? The gunshots in the grove? That wasn't our enemies in gray, was it?"

"You're very astute. I had to explain it away somehow. Most of our men are farmers. Laborers turned resistance fighters. They've never had to shoot a weapon in their lives and now we'll be asking them to go against trained soldiers with submachine guns. Target practice is typically over when the music plays. I signal back if there's any threat on the road to the castle. The deepest part of the woods is the only place the shots won't be heard from the outside, so we have to watch it all the time. And we're always concerned with enemy fire, so the caution you saw wasn't an act."

"But that's why you were at the cottage that day. Keeping an eye on the grounds. And you saw me go into the chapel."

"Saw you pick the lock and break in, you mean? I did." He smiled, a slight twinkle in his eye. "Though one day, I'll have to ask your real name, Lady. Just for kicks, because I know you're too stubborn to tell me on your own."

Vi ignored his cheek, or tried to, by scanning the evergreen depth of woods and murky water that surrounded them. "So we came in at the back of the grove."

"That's right. This is part of the moat. It carries back from the castle ruins, cutting the thicket in half." He pointed out in front of them. "See? We'll come out behind it, and the chapel will be on your left. Then the long stone wall with the arch and gate—it borders the vineyard at the back."

"And the road cuts out, making the bottom of a cross on the opposite side. It leads out to the bridge over the creek, and the high points on the ridge overlook that. The ridge holds the cottage, and the underground tunnel from the estate house leads there."

"You already know your way around. That's good. Keep that map in your head, Lady. We may need it."

Vi's breathing hitched as Julien rowed them around the bend in the water.

It had been all trees, a canopy of blossoms, leaves, and limbs, and the subtle sounds of nature along the water until . . . Looking as if it had simply dropped out of the sky, a clearing opened up and the castle slept, smack-dab in the center island of it all.

"I suppose I don't need to tell you we're here."

"No, you don't. I've seen her before." Vi breathed out, still amazed she could be awestruck by the view. "But she's still breathtaking every time."

It had only been possible to see the ruins from afar last time. But in that moment, being so close, knowing she'd walk through its walls turned into some kind of magic she couldn't explain.

Julien rowed them across the wide moat, then tied a rope round a crumbled stone mast when they'd reached the castle's side.

"Lady?" He'd climbed out, somehow without her notice, and waited on the landing, his hand extended over the water. The lip from boat to ledge was small, but Vi nodded and leaned in to him, borrowing his strength to lift up and over.

A stone gave her trouble, lodging under her oxford on the first step to the terrace. It wasn't a full stumble, but Julien caught her against him, holding tighter than she'd expected. His grip was solid, the fit of his palms natural as his fingers wrapped around both of her hands and steadied her on her feet.

He looked down on her. "Alright there?"

"Mmm-hmm." Vi swallowed hard. Looking away from those eyes. So sure he could see the awakening of something within her, and that it must have shown in a blush upon her cheeks.

He squeezed her hand, then let go on a nod.

Whatever magic beheld the place faded as Julien fell back into the business nature of their visit. He'd say, "Watch your step," or "Low ceiling," when she'd need to duck under something, leading her on, obviously not as affected as she.

The castle had remarkable bones, centuries later, stretching out all around them.

Windowsills, engraved and once lavish, had their edges dulled from years of exposure to the elements. The sky poked through the clouds overhead, mingling freely where the roof should have hemmed them in. The ghost of what it once was still lingered, and Vi could imagine how great it might have been, in etchings and arches, and the shell of grand rooms now covered over with thick ivy and moss, and a clear blue sky.

They ducked through an archway, and though it took a bit of attention to hold his hand and climb up surefootedly, Vi followed Julien through a turret to an open-air courtyard. Young trees had taken root in cracks in the floor, growing up to form a bower of green, in which birds had made their sanctuary. Tiny wings stirred as they walked through, Julien leading her to a sun-drenched tarp covering something in the center, a metal barrel cutting up high, glinting in the patches of sun.

"Julien . . . what is this?"

"You're standing in what once was the grand ballroom, and for some time after that, a library." He winked and swept the tarp off the biggest weapon she'd ever seen close up. "And this is our guest of honor. Lady, meet Gertie."

"Gertie is a machine gun?"

"A 20mm antiaircraft weapon, actually—the Tarasque Type 53 T2 to be exact. She's French, but we gave her a British name because she's going to join in the fight when the rest of the chaps get here. And if all goes well, Victoria will join us soon. She's Gertie's twin, from some neighbors in Loudun. We're waiting for her to arrive because she'll give us a critical point of defense at the cottage. That way, we can do what we need to once the call goes out, and the ridge will help us defend against any attacks down below."

Julien folded his hand across his chest, pride holding his stance firm. "There's an old Matford stowed along the road leading to the castle. She's a bit worse for wear, but she's got a strong engine and four tires that work, so she can pull Gertie here out in the open. We can have her operational in a number of minutes if we have to. The other tarp in the corner of the ballroom covers the weapons we haven't distributed yet. In addition to the plastic explosives we get for Brig, we have a cache of Stens and Welrods—both sturdy weapons with simple designs for wide use. We've also stocked enough ammunition to keep us in arms for days, if necessary. And we've stockpiled cans of paint, so we're all set."

"Paint?"

He nodded. "That's right. When le Professeur gets the call through the wire, we paint the largest *V* we can on the castle façade—for *Victory*. It's de Gaulle's sign for the resistance to rise up. Elder will see it from the woods and know it's time to call the fighting men and women to arms. That's what I meant when I said we know the Allies are coming. We just don't know when. But when they do, we'll be ready. The castle is the heart of everything we're fighting for in this place."

When Vi didn't respond right away, he leaned in, meeting her gaze. "Well, what do you think?"

"What do I think?" Vi ran her hand over the cold metal of

Gertie's side and around the rough divots of the two-wheeled cart's tire. "I think . . . you're anticipating far more of a fight than I did."

"Anything wrong with putting up a fight?"

"No. It shows real courage that you wish to fight back."

"But . . ."

"But what I still don't understand is why you'd let me stay here when so much is at risk. It breaks my heart to see what's happened to this castle. To your family. To the land and the people here. But if the fight comes, God help us, what will be left?"

"What's left when the smoke clears isn't nearly as important as what you're fighting for to start out with. Sometimes we have to choose between what is easy and . . . what we know is right. The entire war has been anchored by men fighting for the notion, and I believe in it."

Birds flew overhead, little wings carrying the hint of sound to cut the silence between them. It hushed them, the mix of nature and talk of humanity in the same breath.

Julien took a step closer to her.

He shook his head, lowering his voice to a whisper. "Lady, you can trust me. I don't know what you've been through, don't know what's happened to you—"

"I cannot tell you."

"And I'm not asking you to."

"But why put up a fight that you can't possibly win? When there's so much at risk?"

His brow darkened a shade as he looked down on her. "Who says we can't win?"

Vi blocked out the harsh reminders of death, of fighting and loss that permeated every moment of her recent memory. The whistle of bombs falling over London . . . the cries of the injured at the RES building as it burned around them . . . the cocking of a pistol and a series of shots as an SS guard fired into the skulls of the other secretaries at Château de La Roche-Guyon . . . and she got away.

Fled, while others died.

"I've seen what the Nazis can do, Julien."

"As have I."

"Then you know it will take more than Gertie to hold back what they'll bring. I worry that you're getting into something that's far over your head. The estate has children. Think of Marie. Her baby and Criquet. And everyone here. If the Nazis find Gertie, you'll be hanged. Every one of you. And if they find me . . ." She shook her head, fear penetrating the confines of her chest. "They'll do the same. All of you are at risk by having me here."

"I didn't let you stay because we need another man in the fight." He smiled down on her, his hand reaching up to tug a lock of hair that had swept over the apple of her cheek. "Is that what you think?"

"Why are you showing me all of this?"

"Because I saw your face when I walked in that chapel. I knew you needed someone to help you, and I made up my mind then that I wanted to be the man to do it. You're a part of our makeshift family here, if you want to be. We'll protect you, even if all we have is Gertie to do it."

Julien looked at her with the same eyes he had the day they'd met in the chapel. Kindness emanated from them, looking on her with an openness and bringing a calm like she'd never known before. In his eyes she saw earnest belief, courage, and selflessness, all in a single, heart-pounding look.

It made her want only to believe in him—to trust him without reservation.

"I'd die before I let anyone hurt you, or anyone else at this estate." He reached out, pressing a palm to her cheek. His thumb brushed an invisible line to her jaw. "Did you need to hear that, Lady? That we won't back down?"

"And if the worst happens? If the Nazis come before the Allies do. What then?"

"Then our mission is to blow up the bridge to Loudun and hold them off at the castle. It won't be easy, but it's right. And if it comes to that, I intend to see it through."

NINETEEN

"They called it the *Serment du Jeu de Paume*—the Tennis Court Oath. The king had to take drastic measures, locking the beasts of the Third Estate out of their Versailles meeting hall altogether." The nobleman took a snuff box from his vest pocket, then coughed along with a sniff. "They say the men had to go to tennis court, of all things, and made an oath as the National Assembly, not to disband until a new constitution is drawn up."

Aveline sifted her gloved palm along a line of hanging ribbons in Rose Bertin's Le Grand Mogol shop, pretending to find the array of peach and rose hues most fascinating. Instead, she was far more interested in the hushed conversation between a shopkeeper at the high-end clothier and a gentleman adorned in robin's-egg satin who stood by, nodding to the notion that the king would soon put a stop to the audacity of the Third Estate to take state matters into their own hands.

It was morose talk indeed at the early morning hour, and for the general fluff of their surroundings. Aveline hadn't expected to hear anything save for blather about plumes and chapeaus, so to have discovered talk of the latest events in a ladies' clothier shop was a stroke of genuine luck.

"But the king has sent out royal guards to quell insurrection before, and no doubt will do the same to prevent further infections of violence across the city. May the king string up gallows at the Élysée Palace if necessary to silence the devils who make up the discontented rabble. We should soon find the streets outside your shop peaceful again."

"Quite right. Madame Bertin is most aggrieved at the rumblings of violence, even in this most genteel part of the Rue du Faubourg Saint-Honoré."

"Then let the king eliminate all impediments to keep it such. And if necessary, lock all the doors of Versailles in the process!"

While the talk of affairs in the National Assembly was nearly inaudible, the merciless laughter of "gentlemen" was not. They made no effort to hush that from the delicate ears of women who browsed through the famed designer's boutique, flitting over ribbons and plumes made famous in Marie Antoinette's court.

Aveline closed a fist around a handful of ribbons, squeezing in a tight grip.

"Pardon, mademoiselle. Were you looking for something?"

Aveline glanced up. She'd drawn the attention of the men with her ireful response. She shook her head, placating them with a sweet smile of naivety as she released the ribbons back to free-floating from their wooden harness overhead.

"Oui, monsieur. It is said that Madame Tallien recommends a pale-blue cotton for the aprons similar to those in *The Marriage of Figaro*. I understand the Duchess of Chartres has one with two rows of ruffles. I should like to see the choices for the pattern I've selected so I may order one identical to hers."

"*C'est bon*, mademoiselle. You are the third lady to request such an adornment today. We have them right over here."

The inflated nobleman in blue satin and his inane chuckling moved on then, no doubt to reunite with a wife or daughter who was also sifting through the luxury of wares around them. The shopkeeper bowed, scurrying off to a ream of fabric samples in an array of sky colors stacked on a far wall. He returned not long after, exclaiming over the bundle of fabric in his arms.

Aveline selected a shade of blue cotton without looking and told the gentleman to which account the request should be billed. He scurried off to document the sale and would be pleased, no doubt, to come back and assist her once he learned that she had a near inexhaustible account to fund the purchase of her trousseau.

It was remarkable to think that from where she stood, the world was all pastels and plumes, while a mere carriage ride away stood the street market where she'd traded her gloves. She'd not returned since that day.

"Mademoiselle, I shall personally see to the procurement of your requested item." The shopkeeper bowed low, his simper sweet to the point of nauseating. "And may I congratulate you on your impending alliance with the family of the Duc et Vivay. I am most honored to wait on you."

"Merci," she sighed out, upholding the dictations of her mother's instruction only as much as required to slip from the shop without boxes of fluff sewn to her person.

"Will there be anything else, mademoiselle?"

Aveline scanned the shop, her gaze sailing over hats and plumes, jumbles of waxed fruit for the adornment of courtly pompadours, and a seemingly endless array of brocades and striped satin. Until . . . gloves. Scores of them lined up in tiny boxes with lavender-scented paper and courtly hues of blush, chartreuse, and bright azure. There among them, dove gray—innocent and subdued, and paining her with their very existence.

An idea struck then, one she knew her father would abhor were it made known, unless she were to proceed with the utmost care.

"Oui, monsieur. I wonder, did you happen to see the extent of my father's account at this shop?"

"I may have become aware of it, mademoiselle."

"Bien. I have been told that my mother has already ordered my gowns. But as to the rest, please do find a parchment and quill to document all that I request in earnest. I shall need whatever you currently have in stock of a number of items." She gave him a pointed look and walked over to the gloves, picking through the brightest colors of the lot. "I shall be making a very large purchase today. A very large purchase indeed."

AUGUST 9, 1789
LES TROIS-MOUTIERS
LOIRE VALLEY, FRANCE

Aveline's view from inside the fire-ravaged castle was worlds away from a clothier's shop in Rue du Faubourg Saint-Honoré.

No frivolities were left to the eye here—only the evidence of the wretchedness from weeks before. The beautiful linens and fabrics, inlaid floors, and sumptuous furnishings that had adorned the halls around her were now marred by bled dyes, water damage, and a layer of soot that painted nearly every surface in a thick, black grime.

Robert had allowed Aveline and Fan to accompany the men

who were to finish clearing the castle. She'd been pleased to fall into the ranks of those able to go, that is, until she beheld more than just the remnants of the felled entryway. Questions of stability around the façade would have to come later. But this time, the task was to sort through the remaining rooms at the back wing—those that were heavily damaged by water and smoke—to see what, if anything, remained to salvage.

The men lined up in boats along the stone landing, ready to transport any remaining wares that might be saved. The ones that couldn't would be piled in a great heap by the road. The ones that could would be stored at a neighboring estate until such time as they could be used again.

Aveline's shoes echoed as she walked the grand hall in the back wing, facing the moat. She gazed out to the terrace, moving along by a row of open-air frames. No glass remained; they were likely broken in order that the castle might air out. Sunlight fractured a curious pattern of light at her feet, cut by the moving shadows of men in their boats along the castle's back side. Curtains still hung on gilt rods at one end, with colors bled down to the tips as if water-color paints had been left out to dry upon them. Settees that had once lined the walls. Sideboards and mirrors too; she remembered those from the night of the party. They'd all been cast out—likely already taken over by the pungent enemy of mold. Silver candelabras were piled in a heap against the wall, blackened from soot but still alive. They could be reused, and perhaps play host to new flames one day.

"Here you are." Fanetta's voice rose in the empty hall, echoing against the high ceiling. She'd nearly passed by in the service hall but stopped and whisked in when she saw Aveline.

"I can't believe these rooms survived," Aveline said, looking up to the engraved ceiling that remained. So meticulous in design and exquisite in its rendering. She hoped it could be saved under the layers of smoke and soot. "They're a ghost of what was here only a few weeks ago. It's as if everything was plunged underwater and time simply . . . stopped turning."

Fan brought a hand up to cover her nose. "You can smell the fetid water, that's for sure."

Aveline smiled. "Oui, decay does have a certain aroma. We'll have to do something about that if these rooms can be used at all."

"This one I'd love to abandon with all haste, if you please." She swept in, hooking her arm around Aveline's elbow to pull her from the hall. "The men have already cleared this hall. But come with me. We found some things in the portrait room Robert thinks still might be saved."

Realization fell like a shadow.

The portrait room . . .

Aveline had forgotten until that very moment.

With a tight squeeze to Fan's arm, she eased back into the shadows of the hall. "I can't go in there. Not now."

"Why ever not? Master Robert says it's safe. There's no structural damage to this part of the castle, and all the rooms have been aired."

Aveline shook her head like mad, a sense of panic rising from her midsection. "You don't understand. I'm in there. My face is on the wall—a portrait that my parents commissioned in Paris. It was to be a wedding present for Philippe. If anyone sees it, they'll know who I am."

Aveline swallowed hard, willing fear to be held at bay. She steadied her stance, staring back at the growing worry upon Fan's face. "If what you say is true, that the people are looking for the betrothed of the son of the Duc et Vivay's, even with the scars, it would be possible to compare the likeness."

Fan's eyes widened. "You're certain of this."

"I am. I was told upon my arrival that it would be done, though I hadn't the chance to see it. I'd made plans to stop by the portrait room before the ball began, but I received my sister's letter and then everything happened so fast."

"Then I wonder . . ." She looked to Aveline, clearing her throat as she searched for words. "Where was it to hang? Do you know?"

"Over the mantel. They'd moved the former duchess's portrait to accommodate mine, or so my mother relayed."

Aveline shuddered, thinking the honor of its placement shouldn't have belonged to her. She'd done nothing to earn it. And now, if the castle were rebuilt, Aveline feared seeing her likeness hang anywhere, not with scars and red pigment slashing over her porcelain skin.

She pushed the thought away.

Perhaps Philippe would not want her as she was now. That would abate the fear and the problem itself in one fell swoop.

"If your face is to be hanging upon that wall, then I'm afraid someone may already know you're here."

"How can that be?"

She squeezed Aveline's hand, her brow etched in distress.

"Because, mademoiselle—your portrait is missing."

TWENTY

Butterflies danced through the patch of wildflowers that had sprung up along the road to the winery—bright buttercup-yellow blooms and sprigs of wild violets that poked up from the field grasses. A sudden crash penetrated the air, stirring the winged creatures to carry their colors away.

Ellie looked up, heading in the direction of the thatch-roofed barn on the hill. The setting sun cut past open doors, illuminating weathered wood in a small alcove of the entry. Quinn knelt before a rustic potter's table, jeans ground against dust and stone, his attention fixed on digging through a crate of old wares stowed underneath.

He'd managed to break an impressive amount of pottery, the evidence of the crash strewn about him like sharp clay land mines.

Ellie rapped her knuckles on the door frame. "Titus said you might be here. I didn't think you'd taken to outright mutiny though. This really isn't the way to get through to him."

"You've found me." He sighed. "And not quite a mutiny, yet. But 'tis still a royal mess."

"Can I help?" Ellie knelt alongside and swept up the pottery shards in her palm, discarding them in a wastebasket nearby. "What were you doing out here? It looks like this old place hasn't seen any visitors in a while."

"Doesn't usually. But Titus had me searchin' for somethin' I'll never find in this graveyard for old tools. Wants a set of shears that have been gatherin' dust out here. Says he can't keep up in the harvest without 'em. But tell me how dull blades are goin' to help cut through grape tannins?" He tossed a span of twine and rusted garden tools in a crate, then rocked back on his heels, running his hands through his dark hair in frustration. "I think he sent me on a goose chase. But the question is why."

"Well, at least you tried. He'll know that."

"Ah . . . I have my doubts. But then, I had to inherit my olagonin' from someone, yeah? Seems logical it would be a stubborn old Frenchman."

Ellie stood on a smile, brushing her hands on her jeans.

Though she hadn't noticed when she'd come in, the cast of sunlight glittering against glass drew her attention to a host of bottles, beakers, and a cast-iron scale lined up on the potter's table. She brushed her index finger along the edge of the tabletop's aged and scarred wood, looking over the setup.

"What's all this?"

"Titus's workshop. Not used as much now, with the added hurdle of his eyesight. But he still has his way. His method for determinin' when it's time to harvest and what the wine should become from it. It's why we all use baskets in the arbors instead of plastic bins, and old trucks instead of newer machinery. It took an hour of convincin' to get him to agree to ice trucks now that I'm here this season. He's just bound and determined that the wine demands the old ways."

"And you'd like to modernize things a bit?"

He tipped his shoulders in a shrug, rising next to her. "Maybe. But what do I know? Only been here a few months, and at some point I expect I'll be movin' on again. What good would it do to force changes that won't stick?"

"So you never stay anywhere long enough to let roots grow, hmm?"

"This place has enough of them without addin' another hot-headed personality to the mix. Can you imagine bringin' in the harvest each year with an Irishman and a Frenchman at the helm?" He shook his head. "That's askin' for another war if you ask me. His way's a little more art and age than it is science, though Titus would swear on a stack of Bibles it's how all wine is made. Better than that—he'd believe it."

"If you'll be moving on soon"—she rolled up the sleeves of her button-down to the elbows—"then I guess you should teach me now."

He tipped an eyebrow. "You want to learn about wine-makin', but from my grandfather's view. Have I got that right?"

"Well, you're my tour guide, aren't you? I put in a full day's work. I think that entitles me to ask. You said no to the castle again, so this time, I want a tour of Titus's mind."

Quinn laughed, a carefree chuckle that resounded from his chest. He wasn't taken with humor; subdued was more his way. But in that moment, he'd given her a glimpse of the real man behind his grandfather's shadow. If authentic, Ellie liked what she saw. It seemed the Irish drifter was willing to consider the roots of the past, that the art of Titus's storied methods could hold some measure of validity, even if he hadn't fully subscribed to them.

"Alright. Close your eyes."

Ellie took a turn with showing him skepticism.

"Humor me? Titus would say your hesitation is akin to dis-belief. His passion for the land has no method that's goin' to make a lick of sense to ya. But this is how it's done. So close 'em."

Ellie shed a playful sigh and obeyed, but not before she rolled her eyes for good measure. In the next breath the warmth of Quinn's fingertips brushed against hers. She covered a hitch in her breathing at the surprise of it, as a small glass vial eased into her palm.

He edged her fingertip over the rim, so she'd know where the glass ended.

"Smell this. But don't name it yet."

Ellie brought the bottle to her nose and drank in a breath, the obvious softness of vanilla filling her senses.

"Good." Quinn exchanged the bottle in her hand for a new one. "And this?"

Its scent was deeper. Musky, almost. Rich and somehow famil-iar, but not enough that Ellie could name it outright. He seemed to expect it and moved on.

"And the last one."

The scent was familiar, all right.

It had drifted over her the moment she'd stepped from her car in the estate house circular drive. It was soft and lyrical, mild and inviting. Familiar and oh-so-French. The floral aroma was as wist-ful and romantic as the idea of a fairy-tale castle nestled in a deep wood. It was the perfume of France: lavender, mixed with an air of something fruity on its notes.

"Right," Quinn noted, and she heard the sound of a bottle's uncorking and the *glug glug* of wine being poured into a glass.

Before she could even ask the question, he answered, "Don't open. Not yet." Ellie felt his hands find hers again, replacing the vial of lavender scent with the bell of a wineglass. "Smell first. And then sip."

Ellie tipped the glass, bringing the layers of scents to her nose, and the dark smoothness of the wine to her lips. Never had she expected that the scents could have fused into taste, becoming the richness of the land on her tongue.

"Keep 'em closed."

She heard the opening of a door—rollers squeaking and the flip of a light switch or two—but didn't look. After a moment of the odd sounds, Quinn gently instructed, "Now, open."

Ellie opened her eyes to find that the rest of the barn, and an added warehouse space behind, had been illuminated with the storied past of the Vivay family legacy lined up in neat barreled rows. Wine barrels soared behind them, stacked five high, and she couldn't count how long, taking her breath away with their uniform beauty. The air was tinged with fermented grape and berry, sweet vanilla, and the woodsy smell of the other scent she still couldn't name.

Electric lights glowed against the aged stone walls of the barn, and the metal of the newer warehouse addition behind. Stainless-steel tables and machinery contrasted with the vintage feel of the potter's table. The concrete floor—a more modern update to the vineyard—had been swept clean. A vintage radio was tucked on a corner shelf, rounded on top and missing a dial on the front. It probably hadn't been used in decades, but Ellie couldn't help but wonder if its sound hadn't once filled the rafters of this place. Had some couple, maybe Titus and his wife, danced in the center of the room?

"You've smelled the earth. Tasted the harvest. And delved into the murky spots of my grandfather's methods. So what does it tell you? As Titus would say, what did the Master craft from His land?"

"Vanilla, to start. That was easy."

"Mmm-hmm. And?"

"Lavender? But I thought it didn't grow around here."

"That's right. But he swears the wind carries the scent up from the south. It's still French, even if it's not Loire Valley. What else?"

"Fruit. A tartness. Tangy?" She tasted again. "Raspberry, maybe. Or a different variety of grape I know absolutely nothing about? One of the sweet varieties of dessert wine those American tourists buy up at le marché nocturne each year."

"*Très bien*. For a novice, I'm quite impressed."

Ellie set her glass down, drawn to the rows of barrels. She walked over, curious, peering down the remarkable length of a row. "So, the second vial. What was it?"

Quinn followed, hands in his jeans pockets. "That would be hickory. The trees are all over Fox Grove. Titus has the barrels specially toasted with it, to give an edge of flavor that can only be found here. On this land." He ran his index finger over the burned marking on the barrel. "See? We stamp the barrels here and ship all over. To wineries in the States. Throughout Europe. Even Australia and South Africa, so their wine will have a bit of authentic France in it too."

Ellie ran her hand over the stamp, as if she could feel the legacy burn beneath her fingertips.

"Titus says the land is a witness of the generations who have come before. That it stands resolute. It's the same yesterday. Today. And who knows what tomorrow will look like. He likens it to God's influence over creation. That He's immovable. Steady. Watching from a distance, yet ever involved. A bit like your lost castle, hmm?"

Something changed in the air when Ellie looked up.

The sweetness of vanilla and wine still lingered, but Quinn's words kindled something between them in a way she hadn't expected. He stood nearby, his hand on the barrel, fingertips hovering dangerously close to hers. With her eyes open this time, she stared back at the ease in his. Considering his words. And a free hand, with no vials to take up space.

While she didn't move, he did. Sliding his fingertips down the arc of the rim until the warmth of his touch seared her skin, brushing over her thumb.

Quinn's gaze drifted up to the scarf that still held ebony waves back from her face. "Why did you wear that?" He'd chosen to murmur the words.

Soft and open, they were meant in kindness, without an ounce of teasing or reproach. Quinn simply wanted to know why. And heaven help her, but Ellie couldn't bear to tell him.

With the small of her back fused to the wine barrel behind, Ellie fought the urge to fall into step with him and edge closer. But what good would it do to form an attachment that wouldn't last beyond a few weeks of the harvest? Quinn had said it himself—drifters moved on. They didn't plant roots. And they certainly didn't take interest in those who did.

Ellie had so little left to anchor her, she was holding on to life with a death grip. It was far different from how easily Quinn seemed to let go of anything that could seek to hold him. But in that breath, all that held her was his hand upon hers.

"Wasn't I supposed to wear it?" She swallowed hard. "I thought it was a gift."

He nodded, green eyes locked on hers. "To take home—yeah, it was. But you're still here."

Ellie left her hand under his and kept her feet iced in place. "I couldn't see taking it home, shutting it in a drawer, only getting it out when I wanted to remember." A light tip of the shoulders, the bearing of truth, and she whispered, "We live where we live, Quinn. And I have to live in the moment. Now is all I've got."

He cleared his head of the edge of a barrel overhead, his whisper close now and so warm she could feel it pinging off the skin of her collarbone.

"Why are you here, Ellie? The truth."

"I thought I was here to see the castle. To uncover a story."

It was so like him to shake his head. To almost read her thoughts. To determine when she was posturing and challenge her in the face of it.

"I didn't ask about the castle. I want to know why you're standin'"—he pointed at the tips of her boots as his shoe nudged them—"right here. Why did you come lookin' for me?"

"It was something Titus said in the arbors. He wanted to help. To open the castle again. And he said that if I asked you something, honestly, that you'd help too. He made me promise I would."

Quinn leaned down until his forehead was close enough to graze hers.

"So ask me."

Even with the hope of the castle and the secrets it held, the fear of breaking their closeness in that instant—it shocked her that his nearness could matter more.

"What would Juliette want you to do?"

The muscle in Quinn's jaw tensed. He eased back, leaving a cold void between them, and an empty place where his hand had been.

"Quinn, I'm sorry." Ellie took a deep breath, shaken as he edged away. "Did I say something that—?"

He turned his back on her, stalking to the potter's table to clear the remains of the tasting. "Let me guess, Titus told you I'd crack if you mentioned her? That I'd finally bend the rules if I thought it's somethin' that she'd want?"

"He didn't tell me a thing, except to say it. And he said it was time . . . that it had been too long and it was somehow your choice whether to let me in or not."

Quinn brushed by her, carrying wineglasses to an industrial sink in the corner. He blasted the water from the faucet, rinsing, still facing away.

"You think I own that castle?"

Ellie shook her head. The questions were flying too swiftly, her heart beating too fast.

"I know you don't. I went to the *l'hôtel de ville*. It wasn't easy to step into the courthouse and sift through public land records written entirely in French . . . but no. Your name wasn't listed."

"And let me guess—my grandfather's was. He's been playin' us both for fools?"

"No. I don't think so. He owns the surrounding land, but the castle's island, surrounded by the moat—no. That plot is missing from the public record." Ellie swallowed hard, knowing what it could break between them if he answered what she needed to ask. "I don't understand any of this. Who is Juliette? The way you're reacting, she must be . . . Was she your wife or—"

"She was my mother." He stopped, shut off the water, stared down into the depths of the old copper sink. "Titus's youngest daughter. From his second marriage—my grandmother."

"Juliette *was* your mother?"

It made sense. Quinn's pain masked as the apathy of a free-fall attitude. But the shoulders that had turned against her weren't free. They were drooped, ever so slightly. And burdened, despite what he wanted the world to see.

"What happened to her?"

"What do you think happened, Ellie? She died. Cancer. Eight years ago in a horrific battle that I'll spare you the details of. My grandfather may own this land, but he does not own me. I choose where I live, and for how long. It's been the way of it since I was old enough to know how this world works. And openin' the castle is not my decision to make. If someone wants their privacy, whoever they are, I mean to honor it. I honor it because it's what I want too— the privacy to choose my own life."

"Quinn, I promise. If I'd known . . ."

"You wouldn't have said anythin'. I know." He turned on a sigh, arms crossed over his chest, and leaned against the sink. "And the goose chase makes sense now. Titus didn't have me come lookin' for shears. His agenda's a little more basic. He wanted me to find that."

"What?"

Quinn darted a glance to the corner of the barn, to stacks of wood lined against a tarp-covered crescent—the perfect shape of a boat.

"You said you lost your parents, so I won't pretend that you don't know how this feels. If you can tell me I'm wrong, I'll drag that thing out, and though I may regret it, I'll use it to take you in."

"Tell you you're wrong about what?"

"Ellie, I see a woman before me who thinks a story will save her. But in the end, whatever the story is, it won't be enough to make you happy. Are you willin' to risk gettin' hurt to find that out?"

Ellie's heart beat faster, flip-flopping in her chest for a second time. "I think I already have."

His nod was curt, and final. "Fine. Midnight, at the back of the arbors. Along the grove. It's our only way past the cameras." He shoved his hands in his pockets—aloof and distant—back to where they'd started. "Can you swim?"

She nodded. "Like a fish."

"Well, let's hope we don't have to test your skill." He tapped the toe of his boot against the corner of the tarp that just tipped the floor. "And do me a favor? Leave the scarf at home."

TWENTY-ONE

DECEMBER 11, 1943
LA ROCHE-GUYON
GIVERNY, FRANCE

How a British linguist with enough espionage training to fit in a thimble was expected to infiltrate one of Hitler's highest-ranking command centers, Vi hadn't a clue.

They didn't know who she was—that much she had confidence in. Had they known, she'd have received a bullet to the head the moment SS guards had escorted her out onto the Paris street, instead of being loaded into the backseat of a waiting vehicle.

Andrew's contact at Baker Street did find her skills an asset. In fact, Garrick Moran remembered her. He said Vi was just innocent but also wicked-smart enough to be useful overseas. After a brief course in how to use a microfilm camera, she'd been sent to France. It took some time to procure travel papers and get assimilated to life in occupied Paris. She'd worked in a newspaper office, keeping a keen eye on who came in and out through the *fleur* shop on the ground floor. Sunflower or lavender bouquets didn't enter and exit nearly as often as unnamed visitors.

But on that day, she'd been singled out from the other secretaries. Without explanation Vi had been escorted past the fragrance of flora in the quaint street-facing shop and loaded into an automobile that ushered her deeper into the Nazi stronghold of northern France.

Dusk had fallen into night on the drive from Paris to Giverny.

The world outside the car windows was layered in shadows—silver-gray from a recent ice storm, and the glow of a full moon peeking through the clouds. She recognized remnants of the Paris migration from 1939, lining the roads in ice-covered graveyards of metal and wood, shining like glass beasts guarding the road.

Vi battled the angst that grew with each kilometer they traveled, keeping gloved hands still in her lap. Were her driver to glance in the rearview, he'd see none of it. To him and anyone else she might meet on the road, her demeanor would read stark.

A lady never fidgeted, unless of course it was on the inside.

Her will would remain steadfast and orderly; whatever was brewing behind the Nazis' plans for her, Vi would be faultless in assisting them. She would be as French as they thought. A secretary whose forged papers said she was of German descent on her mother's side, and therefore could be trusted to translate simple missives coming in over the newswire. That's what they were to think, anyway. And that's what she'd show them—or, heaven help her, die trying.

Their car was waved through a heavily fortified gate without the slightest impediment, then slowed to a stop. A tidal wave of panic threatened Vi once she recognized the building before her, one she'd only seen in photos.

God in heaven . . .

One moment she'd been a humble secretary, an undercover agent looking for any meager scraps of intelligence she could relay back to the war department in London. But in the next breath, she'd been taken straight into the eye of the storm and deposited on the front doorstep of the Château de La Roche-Guyon—French headquarters for Field Marshal Erwin Rommel himself.

The stone-wall façade was covered in red Nazi flags—that she could see even through the darkness. They'd been strung up on either side of the front steps like banners, rolled down in a blanket of blood-red spanning roof to ground. She drew in a steadying breath at the sight and scanned the scene of black uniforms blending in with the night around them.

It was impossible to count how many SS made up the swarm of guards padding the building's front façade. The only distinction between the sea of uniforms and the night was black boots lined against latent drifts of snow and red armbands—swastikas that shone out from their left arms like floating red squares in a sea of black and white. They'd lined up against the front of the château, staunch and still, standing watch despite the cold.

An SS guard swung a rifle over his shoulder and approached, then opened the door for her.

"*Sieg Heil!*" A man of some stature, obviously a commander given the uniform, approached from behind and straightened the men to an even more rigid call to attention.

Vi stepped out of the car, praying she appeared unaffected as the commander thrust his right arm in the Nazi salute, though inside she was screaming.

It felt black and evil to have to respond with a *"Heil Hitler"* of her own, but Vi did so without hesitation, pushing away thoughts of bomb-ravaged London from torturing her in the moment.

"*Zeigen Sie mir Ihre papiere.*"

Vi unlatched her clutch, took out her travel papers, and handed them over. She held her breath and issued an emotionless stare while he inspected them.

"Fräulein Karine Laurent."

A curt nod. *"Ja."*

He studied her openly. With rough eyes, he took in the mannerisms of her response. Her insides burned with resentment when his eyes landed lower, slowly taking in her figure from under even a modest navy suit and traveling coat of thick wool.

Vi held the visceral response secret, determined to show no emotional response to his intrusion. Not fear, anger, or—may God prevent it from showing on her face—the intense loathing she felt for the man standing before her.

He kept hold of her travel papers and turned toward the château. *"Sie wollen dich innen sehen."*

They want to see me inside? Who even knows I'm here?

Vi nodded, gathered up her clutch, and ascended the row of steps behind him, careful to keep her heels from slipping on the ice. She wasn't sure how many pairs of eyes followed them inside, but she was fairly certain she could feel every single one boring into her back until the front door was closed and bolted behind them.

The commander stopped her in the entry, pointing to a spot at the bottom of a grand, winding staircase. She obeyed, waiting as he went into an adjoining room, leaving the door cracked. Another man stood before a desk. She could see him only from behind, he too dressed in the Nazi finery of a high-ranking leader.

A fire burned in the hearth, warming the room with orange-yellow flames.

She shuddered with the comparison her heart made to seeing the fire burn, as if she'd been pulled into an inner chamber of hell. The entry, too, was as she'd expected: closed off and cold, doors leading to who knew what, the staircase exacting with stone steps that led to more rooms on an upper floor.

More uncertainty.

More of the Nazi world pulling her into its clutches.

The commander returned, barking a *"diesen Weg"*—this way—as he marched up the stairs. He led her to a room at the end of a stone catwalk and opened a heavy door to a library. She stepped in and, without explanation, was shut up, a bolt locking into place on the outside.

And that, Vi would remember, was the first night fear overtook her and the last time she'd see the outdoors again for months—until the day she and three other secretaries were to be marched out to a courtyard, lined up, and shot to death.

JUNE 5, 1944
LES TROIS-MOUTIERS
LOIRE VALLEY, FRANCE

The lightbulb hadn't blinked with a pulse of electricity, so Vi had no indication anyone was in the cellar tunnel until the bunker door creaked open behind her.

With a swift move, she flipped the transmission connection back to receive and slid the headset down around her neck. Whether Julien had noticed her sleight of hand, she couldn't guess. He simply walked in, greeting her with the ready smile he always did.

"I didn't mean to startle you."

"It's alright. Just on edge, you know. I'm down here alone until Pascal returns. It's natural to jump at every sound." She glanced up to the dark bulb in the bunker's corner. "You didn't come from the cellar. I'd have noticed if the door had been tripped."

"I came from the cottage. But I'm glad you're watching for it. And as a matter of fact, I think we should keep a rifle or two down here. I should have thought of it before now, but I'll bring them back through tonight." He walked closer, leaned in to look over her shoulder as he scanned the exacting block letters of Pascal's notes and her more elegant, looping script. "Anything new this afternoon?"

"Transmissions coming in almost too fast to count. There's a lot of static mixed in, but at final number, we had almost two hundred yesterday."

"Anything for us?"

She shook her head. "Not specifically, no."

There'd been no mention of *The Sleeping Beauty* since Vi's first days at the estate, and she knew that troubled him. But lately, transmissions for their castle crew had been few and far between, peppered in with static and background noise that amounted to little more than nothing.

Julien would ask about Victoria, and each time they'd have to tell him no.

He'd crease his brow, absorbing the concern, no doubt locking worry deep inside where only he had to endure the burden of it. He'd review Pascal's notes, ask questions, and focus on every word taken down. Listening. Waiting for news that would tell them anything concrete—that it was true, and the Allies really were coming.

What Vi couldn't say was that she was troubled too.

She'd been sending transmissions out, trying in vain to reach anyone at 64 Baker Street to let them know she was alive and relay what had happened to Clémence and the other SOE operatives who'd disappeared at Giverny. So far, she'd been unsuccessful. If a connection didn't pan out soon, Vi would likely have to make the very difficult decision of whether to keep waiting or to leave and take her chances on foot once again.

Julien sighed, having read nothing of consequence, and righted to standing again.

"I came to fetch you to the castle. Le Professeur is on his way back to relieve you on the radio."

"Fetch me for what?"

Julien reached out and, with care, eased the headset from around her neck. "You can't stay buried down here all day."

Her hair was still too short to pull back in a tidy bun, so the wires stirred it, casting waves down over her eyes and cheek. Vi set about calming it behind her ear but paused when the sound of music filled the room. She turned, seeing Julien's hand upon the volume knob.

A French lady belted out a rousing rendition of "Le Chant des Partisans"—Anna Marly's popular resistance anthem.

"Honor me?"

"You want to dance." Puzzled, she glanced around. "Here?"

"Oui. I want to dance with you."

The tune was a bit too jaunty for a proper waltz, and she doubted Julien's leg could keep up with the jitterbug like the Yanks did it. And though he owned an easy smile at the moment, playful wasn't really his way. He was a leader, young and confident, and smiled often, but he hadn't broached the line of familiarity with her at all until that very moment.

She bestowed a deep curtsy, fit for the king of England himself, and Julien replied with a proper bow.

He gathered her up in his arms and they could have been guests in a grand ballroom, like the one at the castle, without a care in their war-ravaged world. Lost in turning circles around a windowless bunker, Vi could pretend he was bedecked in a white tie, and she draped in a ball gown of spilling satin, instead of always wearing her oxfords, houndstooth trousers, and an old blouse that had seen far better days.

"So what is it we're celebrating?" She paused, instantly hopeful. "Victoria?"

He shook his head. "Not yet."

"Then what?"

"Life. That we're here to live it." He spun her under his arm, then gathered her back with a smile. "And the fact that we'll feast tonight—at least on more than potatoes and leeks for a change."

"We have had another supply drop then, even if Victoria didn't come with it?"

"The team's sorting through the lot of it now." Julien dipped her, rousing an unconscious smile from her lips. "We'll be full on canned meat and peaches tonight. And some of those pears you love so much."

Somehow he'd convinced her, carrying Vi away until she was laughing and twirling along with him, delighting in the happy circumstance of their meager provision.

"Ah . . . French cuisine. Tell me there will be walnuts and contraband wine, and I'll be yours forever."

Julien led an army; dancing should have been traded in for valor long ago. Along with teasing about tomorrows. Yet he'd gathered her up in his arms anyway, and Vi found herself staring up in the eyes she'd come to know so well. The gold spoke volumes as they studied her now, layered over with a seriousness she'd not expected, as if he'd stopped to earnestly ponder the quip she'd made in cheek.

The music ended, once again fading into static.

They stood, feet slowed to a stop. Arms holding fast. The good fortune of their feast suddenly forgotten.

"But there's no time for dancing these days, is there? Not when the music stops."

"No." Vi swallowed hard. "There's no time for dancing." The whisper of tears bathing her eyes shocked even her.

They'd been banished so long ago. In the thick of bombs raining on London. Again in Giverny and at the lovely haven of the castle's hidden chapel. Vi wouldn't allow them back. She'd vowed it with resolution. But somehow, they'd overpowered her in his presence and chose that musty underground cellar to reemerge.

She closed her eyes, tried to look away, shamed that Julien might find weakness in her. Or worse, see the truth she'd been keeping from him. That she wasn't who he thought. That his arms held a lie.

He tipped up her chin until she opened her eyes again. "Why the tears?"

"I don't know. I don't cry. Not anymore. I promised myself I wouldn't because it's the only way to keep going. To pretend death isn't chasing us all. If I give myself no reason to care, then I don't cry. And if I refuse to cry, then I survive. My will keeps my heart beating."

"What if . . . you had a reason to care?" He stopped.

Backtracked.

Took a long pause to brush a lock of hair back behind her ear, like he was stalling over something.

"Julien, I do care. About all of you. I'd have died out there in the woods. Or on the road to Vercors. Or any number of other places my fate could have played out in the worst of ways. But you provided a haven here at the estate, at great risk to your own safety. You saved my life and I'll always be grateful."

"I don't want your gratitude." He searched her face, holding fast, his face downturned until he was a breath away from hers. "I want you to stay."

"I said I would, as long as I'm able."

"No, I want you to stay when this is all over. I can't think about life after the war. Not because of what's coming or what we stand to lose. But because I don't want to imagine this land without you a part of it."

"Julien . . ."

"Do I have this wrong? That your eyes tell me you want to stay?" He swept a hand around the small of her back, face drifting, mouth easing a breath away from hers. "Because if you tell me to go, I will. I won't dare look into those violet eyes and read that you want me to kiss you right now."

It felt right to say nothing. She couldn't have summoned a thought to her lips anyway, not with his taking possession of them. Not with the security of his arms crushing her, and the breach of affection she hadn't known she so desperately needed, claiming her from the ravages of war around them.

A transmission cut in, haunting the moment of a first kiss that should have been infinitely tender, with the shock of a Frenchman's words bleeding over the radio.

"*Les sanglots longs . . . Des violons . . .*"

Julien stopped, his lips pausing in their brush over hers.

"*De l'automne . . . Blessent mon cœur . . .*"

Vi's heart plummeted. She nearly crumpled in his arms, shock pulling her back when she recognized the poem as Paul Verlaine's "Chanson d'automne."

"Julien." She looked up into his eyes, a tear left free to cut a path down the side of her cheek. Wanting to go back to the whisper of a kiss. A moment of sweetness that had been so welcome, and then suddenly robbed from them.

The voice continued, "*D'une langueur . . . Monotone . . .*"

"You know what this means?"

"I think so." Her chin quivered, and her voice nearly faltered over the few syllables.

"It's a call to arms. If we hear Beethoven's Fifth, the Allied invasion will begin in twenty-four hours." He pecked his lips to hers in a casual way. As if they belonged together and had been doing so for years. "We'll stand here and wait. Together. Oui? I won't let you go."

They stood silent, his golden eyes looking down on her with forbearance, and strength, and such hope as they waited together, seconds ticking by on the clock. Vi gripped his arms, heart blasting in her chest, listening as static continued coughing from the radio speaker. And then the lilting melody of classical music reached out and pierced her heart.

The recognizable drumming of Beethoven's symphony cried out, the first series of notes corresponding to the letter *V* in Morse code: the resistance code for Victory.

"No more tears, Lady. Not today." Julien perked up with a characteristic smile. "We have twenty-four hours. Tonight we dance and feast like kings. Only God knows what tomorrow will bring."

TWENTY-TWO

Ten pairs of gloves. Six hats. Five dainty bottles of eau de parfum—
the most lavish and so-priced scent available in Rose Bertin's shop.
And reams of satin and brocade, wrapped in lavender paper and
boxed up in her carriage.

Aveline rode away from Le Grand Mogol shop in possession of
it all.

It wouldn't take nearly as long to dispose of the lot as it had to
purchase. Of that, she was certain. And in a matter of an hour's time,
she'd been relieved of the burden in trade for a chartered wagonette
and an overflowing load of wheat and salt. A second wagonette followed behind, stocked with bread, cheese, and wine. And due to her
father's standing in the Second Estate, she was not required to pay a
tax. The people would receive every ounce of its worth.

It was the one and only time Aveline could applaud a lack of
taxation.

Knowing she could be spotted on sight and remembered,
Aveline instructed Durand to pull the carriage only close enough to
watch from the shadows. The wagonettes pulled up to the market's

edge, as she'd instructed, and stopped in front of the courtyard gates of the Sorbonne. Though the clergy would have expected they'd be called upon to distribute any donated alms to the poor, the men of the cloth were not asked to intervene.

Not this time.

Aveline's heart thundered in her chest as she peeked around the carriage curtain. Children . . . men and women . . . the forgotten—they came forward.

Cautious and questioning at first. Was this a trick? They looked around, bewildered. The king's guards hadn't been summoned. And the merchants, too, were unaware of the source of the goods. Was it real? A gift from God, perhaps? The hired men, paid for their silence, offered the goods without debt. Then, smiles. The filling of torn aprons and weary arms—all to brimming. The men she'd hired distributed the wares: satin for salt, plumed hats for bread, and gloves traded in for the rich color of wine.

It was a sight Aveline would never forget. For each pair of hands that opened to receive, another reparation had been selected, paid for, and freely given.

A single violet: more color for their world.

AUGUST 9, 1789
LES TROIS-MOUTIERS
LOIRE VALLEY, FRANCE

"If the painting is not hanging in the portrait room, you should be relieved for it. Not left in fear. It means your likeness is protected."

Fan had stolen Robert away from the rest of the men the instant they'd realized the portrait was missing. Her argument held some comfort, though Aveline still felt a knot of worry that continued its relentless tightening in her midsection.

She gazed around, eyes sharp to the bustle of the workers below the front steps, as they piled a great mound of splintered wood on the road to the castle. They strong-armed bed frames, settee limbs, wingback chairs, and tea tables. All the while, Aveline wondered if each was a man privy to the knowledge of who she was.

"But if someone should learn that I'm still here . . . Anyone in possession of it may try to use it against us." Aveline turned her face to the paved stone beneath their feet. "I have acted in haste. I should have listened to you, Robert. Should have stayed at the cottage until Philippe returned. Or fled back to Paris after my mother left."

"You were not well enough to do so, mademoiselle. And I would put forth that you may not even be well enough to do so now. A cross-country journey by coach holds its own dangers."

Aveline met Robert's gaze, noting he'd seen fit to address her in a more formal manner, at least for the benefit of Fan's ears.

The maid nodded, enthusiasm agreeing with Robert's logic. "Yes. As the castle will heal over time, you will also. Look at all that's been lost. Many goods were tossed away immediately after the fire, and an equal amount today. A great number of portraits were among the items that could not be saved. Isn't that right, Master Robert?"

He paused, gaze moving from the activity back to Aveline. "It is."

"See? There you are. You're not even certain that your portrait was hung in that room. Isn't it possible the painting was still boxed up, waiting for a grand debut after the engagement ball? Most likely it, too, has been lost in the fire."

Aveline steadied her breath, wariness still there, but the arguments of those she trusted were managing to win over in some small measure.

A gentle rumble cut the sky—a sure sign rain would soon be upon them.

Robert noticed, of course, that time was wearing thin, and shouted at Gabin to ready the men around the pile. The instruction set about more activity with boats backing away to the outer circle of the moat and men readying buckets of water, tying linen strips over their mouths to protect from smoke.

Aveline's heart squeezed. "You're going to burn it?"

Suddenly, the intent felt barbaric. The wares couldn't be used, that she knew full well. But to see the family's loss on display and then to have it ravaged all over again . . .

Robert braced his hands behind his back. "Fan, I wonder if I may have a word with mademoiselle." He cleared his throat. "Alone."

"Certainly," she whispered, and dropped into a soft bow. She locked eyes with Aveline before whisking away—the tiny impression of a smile brushing over her lips.

Robert waited patiently, still, until Fan rushed down the steps to join the others on the road. It wasn't until the rest were a safe distance away that he continued.

"Aveline, you have nothing to fear. I've ensured that your portrait was put back. It was damaged, but—" He looked away from her, settling his gaze on the safer view down the castle steps. "It's still private enough that it should be for your betrothed to decide whether to keep it or commission a new portrait sitting."

She exhaled, a small measure of comfort allowing her to do so. "You didn't wish to say so in front of Fan."

"No. I didn't want to add injury to what you've already been

through, so put it back upon discovery. My apologies. I hadn't considered how any of this might pain you. But as for the fire—it's the
only spot not covered over in trees, and I can't risk setting fire to
the grove or the vineyards behind. I'm happy to take you back to
the cottage if you don't want to be here, but this must be done—
damaged portraits and all."

Aveline nodded. Though his offer was a comfort, the sentiment
was misplaced.

"I thank you for your generosity, but you misunderstand. I
don't fear the fire. In fact, I wish I were more delicate, but my father
always said I was too unyielding to be a placation at court. Perhaps
it's why I'm beginning to feel at home out here in the countryside."

"You're at home here?" Robert's eyes calmed, concern replaced
with the edge of a smile at their corners. "That's good. Philippe will
be pleased to hear it."

"Perhaps. But what pains me is that I can't bear to watch it again.
Not when your family has already lost so much. It's a blackness I
don't wish for you, or for Philippe. Who knows what will happen
now? Paris is in upheaval. And the king's rule will be challenged
more than it already has. I fear this is the first of many fires of the
past we'll be forced to watch before France can heal. Smoke . . ." She
sighed, spilling into a laugh to cover the threat of building emotion.
"More blackness. Why can't the road be bathed in color?"

"It is in the spring. Wild plum trees blossom all the way down
to the gate."

"But that's for such a short time, and it's always above us. Why
not violets? They're wild and resilient. They could flourish in a
place like this. And they keep their petals close to the ground, so
they'd add color whenever one looked down in sorrow."

"Violets stealing away sorrows?" He tipped his brow in consid-
eration, nodding along with her.

"Yes. Like Paris gardens that bloom in the spring. You should see them. Violets bring the most remarkable color to the places that have none. I think they're God's gift to a burdened world. If I could, I'd plant violets over every inch of the grove to remind those visiting the castle that there will be life and color here again—especially in those times when sorrow reigns."

The *whoosh* of wind drew Aveline's attention down below. The pile had been lit and was fast being consumed, eaten up in orange flames that licked the sky. The crackling sound she remembered. Smoke and ash tingeing the air, a sudden familiarity. She wrapped a hand around her waist, leveling her breathing against the sight.

"I saw Philippe's portrait before you had it carried out." She cast her gaze out on the fire. "What a relief that it could be saved."

"So he is faceless to you no more. Must be some measure of relief. My brother is said to have a noble brow."

"Oui. A very noble brow . . ." She thought it over, how Robert had a likeness not far off from his elder brother's. They were quite obviously family. Same lean build. Similar dark hair. An intense, brooding glare. Save for the eyes. Robert's owned the subtlety of kindness that paint could never capture. "The heritage of the Vivay family, no doubt."

"And it will be your heritage now too."

The last thing Aveline had expected was to feel the warmth of Robert's hand covering the fingertips of her damaged one. He held them gently, but not laced in an intimate way—anchoring in a show of solidarity. Of family they'd one day become. Without the necessity of words, he'd reminded Aveline that she wasn't alone. That in a new life, she would rise from the ashes. That the castle, too, would awaken again after a cleansing by fire.

"I beg you to forgive me, but—" Robert didn't look at her but paused, his voice an odd combination of strength and wavering at the same time. "I should have told you something the night of the celebration. But you were so happy. I was afraid it would break you, and I couldn't stand to be the harbinger of more pain upon you."

"Tell me what, pray?"

"The missive about the meeting of the National Assembly on 4 August arrived from your father. It was addressed to you. As the ranking member of my family here, I had to open it. I didn't know whether it held news of your family or mine—perhaps even Philippe's death. And I meant to tell you gently if that were the case."

Aveline nodded understanding. And she did understand. More than he realized. "But he mustn't be dead. Surely you would have told me."

Robert squeezed her hand and, with a cold absence that cut through her, let go. "I thank God, he is not. Both he and my father are quite well. In Paris these last weeks."

It took little to read between the lines and understand what he was trying so hard to avoid telling her.

"But the missive said I am leaving, didn't it?" She brushed a tear that threatened to drop from the tips of her lashes. "I'm to return to Paris too."

"Oui. Eventually. What with the fall of the *ancien régime*, they fear Paris will be a risk for the nobility. Philippe and your father will return to fetch us north to Lisieux, where we have a family estate. We will rendezvous with your mother there, and you and Philippe can be married. Arrangements have been made for your family and mine to go on to the port at Le Havre, in the event that a sea voyage is necessary. It is a sound plan, at least until the madness in Paris is settled."

"A plan to sail to England. Is that what you're telling me? That

I'm to leave the only home I've ever known and cross the sea to a country of our enemy?"

The tear that had hidden on her lashes so convincingly moments before now edged out and left a trail down the side of Aveline's cheek. She left it, unable to let go of the connection of where his hand had been, even to swipe it away.

"It's a remote possibility only. Just to ensure your safety."

"But you're not going, are you? You're staying here."

"The people here, Aveline . . . the vineyard . . . even this castle— they are my home. I cannot abandon them."

"Yet you'd ask me to do the same."

The storm grew closer. Thunder rumbled, cutting the sky in two with its warning. She shivered, despite the thickness of the air.

"You sent my father a missive in reply?"

"I did. The night of the fête on the ridge."

Aveline drew in a breath, willing herself to be brave and ask the question. He must have known it was on her mind—her scars—or surely he would have already addressed them.

"And you warned Philippe about me?"

Robert turned, an abrupt face-to-face, his eyes searching her with ardent attention and his stance dangerously close to hers.

"And what would I tell him, Aveline? Save that he may rejoice that his betrothed is still alive and well? And healing from something that never should have happened to her while we still had breath in our bodies? Believe me, it took everything I had to relay events with even the smallest measure of civility after what he's done. Do not make me dishonor you further by relaying scars of a nature that are mere surface affectations. Forgive me—but they should never matter to the confines of a gentleman's heart!"

The sky cried, gentle drops of rain tumbling down in a soft veil between them. Uncaring for their intrusion, Aveline stared back, her eyes following his through the building storm between them.

"Philippe knows nothing of me outside of the virtues my father relayed when he brokered our marriage arrangement."

"That is meritless."

"But I am altered. Forever, Robert. You dare speak of the heart against a man who has yet to meet me or accept me as I am now?"

Robert swallowed hard as rain collected and dripped off the bottom of his chin. He chose to ignore it, as if seeing only her, for long seconds afterward. "No. I speak with the knowledge of a man who already has."

He backed away.

A clear step when he might have brushed forward a tiny breath and simply pressed his lips against hers. Instead, the convictions of propriety put a solid barrier of rain and much-needed space between them.

The fire burned, illuminating oil-painted faces of past generations of Vivays, as raindrops sizzled in gray smoke, instead of the deep black cloud that should have consumed the sky.

Aveline watched the glint of firelight illuminating Robert's profile. There was no doubt he owned a noble brow. But it was made more so in that he stood on the steps of his father's castle, resolute where Philippe had lacked, and impassioned in his convictions, when her own fiancé's heart was still a mystery.

Even then, she clung to the hope that when reunited with his brother, the affections of her heart would no longer be softened by the man who stood at her side and would no longer ache to watch the legacy of past generations burn.

TWENTY-THREE

"Trespassers—especially the enchanted American kind—are fair game for the police. Best to be keepin' that front of mind while we're here."

Best-case scenario, they'd spend the night in jail.

It's what Quinn warned her, among other things. To stay still. And quiet. To keep their voices low as they traversed the wide moat to the castle ruins and certainly avoid making any hasty movements in the patched wooden dory, or the two of them could end up in the water.

He said he could sneak her in, sight unseen. But sink the boat in a great splash and there'd be little he could do to ensure their undertaking remained a secret. He'd agreed to the midnight excursion reluctantly, and with repeated deep sighs, only when Ellie reminded him they'd accepted her payment for a tour in advance and promised her full agreement to follow orders once they were on the water.

Quinn sat behind her, steady and silent, rowing them headlong into the night.

"So this is Fox Grove?" she breathed out, her words fogging to a slight cloud in the night air. "It's bigger than it looks from the outside."

The boat creaked as Quinn stretched back and rowed again, the oars cutting a lilting refrain of wood to water. "That it is."

"And how do you say it?"

"Bosquet du Renard," he whispered back, his Dubliner upbringing somehow managing to cling to his words even then.

"You've seen this before? You know, the view of the grove from the inside?"

She turned, having expected Quinn's reply, but caught only his quarter-profile, etched in silence as he rowed on. He'd pulled his hair back, tucking it behind the ears, and still hadn't shaved. Probably because he was at war with the expectations of his grandfather's world, and it was a show of defiance to cut his own path in something.

He cleared his throat but didn't answer—just kept rowing.

A muffled laugh, perhaps? Maybe he'd seen an American tourist's reaction too many times before. It must all seem cliché to him. Countless boat rides across the moat and somewhere along the line, even a fairy-tale castle can manage to lose its luster.

"Something to add, Mr. Foley?"

Quinn paused, long enough that she stole a full glance over her shoulder to see if her instincts had been correct. He didn't appear to be laughing then, but he was waiting this time, like he knew she'd turn back. He met her with the oars resting in his lap and the green pools of his eyes staring back. His typical buttoned-up nature might have kept him glued to short answers, but he could punctuate the words with a single look.

"Just that I've seen it. Once."

"You mean to tell me you live here, have tourists stopping by the vineyard every single day, and yet you've only been out here once?"

He shrugged it off. "That's right."

"How is that even possible, that you can know this place exists, see it staring back every time you look out your window, and not want to come here every day? I think I'd *live* here if I had the chance."

"We live where we live. Isn't that what you said? But you forget, I'm not in the habit of trespassin' upon private property. I don't take this trip lightly."

"I haven't forgotten."

"You're still darin' though, yeah? The letter of the law doesn't stop Ellie Carver."

"Has it stopped you?" She pitched an eyebrow at him, firing his question back. "And if you've only seen it once, then why choose now to see it again?"

"Let's just say that your persuasiveness won out, mainly so I wouldn't have to hear you ask for the hundredth time. But I warn you that others have come and gone, lookin' for the same thing you are. The ruins won't be disturbed. You'll find yourself disappointed if you set your heart on rescuing this place."

"Rescuing?" Ellie waved him off with a flick of her wrist. "Don't be ridiculous. I just want to see it."

Quinn stopped, bracing the oars on his knees again, but leaned in far this time, as if she'd struck a chord somewhere inside. He sent her a knowing look and tapped a fingertip to his temple. "Tourists always want to see it. And whether they say it aloud, it's always what they're thinking. Admit it—it's what *you* were thinkin'. See the ruins first, then spearhead an international social-media campaign to garner support and return an important historical landmark to its former glory. If you sell mountains of tourist tickets afterward, that's a *craicin'* outcome for the cause."

"Craicing?"

"Yeah. Since you can't look that one up in your Irish dictionary at the moment, it means a good time, to you Americans."

"Wouldn't be the first time someone's found a good time in doing something positive."

"And here I thought you wanted more than a good time. That plan may have worked for other castles in the Loire Valley, but I told you the property owner wants nothin' of it. And he's persistent enough to employ security staff who are passionate in ferretin' out intruders on the grounds. So no, I don't come here. I live on the other side of the estate, let the castle be, and I'm quite content with that."

"I'm sure you are. And I'm not a lawbreaker either, come to think of it. Just the opposite. We homebodies don't pick up and go that often—certainly not as far as France. But I'd still come back here. To this place," she confessed, enchantment pulling her back to the landscape ahead of them. "I'd have to."

Ellie turned around for a breath, somehow unafraid to show her excitement this time, even if he would mark it as vulnerability. Or cliché. Or whatever might make a Loire Valley vineyard owner find humor in a tourist's dumbstruck moment. It was enough that they were here, dancing around the edges of uncovering the castle's secrets.

Whatever response he chose, Quinn couldn't make her sorry for it. Not now.

"I wanted to know what might have been in this place—what story was here in the valley of castles and kings. I never even knew *The Sleeping Beauty* existed until a couple of weeks ago. And now that I'm here . . . she's all I see."

Ellie pictured her Grandma Vi, the proper English lady, leaning forward in the dory with the same excitement she felt then, like a child at a thousand Christmases. This was a fairy tale come to life. It was generations past. The foundation of another time, another place, daring to reach out and ripple the cadence of their present.

"It's better than I ever could have imagined."

Quinn leaned in slow, the boat creaking with the shifting weight. "Look over there." He pointed into the trees to their left. She turned with him, peering through the mingling darkness. "Buried off in the woods behind. See it?"

Gangly trees tried to hide it. Ivy delighted in blanketing its sides, just like on its larger sister. A tiny cross and spire rose out of the overgrowth, and Ellie followed it down with her gaze until it connected to stone walls and a pitched roof lined in haunting portals of rainbow-stained glass. The windows were narrow, aged and unkempt, with a noticeable break dominating the corner of one. Fractured glass stole no beauty from the forgotten place; it meant life had happened there.

Her heartbeat quickened. "There's a chapel . . ."

"The castle burned—was gutted from the inside centuries ago. It's been rebuilt o'er the generations, and abandoned after a fire in the 1930s. But the original chapel survived. Through World War II and the fightin' that took place all around it. It's had a new roof or two, but who would've believed it's still there after all this time? Just peekin' through the trees."

Exhilaration rolled under her skin like ice water pulsing in her veins.

"Please tell me we can go inside." The statement fell from Ellie's lips like a question, her tone rising at the end. She turned back from the chapel to look him in the eye, hope taking precedent.

Quinn braced his arms to keep the oars stilled against his knees. "Sorry. Couldn't take the chance it'd fall in on us."

"And . . . if a tourist is fully aware and willing to take said risk, without suing you should she receive even a scratch from a rogue thornbush?"

"The no is with full knowledge that you'd always take the risk for somethin' you truly want, Ellie. That much I am certain about."

It wouldn't have been the right time for Ellie to remind him she wasn't one to accept defeat. She'd traveled thousands of miles and put her whole life on hold in the process to avoid doing just that. The no wasn't a no at all. In her view, it was simply a "not yet" with the ever-present possibility of negotiation.

She clicked away at mental snapshots: the layout of the trees leading to the chapel . . . the windows facing the water—especially the broken one, nudged up to a tall shadow on one end . . . probably a door—an entrance into the heart of the hidden place. She'd remember it all for when she returned. And return she would. Once they were back on dry land, all bets were off. Now that Ellie had seen it, she couldn't possibly stay away.

And then . . . Ellie stared at a sight she'd seen before.

The rock wall. The rounded arch and the opening for a gate that was now missing. Arbor rows spread out behind, a vineyard rich with the harvest to come. Though time weathered and now buried under thicket and thorn, this place was familiar, already etched in her mind.

A forgotten photo had been taken there in summer 1944. The very place her grandmother had once sat.

The scene where her own story had begun.

Forget the wobbly dory. Quinn's warnings about trespassing. Even the plan to return and investigate the romantic little chapel on another day. In a blink the moment shifted, like lightning had just split her in two.

Overcome, Ellie shot to her feet, her heart dancing wild in the confines of her chest. "What is that?"

"Ellie! Have ya gone mad?" Quinn reached for her hand, no doubt to keep her from pitching over the side. "It's taking everythin' I've got to keep this rig from overturnin' us when you aren't movin' about."

"What is that stone wall? See? Far off behind the chapel. There. Through the trees."

"I don't know—some leftover structure of the castle gardens?"

The boat wobbled to start, then pitched violently to one side. He eased forward, balancing with care, and wrapped his forearm around her waist from behind, trying to stabilize them both.

The rush of Quinn's arm enveloping her couldn't hold her back. In truth, she wasn't sure anything could. If the castle had whispered to her before, the chapel, and now the view from the photo, were crying out, drawing her in. She was too close to turn back, too aware of what finding the stone wall could mean.

He whispered, breath warm against the back of her ear: "Ellie, if ya don't calm down this instant, you're going to send us both over—"

With one wrong, eager step forward, she was close enough to see clearly, and then . . . only water. She'd been at once above and then submerged in the depths of it.

The shock of cold stunned her senses, dulling the bearings to determine right side up. At least it wasn't like being in the ocean, where waves battled against the swimmer's kick. This was calm. Cool and dark. Velvet water that pulled her in and then allowed her to float back to the surface again without having to put up much of a fight.

Ellie poked her head up out of the water and sucked in precious air, a deep onslaught of fresh oxygen to fill her lungs. She looked around as she breathed, treading water with an enchanted castle and overturned dory looking on.

Hair trekked down over her eye, sticking to her face. She slapped it back, coughing at the mouthful of water she'd swallowed on the way down.

"Quinn?"

Her jacket ballooned up against the surface, and she freed herself from it, slipping her arms out. Her body took to shivering as she kicked through the water, her skin prickling under just a tee and jeans, and her heart a little too frantic to find him.

"Quinn!"

Relief flooded her when she saw him—for a moment anyway.

Quinn was fine. More than irritated, but fine, by the looks of him. He'd been pitched to the opposite side and was treading with one arm waving under water, the other fused to his grandfather's overturned dory.

It was feeble, but she tried to offer a faint smile. "Sorry?"

If looks could boil water, they'd have fallen into a Jacuzzi for the way his green eyes pierced through her.

"While I'm delighted to know you weren't lyin' about your ability to swim, I'd have preferred to avoid this. Even though I had a feelin' that with you, it was sure to happen."

"I had no intention to try it out, honestly." Ellie breathed, adrenaline pumping and limbs tiring in the water, trying to sort her thoughts into words that would make sense to him. She grabbed onto the side of the boat, patch-side up to the sky. "But I have this photo, taken during the war . . . I should have told you. I didn't know if you'd believe me . . . and even if you had . . . But it's that."

She tried pointing out of the water but got lost in treading again. "Right there. The stone wall and the arch, the vineyard behind— everything. In a photo taken of my grandmother from June 5, 1944. She was there! Sitting on that rock wall. I know it now. Her story is buried here somewhere, at this castle. At *your* vineyard. Now that I know it's here, I have to find it. I can't give up now. Not when we're so close."

"So close to what, Ellie, that would send you all this way? Because it's got to be more than just diggin' up the past."

Don't say it out loud . . .

Don't say it out loud because that will make it true . . .

"She's dying."

Ellie clamped her eyes shut when she said it. Just let the weight of the words fall as she kept treading water. Arms tiring and heart stinging in her chest.

"I have nothing left but her. My parents were on their way home to me. That's why it happened—I had a youth soccer game, of all the stupid things. They were rushing so they wouldn't miss it and took a company plane. And I never saw them again."

Quinn shifted his glance from her to the stone wall and arbor rows as she spoke. He waited a moment, then simply shook his head, his chin, still defiant and unshaved, tipping just under the surface of the water. His brow creased, something evident. Sorrow? Pity? *Please, God, don't let it be pity.*

"It's not your fault, Ellie."

She shook her head, water stirring around her chin.

"Look at me." He paused until she dared to lock eyes with his. "Did you need to hear that? That it's not your fault?"

"I know—or, my head does. But my heart is telling me that if I lose Grandma Vi, I lose them all over again. And then I'm alone. So it's not just a story, not a castle or a rock wall that I need. It's her. *All* of her. And I know if I look past the weathered stone, she's here. Waiting for me. That somehow, this story will have a happy ending because I know that's what's coming. An ending. And I'm not ready for it."

He ran a hand over his brow, slicking the hair off his forehead.

"Well, that changes things a bit, doesn't it?"

"I know it does. And I should have . . ." She stopped. Redirected her thoughts to what they could control at the moment. "Do you think we can see it?" No—that was weak. She wouldn't ask. "We need to see it. Please. The boat's already overturned. And we're soaking wet. What does it matter if we swim to shore and take a look around now? We'll have to walk back anyway. At least the trip won't have been wasted."

Leveling her chin in confidence wasn't the easiest thing when she was trying to stay above water, but she did it, straightening her spine all the way up.

"I think you'll find your plan difficult, Ellie."

"Why? You think I can't do it?"

Quinn did laugh then. A light chuckle he didn't try to hide in the least. "I'd be a fool to doubt you. You're quite clever enough to find your own way. But I know you can't do it—at least not tonight, because . . . *On nous arête.*"

If Ellie's heart could have sunk to the bottom of the moat, it would have. Her French was worse than rudimentary, but it still didn't take much to pick out the meaning of the final word.

"Quinn . . ."

Flood lamps clicked on, engulfing them in light.

A small fishing boat appeared off behind them, the engine cut and three uniformed officers standing in its belly. They directed their searchlights in a beam along the side of the overturned dory, illuminating their faces.

Ellie pulled her palm up to block the piercing light from her eyes.

"*Salut*, Michel," Quinn called out over her, a hand raised in a lackluster wave to one of the men in the boat. The man nodded back, a rather sorry-looking simper fused to his lips.

"Do you know them?" Ellie whispered, keeping her death grip on the dory. She looked from Quinn over to the men, noting that their faces seemed to reflect similar amusement.

"Chaps from Loudun."

"And these chaps are . . . ?"

"Police. And they've arrested dozens of tourists just like you. Can spot a trespassin' American with an eagle eye, I'm afraid, even in the dead of night and with careful steps to subvert a few security cameras." Quinn held his hand out to her so he could ease her over to the side of the security boat and help her climb in.

He leaned in close, whispering, "So your castle will just have to keep her secrets hidden a little longer, yeah?"

Ellie placed her trembling hand in his as he led her over to the side of the boat, then she climbed up. Quinn followed, easing onto the bench beside her. She turned back as the motor started and they began to drift away, her heart sinking like a stone under the water.

Even as an officer handed her a life vest, Ellie slipped it over her head, refusing to look away. With one final ardent glance at her castle, she whispered her promise.

A promise to come back.

TWENTY-FOUR

Heavy oak doors crashed in at the center, splintering wood across the basement floor.

Heavy bolts had locked the secretaries in the lowest level at Château de La Roche-Guyon, but the doors were shocked on their hinges as a horde of SS guards flooded into the warehouse-style room like a plague of wasps infecting the air.

"*Aufstehen!*"

Calls rang out, telling them to *Get up! Get up!*

Where there had only been the *click-clack* of typewriter keys, the room was flooded with heavy boot falls, shouts from guards with guns drawn, and frightened shrieks at the sudden intrusion. Women obeyed at once, front to back in the room, standing with their hands raised.

Vi had been sequestered in the wide basement room with the legion of other secretaries conscripted into the Nazi ranks. They were fed water and bread, and watery stews on occasion, and forced to work day and night, toiling over transmissions. They hadn't a clue where the messages came from, nor where they were going. They simply changed French for German, or the other way around, and submitted bizarre missives that meant nothing to them at all.

And so she, too, had been absorbed in the yoke of terror since she'd been brought here months prior—most French women, but some German and probably another Brit or two hiding in the lot just like she was. To the SOE in London, she must have simply dropped off the face of the earth. For months, she'd not been able to send word of her whereabouts. But to the other forced laborers in the room, she was as alive as they—locked in an underground prison of work, with the prospects of survival darkening by the dreary second.

The sight of so many SS, tromping through the rows of desks and typewriters, grabbing women out of line with seemingly indiscriminate fervor, sent fresh waves of terror pinging through her body. With guns drawn and eyes cold as death, they chose their targets. Mercy would have no place among them, not when the wasps were ready to level stinging punishments for something. What had triggered the attack, they might never know—save for the outcome of it.

"*Karine!*" Clémence's whisper was rough, immediate.

Vi turned around at the use of her false name to see she was being summoned by the friend behind her.

Clémence was a secretary too—older than Vi by some twenty years and downgraded from her former life as a mathematician at a Paris university to work in the doldrums of a château prison in northern France. She was wicked-clever, of course, or she wouldn't have been counted among the women in the room. But instead of standing as the rest did, she'd ducked down at her desk, watching the activity over the top edge of her typewriter, all the while untying the string-thin laces on her heeled oxfords.

"Change shoes with me."

Flitting her gaze between the woman furiously freeing her shoelaces and the advancing swarm of SS guards, Vi shook her head. How could she think of something so odd at a time like this?

The guards had done the same before. Women had been pulled from line weeks back, for no apparent reason then too, and never returned. Though they hadn't seen the outside for months, the women all knew a walled courtyard couldn't be far off. They'd heard the deafening pierce of gunshots fill the air outside, even from their basement hollow. It served as a warning that with their Nazi captors, there were not to be second chances.

"Clémence, what are you doing?" Vi whispered, keeping her head level to the activity in front of them. "They told us to—"

"We haven't time to waste. Do it now, Karine. Give me your shoes before they reach our row."

Clémence pulled the heels from her feet, passing them to Vi under the desk. She waited a second, watching the guards with an eagle eye. When Vi didn't respond right away, she snapped her fingers. "Quickly, Karine!"

Vi responded, though flustered, and eased down to pull her T-strap heels free. She scrunched down under the desk to exchange them for Clémence's—sturdy oxfords with a thick heel and rows of laces that locked the shoes up to the ankle. She'd have precious seconds to tug them on, but with fear manifesting itself in sweaty, shaky palms, doubted she'd be able to lace them.

"Listen to everything I say." Clémence spoke through gritted teeth, keeping her eyes trained on the black boots that were but three rows in front of them. "Do not let those shoes out of your sight. No matter what happens, keep them on your feet. I pass this responsibility to you."

"What? Why?" The SS drew near, scattering papers and files from desks, shouting at the women in their row to stand. "What's happening?"

The swarm advanced, and Vi gave up on the laces or else be picked from line for remaining behind her desk. She stood behind the rest of the women and eased back from her desk with hands in the air.

Clémence leaned in behind Vi's head, whispering in her ear. "There is a door at the end of the hall, marked *Achtung*—a sign warning danger of electrocution. Nod if you know which door I speak of."

Vi knew it. All the women did. It was kept under guard by at least one SS guard at all times. They were marched by both morning and night, past the door and a hall that led somewhere deeper into the depths of their château prison. They never questioned it, just passed by on their way to see to their duties.

But now, the mystery portal took on an entirely new meaning.

Vi nodded in as slight a manner as she could.

"There is a five-minute window when the guard shift changes. Five minutes only, at the midnight hour. Maybe less, but never more than that amount of time."

"How do you know this?"

"*Shh!*" Clémence grasped Vi's shoulder from behind, a gentle tug drawing her back against the wall. "Listen only. There is a muslin pouch in the floorboard under my bed. In it is a small, leather-bound journal and a package of soap shavings. You will fall ill tonight. Foam at the mouth and make it convincing enough that they will take you to the hospital wing. The doctor will not see you until morning, but by then, you must be gone. Tie the journal to your thigh so it's not discovered, and memorize the halls from our room to the hospital—how many guards, which doors have wires running to them, and which do not. You must make it back to that door without tripping their notice in the dark."

Vi shuddered as a woman was grabbed from the row in front, guards pressing the cold metal of a barrel against the back of her skull as they shouted accusations and marched her toward the doors.

"You will contact the Baker Street Irregulars and give them the contents of your left heel."

The cold reality of their situation washed over her, and Vi lifted her left foot, instinct feeling whatever was hidden there had grown like a stone out of thin air.

"There is a secret undertaking. A massive ruse operation to fool the Nazis into thinking an invasion is certain. The Allies are coming. Soon. But not when or where these heartless beasts expect. Your chaps in London have done their job with falsified chatter over the wires, and managed to hide what's really coming."

"How do you know this?"

"Hush—we haven't time. A coded message will go out over the underground wire. When you hear Beethoven's Fifth, you'll know it's time. Get to the Resistance. Stay there until you know the Allies have landed. Then, as soon as you can, find the boys from Baker Street and give them the contents of your heel."

Never had Vi guessed Clémence was aware of 64 Baker Street.

Suddenly, she wished they had but a few precious moments to exchange stories, to look in each other's eyes and know that what was happening could not be final. Was she an operative from the SOE, working in the same row as Vi for months and never saying anything? Sifting through the work of translating French to German and back took on new significance. It was more likely that Clémence had been battling to send secret transmissions from inside enemy lines, and Vi hadn't known a thing about it.

But somehow, the SS did.

"What is it?" She swallowed hard. "What's in my heel?"

"Proof—" Clémence stopped short, both of them jumping slightly when a guard shoved a typewriter on the ground with a great *crack*. She leaned in closer to Vi's ear. "Rommel is plotting to assassinate the Führer."

Vi's breathing hollowed out. She lowered one of her arms and grasped the wall for support, digging her fingernails into cold stone behind her. "Then this is for you?"

"There are a few of us here, yes."

"What have you done, Clémence?"

"Only what was required of me by God—for king and country. And now, the cup is passed to you." Vi could hear the smile in the woman's voice, defiance tingeing her every word. "Just promise me. You'll get to that door tonight. You'll go through it and no matter what happens, you'll keep running after you do." Clémence pulled Vi's arm away from the wall, then squeezed her wrist and hand in solidarity. "Promise me this."

Vi's breaths swept in and out in a flurry. She trembled, turning for a last look at her friend, and nodded—once.

What audacity it was to think that at one time, Vi could judge courage. And character. And even faith, and that she could claim all three. That bravery owned a pedigree of fighting men in uniform, or survivors like her, who'd endured the worst of the Blitz and turned to run back into the fray. But that moment was one she knew she'd never forget, as the dauntless nature of courage took shape before her eyes, molding into the form of a woman she'd known for mere weeks, and now, the world was poised to lose altogether.

It cemented Vi's resolve that not only would she make it to the door, but whatever lay beyond had better be prepared for a fight.

The one thing she refused to do was fail in the eyes of the most courageous person she'd ever know.

"What's on the other side of the door?"

"Make it through, and the rest of your life will be waiting. Live it for us."

Clémence straightened, infusing her stance with iron as the SS came to their row, then tendered a gentle squeeze to Vi's shoulder and finally let go.

JUNE 5, 1944
LES TROIS-MOUTIERS
LOIRE VALLEY, FRANCE

"Lady, come quick."

Camille knelt over a crate, her deep-chocolate hair falling down to shield her face as she dug through. Vi hurried over from organizing the paint supplies to the back corner of the castle ruins' grand ballroom, meeting her with an anxious heart.

"Whatever's the matter?"

"Nothing's the matter." Camille grinned, lifting a span of soft mint fabric from the depths of the wooden box. "Except I found this."

"A dress? How in the world . . . ?" Vi ran her fingers over the bottom edge of the fabric as if it were made of spun gold. It was a mite wrinkled and not the most couture of cuts, but a dress of any kind was a luxury set aside for the likes of queens. It was something they never should have found buried in wares dropped from their friends across the Channel.

"Mounds of coats and trousers, and old work shirts, and someone slips this in. It must be fate." She winked and tossed it in Vi's arms. "Why don't you try it? Looks like your color."

Vi rolled her eyes, even though she held tight to the fabric in her arms. "What would I do with a dress? We have preparations to make. We have to get ammunition up to the cottage, make ready for when Victoria lands . . . take extra weapons through to the bunker. How in the world would I go tromping through the grove in a dress like this? And look at my shoes. Ruddy oxfords don't exactly match the sash."

"So go barefoot for a while. It's warm enough."

Camille was softhearted. Lovely and, Vi forgot sometimes, as young as she was. War had an odd way of making adults out of barely grown girls and boys. It was normal for a young woman to desire some frivolities, even given what they might be facing in mere hours. Of course she'd see merit in donning a lovely dress and living in the moment.

"Look, you've been wearing trousers for weeks and even I forgot you probably once owned a tube of lipstick." Camille braced a hand on her hip and, in the other, raised the curious find of a camera. "You don't want to look shabby for our photo album, do you?"

"You found a camera?"

"Uh-huh. And a roll of film." She winked. "Now get a move on. We don't have much time to get you ready. I'd like to document the look on Julien's face when he sees you in that."

Vi bit her bottom lip over a smile, then whisked away into the back of the ruins.

The turret surrounded her on all sides, a rounded semicircle of stairs that cut up for some six stories, with window cutouts rising to the top. She stopped in the shadows, shedding the old clothes in an instant, and pulling the delicate fabric up over her hips and shoulders. Mother-of-pearl buttons lined the front, and she tied the sash, nipping tight around the waist.

A sound startled her from behind—a slight scratching that sent her whirling—and her eyes met with the most curious sight.

A fox.

As if written from a fairy-tale world, he'd managed to climb up to a second-story window ledge and stretch out in the sun. He snoozed, swishing his black-tipped tail over the sill, brushing against the ivy that clung to the outer walls as if he cared not to have been seen. Clever and careful he was not.

"Lazy creature," she scolded on a smile, and gathered her things.

But the cheek died away as fast as it had arrived. Theirs was not a castle in a fairy tale, and war didn't promise happy endings. Odd that he'd chosen that very moment to bring whimsy to the world around her.

"Lady!" Camille's voice drew her back.

"Coming," Vi called over her shoulder, stirring the fox from its slumber.

The animal darted out of sight in a heartbeat, scurrying off beyond ivy-tipped walls.

"You'll want to find a place to hide, little friend." Vi sighed, ducking back into the depths of the castle. "Before tomorrow, that is. Hide in your grove, and wait it out. Help is coming soon."

Vi told herself it was foolish to have pinned her hair in rolls at her temples, when it was only long enough to tip her chin. A girlish folly. Oh, but what she wouldn't have given for a tube of lipstick, like Camille had mentioned. Or dainty heels and a flashy new hat to tip down over her brow in a coy show of confidence. But it didn't matter now.

The team had gathered along the stone wall behind the castle, all except the still elusive Elder, who was readying the men deep in the heart of the woods. And though Brig was making final preparations on her explosives under the bridge, even she'd emerged to share a ration meal with the others.

Vi took a deep breath and stepped out, oxfords in hand, the feel of the stones cold against her bare feet as she walked down the castle's front steps. Julien must have found the gramophone; music lilted up to touch the canopy of trees overhead. Light laughter drew her to a path through the old gardens, to the ancient stone wall and arched gate overlooking the vineyard rows.

The long walk was humbling in a way, reminding her that time was short, but hadn't it always been? The castle was a witness to the speed of life, and the generations that had passed around its walls. And so it was again that in a matter of hours, or days, all that surrounded them could fall away too. Bombed flat. Burned to dust. The castle's world changed once more.

She forced the thought away, instead smiling when she saw the boot of Julien's left foot hanging out from inside the gate. Vi kicked it in her path, gaining his attention.

"Lady." Julien shot to his feet—fast for him—and, to her delight, stood with jaw dropped for the seconds it took to recover at the sight of her in the creamy mint dress. He grasped his wits enough to offer her a seat and helped her ease down on the large pile of stones at his side.

Camille's muffled giggle followed the click of the camera. Brig's aghast visage and Pascal's approval, too, as they made room for her at the makeshift table on the forest floor. Marie eyed her, keeping her cool nature affixed no matter the build of the clock ticking toward tomorrow. Criquet smiled and stuffed a peach in her mouth, then tipped a tin can up to drink what remained of the sweet in its bottom.

It was in those moments Vi thought of the memories of the last weeks, and months, and then before that, the London years of her life. Sifting through moments in her mind. The good and the bad that made her the woman she'd become. The beautiful, the lost. And as the dwindling light threatened the reminder that dusk was drawing near, she looked to the sky, the sun waving farewell, wondering when would be the last time they'd see it together.

Julien seemed to notice too and, without fanfare, reached over and laced his fingers with hers. He ran his thumb over the long scar that curled over her hand and wrist.

"What's this? Pear bite you?"

It had been years since the bombing in London had branded her with the scar. Vi rewarded him with a smile, grateful that the time spent at the castle had helped her forget.

"No pear stealing. Just a bit of leftover courage, that's all."

The makeshift family broke bread over a table of stones. Julien poured wine in tin cans—the *L'Aveline* label, their best vintage. The one that had become the lifeblood of the Vivay land. And they feasted like royalty, just as he'd said. Dessert was canned fruit, if Criquet had left any for the rest, and after, they became artists, climbing ladders and donning brushes with red paint, covering the side of the castle in a grand *V.*

This was life. Living right where they were, stepping out into the unknown together, without an ounce of regret because they knew what they were doing was right. Camille snapped photos. Pascal supervised Julien's every move. Brig took chances with her painting, hanging out windowsills and scaring the lot of them half to death. And for her ability to bristle, it was a consolation to see Marie smiling, making a game of it all, telling Criquet they were "painting the roses red" just like Alice did when she'd fallen into a Wonderland world.

Vi knew she'd never find a grander meal or a lovelier memory in all her life.

The evening wore on and Camille convinced them to pose for final photos before the light left. It was Julien's idea to level Vi's height with his, and he lifted her to sit on the stone wall at his side, whispering, *"Belle . . . Belle, Lady . . . ,"* in her ear.

"Look to the camera," he said, and slipped the subtle luxury of his arm around the small of her waist. "And smile, Lady."

She did smile, but the camera wouldn't know it in full.

Vi looked up, memorizing the strength of Julien's profile in that snapshot of time, finding that she only had eyes for him.

TWENTY-FIVE

The vineyard had received Aveline's attention much of the morning. She'd tended to the arbors with Fan and the others, cutting back the leaves in areas of overgrowth so the abundance of grapes on the vine could soak up the last weeks of precious sunlight before the harvest. The sun was high overhead now, baking down, and she was relieved to spend time in the grove, tending the castle garden under the cover of shade trees.

"I apologize for the intrusion, mademoiselle."

Aveline leaned her spade against the stone wall and turned with a smile, glad for the sound of Robert's voice. "There you are. I've wanted to show you what we've accomplished—"

Her voice was silenced by a man who hadn't come to help break soil in his mother's garden, but by the authority of his rank, suddenly on full display.

Robert stood along the hedgerow, turning a cocked hat in his hands. The black beaver skin stood out as formal, as was the rest of his attire—crisp shirt beneath a vest with gold buttons, covered over with a jacket bearing the Renard crest, and black breech trousers. Certainly not attire she was used to seeing on the man who was tireless in laboring upon his father's land.

With an apron and linen work dress dusted over with earth on the front, Aveline couldn't hope to match him. She wiped her hands on the apron, then smoothed it out against her skirts. "It appears as though I am unprepared for the formality of this meeting."

Something told her to reach for her hat. Straw and light-blue ribbons were paltry adornments compared to the nature of propriety he brought, but it would have to do.

Robert shook his head. "I'm not here to work. Not today."

"Oh. I see. But Gabin has been making plans to break down the stone wall—for the gate we talked about? Over there, by the void in the tree line. I wanted to show it to you. He said we could fashion a wide arch, so it would still be possible to see the arbor rows in the fields behind it. And when visitors come down the hill, they should see the colors bloom on this side."

She tipped the hat low on her head, smiling under its brim, still trying to find lightness in him. The capriciousness of his features, hardened over and foreign, stirred the flutter of doubt in her midsection. "Unless you think it a poor idea . . ."

Another turn of the hat in his hands caused a flip-flop of her heart.

"No. It's a fine idea. I'll see that Gabin begins work on it right away. And Fan will plant seeds so that come spring, the garden will look as you wish it to."

"I should like to help her. And I thought we'd settled this. You are free to address me as Aveline. You can't think me that formal when I'm layered under a veil of earth."

"Not free, mademoiselle. It would not be appropriate now." He cleared his throat. Shifted his stance a step. "I have brought something for you. It was kept safe until you had need of it again."

Robert set the hat upon his head, indicating he intended to take his leave momentarily. He tucked a hand in his vest pocket and opened it, revealing the fox brooch glittering in his palm.

Aveline stepped forward, not understanding how he could stand so unaffected before her. With a stark coldness he stood, not flinching as she took the brooch from him, even when the scars on her hand brushed his skin slight as a butterfly's kiss.

"Robert . . ." Aveline gripped the brooch, precious stones cutting into her palm as she watched him retreat. Step by step, he eased back. "If I've done something . . . said something wrong . . ."

"You have done nothing." He clamped his eyes shut, as if suddenly pained, his back fusing against the stone wall. "Nothing at all."

"Then why—?" Aveline took a step forward, hoping only to go to him. Eager to resume the warmth of familiarity they'd exchanged in weeks of laboring side by side.

But her path was cut short by another gentleman who'd stepped from the castle road into the garden's haven.

Sunlight rained down upon the shoulders of Philippe.

The shock of seeing him—as more than the ghost of a fiancé but a real gentleman—rendered her speechless. His was the noble brow she'd seen once before, in a portrait salvaged from the castle. Not as tall as his younger brother but adorned as formally, quite distinguished in a French naval uniform.

"Aveline?" He removed his hat, bowing before her.

Warmth shone in the gentleman's eyes. Though they were seeking, and surveyed the side of her face in earnest, then fell to the damaged skin of the collarbone exposed above the bodice of her dress. Aveline's first inclination was to hide her face, so she turned away, chin tucked, hat working as a straw shield over the harsh pigmentation of marred skin.

"No, it's alright." He stepped in farther. She heard careful boot falls approaching her from behind. "Robert has already told us what occurred here at the castle. You needn't hide yourself. This is not your shame to bear."

"Shame?"

"I meant there is no shame for what's happened," Philippe coaxed, his voice tentative as he walked round to face her. "It is evidence of the rabble's petulance that nearly felled the estate. But thank Providence your life was spared in the midst of it."

Philippe approached and her gaze drifted over a blue coat and red vest, both with embroidery and buttons of finely polished gold. A uniform of some stature, it seemed. And then—a purse to his lips, in what she hoped was authenticity rather than charity.

"You have joined the king's forces?"

"Oui." He flashed a malleable smile and brushed a hand over his lapel. "I am the Duc et Vivay's heir. As my brother hadn't the inclination to pursue the military duty of a younger son—this vineyard holds him fast—I will fight in his stead. It is believed by some that officers of noble lineage are not seen favorably by the masses. Nevertheless, I have joined the Royal Navy, to take up that yoke for our king and our family name, and I intend to rise in rank with all due haste. After what's happened to you here, on my family's own land, and now with the insurrection in Paris, the navy needs men who will stand up to our enemies, both in France and abroad. I mean to restore my family's honor."

"Honor? Isn't such earned by caring for those closest to you?"

"Events have occurred across the country. Just two days ago, a peasant assemblage forced nobles from their estates at Liège. Even César-Constantin-François de Hoensbroeck was made to leave. Imagine—a prince-bishop of France forced out! Our fathers have attempted to quell the insurrection with others of the Second

Estate, but Paris has fallen into disastrous unrest. We are to sail to England where we are assured safety."

"England? But who will defend your home if you leave? If there is insurrection in Paris and Liège, it will most certainly revisit the Loire Valley. What's to become of the castle? And the vineyard? What of all the people here?"

"My father lays claim to multiple estates, Aveline. This is merely one of them. I thought it was understood. This is a country château. An amiable place for a wedding no doubt, but not a permanent home. The vineyard is nothing but a . . . provincial amusement."

"It is not an amusement to the people whose livelihood is rooted in this land."

"And we will keep the land—Robert may work it for us, if it pleases him. We could even gift it to him one day, seeing as he has nothing to inherit on his own."

"How easily you discard your family." Aveline felt her heart drop from her chest. "You never intended to set up residence here?"

"No. And certainly not now that the only suitable residence is in ruin." His gaze drifted to the castle spires and his jaw hardened, anger bleeding into the lines of his face. "It is a total loss. And a contempt to the king. But the people will pay."

"The people here?" Thoughts of hiding her infirmity from him faded, and she leaned in, challenging the cold affectations of his manner. "You mean the laborers in the vineyard? You don't mean to seek reprisal against them. I do not believe it is their doing."

"I will seek justice against anyone I deem responsible."

"But what of rebuilding? The castle can be saved. I've been inside. Did Robert not tell you? We have been working together to help her rise again. It's why you find me in the garden at this very moment." She stepped to the wall, her scarred hand pressing over the stones like a lifeline. "This was your mother's garden, was it not?"

"I can't say I remember her ever stepping outside for a jaunt through the woods to know of a garden or not. But you needn't worry over such things. I've come to escort you away from this depravity, to see you to your new home. Your father and sister are waiting in the carriage at the castle gates. We will take you away from here. And once we are married, you and I needn't come back to the place again. I will not allow this tragedy to haunt us."

Aveline turned her gaze up to the castle spires, the blackened but beautiful turret rising over the trees. Her family was but a few steps away. They were home, weren't they? Or had the land around her—the ruins and a grove laden with fox, and the arbor rows teeming with the smiles and determination of laborers cultivating the land—become a home too?

"But I do not feel haunted here."

"After the beastliness of that night and now with what is happening in Paris . . ." He shook his head. "We haven't time to waste. What have you to take with you?"

Aveline looked around, as if her meager possessions would be counted somewhere among the trees. "I haven't much. A brush, a vanity stool, and a stack of books at the cottage. But everything else was lost in the fire." She pressed her hand around the brooch, holding it like a lifeline. "Save for this, of course."

His brow edged up. "A brooch? That is of some consequence."

"The one you gave to me. The night of our engagement ball?"

Philippe's brow turned quizzical.

Aveline looked to the stone wall, wishing to see if Robert's eyes would contest that Phillipe had given the brooch that night. But he'd slipped away and the spot lay bare, covered over in earth and underbrush instead of a gentleman's boots.

"I know the note of warning was penned by Robert, but I just assumed the brooch was from you. A fox of gold and citrine . . . for the Renard family crest." She slipped her hand into the depths of her apron pocket, burying the sentiment of such a gift.

"Possibly. My betrothed would have any number of jewels at her disposal, selected from those of my mother's family heirlooms. Who brought it to you?"

"Well . . . it was a lady's maid."

"There you are. She would have been instructed so by your mother." Philippe reached for her hand—not the one that floated freely at her side, but the scarred one she'd buried in her apron.

Aveline released the brooch as a deadweight in her pocket and allowed him to grasp her bare skin.

"I'd have selected a tiara for you, as the future queen of this castle." He didn't shudder when he'd taken her hand and pressed scarred fingertips to his lips. "But I promise you'll never have to wear the brooch here. This chapter will be buried and we can start anew."

The light kiss was meant to calm any misgivings she possessed. He'd shown intention with the move, a great generosity that he wouldn't find her scars a revulsion.

Philippe hooked her arm around his elbow, leading her back to the road. She turned for a farewell glance at the garden, the thought pricking her heart that the spade, too, was gone. Robert must have taken it from leaning against the garden wall.

Aveline saw a carriage up ahead, a wheeled prison in which she, too, would be taken away—to till earth in another home.

TWENTY-SIX

PRESENT DAY
RUE DU MARTRAY
LOUDUN, FRANCE

"To be in police custody is *garde à vue* over here, which means they could keep us for twenty-four hours if the owner of the property wanted to press charges for trespassin'."

Quinn opened the door for her, letting her swing through in front of him.

"But they're letting us go anyway?"

He nodded, following her out into the sunshine. "Titus must have spoken up for us. Good thing, because the owner doesn't want to press charges, apparently. So the prosecutor is lettin' us off the hook with a warnin'. But what say we shake this off and go get breakfast? Maybe regroup on all this. I need some coffee and we can call Marcel over from the vineyard to pick us up at the café."

"That'd be heaven. Because I can't think about anything but a strong cup of coffee at the moment." Something told Ellie she'd just scored points for honesty and she turned, sending a tentative smile his way. "You?"

"Praise be. Because I just wasn't in the mood for French tourism right now."

Ellie gazed down the length of the street, a curve that rounded the hill with shops and businesses and a moderate bustle that kept patrons moving all the way down to an ancient stone gate at the end. A mounted plaque stood out along the way, the bronze corners shining in the early morning sun.

She placed a hand on his elbow. "Quinn, what is this place?"

"The gate is *Porte du Martray.* Historical landmark here in Loudun."

"I've read about it. But what is that—the plaque halfway down the hill? In front of the church? I've been looking through the historical records in Loudun, visiting every monument that might mention the castle. I didn't find a thing. But I never came this far through the gate, so I missed that one."

"Ellie . . ." Quinn shook his head and sighed, kicking his shoe against a stone that dared cross his path on the sidewalk. "I must be mad, but let's go then. Lucky for you the café's on the corner behind it or I'd have said no."

The walk was bright. And Ellie felt a little drumbeat in her chest with each step along the sidewalk. Quinn had, in his own stubborn way, bought into the curiosity of the what and how in the castle's story. He pretended to bristle of course, with hands buried in his pockets and reticent manner in place. Though if she had to judge, he just might have been a half step ahead of her the entire way.

They reached it, and Quinn gave a rough translation. The plaque didn't mention the castle, but Ellie ran her fingertips over the blue-green patina of the one engraving she did recognize: 1944.

"It says a band of French resistance held off a German attack at the bridge to Loudun. This chapel was used as a hospital during the war, and for many months after the Allies liberated Paris in August 1944." Quinn tipped his shoulders in a light shrug. "Well, there's 1944. It's worth a shot, isn't it? That's the year on your photo.

Maybe they'll know somethin' about what happened to the castle. It's not that far away."

Not far away . . . The thought sent fresh prickles of doubt to provoke her. To have been so close a number of times, yet so far away from the truth in the same breath—Ellie wasn't sure of anything anymore.

"What do you think? Should we go inside? It could be another dead end."

"And you won't have any peace until you know for sure." His smile was a gracious one, a sign he wanted to step through the doors maybe as much as she did—if only to make her happy. "That much I do know, Ellie Carver."

"I suppose I wouldn't."

"And you didn't come all this way to France just to get arrested, now, did ya?" He released a quick wink as he reached for the scrolled iron handle on the front door and opened it wide. "Come on then. I'll see if we can find someone inside to answer your barrage of questions."

The chapel's street-side façade was deceptive; it boasted a nave nearly three stories in height, with long, chair-lined alcoves on either side and a grand central altar set far down at the front. A rose window—impressive for the small provincial town it was— dispelled the color of light piercing through stained glass.

While Quinn wandered to a tourist counter and began flying through an explanation in his quirky Irish-French accent, Ellie explored the wings at the back, looking over display cases with heirlooms of the chapel's history: Relics for the Sacrament in silver and gold. Illuminated manuscripts, exquisite in their hand-tipped details and, if one could guess, quite old. There were a number of portraits of chapel patrons and stained-glass windows backdropping the arrangement with fractured color.

"Quinn!"

Ellie froze for the seconds it took to process the contents of the case at the end of the row. She turned, saw him trotting in her direction.

"What's the matter?"

"She's . . ." Ellie pressed her palm to the glass case. "Here."

Ellie pointed to photos—dozens of them, hung in neat rows behind plate glass.

There was a straight razor and leather satchel. A 1940s Mycro brand camera and leather case. Even a rifle, the wood now aged. And there, smack-dab in the center of the display for the French Resistance in World War II, was the photo image of a British lady with ebony hair and a telltale dimple in her left cheek. There was a team huddled in front of a stone wall. A distinguished-looking man with a bow tie. A young girl with long, dark hair. Another photo of the team at the ruins of a castle, the majesty of its façade painted over with a garish *V*. And another of the group standing in the woods, weapons resting on shoulders or raised above their heads.

"Quinn, look," Ellie breathed out, her fingertips drifting from photo to photo, moving along the glass, as if she could reach out and grasp the memories. "It's Grandma Vi. The dress she's wearing here matches the photo I have. But the rest . . . I've never seen her like this. She's poised for battle. How could my grandmother have fought in the French Resistance, and I knew nothing about it?"

"You look so much like her. I wondered." Quinn eased in beside her, his shoulder brushing against hers. "Well, you did it, Ellie. Look at all this. You found her."

"Did I really? She's in these photos, but did I find her, or more questions? Because I'm no closer to the truth than the first day I came here. She's a completely different person than the woman I know."

"But isn't that your castle?" He pointed to a photo of a group of fighters posted in front of the Château des Doux-Rêves' six-story tower.

Ellie traced a faint *V* on the glass, following the lines on the photo. "I think it is. Yes."

"And that's your grandmother standin' in front of it, yeah?"

"It's her. There's no question about it."

He sighed. "Then I'm sorry. It looks like we're going to have to get our coffee to go. You want answers, then we need to go home and talk to the source."

Quinn eased his palm over hers, directed Ellie's index finger to press the glass over the photo's caption. "Because this one says the commander of the Maquis resistance at Château des Doux-Rêves was this man—by the name of Julien *Vivay*."

TWENTY-SEVEN

The sound of planes flying overhead in the middle of the night couldn't be drowned out, even from inside the bunker.

Vi glanced up to the bulb in the corner.

Dark . . .

That was good. They had a protocol in place that unless it was an absolute emergency, they'd maintain radio silence and no one was to trip the cellar door. From there on out, the entrance to the bunker was to remain sealed, accessible only by means of the tunnel to the winemaker's cottage.

They'd been on edge, buried underground most days since the Allies had invaded the beaches to the north, Pascal and Vi working together to track the Allied armies' progress through France. But the advance was slow. The battles, bloody. And the transmissions from inside the estate house cellar, discouraging at best.

They watched the vulnerable bottom floor of the estate house, Julien tasking himself with keeping an eye on the vineyard hills below and sequestering the women and children behind the relative safety of locked doors. Brig had taken to sleeping in the grove, watching her bridge from the vantage point of the cottage. And Vi and Camille took turns in the bunker, listening to the transmissions come in, waiting for the call for Elder to draw the *maquisard* fighters out of hiding. And if a bomb blast hit them or, God help them, the Boches tried to overtake the house, the fight plan would be set in motion.

Whoever was in the bunker at the time of attack would defend it at all costs.

Vi breathed deep, listening through the deafening silence overhead. She checked her wristwatch—nearly midnight. A bomb blast railed somewhere up above and shook the estate house, raining down dust from the plank ceiling.

The lights flickered and pulsed, the electricity threatening to plunge her into darkness.

She glanced up.

Still dark . . .

A second blast screaming and tearing at the world above her sent Vi to her feet, regardless of whether the bulb came on or not. She'd already dressed in trousers and shirt, with a vest buttoned down the front and a Basque beret to hold her hair out of her eyes. Her oxfords she always kept on, even while she slept. Every day was spent in preparation for battle mode.

Vi pulled her messenger bag over her head and crisscrossed two bandoliers of bullets across her chest, one resting on each shoulder. She reached for the Sten 9×19mm Julien had given her, and she raised it just as the bulb in the corner flicked on.

Her breathing quickened and blood thundered through her veins.

It was a far cry from waiting for a member of the SS to come into the chapel that first day. And she'd only had a board and two rusty nails to aid in her defense then. This time, she'd be ready for them. If the cellar door had been tripped, they'd find Lady, a stalwart maquisard fighter from the house of Vivay, instead of the former linguist named Viola Hart.

Easing into the corner behind a shelf, Vi raised the submachine gun chest high and trained her eye on the door as more plane engines gutted the sky overhead.

"Lady!"

She could breathe again when she heard Julien's voice carry down the tunnel.

"Julien?" she called back, waiting for an answer that didn't come.

God help me . . .

She blasted through the door, turning to both sides, expecting him to be there. The tunnel was dim as usual and deserted, but too bright at the end where the shelving unit should have blocked out the light.

Vi eased out, slow and steady, the strap of her Sten wrapped tight around her flexed arm. "Julien?"

"Lady! I need you!"

The moments that followed passed in a blur.

Vi tore up the stairs to find a hollow made out of the farmhouse kitchen. A small fire ravaged the stone outside, sending smoke in a billow over her head. Sparks flew from a wire laid bare in the broken ceiling, stone and splintered wood tumbling down over itself. She shrieked, ducking under the pulse of electricity, spilling her hair about her cheeks when the beret went flying.

Gut instinct told her to flee from the fire and smoke, so she fled around the corner, then slammed into a moving wall.

"Lady." Julien crushed her in an envelope of his arms. He pulled her back, hands pressing against her cheeks and brushing her hair back so he could look fully in her eyes.

"Es-tu blessé?" Over and over he asked if she was hurt, pressing her in a kiss and then begging her again to tell him that she was whole.

"No." She shook her head. "I'm not hurt. See? I'm fine."

He absorbed her words, golden eyes stormy as they checked her limbs over, seeing that she'd escaped from whatever it was, unscathed. Unlike the library, the kitchen and the entire side of the estate house had been ravaged in one fell swoop.

"What happened?"

"There's no time. Just listen to me—Pascal is dead. In the first blast."

Shock penetrated skull-deep.

Vi's mind kept calculating but numbed her from the inside out regardless. Words wouldn't come, so she nodded feeble understanding, trying so badly not to want to retaliate with the Sten gun in her hand should she dare see a Nazi uniform.

"And Marie?" She looked to the shell of the kitchen, sparks still pulsing. "The children?" Her hands shook as she gripped him, fingernails digging into his forearms. "Criquet! Where is she?"

"They're fine. In the mudroom. We've sustained a hit here, as you can see. And there will be more. So I need you to take the children down to the bunker." He showed her the key, then pressed it into her vest pocket. "Lock the cellar door from the inside. It's only plated in oak but it's metal at the core, so it will hold back any fire. And keep the Sten with you."

"I'll take them down, but I'm coming back. I want to fight with you."

"No, Lady. I need you to do this. This will help the fighting more than anything else."

Vi shook her head in furious denial as the smoke began to build around them. "I'm going with you."

"You're not. Not now. Brig is at the bridge. If the fight comes that far, we can't take the chance that she'll be killed before she hits the trigger on her explosives."

"Camille?"

"Already gone to the grove. She'll meet up with Elder, divide the fighters between the bridge and the road, and then she'll man Gertie at the castle. Now, I promised my brother I'd keep our family safe, but I can't do that if I'm worried that something's happened to you." He looked down on her, strong in battle, as she expected. Eyes sharp and unyielding. Brow creased and begging her for an answer. "Please—protect our family? I'm entrusting them to you. You're a part of us now." He paused a long second. "You're a part of me."

Planes seared the sky with the roar of engines, and a fresh blast shook the library windows. Vi shrieked as Julien covered her head, ducked them into the library doorway, and slid them both down to the floor in an alcove with empty shelves. The planes passed by, merciful to the estate house a second time. But a fresh blast broke far out beyond the vineyard, orange lighting the sky on the horizon in a series of booms.

A painting she'd noticed before hung in the darkness—a lovely lady of the eighteenth century keeping watch as the eerie orange-yellow blasts reflected against the painted canvas.

"Take this."

Julien eased the cold metal of the Sten from her palm and pressed something in its place, curling her fingertips around it.

It, too, was metal but oval. With tiny beads or rocks that pricked at her skin. Vi would have looked at it, but a blast shook them again, closer this time. Julien waited, eyes watching the ceiling for seconds only, to ensure the planes wouldn't bombard the estate a second time. "Do you remember what I asked you? The day in the bunker?"

Vi nodded, smoke and tears burning her eyes.

"If you're wearing this the next time I see you, I'll know your answer." He pressed a hand to the apple of her cheek. "And I'll know you want to stay here with me, Lady, and together we'll rebuild. We'll take that castle and make it our dream. Together."

He kissed her then, the kind of defiant embrace that had little to do with momentary passion and everything to do with survival, and love they'd been too afraid to confront until that moment. For the seconds it lasted, the connection as they fell into one another and he threaded his palm through her hair became all there was in the world.

"I wish there was more time. I'd give anything for it right now." He drew back, eyes locking on hers.

"I would too," she murmured, hands shaking as her fingers found his palms, lacing fingers, pulse to pulse.

"I need you to take the children down, lock the cellar door, and keep it sealed at the cottage end. Promise me you'll stay safe. All of you."

Vi nodded. "I promise."

"And if you must find me—*only* if you need help—I'll be at the chapel. You can find me there at dawn."

"The chapel. At dawn. I'll remember."

"You'd better believe we'll chuck all of this back at them—and then some."

Julien branded a final kiss to her lips and, with a stalwart smile, swept off through the cloud of smoke floating in the hall. She watched as night carried him away. And then she was alone, as the estate house groaned around her and fresh blasts shook the ground outside the windows.

With hands shaking, Vi leaned against the wall and opened her palm. In it, she found a brooch. A fox, the symbol of the Vivay land, gleaming in gold and amber stones that reflected the firelight against her skin.

Resolve took over.

Planes could rail against them and bombs could fly, but they'd never win. Not as long as the people fought back. Vi pinned the brooch to the front of her collar, and with a strengthening of will she hoped Julien would be proud of, she swept up her Sten gun and flew into action.

She was a maquisard fighter now, and battle number one was to shuttle their family down the cellar stairs.

TWENTY-EIGHT

Aveline didn't mind the rain.

The Château des Doux-Rêves stood at the end of her long walk, proud with sections of a new roof sloping its highest floor. She stared up at the façade, heedless of the rain collecting on her cape. From where she stood, only beauty emerged with the transformation. The rich smells of freshly cut timber, the cadence of raindrops hitting stone, and the glint of leaded glass panes back in the window frames all drew her.

The front doors had been replaced with hickory—an homage to the grove—and scrolled door handles that parted in the center with the Renard crest fashioned in iron. She pulled the door open, a rush of new overtaking her.

No longer open air, the foyer had been roofed and refinished first. Its former winged guests had been banished back to the trees. A magical addition of a chandelier hung with prominence, fashioned not of crystal, but iron made to look like twigs had grown out of the ceiling. The floor had been blocked, checkered in black and bright white marble, all the way back to a reception hall that had once been the grand ballroom. Now it stood humble, empty save for unadorned windows overlooking the water, and hickory shelves with row after row : . . of books.

A single looking glass hung above a sideboard on the wall. Instead of greeting guests with a succession of gilt mirrors as before, the castle would offer only one, arched at the top and engraved on the sides with long rows of violets stringing down the wood.

No longer concerned with the pigment of her skin, Aveline stopped before the glass. Only then did she see her image staring back—not as a woman scarred, but a reflection of the portrait she was once to gift Philippe, which had been hung on the opposite wall, tucked safe in a high alcove created by the curve of the stairs. And then, movement. The edge of a shirtsleeve clouding the side of the mirror's reflection in white.

She turned, her breath arrested.

Robert walked toward her, a book in hand and a hint of astonishment showing in his smile. "I heard someone come in."

"I didn't expect there to be a door at the top of the steps. So of course the instant I saw one, curiosity took me through it."

Rain tumbled down, a backdrop of pitter-patters on the front stoop from the door she'd left ajar. Aveline slid her cape hood down from her brow, laying lavender velvet down across her shoulders so she could look about freely. "I can't believe all you've done."

"You should have said you were coming back. We'd have had everything ready for you."

"I didn't know I was. The Society of the Friends of the Rights of Man and of the Citizen convened in Paris three days ago. And before you ask me to say that ridiculously long title again, I'll tell you they've shortened the name to Club of the Cordeliers. It was a political meeting of the populace and women were encouraged to attend, so I did. Without my father's approval, I might add."

"But Philippe approved your joining the cause of the people?"

"Not quite. I do not support violence in any way. The nobility is still being railed against, and there is rumor that the king will be forced from his throne. But I am merely trying to listen to both sides. That is not altogether dissimilar to the son of a duke rebuilding a castle and defending his land for the benefit of the people, is it?"

"It's not done, as you can see. The rooms are barren. But at least we keep the rain out. The entry and upper floors behind the façade have been enclosed and the library is new, of course. I'm just shelving some of the books now. But the remainder of the castle will take time to bring back."

"Quite a luxury. No furnishings, yet you possess a room for books." She looked out the front window, to the green of the woods beyond. "A stone wall with a wide gate . . . and a portrait."

He set the book on the sideboard, fingertips drifting along the edge of the wood. "Oui. A portrait."

"I'd forgotten all about it."

"As you are the future Duchess et Vivay, it's not appropriate for public display. I didn't think it right that anyone should see something so private before your husband. So it's been held in wait here, safely tucked out of sight, until Philippe should return for it."

"But with a felled castle and only a humble winemaker's cottage to take up residence, I'm not certain the future Duc et Vivay should like to spend much time on this estate. He told me such the day we left."

"And yet he approved of your travel here?"

"No. He never would have approved. Nor my father. I have lately broken with my parents and my father has given me the sum of my dowry to let me go." She raised her chin before him, willing herself not to feel her scars an infirmity. "So that is why I summoned a carriage and came on my own."

"On your own?"

"Well, almost. There is a coach and four at the gate, with Durand—my father's coachman, who's looked after me since childhood and insisted that both he and his musket make the journey. I had interests in Paris and it was of my volition to stop here."

"You will stay in Paris now?"

Aveline didn't answer. How could she tell him that Paris was no longer her home? And as England would never be, that left few places for her to imagine hanging a portrait.

Robert hesitated, their conversation polite on the surface.

"Philippe may take possession of the portrait whenever he desires. I intend to stay here, restoring the castle, working the land with each harvest. Neither my father nor my brother have much care for it now. So whenever you're ready to return, the portrait will be waiting for you."

"But . . . is it not waiting for me now?"

He started, eyes flinching at the implied meaning of her question.

It was easier to look to the girl in the portrait. Her creamy skin. Lavish gown with russets of satin and gold furnishings fabricating a world of courtly perfection around her. Outside of the painted likeness Aveline was not the idealized image of perfection, not the subservient bride of her parents' ambitions, nor a great lady of the French peerage.

She dusted her scarred fingertips along the front edge of the sideboard, stopping short of Robert's hand. "I have come to tell you the joyous news that you and I are now related through marriage."

He nodded. "I received no missive. But I assume congratulations are in order."

"They are, perhaps—but not to me. Your brother and my sister have been married just this month. The carriage waiting outside holds me alone."

Aveline untied the cape, letting the waves of velvet fall to the floor. His gaze fell to the collar of her traveling dress, and the brooch that was the lone adornment she'd pinned there.

"It was you who chose the symbol of the Vivay land for me to wear, isn't it? When I realized that, I couldn't conceive of living a life with a man who would not allow me to work at his side. I want an equal partnership, not a husband who is merely willing to overlook the disfigurements of my skin, or my will."

Robert took an authoritative step forward, his hand brushing the scars on hers. "But you're not—"

"I know." Aveline paused, searching him. Eyes misting as hope grew. "But you see *me*, don't you?" She took his palm, eased his fingertips to her face, slowly, hand trembling for fear she'd been wrong, that his affections hadn't grown to the same depth as hers. "Where others only seek to build walls, you succeed in tearing them down."

"Aveline," he breathed out, eyes softening, face lowering. "I would tear down every wall. Every one, for you. You have but to wish it of me."

Robert stopped time, pressed his lips to hers, arms hemming her in with strength, the way he'd done so many months before when she'd broken apart. His fingertips, not abhorred by the touch of her skin beneath them, just as the day they'd stood side by side and he'd held her hand, watching the smoke rise as the history of the castle burned.

Aveline smiled before him now, thinking how right it was that the castle and the people supporting it should no longer find an impasse of stone between them. Whatever may come with the crumbling of France, they could see to rebuild everything together.

"I do wish, Robert. I wish to stay here, at the castle. With you. To be the lady who disappeared into the grove one night, and never returned."

TWENTY-NINE

PRESENT DAY
LES TROIS-MOUTIERS
LOIRE VALLEY, FRANCE

The scrolled-iron gates were parted at the center of the long road, as if the castle waited for them. Maybe even welcomed their return.

Ellie and Quinn paused, hovering at the threshold of the road to the ruins, both staring down a long path broken by fractured sunlight cutting through the trees.

She grinned, rolling her palm over the curve of a rusted scroll. "Titus?"

"And to think I was goin' to give you two guesses this time."

Quinn met her smile with an easy one of his own, but the air turned sober as he tipped his head and looked down the road once more. He ran a hand over the back of his neck for a long moment, refusing to look at her, like he was battling in some way.

Hands in his pockets, he asked, "So, you want me to go along with ya then?"

"Well, you are my tour guide."

"I don't know this place well enough to give anybody a tour, Ellie. Told ya—this would only be the third time I've seen the grounds from inside. Twice with you and just one other time before that."

"But that one time . . . it was special, wasn't it?"

Ellie watched him stare out beyond them, the moments they'd shared in the winery suddenly making sense. Emotion could be wrapped in detachment as easily as a zealous pursuit of truth. Quinn was running as much as she, only in the opposite direction. With his quiet way and casual approach to life, she'd judged his flight as apathy when all along, he'd been fighting to exist with both roots and wings.

"The one walk you made here was with Juliette—your mother. That's how Titus knew you'd change your mind about taking me in to see it."

He nodded. "She was everythin'. Used to tell me and my brother stories about the castle when we were young. Cormac's a bit older, so he wasn't sold on them like I was. But she said there was a princess once who'd been lost somewhere out in the fairy-tale wood. She disappeared. Never came back, and the castle was named for her— *The Sleeping Beauty*, because she wouldn't tell her secrets. Just like the ruins. Now that legend is hauntin' the land with stories of the past." He shrugged it off, maybe not ready to talk about the family dynamic that had shut down areas of his own past. "Childish tales."

"Childish or not, they matter to you."

"Yeah. They do. And I haven't thought about 'em in a long while. I suppose I have you to thank for that." His gaze searched Ellie, drifting from her eyes up to her brow and her hair, spilling out over her shoulders. "She said every woman needs a scarf. A real one, from France. That if a lady was ever gifted one, she'd remember it for the rest of her life."

It wasn't like Quinn to stand defenseless before anyone. But something about the moment felt like a wall was tumbling down. For him. For her. Both of them, choosing to travel that road together because they were no longer content to walk alone.

"Sure you're wantin' to do this?"

"Yeah." Ellie drew in a deep breath. "I'm ready for answers. Whatever they are, I can't leave without them."

Ellie couldn't think of going home, or of the e-mails that had increased, Laine calling her back to face Grandma Vi's decline. She knew she'd have to go, maybe tomorrow. And at his own admission, Quinn would be packing up his guitar case and drifting off again soon. They'd been tossed together by a story and would be separated the same way. He must have understood that it meant they'd walk together in the moment and then walk away after, because he spoke to her heart, so gently, without the necessity of words.

He just reached for her hand.

It felt safe, and right, and . . . like home somehow, to lace her fingers with his.

Quinn was content to walk at her side, as slowly as she needed to absorb every detail of the castle they'd seen rising out of the trees.

The overhead canopy mingled with birds, and the leaves with late-autumn breezes. Timber snapped somewhere in the depth of the wood—one of the fox perhaps, creating mischief in Titus's Fox Grove. The sound of their shoes against the road . . . somehow, even that became magic.

Ellie's heart swelled to see the chapel, its spire and moss-covered roof peeking through the trees to her right. And then the long span of the rock wall and gate, creating an enchanted garden boundary all along the edge of the arbors behind.

Quinn let go of her hand, pulling her attention back.

"What in the name of St. Patrick do ya think you're doin'?" he shouted, racing up the castle steps.

Titus waited beneath the castle's grand façade, patient and

resolute as always, his walking stick buried against the stone at his feet. He held his palm on air until Quinn found it and moved to support his forearm.

"Are you mad? You could slip on the rocks, fall in the water, and drown before anyone could get to ya, stubborn old goat."

The hint of a smile swept Titus's lips. "I believe I am acquainted with this castle a bit more than you, my boy. Even blindfolded." He nodded, then reached up until his palm met Quinn's cheek and gave it a light tap. "But I'm warmed by the concern. And when I received the call from the *Gendarmerie* that they had indeed let you go, I knew I should wait. I wanted to personally welcome Lady Vi's granddaughter for her first visit to the Château des Doux-Rêves."

"*The Sleeping Beauty . . . ,*" Ellie whispered, climbing the steps.

"That's you gasping over there, isn't it, Ellie?"

"Oui, Titus." She eased up the last step and accepted his hand. "*C'est moi.*"

"Your Français is improving," he teased. "Soon you'll be teaching this boy a thing or two about a proper accent."

She flipped her gaze to Quinn, who rolled his eyes heavenward.

Titus raised his eyebrows. "And have you seen the fox yet?"

"No." Ellie looked around even then, always hoping to catch a glimpse of rust and a black-tipped tail darting through the trees. "Not yet."

"Give it time. They will come to greet you after a while. But they are not why you've come. You young ones must have had to walk by the Cathédrale Espoir Sacré, or you would not be here now. Hmm? So tell me—what did you find in Loudun?"

"That was you?" Quinn leaned back against a ledge of stone and let out a hefty sigh. "You called the police. I might have known my own grandfather would one day be responsible for startin' up my arrest record. I'm tellin' your wife, make no mistake."

Titus brushed off the threat with a wave of the hand. "Hush. Let the girl answer."

"Everything, Titus. We found everything. She was *there*. In old wartime photos on the wall. I saw Grandma Vi in the dress, the same one from the photo I have. And then in trousers, a vest, and a beret . . . We saw her as I've never seen her before. Standing with the rest of the resistance fighters right here at the castle, bold as they were to defend it. Alongside the man from her photo. Was he your brother—this Julien?"

"It's been a long time." He nodded, pausing on the words. "A very long time. I haven't heard his name in . . . many years." He turned his face out to the grove, the road, and the chapel, as if he could readily see them all. "Yes. Julien. And my first wife, Mariette. She passed many years ago, when our son was young. And Camille. Brig and Pascal. So many names."

"We saw an old camera in a glass case at the church. Was it yours?"

Titus pressed a finger to his lips. Thinking. Remembering. Some evidence of pride washing down over his countenance. "No. It was not. But I am grateful that your grandmother took ownership of it at the proper time."

Ellie walked over to the side of the castle and pressed her palm to the stone façade. Tiny flecks of weathered red still remained; the breath of history beneath her fingertips. "And the *V* you painted on the front. I can't believe it—after all this time, the paint is still here."

She turned a circle. Looking, taking in the art of the ruins . . . loving the feel of the sun on her shoulders . . . hearing the slight ripples of the water on all sides . . . and seeing the length of the long road she and Quinn had walked together.

"There is a history where we stand, Ellie, and I would be honored to give you your first tour of this story. In spring, the road is bathed in blossoms overhead, and violets on both sides. They grow wild through the grove. It is said that a mistress of the castle—the first lady to rebuild it anew after the Revolution—she favored them. She came here, fell in love with the land and the people on it. And she is the reason our wine, and our name, and even this very castle survive today."

"*L'Aveline* . . . the Muscadet." Ellie jumped her gaze over to Quinn, remembering their tour of the night market and the name of the Renard signature label they'd seen at the wine tent. "It's named for her, isn't it? Aveline. Was that her name?"

"There are many names in this place. And Lady Vi made sure to record them all. She spent years writing every name, research-ing every story, so that one day these ruins could be rebuilt upon them." Titus lavished her with a smile and took a small leather-bound journal from the inside pocket of his field jacket. "The job of keeping them safe was passed to me. And now, Ellison Carver, these stories belong to you."

It felt like a kiss from heaven sweeping in, overwhelming Ellie as she flipped through the journal and saw her grandmoth-er's writing. Inked pages, years' worth, filling cover to cover with names . . . and dates . . . and the storied past of the sleeping castle where they stood.

"I wish I could stay. But Grandma Vi hasn't been well, and if I have any time left with her"—she paused, hugging the journal to her chest—"I want her to know I found the truth. About her. And Julien. And all the people who have lived here and loved this place. She needed me to find this story, and now that I have, my job is to bring it back to her."

She locked eyes with Quinn. There was one question left to answer, and somehow, what he would think about it mattered more to her than having it confirmed.

"There's one thing I need to know before I go. You are not the owner of this *Sleeping Beauty*, are you, Titus?"

"No. I told you that I am not. But then who is, Ellie? Because I think deep down, you already know the answer."

She swept a palm under her eyes, emotion having crept in, and brushed at the wetness beneath her lashes.

"I am."

THIRTY

Julien stood along the road to the castle as an eerie morning mist rolled in from the trees.

Vi recognized his gait, even from far away—the slight hitch of a limp, the tall form and broad shoulders—and lowered her rifle. Relief prompted her to walk faster. To run if she had to, desperate for her legs to pick up and carry her to the safety of his arms. He was alive, and it was all that mattered in the world.

"Julien!"

He turned, slowly.

Too slow for what was normal, without his usual flash of a smile. There were no words. No voice returning the call of her name. And no relieved-to-see-you glimmer in the eyes she knew so well. Instead, agony washed over his face at seeing it was she who was rushing toward him.

Julien raised a hand to stop her advance.

His palm was blood-red in the early dawn light, glistening as the drizzle of a cool summer rain fell around them.

"Julien . . ." She restrained a sob, dulling it to silence upon her lips.

Vi raised the rifle, keeping her sight sharp for any movement around him.

She took slow, even steps along the road. Watching. Defying his request to stay because she knew if she could just get to him, surely everything would be alright. They could stay at their castle. Dream together. Rebuild the ruins from the ground up.

She glanced down, marking her steps as she drew closer.

The fog began to fade in the rain, and she swallowed hard as crumpled bodies in Nazi uniforms, others in street clothes of the maquisards, began to take form on the road between them. Rifles discarded. Helmets gathering raindrops. Blood mixing with water and mud and pink blossoms that had fallen to the ground.

"Stop, Lady," he whispered. Pained, shaking his head. "*Please . . .* stop."

Vi froze, her boot kicking against something as she halted her advance on the road. She dared to look down, hands shaking but sure as she gripped the rifle. She took her gaze off him long enough to see . . . a camera.

The camera she knew well.

Her heart sank deeper; the strap was still entwined round the wrist of a girl with chocolate hair who lay facedown on the road, her body entangled with a jumble of others. She resolved that grieving would come later; for now, she'd take charge of the camera's witness.

Lifting Camille's wrist with care, Vi pulled the strap free and swept it over her shoulder, tucking the camera behind her back.

A shot rang out before she could right herself. Then another, echoing through the trees. Vi fell, facedown in the road, her hand clinging in a white-knuckled grip to her rifle as her cheek ground into stone and mud.

It took split seconds to realize why Julien had asked her to stop; they were being stalked like prey in an open field. Though fired at, she was unhurt. Limbs were all accounted for and nothing seared with pain, which meant any shot fired must have missed its mark.

Unless . . . *Julien.*

Vi raised her head enough to see through the mist, though her chin still lay buried in the mud. But he was still crouched and moving in her direction along the trees.

Breaths rocked in and out, terror cinching her chest as she lay pressed against the ground. She watched as Julien backtracked toward her, his shoulders hunched and a pistol raised in his left hand. Blood trailed down the other, stabbing her heart each time liquid red dripped from the curl of his fingertips.

He stopped before her, the backs of his military-issue boots within reach of her hand.

Vi gripped his ankle and squeezed, letting him know she was alive. He eased back and knelt, legs braced in a protective haven, his head and shoulders absorbing the rain over her shoulders.

"*Diables verts,*" he whispered down at her, eyes trained on the darkness of the trees on both sides. She closed her eyes and nodded.

Green devils.

It's what they called the Nazi paratroopers—the savage fighters uniformed in forest green. No doubt that's what they'd heard the night before, planes dropping more than bombs over the estate house. The Nazis were desperate to hold France from the Allies and dropped reinforcements in known areas of resistance or strategic points of defense.

Turned out, the castle and the bridge to Loudun were both.

"We were ambushed at the bridge. Brig pulled the trigger before they could come over, but the green devils were already here." It was a short summary for the evidence of the fight all around them. In the next breath his voice softened with, "Are you hurt, love?"

"No," she whispered, rain splattering mud sprays against her lips. Vi feared she knew the answer but begged, "Are you?"

He ignored the question, keeping his gaze moving along the trees. "See the Matford on the side of the road, to our left?"

It was a skeleton of metal riddled with bullets, but still there.

Gertie was mangled, her cart flipped and torn into a pile of scrap metal. Vi could only imagine the fighting that had gone on to defend the estate house. Hold the bridge. Fend off an attack on the castle ruins, and protect the ridge that led to the cottage and the underground bunker, and she who'd been inside it.

"Yes. I see it."

"Rise up. Just enough to crawl, but stay behind me. We're going for cover. Over to the car." He reached his hand down, palm open to her. Vi obeyed and took it, feeling relief at the strength of life still in his grip but worried that it would cause pain if she were to hold too tight.

"Together, oui?"

There wasn't time.

Not to crawl an inch or even nod her answer to him.

A Nazi uniform emerged from the cover of trees, with a pair of devilish eyes and a rifle trained on them. A lone paratrooper, ready to claim his prey.

Julien raised his pistol but still braced in front of her and absorbed a bullet that tore through the air, spinning him at the shoulder. Vi screamed and caught him as he fell, trying to cover him so another bullet couldn't tear into his flesh.

Two shots, one piercing echo after another, blasted the air. The paratrooper fell forward and then . . . only deafening silence.

And the sound of rain.

Vi pulled Julien back with her, realizing the final shots had found their target, and it wasn't them. She lay Julien across her lap and raised the rifle, training her sight on the form of a man cutting a path from the castle steps, trekking down the center of the road with weapon raised.

With hands shaking, she gripped the rifle, index finger hugging the trigger.

"Ne tirez pas!" he called out, telling her not to shoot. "I'm Elder, and that was the last one."

"Elder . . ." The name sparked something familiar, the code for their general in the woods, though he'd been a ghost until that very moment. Tall, broad shouldered, with a thick coal beard covering his chin, he stalked forward, moving in their direction while shifting his shoulders to scan the tree line on both sides.

"Stay down!"

Vi obeyed, dropping the rifle at her side.

She slid her fingers under Julien's neck, supporting his head. His eyes followed her, thank God. He was awake and she could have smacked him—for he'd chosen that very moment to lavish a boyish smile up at her.

"Lady . . ." He reached up, twirling a lock of her hair in bloodied fingertips.

"This is my fault," she sobbed, sliding him onto the ground to make a rain shield over top of him. Vi tore the buttons on her vest and shrugged out of it, wadding the fabric to press against the wound in his shoulder. "If I'd listened to you . . . gone straight to the chapel . . ."

"No, Lady. It's not your fault. I wouldn't have been there. This way, I get to see you," Julien whispered, dotting a finger to the dimple in her cheek to get her attention. "You have dirt on your face. Remember? Just like the first time I saw you."

"And I am delighted to see you too." Vi lowered her head and pressed a kiss to his lips, tasting the salt of her own tears upon them. "But shh . . . let me see to this now. Teasing later."

Elder appeared, swung the strap of his rifle over his shoulder, and knelt at her side.

"Help me," she cried, looking to the man. She shuddered at the blood covering her hands—Julien's—as she pressed the vest to his shoulder. "Please, I don't know what to do."

"Didn't I tell you?" Julien cut in, looking up to Elder. "She's beautiful, isn't she?"

Vi wished she could ignore the comment as Elder did; it blistered her heart. But Elder was calm, going to work on the compression at Julien's shoulder. He inspected the wound only briefly, then, brow furrowed deep, he turned his attention down, instead looking over Julien's torso.

Vi studied him, not understanding. "What's the matter?"

"The shoulder's just a flesh wound. A nick shouldn't be bleeding like this." He tore at the black vest buttoned down Julien's middle, revealing a deep wound to his right side, his shirt soaked in crimson.

"Julien . . ." She covered her mouth, her chin trembling beneath her palm. "Oh no . . ."

"I knew you took a bullet in the side before you ran down the castle steps, but you wouldn't stop. Brave fool." Elder looked to her. "He went after the team."

Vi turned around, seeing Camille . . . probably Brig, and countless other maquisards from the woods, their bodies strewn along the road.

Elder wasted no time, pulling Julien's vest tight. "Deep breath, my brother. We're going for a walk." Then he raised Julien, lifting him over his shoulders.

Julien cried out, a moan tendered with each running step to the car.

"Brother?" Vi grabbed up the rifle and her vest, following behind.

He nodded. "I'm Titus." He eased Julien in the front of the car to lay him out on the seat. "If we were going to put up a fight, it was safer for everyone if the Boches thought I was already gone. Or dead."

"You're Julien's brother . . . All this time, you've been leading the Maquis in the grove."

Suddenly, thoughts hit in a barrage.

Marie and the baby flew back to her mind, realization that the short time she'd promised to be gone from the bunker had turned into a nightmare of moments she'd lost track of. That in the very moment they stood beside her love, bleeding and moaning in a front seat, Titus's love could be in just as much danger.

"Titus." Vi reached out, grabbing his lapels. "Your wife is in labor. I came to get Julien, never expecting to find you instead. But she's calling out for you. She won't calm for anyone else. I would have delivered the baby myself, but it's been hours and I'm worried that something is wrong."

His eyes, so similar to his brother's, deep and gold, and pained beyond anything, looked to his brother's boots sticking out of the car. "Where is she?"

"The bunker. With Criquet and the rest of the children. I swore I'd only be gone long enough to bring help back. But you have to go to her. I can handle this." Vi looked down in the car, relieved that Julien's chest was still rising and falling at a steady pace. She turned back, pulled the cellar door key from her vest, and pressed it into his hand. "Now, tell me what to do, and I'll do it."

Titus shocked her. A man of strength, a shade taller and thicker than his brother, with a steely resolve to lead an army in the woods, couldn't keep tenderness at bay enough to keep his bottom lip still.

"I think you should make him comfortable." He swallowed, a long pause of emotion. "Just stay with him. Please."

Vi shot back a denial, shaking her head with the force of everything inside her. "No. I said tell me what to do. You go back to the bunker and I will look after your brother." She swept the strap of the rifle over her shoulder, determined to move. "Look at me, Titus. What do I do?"

Titus glanced at the car, then sighed deep. "Take the road leading out from here, past the estate house. The bridge is bombed flat so it's the only way out. Left at the big fork, all the way into Loudun. That's ten kilometers, Lady. Through countryside that could be overrun, so don't you dare stop for anything or anyone. I can't promise you'll make it—"

"We'll make it." She notched her chin. "What then?"

"Look for the *Porte du Martray*—a medieval gate at Rue du Martray. There is a chapel beyond it, buried in the street on the hill. It's *Cathédrale Espoir Sacré*—Cathedral of Sacred Hope. Medics were dropped in France weeks ago, in preparation for the invasion we didn't know was coming. They're already taking wounded. If Loudun is not under siege, it'll be the best chance for him."

"Then I'll get word to you when we're safe."

Vi ran to the driver's side and climbed in, settling Julien's head in her lap. She braced the rifle on the floorboard, leaning it against his shoulder for quick access, and steadied her hands on the wheel.

Titus eased Julien's boots in, clicking the door closed behind them. He braced his hands against the door, holding fast. "You're in good hands, Julien. If what you've said about her is true, then she's the toughest Lady we've ever had at this castle. If anyone will get you through, it'll be her."

Vi felt the soft nod of Julien's head against her thigh. He watched his brother out the window, through eyes that were turning glassy and unfocused, warning that time was wearing thin. She fired up the engine, and Titus backed up, only to be summoned back when Julien called his name.

Titus reached in, grasping Julien's bloodied hand through the open window. "Oui?"

"Titus? The castle . . ." Julien looked up at her, his eyes locking on the brooch pinned to her collar. "It's hers. Lady gave me her answer. Said she wants to stay. So I want her to have it. The chapel, the rock wall, and the ruins—all hers."

Titus glanced over to her as rain dripped in through the open window and cried latent streams of water over the bullet holes in the windshield. Vi hadn't thought anything about staying, not on her own. Not for a castle; only for him. But she nodded, willing it would make Julien happy in that moment.

If he needed a dream to fight for, then she'd agree to anything.

"Promise me, Titus."

"*Je te le promets*, Julien," he whispered back, setting the promise in stone with a shake of his brother's hand. "Always, I promise you this: *The Sleeping Beauty* is hers."

THIRTY-ONE

An assemblage of men, women, and children—a mass nearly a hundred thick—poured down the road to the castle. Aveline gripped tight to Robert's forearm, fingernails digging into the sleeve of his morning coat.

The last memory they had of an assemblage descending upon the castle was the night of the attack. And now, even as they'd stepped from the chapel christened as husband and wife that morning, the savagery of France's bloody battle for independence seemed intent to strike at them again.

"It's alright," Robert whispered. His solid tone did little to convince Aveline, however, as he'd stepped forward, edging his shoulder to ease his body in front of hers. "I will speak with them."

"*We* will speak with them." Aveline slid her hand down to grip his. "That is, if you believe we can reason with an assailment of a company this size?"

"They're not carrying torches, Aveline."

"Perhaps not, but look—" She pointed to a number of horse-drawn wagonettes, filled to the brim with sacks of grain and wooden handles hanging from the end. "They carry tools of some sort."

"Garden tools. And children. I don't think they'd arrive to attack a couple on their wedding day with their families in tow."

"Robert, the last time the populace came down that road, the castle was nearly burned to the ground. The Second Estate may not exist any longer, but the hate remains. In Paris, it is growing. You know the *Commune de Paris* holds the power of the government now. Even with the municipalities redrawn, the king's rule is in peril. Why would they come here if not to threaten us as members of our families' former rank in the peerage?"

"You know how I appreciate your interest in politics, my love." He pecked a kiss to her lips. "But la noblesse is dead. And we are not in Paris now. These people are our family. Philippe has no interest in this estate and has given it to my charge. That means I am still master vigneron here. If they wish to speak with me, then I'll allow it." He laced his fingers with hers, squeezing a light tap against her fingertips. "I will not live in fear for our lives. And I won't give them a foothold against us, even on a day as special as this."

Aveline's heart jumped in her throat when Robert took a step forward, cutting the people's advance to the castle.

The gathering slowed to a stop before him. They were restrained, as if forbearance held them to a hush. Robert stood before her, legs braced in a wide stance in the center of the road. He waited, hands at his sides, open to the crowd.

"Master Robert, vigneron and son of the Duc et Vivay." Fan stepped out and bowed in front of the group, a smile lighting her features. "We have come to speak with Madam Vivay."

Aveline swallowed hard. It was the first time she'd been addressed as Robert's wife, and though the sentiment should have warmed her heart, caution overwhelmed it instead.

"My wife is here." Robert eased to the side, hand extended to her. "If you wish to speak with her, you have but to ask. It is to her to decide who she will take audience with."

"It is because of who she is that we are here."

Fan stepped forward and took a span of folded paper from her apron pocket.

"Some time ago, a rumor persisted in Paris that a woman of great wealth and rank in the king's court had once attended a pau-pers' burial in the heart of the city. It was said she was so moved by what she'd witnessed that she sought to tear down a wall between the nobility and the people. She purchased a very large trousseau for her impending marriage to a high-ranking member of the French peerage. But instead of keeping the wares she'd purchased, she bartered them and sent wagons of provision to the people, instructing that a bundle of color should go into the hands of each one she'd blessed.

"She thought to stay out of sight, but the men hired to disperse the goods hadn't payment enough to quiet their tongues to keep it secret. And her family's coachman has confirmed what he, too, saw of her actions." Fan placed the missive in Aveline's hand, tendering the exchange with a gentle squeeze. "This letter proves that woman is you, madam, and we would like to convey our happiness that you are here, and our wish that you should always remain."

Fan stepped away, easing back toward the group.

"Gentlemen? If you please?"

Men opened the wagonettes at Fan's bequest, and the people went to work unloading sacks of seed, opening them, filling seed-ing bags, and, with the children at their sides, dispersing the promise of wild violets all along the road to the castle. Spades cut earth in the garden. Hoes and picks tilled the ground along the stone wall. And the laughter of men, women, and children rose up, carrying through the gate; a harvest as great as the arbor rows owned beyond.

"Aveline?" Robert stepped forward, easing the letter from her hand. He scanned it, brow furrowed as the words sank in. "Is this true? I'd heard rumors. They came all the way from Paris here; the lady and her violets are known as far as the Loire Valley. But I never imagined . . ."

He stood back, staring, the usual kindness in his eyes a comfort to see once again.

"Félicité's letter," she cried, tears bathing her eyes. Aveline took the letter and pressed it to her heart, covering the fox brooch she'd worn for the ceremony that morning. "After all this time, I'd forgotten. I thought it was lost in the fire last year. But Fan saw I'd dropped it, right before I received your note . . . and the gift that saved me."

"You are remarkable." He leaned in, his arm collecting the small of her waist, and pressed a kiss to the base of her neck where the scars met her gown. The praise he'd whispered, but she felt it soar high as the canopy of trees overhead. "And a treasure, worth more than any jewels to which the Vivay family could lay claim. It is you who saved me."

It was all Aveline had wanted, to come back, walk the road to their castle, and see him standing in its path, looking on her as though beauty were more than skin deep. It was true that scars could heal to make something exquisite again; the castle would be brought back to life in the same way—scarred by stories in their generation and perhaps rebuilt in one they might never know.

If the smile of a bride on her wedding day is felt on her face even more than it is seen, Aveline looked to Robert, knowing it was true.

"I wonder if I might make a request before we, too, pick up tools and go to work in our garden?"

He laughed, no doubt because what bride would till the earth in her wedding gown, save for one who had a voracious love for violets?

"Anything."

"I would like to sit for a portrait, as soon as it can be arranged."

"Another portrait?"

She nodded to him. "We don't need the old one. I should like to be painted as I am now. I don't know the lady in the former portrait any longer. I only know the one who stands before you. The one who loves this place, and loves you in return."

"Is that all?" He paused, brow tipped, thinking it over. "Then if we're agreeing on the making of concessions, I would request one from you. To start off on the right foot as a husband, of course."

"Very well."

"The Renard Reserve . . . You know of it?"

Fanetta had mentioned it. Once, quite some time ago.

"I do."

He tightened his hold around Aveline's waist and with softness added, "Bien. Then our most renowned label should be yours. Just like the castle . . . this land . . . and the people in it. I want the evidence of your heart forever tethered to the Vivay family. So— *L'Aveline*. That's its new name."

L'Aveline . . . She'd not have smiled at the sound of her own name, had he not said it in a shiver-inducing whisper against her ear.

"Then we should start anew while our *Sleeping Beauty* takes her time to awaken. Perhaps christen a new wine with a new life entirely. I favor the site on the ridge. We could build an estate house where we first dined and danced with the people. With a dining hall large enough to accommodate our friends. Where we can open our doors, work side by side, and celebrate when the harvest is drawn in, and when the wine flows in abundance. We have a gate now, between former worlds. You've opened it to me, and I pray it will never be sealed. I would like to know that we breathed life back into the castle."

She paused, watching as beautiful, laboring hands scattered seed on the grove floor.

"I want this place to always tell the story of God's faithfulness, just as we've received it here."

"Aveline, if the presence of your beloved violets is any indication, it always will."

THIRTY-TWO

"What did you say about me?"

Vi jiggled Julien's uninjured shoulder, then pressed her toe down to give the car more gas. Her hair whipped against her face, the wind playing at will.

"Come on, Julien. Talk to me. I said, what did you tell your brother about me?"

The road to Loudun lay ravaged.

The carcasses of cows, bloated in the summer heat, lined barren fields. Smoke rose from somewhere, cutting a black line across the sky. Trees flew past the windshield with its glass all but shot out. And Julien had begun to fade. Even then, his gaze drifted out the window, and that terrified her more than any barren landscape could.

"Fine. That'll be your secret. Brothers are entitled." She turned around a sharp bend, swerving to avoid an abandoned vehicle in the road.

"I want to know about the painting. The one in the library, of the woman with the scars on her face. Can you tell me who she is?"

339

His eyes drifted closed.

"Please. Julien, talk to me."

Tears and rain, they swept over her face, blurring her vision and choking any words she could find. She swiped at the wetness on her cheeks and kept driving.

"What if I tell you my name? Hmm? My real one. Would you talk to me then?"

They eased up over a rise, past trees and the heart-stopping sight of sandbag barriers, and came through the edge of town. A medieval gate rose beyond it; that must be the Porte du Martray.

Please don't let them be under siege.

"Viola . . ."

Vi had been so desperate for his voice that she nearly turned them into the side of a building at the sound of it. "How do you know my name?"

"I've known it since the first day you broke into my chapel."

"But how? You never said."

The cathedral—her heart raced when she saw the spire rise over the buildings. She turned down the street without care. Not knowing if they'd be shot at by hidden enemies in buildings lining the drive.

"Last winter. Viola Hart disappeared in Paris. The SOE sent out word about a missing linguist . . . black hair . . . violet eyes," he whispered. "If we found you . . . we were to keep you safe until the Allies could get you out. I let them know you were with us that first day."

Vi pulled up to the front of the cathedral and pulled to a stop, blasting her horn.

"That was my job . . . Lady . . ."

Heaven help her, but Julien was shaking so badly, she could scarcely understand him.

"To . . . keep you . . . safe."

"And you were brilliant at it, my love. I am safe now. See? We're at another chapel." She banged the door open and swept out, enough to stand over him and press an upside down kiss to his forehead. "And I'm wearing your brooch, so I'm staying at your invitation. My heart will never leave."

Vi struggled to lift Julien out, his shoulders a deadweight as she hooked her arms under them. She blasted the horn again, and heavy doors opened. A man ran down the steps, meeting her, working at once to shift the bulk of Julien's weight into his arms.

"Please, help us," she begged, the sight of so much blood causing her own voice to shake uncontrollably. "He needs a doctor."

The man started when she spoke but called out over his shoulder, drawing men and a woman with a cloth pallet stretcher from the inside. They swarmed the car, rushing on all sides of her, lifting Julien from her.

"Please . . ."

"What is it?" When she didn't answer, the man blasted again. "Quickly! Shrapnel? Gunshot?"

"It was a paratrooper . . ." She battled to think, trying to stay close even as they eased her back. "Um . . . gunshot from an FG 42, I think. His right side."

She didn't need to be told that life could slip from him; Julien had never held her hand that way before. Vi gripped his palm as long as they'd let her, until they moved up the steps and she finally lost the warmth of his skin against hers.

"I have to go with him!" she cried, her gaze following the path of the stretcher until it faded into the depths of the chapel.

Vi pressed fingertips covered in dried blood and dirt, brushing them to her lips, kissing their last connection.

"Miss?"

Devastation. Exhaustion and shock—they hit her at once. Trying to look up at the man who'd rushed out to them caused her to falter on a stair. She fell down, knees smacking on the steps as she crumpled. He moved with quick reflexes, catching her at the elbow, helping her sit. He slipped a coat over her shoulders, even as they still trembled.

"We're your friends here, and we will help you both. But I need to know if you're hurt too. Now is this your blood or his?"

Vi stared over her shoulder, the darkness of the chapel an abyss. "Why can't I stay with him?"

How quickly she'd forgotten everything, that she was soaking wet, covered in a horrific mix of mud and blood-red stained upon her clothes, with her senses faded to listless.

"Don't worry about me." She swallowed hard, feeling her hand form a fist on its own, as if she were ready to fight the world if he dared try to help her. "Just get him to a doctor."

The man reached out, hand on air, trying to calm her.

"I am a doctor—Captain Frederick Carver, American OSS. I'm one of the medical staff here. He'll receive the best care, I promise you. And I'll take you to him as soon as possible. What's his name?"

"Um . . . Julien." She sniffed, trying to find her wits enough to think, let alone speak. Courage felt lost and she feeble in trying to summon it. But Julien deserved better, that his name be spoken in accordance with who he was and what he'd done. So she notched her chin. "His name is Julien Vivay, commander of the Maquis resistance at Château des Doux-Rêves, and winemaker at the Renard vineyard in Les Trois-Moutiers."

"And your name, miss?"

"My name?"

Vi looked up at him, wishing it were as simple to answer as

giving her name. But she wasn't Viola Hart anymore—just Lady. A hidden chapel . . . a photo taken at castle ruins . . . a family and a man she'd come to love in the mere weeks she'd known them—they'd changed everything about her, who she might have once been.

All of it started with her name.

"You spoke English over there and with the accent, I have to ask. Are you a British citizen? How did you end up here, fighting with the French?"

With a deep breath Vi slipped the strap of Camille's camera over her head and set it on the steps beside her. She reached down, twisted the heel of her shoe until it unlocked and came off in her hand. Turning it over, the tiny black witness of microfiche film spilled into her palm.

"I am French now. I'm Lady Vi Hart. And if you are our friend, Captain, then you can help me get this to 64 Baker Street in London as soon as possible. It is intelligence information from the headquarters of Field Marshal Erwin Rommel, of the Third Reich's 7th Panzer Division."

"Hitler's commander?" He paused a breath when she didn't confirm he was the same. "His car took a direct hit from a 20mm in Sainte-Foy-de-Montgommery just yesterday. It's said that his injuries are near fatal. And the Nazi strongholds are falling all over France. We may still have a fight ahead of us here, but after Normandy, we believe the war could turn. You really didn't know?"

It must have shown on her face, the shock of the world going on outside of what had occurred at the castle ruins. War was happening everywhere, but it was so much more personal in her small view of it that she'd nearly forgotten it wasn't over yet.

"No. We didn't know anything. We were fighting our own battles just then."

"But you're with the SOE? Is that what you're telling me?"

She stretched out her hand and rolled the film cartridge into his palm. "Four SOE operatives at Château de La Roche-Guyon in Giverny, and countless maquisard fighters at the Château des Doux-Rêves, gave their lives to get that into your hands and out of France. I have their names. I have photographs in this camera, and their stories recorded in a journal. Their families and their government will want to know what's become of them all."

He stared down at the film cartridge, then turned it over in his hand. "And you, Lady Vi? What should I tell London has become of you?"

Vi pressed her hand over the brooch pinned to her collar, looking out over the span of Loudun's townscape before them. Would it be overrun? Would the people living and fighting and dying behind its sandbag barriers have a record of their stories too?

"Tell them the people here made certain I am safe. I will fight in this place until the last battle has been won. And now that *The Sleeping Beauty* is awake, I intend to ensure that her story never dies."

THIRTY-THREE

"June 19, 1944 . . ."

Ellie paused in reading the journal entry long enough to look over at the form of her grandmother, sleeping in the bed.

It wasn't clear whether Grandma Vi could hear anything she said.

Maybe reading the castle's story aloud was for the benefit of her heart more than her grandmother's. But somehow, in the depths of a sleep that refused to wane in recent days, Ellie hoped she could hear her voice. That Lady Vi would know her granddaughter had uncovered the story of the Château des Doux-Rêves, and that she finally understood what it meant:

> Julien died on a Monday . . .
>
> He slipped away, just as the sun rose and cut light through the chapel's stained glass. I'd held his hand through the early morning hours, thinking how rare it was that peace should belong in each tick of the clock . . . and how kindred the view was to the hidden chapel where we'd first met.

I told him that the wire carried news he was an uncle, that Titus and Marie had a healthy boy to carry on the Vivay name. I talked about his remarkable sister, little Claire—Criquet, as he liked to call her. I said she owned grit similar to her older brother, for she'd stood unflinching in the face of fear as he'd always taught her to and gifted me with her most prized possession—a book of fairy stories. I told him about where I grew up, of my parents and Andrew, my only brother—the one person in my life who had always supported me without fault. And how I had a niece and a nephew, Pippa and William, who'd have loved exploring the hidden corners of our castle ruins.

I dreamed aloud, my voice battling against the speed of the clock. I told him how one day, we'd restore the castle together. I promised him that if he'd only open his eyes and look at me, he'd know my answer. That I'd never leave this place, and he would have my heart as long as I lived.

We heard over the wire that a great battle had begun at Normandy on the 19th of June. And through clapping and cheers in the sanctuary at Cathédrale Espoir Sacré, we celebrated the Allies' liberation of Montebourg that day. And I kissed his hand, whispering, "Remember this, remember this . . ." because I knew one day I'd give anything to return to this one moment.

I said good-bye, and never saw those golden eyes again.

Ellie closed the journal and looked up, watching the even up-down cadence of breathing from her grandmother's petite form.

"So that's what you meant. You told Grandpa that in a way, you would always love Julien. And he married you still, and the two of you made a beautiful life together. Julien wanted you to have the castle, but you just couldn't love it without him, could you? You knew when the diagnosis brought you here that the castle would one day go to me. And you didn't want me to have it without the story you held dear." Ellie kissed the fox brooch and leaned over, pressing it into the faint warmth of her grandmother's hand. "You've lived *une belle vie*, Lady Vi. And I am so very proud of you."

"Ellie?"

She brushed a tear from her cheek and turned in the chair, finding she hadn't imagined the whisper from the doorway.

Quinn was really there, as she'd hoped to find him—unshaven as usual, clad in an Irish pub tee and gripping a guitar case instead of luggage. He set the case on the floor and nearly dropped a delicate paper-wrapped bouquet in the process, catching it with all thumbs.

He smiled, exposed and real, the softness in his eyes settling over her like a blanket.

"I was thinkin' about that song on the plane ride over. 'Blackbird'? The one your da used to play for ya when you were young?"

"And I have you to thank for the memory. I'd almost forgotten what a guitar sounds like."

"Do you know the lyrics?"

Ellie shook her head. He took a step inside.

"It talks about a blackbird, taking its broken wings and learnin' to fly again. It says, 'You were only waiting for this moment to arise.' Reminded me of somethin'. That I've been walkin' like this for a long while now. Too long. And I think if you were brave enough to walk the road to the castle not knowin' what was at the other end, then maybe I could too."

He eased in the rest of the way and knelt at the side of her chair with the bouquet in his hand: violets and wildflowers, wrapped in lavender paper. They perfumed the air with the fragrance of Fox Grove.

"There's a bit of the old Frenchman in his Irish grandson, so you'll have to forgive me for bein' of the old-fashioned lot to ask." Quinn held the flowers out to Ellie. "But these are for Lady Vi. I wanted to know if I could court her granddaughter. If I promise no more rides in dodgy dories, and if I can keep my olagonin' about the castle to a minimum."

Ellie took the flowers in hand, trying her best to manage a smile and tears at the same time. "Court her granddaughter, hmm?"

"Old-fashioned term." He shrugged. "I think posh people call it vintage, or some such nonsense. In any case, I wanted to hear the rest of it. The entire story of Ellison Carver. And I can't learn that if I'm trekkin' through a vineyard half a world away."

Quinn softened his features as he looked around, taking in the sight of wartime photos on the bureau, the pin-board with post-cards, and shelves teeming with Vi's beloved books. And then Ellie. She'd waited until his gaze returned to her, then drifted to the sleeping form in the bed.

"I've been reading to her." She patted the journal in her lap. "From this."

"Titus said it was all there. The story of your grandmother, and Julien. And the history of the castle goin' as far back as the time of the Revolution. Funny—I never knew how the Muscadet got its name. And now we do. There really was a lady named Aveline, and she was a princess of the castle who was to marry the duke's eldest son but fell in love with his brother instead. I admit to likin' that part, bein' a younger brother myself. But she was the first to want to bring the castle back to life." He smiled, and Ellie thought she read a glimmer of pride in his features. "You are one of a long line of women who fought to rebuild those old stones. Rather remarkable company to share, yeah?"

"Tell me the truth. Are you here because you want to be, or

because Titus made you? I'd wager he doesn't want to see the castle forgotten after all these years."

"Clever, my girl is." Quinn stood and turned, going after the guitar in the doorway. He eased a chair up next to hers and sat down. "Would you believe he and Auntie Claire figured out how to buy a plane ticket online? I swear by the Almighty I'm goin' to have to destroy that laptop, or those two will be the death of me yet."

She laughed. "Why am I not surprised?"

"But there's still truth in it. Titus said I'd be a grand fool if I didn't go on after ya. Flipped me on the back of the skull somethin' fierce, and said I'd learned nothin' from all this. But I would have bought a ticket without his meddlin'. I did, actually. The moment you left. So now I have two return tickets to the Loire Valley . . . and the dates are open ended."

Quinn leaned down and flipped open the latches on the case at his feet. He pulled the guitar into his lap and let it rest on his knees, ready to play. "May I stay?"

Ellie eased deeper into the chair, turning the bouquet over in her hands. She raised the violets to her nose, loving the familiar scent . . . of home.

"It could be a while." She looked up. "Grandma Vi could rally or . . . Either way, the castle will have to wait. At least I know she wanted me to have it. That it's always been a part of who she is and now, it's a part of me. I'll go back one day, but it's not anywhere near as important as what's in this room right now. And I won't leave her. Not for a moment."

"Neither will I." He leaned in, brushed a soft kiss to her lips as he began to play, fingerpicking the melody of familiar notes to envelop the room. "We'll walk this road together, however long it takes."

EPILOGUE

SPRING
LES TROIS-MOUTIERS
LOIRE VALLEY, FRANCE

Ellie and Quinn walked hand in hand through the grove. She ran fingertips from her free hand along the bumpy ridges of the stone wall.

It was her first spring in France. Their first together. And though the castle had slept through a very, very long winter, their *Sleeping Beauty* could soon awaken with the changing of the seasons. With the wild plum trees blossoming along the road, wildflowers picking their spots in the fields, and tiny grape buds just starting to weigh down Titus's vines, the land was exploding to life.

Butterflies returned. The night markets would open in mere weeks. And the sun would sojourn for longer periods each day, to ensure the mornings of sweater-wearing would soon pass into summer. From summer, to harvest again. And while she didn't favor predictability in her new life, Ellie had worn a favorite sweater for their morning walk and wrapped her wine-and-ivory pin-dot scarf around her hair. Ebony waves—barrel-rolled and natural, as Grandma Vi would have worn it long ago, spilled over her shoulders as they moved along, getting caught up in the last chilly breezes of the season.

Soon they could have a garden where they walked.

Ellie imagined lilacs to go with the wild violets lining the castle road. Lovely French peony bushes bursting with ivory and blush pinks and hedgerows of deep evergreen. A stone bench, perhaps in the center of the garden, near where Julien had been laid to rest so many decades before. Maybe they'd engrave the long-ago names of *Aveline* and *Robert*, the more recent *Lady* and *Julien*, *Dr. Carver*, and Titus's nearly forgotten *Elder*—all the names that may have belonged to the past but signified lives that had led Ellie and Quinn to the next chapter in the castle's story.

She stopped, sinking the soles of her boots in the brush. "I think we should start here." Ellie turned a half circle, gazing around the canopy of trees and the lush arbor rows beyond. "Right here, with the wall."

"We have an entire castle to rebuild and you want to start . . . with a pile of stones?" Quinn's tone was less than convinced as he let go of her hand and inspected the crumbling wall.

"Yeah." Ellie raised her palm to shield her eyes, dreaming along with the rising sun. "I do."

Something about it felt right. The photo taken there on June 5, 1944, had turned out to be one of many taken in the days that followed the Normandy invasion. But it was the singular image that had brought Grandma Vi back to life and called Ellie through the castle gates. And she stood happy, her heart somehow full by the measure that life could still breathe through castle ruins, a crumbling stone wall, and an overgrown thicket.

"I love that Grandma Vi stayed in Loudun after Julien died, fighting with the rest of the people until the end of the war. She must have made quite an impression on my grandfather for him to track her down at Cambridge after it was all over. But she never gave up. All those years, she researched everything she could so one day, we could tell the castle's story. And I finally understand. She dearly loved my grandfather. He was a good man. But she also loved this place, and even if it was only for a short time, that time forever changed her. And if it's succeeded, isn't that what a story should do? Change us in some way?"

Ellie half turned, the way she did when she knew she'd posed something Quinn would take issue with and wasn't sure she really wanted to know his answer. Catching him out of the corner of her eye, she nibbled her bottom lip, waiting.

He stood, slipped his hands in his jeans pockets, and remained silent while studying the scene in earnest.

"So, what do you think?"

He gave a hefty sigh. "That it's goin' to be a lot of work."

She nodded. "I know. But you've seen me harvesting grapes. I'm good for it. I won't complain a bit, no matter how many spiders try to make friends with me in the process."

"I hate to tell ya, but there's bound to be more than spiders in those ruins over there." He furrowed his brow, issuing a mock glare. "I can't believe I'm sayin' this, but if your heart's set on reopenin', we're goin' to need funds. We'll have to set up some kind of social-media campaign . . . get the town to agree . . . I don't want to begin to wonder about what kind of permits we're goin' to need. I get a headache just thinkin' about it."

Quinn sighed again and ran his fingers through his dark hair, the way he always did when he bristled but was willing to give a little. Funny how he'd thought his grandfather's ways were the antiquated ones; the mere mention of social media and permits looked as if it pained him considerably, and Ellie had to bite her bottom lip to suppress an ill-timed laugh.

"But . . . you like the idea? And you think the family will agree, to share the story of this place?"

"Agree or not, it's your castle now. I could ask Titus to put his oar in, but mind, once I do, there's no pullin' him back. He'll appoint himself president of this whole operation, and he'll have my grandmother and Auntie Claire feeding every tourist until they pop. That's a great lot of liability you'd be takin' on."

"I know that too. And it's why I didn't just assume you'd be in agreement. I wanted us to make this decision together." Ellie wrapped her arms around her waist, easing into a hopeful smile before him. "So, maybe we take it in stages. Rebuild the wall first. Gardens second. Raise funds through tourism and wine sales. I'd never considered writing when I was young, though Grandma Vi always tried to push me to do it. But maybe I do that too—start a website, record all that we do to bring the castle back to life. Room by room, if we have to. But at the very least, she'll welcome people again.

"And maybe someone will walk down that road to her front doors, someone who wants more than just a calendar photo for a desk frame. Maybe they'll see the fairy tale in this place too. Maybe it will inspire someone else to step out and take a risk for something that truly matters. I know it would honor Grandma Vi. I think all along, it's what she was trying to tell me. That the story we're writing in this life, day by day, it's a gift from God and we can't afford to waste a moment of it."

Quinn listened and nodded, his quiet way fully intact.

"Well, if that's all true, you're goin' to need this." He pulled a brown-paper parcel from his pocket, tied up in a simple twine bow. "Or at least . . . I'm goin' to need it."

"Need what? Despite what that paper suggests, I sincerely hope you did not put a pain au chocolat in your pocket. I'm not that hungry." She took the parcel, then turned to open it atop the wall. The twine gave. The brown paper blossomed open. "And I already have a scarf, so—"

The tiny wink of a row of diamonds on a white-gold band froze her hands in place.

Ellie spun on her heel, finding Quinn's height had been halved by the knee he'd pressed against the forest floor.

"I like the idea about buildin' up the wall again. It's grand. But I thought maybe we could start with the chapel? If you say yes, we're goin' to need it first." He paused, swallowing over his words. "So I'll say yes to all this, if you say yes to me."

Ellie could have cried for how nervous he looked, and did, for how completely happy her heart was in that moment.

Like in every fairy tale she'd ever read, she nodded to the man kneeling before the one he'd asked to be his wife—except she was the girl and he was the boy, and this was real life. In their story, he slipped a ring on her finger and lifted her boots from the ground, turning her in circles as they laughed.

And kissed.

And dreamed of a future where the castle's legacy lived on, and the stories were written in generations of weathered stone.

AUTHOR'S NOTE

Once upon a time, I was an Ellie.

I walked into my grandmother's room at an Alzheimer's care facility, praying she would know me just once more. After telling her who I was a few times, the scene you read in this book unfolded brilliantly. Like Lady Vi Carver, my grandmother, too, had been a college professor and could still claim a spark of the elegant woman I'd looked up to in my youth. As is the story with so many who battle Alzheimer's—whether patient, family, friends, or caregivers—this disease steals indiscriminately. This book gifted me an opportunity to take something back and write about such loss from a place of deep understanding. It's why the dedication goes to the grandmothers in my life, for the legacy of our generation is first written in the indelible ink of theirs.

Several accounts in this book come from historical fact—the first of which provided loose inspiration for Ellie's lost castle. Château de la Mothe-Chandeniers is an abandoned thirteenth-century–castle–turned-storybook château, surrounded by a moat and nestled in the heart of French wine country. It's not open to the public, but at the time of this novel's publication, restoration discussions continue. It felt right that a mix of fairy-tale inspiration and childhood memories should turn into a main character that, surprisingly, had no lines in this book. A lost castle emerged with a hint of French romance, and a beauty that was forced to unfold alongside the grim realities of war.

June 5, 1944—the date on the back of Vi's vineyard photo—was the calm before the great storm of Allied forces who would invade the beaches of Normandy the very next day. Known as D-Day, June 6, 1944, became the largest sea, air, and land invasion in history—and one of the bloodiest battles of World War II. It shed light on the endurance of the French Resistance fighters who had already survived years of war-ravaged landscape in Nazi-occupied France. While the "longest day" was unfolding with some ten thousand servicemen killed or wounded on beaches code-named Omaha, Utah, Gold, Juno, and Sword, Julien's fictional army prepared for a battle of their own—an unlikely family who'd come together to defend their home and cling to hope around the ruins of a castle.

Vi's journey from Cambridge and London to working as an operative with the British Special Operations Executive (SOE) organization in France weaves a fictional story with many well-known historical facts and figures. London addresses like 64 Baker Street (where the infamous "Baker Street Irregulars" originated) and the direct-hit Blitz bombing of the Royal Empire Society at 25 Northumberland Avenue lend heartbreaking realism to fictional characters' worlds during the Second World War.

German Field Marshal Erwin Rommel's headquarters at Château de La Roche-Guyon became infamous as the location of the ill-fated attempt to prevent the Allied D-Day invasion, and as the place where a plot was hatched (with Rommel's involvement still debated by historians) to assassinate Adolf Hitler on July 20, 1944. And though not mentioned by name, Operation Bodyguard—the elaborate ruse to fool the Nazi leadership and provide intelligence cover for the D-Day invasion—was alluded to with the fictional story of Clémence and the other double agents who lost their lives at La Roche-Guyon.

To aid our story, we've bent history just a bit by adjusting the French *duc* to *duke*, and the time a coach and four could travel from Paris in a single day. Also figments of the author's imagination were the Cathédrale Espoir Sacré chapel in Loudun, the centuries-old Vivay family vineyard, and a deep wood named Fox Grove, which worked to keep our castle ruins hemmed in from the outside world. And while the Tennis Court Oath, Rose Bertin's Le Grand Mogol shop in Paris, and the July 1789 storming of the Bastille are all true to history, Aveline and Robert's story in the world of a budding French Revolution is purely fictional. (Though who wouldn't wish a lady who gave away her lavish trousseau to instead feed starving women and children to have been a real person?)

Portions of this novel also rooted in truth remain some of the most precious to me. The light strumming of "Blackbird" on an acoustic guitar is the soundtrack of my youth, thanks to the guitar playing of my own father. And the quiet, 3:00 a.m. moments in an ICU room, holding the hand of a loved one, reminding myself, *Remember this . . . remember this . . .* , were some of the last moments my dad and I spent together on this earth. It ministered to my heart to make them a part of Vi and Julien's heartfelt "good-bye for now" at the chapel in Loudun.

A common thread in both history and fiction, at the intersection of fantasy and fact, is the enduring power of stories. God's story for us doesn't end with a good-bye or the crumbling of stone walls on this earth. His faithfulness lasts through the generations, lavishing hope on a fallen world and love on the most broken of hearts. I'm delighted that you met Ellie and Quinn as they embark on a new journey in this series. It's my hope that to them, and to each of us, God would become the Repairer of Broken Walls as we walk our own story roads.

ACKNOWLEDGMENTS

In French, *merci* is to say "thank you."

Extending a *merci* in print can't begin to go far enough to thank the amazing team I'm privileged to call my publishing family. (But I shall try!) To Becky Monds, the *très* patient protector of words, expert crafter of story worlds, counselor when this writer gal needs to brainstorm . . . and my dear friend: I remain grateful that you stepped in and forever changed the course of my story road—both in books and in this beautiful thing we call real life. To the lovely Julee Schwarzburg: I adore the deep dive of scrutinizing every syllable of a book with you. How could we not be fast friends after all that? (Smile.) To the pub family—Daisy Hutton, Kristen Golden, Amanda Bostic, Allison Carter, Paul Fisher, Jodi Hughes, and cover artist extraordinaire Kristen Ingebretson: You are the best there ever was. I love that I wake each day and get to work with you. To Rachelle Gardner: I will never forget the special day we toured Tennessee's wine country together and managed to forget the weight of the world for a little while. You're a friend first and an agent second; I'm so grateful for you (and that fabulous idea for Ellie and Quinn's wine-tasting scene).

Merci to readers who helped name characters in this book:

Edie M. for her dear Kathy; and Erin M. for Alaina (or Laine)—an important character who will have her own story in the second book of this series. And to the many, many experts who stepped in to answer my questions along this journey (because it's the littlest details that can add flavor to a story), I extend my most ardent thanks: Winemaker Chase Vienneau and the entire team at Arrington Vineyards in Arrington, Tennessee: Thank you for allowing this curious writer to tour the vast array of sights, sounds, tastes, and smells of your wine-making world. *Merci* to associate professor of French at Indiana University, Margaret Gray, PhD, and student Flavien Falantin—whose authentic details of living in France, knowledge of French champagne production, and assistance with French grammar became *très* dreamy for this story! I also thank Brenna W. from the Marquette Maritime Museum for helping me gain my bearings about the street layout of Marquette, Michigan. It was an impromptu call to you that checked another box for clarity with this author's pen. Thank you!

I extend a *merci* also to dear friends who walked through virtual vineyard rows with me, offering support as I fell deeper into this story: the Grove Girls, Katherine Reay, Sarah E. Ladd, Maggie Walker, Sharon Tavera, Mary Weber, Allen Arnold, Joanna Politano, and Colleen Coble. To the owners, crew, and "regulars" crowd at KöLKIN CoFFEE co.: Thank you for the assigned seat at the table beneath the hanging kayaks. You keep me caffeinated (and happy) when I'm wandering through the wilds of my characters' many adventures. And to Lily Wray, the young author who shares my favorite coffee shop corners: Thank you for being my book-loving friend.

To Brady, Carson, and Colt: You are my joys. To Jeremy: You are my beloved. To Jen: You are my beautiful, book-loving sis. To

Lindy: You are my momma and prayer partner . . . I love walking through this life and writing ministry with all of you. And to my Savior—the One who loves, forgives, offers grace, and forever calls the lost . . . thank You for calling me.

DISCUSSION QUESTIONS

1. Ellie's view of her grandmother had been one of shared memories from old photo albums and the limited stories she'd heard of Lady Vi's life during the Second World War. It is not until the discovery of a lost love—and the unearthing of Vi's participation in the French Resistance—that Ellie sees her grandmother in a new light. How might Ellie's memory of her grandmother have been different if Vi hadn't been able to share pieces of her past before the effects of Alzheimer's prevented it? What changed once Ellie learned the full story of the castle?

2. Aveline's interest in politics and her compassion for the peasant class renders her a liability to her family's wealth and rank, and carries her outside the acceptable roles for women in eighteenth-century France. What decisions does Aveline make that positively affect others yet put her own life and livelihood at risk? When is it important to stand up for our beliefs, even when our own comforts may be negatively impacted?

3. Titus holds a deep affection for the history of the Vivay land, and the belief that wine making is far more a matter of art than one of modern science. This view strongly

contrasts with Quinn's and affects his ability to plant familial roots in a way similar to his grandfather. What keeps Quinn from seeing the world as Titus does? How can past hurts affect our ability to heal and open our hearts to new opportunities and future relationships?

4. Julien's band of French Resistance fighters at the castle ruins becomes a makeshift family, brought together by their common bond to fight for survival in a time of war. Have you ever developed a bond with a friend or coworker who held a differing world view? How did that relationship affect the way you see the world around you?

5. As the story of the castle unfolds, Ellie has to acknowledge unresolved pain of her past and realizes that unless she confronts it, she won't find wholeness—or freedom—to love anew. Quinn, too, is practicing avoidance of his pain, choosing to move on instead of planting roots in any spot for too long. How do Ellie and Quinn come together when their barriers to intimacy begin on opposite spectrums? Is it possible to put down roots and still fly at the same time?

6. The visual of crumbling walls is an important image for the legacy of the castle, and the Vivay family through the generations. Aveline wanted to tear down the barrier between the classes, both in Paris and once she reached the Vivay estate. How do we tear down walls of differences with others, whether in our local or global communities?

7. In this story, color is used to convey emotion that spans generations—in the blush-pink blossoms and wild violets lining the road to the castle ruins, the red rust of the fox inhabiting Fox Grove, the rich wine of the land and Ellie's Loire Valley scarf, and Aveline's portrait that hangs in both the castle and the estate house across all three story

lines. How does color reveal the art of God's creation in the world around us? In what ways are our other senses impacted by stories?

8. *The Sleeping Beauty* is more than a lost castle—it serves as an image of God's faithfulness through the generations and His intimate involvement in our own life stories. How can faith be passed down over generations? How important is our own foundation of faith to leave a legacy for future generations?

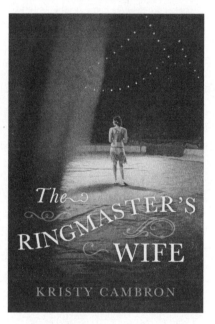

9780718095468-A

Also Available from Kristy Cambron, the

Hidden Masterpiece Novels!

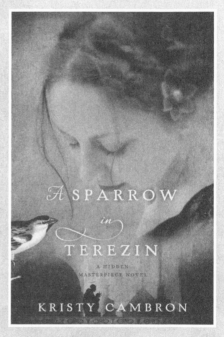

A mysterious painting breathes hope and beauty into the darkest corners of Auschwitz—and the loneliest hearts of Manhattan.

Bound together across time, two women will discover a powerful connection through one survivor's story of hope in the darkest days of a war-torn world.

ABOUT THE AUTHOR

Photo by Whitney Neal Photography

Kristy Cambron fancies life as a vintage-inspired storyteller. Her novels have been named to *Library Journal Reviews*' list of Best Books of 2014 and 2015 and have received nominations for *RT* Reviewers' Choice Awards Best Inspirational Book of 2014 and 2015, as well as INSPY Award nominations in 2015 and 2017. Kristy holds a degree in art history from Indiana University and lives in Indiana with her husband and three football-loving sons.

Website: www.kristycambron.com
Twitter: @KCambronAuthor
Facebook: KCambronAuthor
Pinterest: KCambronAuthor
Instagram: KristyCambron